Two Scholars Who Were in Our Town
and Other Novellas

Two Scholars Who Were in Our Town

and Other Novellas

S.Y. Agnon

NEW AND REVISED TRANSLATIONS
FROM THE HEBREW
EDITED AND ANNOTATED BY

JEFFREY SAKS

The Toby Press

Two Scholars Who Were in Our Town
and Other Novellas
by S.Y. Agnon
Edited by Jeffrey Saks
© 2014 *The* Toby Press LLC

These stories, published by arrangement with Schocken Publishers, are
available in Hebrew as part of the Collected Writings of S.Y. Agnon –
Kol Sippurav shel Shmuel Yosef Agnon, © Schocken Publishers in
23 volumes (Jerusalem and Tel Aviv), most recent edition 1998-2003.

Original publication data:
"Two Scholars Who Were in Our Town" appears here in English for
the first time. *The following stories have been revised and annotated*
for this edition, based upon the following original translations:
"In The Heart of the Seas" translated by I.M. Lask,
originally published by Schocken Books, NY (1947). "Tehilla"
translated by Walter Lever, originally in *Israel Argosy,* vol. 4 (1956).
"In the Prime of Her Life" translated by Gabriel Levin, originally
in *Eight Great Hebrew Short Novels,* edited by Alan Lelchuk and
Gershon Shaked (1983; third revised edition *The* Toby Press, 2009).

The Toby Press LLC
POB 8531, New Milford, CT 06776–8531, USA
& POB 2455, London WIA 5WY, England
www.tobypress.com

ISBN 978-1-59264-355-4

Typeset in Garamond

Printed and bound in the United States

Contents

Preface

In "The Story of the Seven Beggars", one of the Tales of the great Hassidic Rebbe Nachman of Breslov, a hunchback describes his mind as "a little that contained a lot". Since he could hold some ten thousand people in his mind, along with all their desires and problems and needs, all of their trials and tribulations and triumphs, every element of their lives and nooks of their personalities, he presumed that he must be the "little that contains a lot." But, Rebbe Nachman relates, everyone mocked him, saying that those people in his mind were nothing and in fact he was nothing as well.

The influence of Rebbe Nachman on Nobel laureate S.Y. Agnon should not be underestimated. Agnon saw in the Hassidic Master the starting point of what would become modern Jewish storytelling. Gershom Scholem remarked that "if the 'Story of the Seven Beggars' had not already been told by Rebbe Nachman, it could have become an Agnon story and would have taken on a perfectly 'Kafkaesque' aura" – reminding us of that other Jewish surrealist writer, who together with Agnon and Nachman, were all shocked by "the permeability, the loosened state of tradition" (G. Scholem, "S.Y. Agnon – The Last Hebrew Classic?" in *On Jews and Judaism in Crisis*).

And like the hunchback (and his literary creator, Rebbe Nachman), Agnon, too, possessed "a little that contained a lot" – a phrase drawn from the world of Midrash and Kabbalah to describe the miraculous compression into finite space of more than seems possible – that is, an imagination so vast that it contains multitudes, whole worlds of "imaginative history" emanating from and occupying the mind of finite, mortal man. This act of creativity, Godlike in its manner of bringing about creation through word and thought, is precisely the talent demonstrated in the literary world Agnon created.

The four novellas published here in new or revised translations are exemplars of the richness of that literary world created by Agnon, with webs of interconnected locales, legends and leitmotifs. The stories range over a roughly century-long period from the 1820s to the 1920s and are situated in Agnon's ancestral Galician hometown of Buczacz (or its literary doppelganger, Szybusz), or in the Land of Israel of the Old Yishuv and in Jerusalem of the later British Mandate.

The following notes are meant to give background to these four novellas, as well as brief outlines to the major themes of each work and how each fits within Agnon's canon. The annotated bibliography which closes this volume outlines the secondary literature and commentary written on these works in English.

"Two Scholars Who Were in Our Town" (*Shnei Talmidei Hakhamim Shehayu Be'Irenu*) is being published here in English for the first time, in a debut translation by Paul Pinchas Bashan and Rhonna Weber Rogol, who have also prepared the annotations together with this volume's editor. The story tells of the epic clash between two Torah scholars, *talmidei hakhamim*, who according to the Talmudic phrase "cannot abide each other in matters of *halakhah*" leading to the death of one and the exile of the other (see Sotah 49a). First published in Hebrew in *Luach Ha'aretz* 5707 (Autumn 1956) and later collected in Agnon's *Samukh veNireh*, the story is set over a period of roughly thirty years during the mid-nineteenth century in an unnamed Our Town, clearly meant to be Buczacz (as evidenced by the presence of one of Agnon's own ancestors in a cameo role).

Narrating from a point "three or four generations" after the action, the narrator waxes nostalgic – even elegiac – for a time when "Torah was beloved by Israel and the entire glory of a man was Torah, [when] our town was privileged to be counted among the most notable towns in the land on account of its scholars." And yet, as the plot unwinds and insults are traded in the Beit Midrash, the ancient Talmudic curse begins to work its dark power, leading to the tragic denouement. And here we see Agnon's power as a tragedian on an almost Greek scale. With his typical irony at work, the narrator pines for an earlier, more ideal time which turns out to have been rife with flaws and tragic personalities of its own. This draws the reader to question – was it always ever thus? Indeed, consider the Talmudic template on which Agnon sketches his modern tale of scholarly eros, ego, and clash – the relationship between Rabbi Yohanan and Rabbi Shimon ben Lakish (especially as described in Bava Metzia 84a). After reading Agnon's novella the reader might go back and study that primary text and see how he distilled the classical sources of the Beit Midrash into a modern midrashic matrix on which he composed his Nobel-winning literature.

"**In the Heart of the Seas**" (*Bilvav Yamim*), a tale of the journey to the Land of Israel by a group setting out from Buczacz, was Agnon's first English translation published by Schocken Press, in 1947. While originally published in Hebrew in 1934 in a volume marking H.N. Bialik's sixtieth birthday, its earliest fragment was present in a small sketch sent for an unpublished 1926 *festschrift* in honor of the dying Franz Rosenzweig.

Written in the style of nineteenth-century Hassidic tales, the novella's weaving of folklore and aggada into modern literature helped cement Agnon's reputation as the greatest Hebrew author of his time. The story was also singled out for praise for its idealization of the Love of Zion, at a time that the Yishuv was undergoing great struggles. Between 1933 and 1935 over one hundred and fifty thousand Jews had arrived in Palestine, more than all that had arrived in the years of the British Mandate up until that point. (Hitler was appointed Chancellor of Germany in January 1933, leading to a wave of German Jewish immigration). Agnon's biographer Dan Laor shows that contemporary critics were especially mindful that this was the background on which the novella was composed. Agnon's tale is a mélange of both a realistic as well as supernatural narrative of *aliyah*, and was interpreted as a cautionary statement to the immigrants and builders of the Jewish settlement in the Land of Israel: Zionism cannot only focus on the here-and-now, physical construction, but must recall the miraculous story that undergirds our work. It is a vision that emphasizes love of the land over labor, and the supernatural over nature. This may be precisely the reason Agnon chose to retroject himself into the story despite its setting one hundred years before its composition – "Rabbi Shmuel Yosef, the son of Rabbi Shalom Mordekhai ha-Levi of blessed memory, who was versed in the legends of the Land of Israel, those legends in which the name of the Holy One, blessed be He, is hallowed; and when he commenced lauding the Land, people could see as it were the name of the living God engraved on the tip of his tongue" – for that was how he envisioned the purpose of his artistic output.

An attentive reader will notice the dual frequencies on which the story is broadcast and the contrast between the natural travel tale of the group versus the miraculous voyage of Hananiah who floats along "in the heart of the sea" atop his magical kerchief. For the full messianic symbolism of this ersatz "magic carpet" see Agnon's short story "The Kerchief" (in *A Book That Was Lost*, Toby Press). Lask's translation has been revised and newly annotated by this volume's editor.

"**In the Prime of Her Life**" (*Bidmi Yameha*) opens Agnon's collection of "love" stories *Al Kapot HaMan'ul* ("At the Handles of the Lock"; cf. Song of Songs 5:5), and is in many ways the type of psychological love story favored by European realism of the time. Yet, like "*Tehilla*" (which concludes this volume) and "*Agunot*" (Agnon's signature story, from which he drew his penname), it is a disturbed – and, in this case, disturbing – love. One wherein two souls bound or "chained" together (the root of *Agunot* and *Agnon* means "to be anchored together") cannot actualize their love, with disastrous echoes reverberating into later generations.

Although Agnon crafted many fabulous female characters in his writing, this is a unique case of a first-person female narrator – the teenage protagonist, Tirtza Mintz of Szybucz, whose voice lends a youthful, even naïve innocence. Yet Agnon conceals from his reader the identity and gender of the narrator until we are a number of pages into the novella (consider the difficulty of doing this as artfully and seemingly effortlessly as he does given the gendered nature of Hebrew grammar!). When we do discover this fact, the reader of the Hebrew text takes note of the lyrical, Biblical Hebrew style of the story, a departure from Agnon's typical Rabbinic mode. Presumably he does so to echo the elocution of a young girl in early twentieth-century Galicia, the setting for the story, for whom the Hebrew of the Mishnah and Talmud would have been less fluent. Gabriel Levin, in this translation, has done a masterful job of capturing the Biblical rhythms and cadences, so reminiscent of the Book of Ruth (look out for parallels in content and theme as well as style). It is precisely these lyrical weavings of text and master-text, of the modern tale with its Biblical templates, which give this tale of love lost and found its emotional and psychological depth and complexity. The degree to which the reader trusts Tizrta as a reliable narrator of her own unconventional love story will inevitably determine his or her understanding of the whole story. Staking a position in this matter becomes all the more urgent upon reaching the surprising ending and discovering the setting from which Tirtza's account has been narrated.

Israeli novelist A.B. Yehoshua, commenting on "In the Prime of Her Life", suggests that it exemplifies Agnon's ability to bring to life and demonstrate for the reader the complex sub-conscious of his characters. This is what draws us in as readers, and what draws us back again in the ongoing, interpretive endeavor surrounding these stories. Amos Oz has called this novella the "bedrock of modern Hebrew literature" (the interested reader will find echoes of "In the Prime of Her Life" in Oz's novel *My Michael*; see also chapter 11 of his autobiography, *A Tale of Love and Darkness*).

The story, first published in the journal *HaTekufah* in 1923, also serves as a prologue of sorts to Agnon's great novel *A Simple Story* (1935; translated by Hillel Halkin, Toby Press revised edition, 2013), in which our characters exist in the liminal outskirts of that work's plot. "In the Prime of Her Life" sets patterns of Jewish star-crossed love which Agnon expanded on in *A Simple Story* and throughout his entire collected writings.

"**Tehilla**", perhaps Agnon's most beloved tale, explores righteousness, repentance, redemption, reward and punishment. The story is set in the Old City of Jerusalem, and, although exact dates are never explicitly stated, based on some internal evidence, and the fact that the unnamed narrator shares many biographical similarities with Agnon himself, we can establish that the action unfolds between the Fall of 1924 and Spring 1925 (see timeline appended to the story's annotations). However, the emotional force of "Tehilla" comes through the long narrated backstory, in which the 104-year-old title character tells us her tragic life story, going back to events as early as the 1820s.

While not apparent from the first half of the novella, "Tehilla" is also a love story, although a decidedly Agnonian love story – there's no chance for a happy ending. Like so many of his descriptions of love interrupted (again, most especially "In the Prime of Her Life"), it is a tale of a disturbance in first love which haunts subsequent generations. But in "Tehilla" that disturbance is precipitated by the lamentable hatred between Jews (in this case the historic clash between Hassidim and their opponents), leading to a century of suffering. What makes Tehilla so remarkable is her capacity to transcend this suffering. Indeed, the source of her longevity may very well be the century-long attempt to rectify past misdeeds. Tehilla embodies a type of faith all-too unfamiliar to us moderns, certain that she lives in a deterministic world yet still tasked to act as a free agent, responsible for her actions. If her story is a tragedy it is a decidedly Jewish one, and she reminds us of Nietzsche's quip that "The Greeks blame the gods, the Jews blame themselves."

"Tehilla" is also a love story for the Old City of Jerusalem; that Old Woman, who had been living within its walls since before any settlement had been constructed in New Jerusalem, i.e. since before 1860, is herself an embodiment of the Holy City. When Agnon describes her in 1950 (in lines which are among the most famous in all of Hebrew literature) as "Righteous she was, and wise she was, and gracious and humble too: for kindness and mercy were the light of her eyes, and every wrinkle in her face told of blessing and peace" – he was very likely describing the Old City, its inhabitants, society and life, which had only recently been destroyed and barred to Jews with the division of Jerusalem in 1948. "Tehilla" is a lamentation for Jerusalem, as a place and as an idea, embodied in the life of one remarkable woman.

If we consider how these two themes – internecine strife amongst Jews and the loss and destruction of Jerusalem – intersect, we hear the words of the Sages being whispered to us by Agnon from between the lines of "Tehilla": "The Holy Temple was destroyed because of baseless hatred…" (Yoma 9b).

The Hebrew story appeared first in *Me'asef Davar* (1950) and was subsequently collected in Agnon's *Ad Henah*. Translators of Agnon are always torn between a more literal and a more lyrical rendering. This revised version of Walter Lever's translation leans toward the latter preference, while a parallel version by I.M. Lask (which appeared in *Tehilla and Other Israeli Tales*, 1956) was more literal. For those who cannot grapple with the original Hebrew yet want a richer reading of this profound text, engaging with both translations would be an interesting experiment in understanding how translators balance the tension between the words of a text and its spirit.

❧ ❧ ❧

The annotations, which follow each novella, are intended to aid the reader who wishes to more fully experience the profundity of Agnon's writing which is so hard to capture in translation, namely: the manner in which he distilled the language and lore of the Mishnah, Talmud, Midrash, together with the medievalists and Hassidic masters – all recast in the form of modern literature. To explore the intertextual Agnonian matrix is to enter a world of pseudo-Midrash, one which is no mere literary device, but the "very source of his creativity, perhaps its main subject," according to the Israeli critic Gershon Shaked. "To a greater degree than that of any other writer in modern Hebrew literature, Agnon's work is based upon intertextual connections."

Similarly, the notes provide some background on various Jewish rituals, phrases or concepts, which Agnon assumed his Hebrew readers would have been familiar with as a matter of course. (That this may no longer be the case, even for native Hebrew speakers, is a sad commentary on contemporary cultural literacy in the Jewish State, and presumably part of the reason why Agnon and the other Hebrew classics get whittled away each year from school curricula and chain-store bookshelves.) However, because reading Agnon in any language is meant to be first and foremost an aesthetic-literary experience, we have not inserted endnote references into the text itself.

I am grateful to Paul Pinchas Bashan, Gabriel Levin, and Rhonna Weber Rogol, the living translators of two of these four stories, for their creativity and cooperation with this project. Paul and Rhonna's new translation of "Two Scholars Who Were in Our Town" is a particularly welcome addition to the Agnon bookshelf as it is long overdue and has been one of his most important works unavailable in English until now. Their collaboration as translators, which was initiated by Rhonna with the encouragement of Prof. Nehama Aschkenasy, of the University of Connecticut (while discussing the influence of this story on the recent Israeli film, "Footnote"), is a hopeful sign for Jewish and Hebrew high culture in the United States.

The commitment of The Toby Press to continue publishing Hebrew classics in superb English translations is the personal vision of our publisher, Mr. Matthew Miller, and the animating force behind The Toby Press S.Y. Agnon library. I thank him and my colleagues at Toby – Tani Bayer, Tomi Mager, and especially Gila Fine. Various friends and teachers have been particularly supportive, encouraging, and helpful with different aspects of my ongoing engagement with S.Y. Agnon, and I am pleased to single out Avraham and Toby Holtz, Yoel Kortick, Alan Mintz, Avi Shmidman, and especially Ariel Hirschfeld. The friendship, advice, and *havruta* of James S. Diamond *z"l* is sorely missed. My own understanding of the stories in this volume, and many others in this series, has been greatly enhanced through the phenomenal privilege of teaching regularly at the Agnon House in Jerusalem (and via www.WebYeshiva.org/Agnon), and I am grateful to the many students I have encountered there and online, as well as to the staff of that great institution, and to its director, Oreet Meital.

Jeffrey Saks
Editor, The S.Y. Agnon Library
The Toby Press

Two Scholars Who Were in Our Town

"Reb Shlomo was standing and sermonizing and his voice was like that of the humble nightingale on a summer night."

Illustration by Avigdor Arikha for *Kelev Hutzot*

I.

THREE OR FOUR GENERATIONS AGO, when Torah was beloved by Israel and the entire glory of a man was Torah, our town was privileged to be counted among the most notable towns in the land on account of its scholars, who endowed our town with a measure of grace through the Torah that they learned. It goes without saying that Torah had already found pleasant enough accommodations among the elders of our old study house, yet the other study houses that had been built one after another enhanced wisdom even more. And even in the marketplaces and the roads of our town study fulfilled the verse "Wisdom calls aloud in the street, she raises her voice in the public squares." And if people stood around in the marketplace, appearing to haggle with one another over questions of real estate and loan collection and dissolution of partnerships and financial compensation and so on, they weren't really arguing over the monetary issues themselves, but rather about the laws pertaining to them in Hoshen Mishpat. And even those who filled their buckets at the well, used to fill their hearts with words of Torah. Particularly noteworthy was the new Kloyz, which from the fifteenth of the month of Av until the seventeenth of Tammuz never once shut its lights at night. This was the very same Kloyz for which one of the rich men of the town had dedicated space in his courtyard, to ensure that the residence would continue to belong to his lineage throughout coming generations, inasmuch as any dwelling that has a holy place dedicated to Torah and prayer remains in the hands of the family, from generation to generation, for eternity. But, let us now leave aside these matters that will not reappear until the arrival of the Redeemer and tell a little something of what our elders used to tell, about two great scholars who were in our town back in the days when everyone made Torah the essence of their being, because they understood that the saying "the joy of the Lord is our Fortress" refers to the Torah.

2.

One day, between the Passover and Shavuot holidays, a man arrived at our new Kloyz carrying with him a large loaf of bread, the kind that villagers bake for themselves which is large enough to last a man six days, and in his pockets a few fruits and a few vegetables. Since he walked in and saw the bookshelves that lined all four walls, he knew that this must be the place he had coveted and for which he had yearned. But he wondered how this Kloyz, which was reputed to carry on uninterrupted Torah learning both day and night, could be totally deserted. Except on that particular day one of the notables of the town had written a nuptial agreement for his daughter, who had become engaged to the son of an important man from another town, so the entire town had gone out to greet the bridegroom and his scholarly father and not a soul had remained in the Kloyz.

The man put down his belongings, took himself a Gemara, sat down and stayed put, not so much as lifting his head from the Gemara until the men of the Kloyz had returned. People approached him saying, "This is my seat" and "This is my Gemara." He responded that Torah is not a birthright, to be treated as private property. They realized that he was a difficult sort and let him be. From that point on, he did not move from his place until mid-day on Friday. And on Sunday, with the rising of the sun he came back, toting a loaf of bread and a bit of fruit and vegetables, and he sat and learned until the following Friday at noontime, when once again he left off studying and departed for his village. Until Sunday, when with the first gleaming of the sun, he would return to his learning once more. He carried on in this fashion over the course of several weeks, which turned into several months. Every Friday afternoon he would set off for his village and every Sunday return to the Kloyz.

3.

Now we will call him by his name, and tell a little of what we know about him. This man was named Moshe Pinchas and he was a villager, a miller's son. Throughout his childhood he had studied together with the sons of the head of the village, who had maintained good tutors for them. Since the sons grew up and became focused on their various affairs, their father discharged the tutors and Moshe Pinchas was left to study on his own. One time Rabbi Gabriel Reinush came from the nearby city to make the millstones kosher for Passover. This is the great sage Reb Gabriel Reinush, author of *Horeh Gaver* on Yoreh De'ah. One night, during the evening meal, the miller said to the rabbi, "Would the rabbi agree to test my Moshe Pinchas on Gemara?" The Rabbi called to him affectionately and asked him, "My son, what have you studied?" He told him. He tested him and saw that he knew his studies. He told the miller, "Your son learns well. Send him to me in the city and I'll keep an eye on him." So Moshe Pinchas went off to the city and studied under the Rabbi's tutelage. And when there was a lot of work at the mill, he'd leave off from studying to help his father. After a while, a rabbinical post was arranged for the Rabbi in another town. The Rabbi would travel from his city to that other city and leave his student. Moshe Pinchas began to wonder, "Why am I sitting around here?" Just about then, his father died, the mill was sold and the new miller did not need the services of Moshe Pinchas. Meanwhile the Rabbi was totally preoccupied with going back and forth to deal with the demands of his rabbinical post. Moshe Pinchas picked up and came to our town, which is the Torah capital for all the surrounding area. And since a man needs a piece of meat and a spoonful of soup and a clean shirt on his back, and a woman needs to hear Kiddush and Havdalah, every Friday afternoon he would go to be with his mother in the village and she would provide all that he needed for the next six days.

And thus Moshe Pinchas would remain all week long in the Kloyz and on Friday afternoon would return to his mother in the village. When he happened by chance upon a carriage, he'd go by carriage; if not, he'd go on foot. It was a walk of about three parsas from the town to the village and it is nice for a man who is sedentary for six whole days to exercise his legs a bit. In summertime he took off his shoes and went barefoot, and when he got to the river he would take his clothes off and bathe; and in winter he'd rise early and immerse himself in a warm mikveh and enter the Sabbath while ritually pure and observe the Sabbath day with his mother in the village, and after the Sabbath return to the Kloyz. The beadle, who cherished scholars, used to bring him something hot to drink and a pillow to sleep on. If the beadle doesn't exaggerate, we can believe him when he says that Moshe Pinchas didn't drink the hot drinks he brought him until they were tepid and, that as far as the beadle knew, he would never even placed his head upon the pillow that had been furnished. So drawn was he to his studies that he would never take a break, neither for a hot drink nor for sleep.

4.

Our mothers, who had heard from people who knew him, used to say that he was of medium height, with broad shoulders, and a squarish face with small wisps of facial hair that didn't quite mesh into a full beard sprouting on his chin. His earlocks were curled and tucked in tightly at his hairline, his eyes were grey, his forehead arched and he wore a green cloak in both winter and summer. And despite his bulky stature, he was light on his feet. He would pray standing to the right of the Torah podium and during the Shemoneh Esreh prayer he would wave his hand in front of his face because, due to his tremendous diligence in Torah study, conundrums and elucidations kept popping into his head and he would flail them away so that they would not distract him from his prayers. When studying, he would stay put like a stake driven into the ground, never rising except to get a drink of water from the basin, where he would place his mouth near the spigot with one hand on his hat lest it fall off his head, and drink half a sink's worth. They also say that a smile had never crossed his face, and that when anyone so much as made a jocular remark in front of him, he would crinkle his brow, shake his head at him and declare, "Myriad are the needs of your people!" If a householder invited him to dinner, he would decline. And if the householder persisted, Moshe Pinchas would say, "I have what I need and require nothing more." They called him, but not to his face, *der vochndiker bukher*, that is to say "the weekday boy," because they never saw him in the Kloyz except during the days of the week.

5.

Now let's leave aside Moshe Pinchas and go back to the son-in-law of that notable of our town. Not even a year had passed before he had married the youngest daughter of Reb Mordechai Scheiner, an iron and copper merchant, son of wealth, from the line of Rabbi Mordechai Yafeh, Ba'al HaLevushim. This is neither the time nor the place to tell the story of the wedding itself and all of the honor we garnered as a result of that marriage, because of all the rabbis and revered ones who came from near and far. The son-in-law himself, Reb Shlomo HaLevi, was a Horowitz, from the Horowitz family, a direct descendant of the Holy Shelah. It is said that for twenty-six generations back, and some even say thirty-six generations, they were never disconnected from Torah, and that there was not a town in our lands in which one of them had not held the rabbinical seat. And our town was privileged enough to count among its rabbis the sage Rabbi Pinchas Ba'al Mofet, a member of that family. They say that at the time of his death Rabbi Pinchas had said, "I promise you that someday someone very special from our family line will come to reside here." And they also say that he ordered them not to bury anyone next to him until after a hundred years had passed, and that even then the deceased had to be someone from his lineage. Reb Shlomo, the groom, was a son worthy of his ancestors. At the age of sixteen he had already received rabbinic ordination from two of the greatest scholars of that generation. And when he had come before them he had not revealed who he was until they had finished testing him. Unlike most of the well-connected snobs in our land who have made it only on the merit of their fathers.

Already during the seven days of wedding feasts, every single study house in our town was vying for Reb Shlomo to affiliate himself with them. Our old study house, on account of its numerous books; the new study house on account of his father-in-law and his father-in-law's father, both of whom prayed there; the men of the old Kloyz, because it is suitable for a man to pray in the place where his ancestors had worshipped and it was time-honored tradition that the great scholar Rabbi Pinchas Ba'al Mofet used to pray in the old

Kloyz. But Reb Shlomo set himself up in the new Kloyz, because the new Kloyz was situated on a hill and the air was fresh, and he liked to study in a place with pleasant air. When Reb Shlomo entered the Kloyz, he would light up the whole place with the aura of his presence. The radiance of his face, his blue eyes and his chestnut hair endeared him to all who beheld him. His garments were just like those of all proper Jews of that period, short pants tucked into long stockings, soft shoes and a generously cut overcoat, and all of his clothes were of fine silk, as was the custom of sons of rabbis who had achieved a certain stature. His speech was calm and collected and his bearing was one of composure. The elders of the Kloyz prefaced his name with the title of Rabbi and the younger ones tried hard to study each and every one of his mannerisms, in order to emulate him. Except who can really come close to resembling such a son of great scholars, where twenty-six, some even say thirty-six generations or more, were all rabbis and sons of rabbis? Moshe Pinchas, who was so demanding of himself and didn't converse with anyone, would put aside his studies to talk with Reb Shlomo and would accompany him to his house and go in and sit with him and engage him in debate. And he did not notice that Reb Shlomo's wife did not suffer any man coming between her and her husband, like young wives who always like to keep their husbands to themselves.

All this and more. Reb Shlomo was somewhat familiar with German from a translation of the Psalms by Reb Moshe and also from the holiday prayer hymns translated by Rabbi Wolf. And these had not been printed in the German alphabet, but rather in Hebrew characters with Old Yiddish type. Reb Shlomo's wife, being proficient in written and oral German as was the case with most daughters of rich men of our town who used to study with tutors up until the time of their marriages, wanted to teach her husband German writing and pronunciation. But when Moshe Pinchas began coming and going regularly from their house, it diverted them from their studies, and she resented Reb Moshe Pinchas for bothering her husband and disturbing the house with his voice. Because of the story of Michal and David (Samuel II 6:16) she didn't say a word about it. Reb Shlomo would try to appease her (with the same words he himself failed to heed) saying to her, "Is it not an honor that this wise scholar who doesn't enter anyone else's home is comfortable calling so frequently at yours?" And she was thinking to herself, "If only he'd go more to everyone else and less to us!" And Moshe Pinchas was thinking, "If I, who am not in the habit of going to see anyone else, call upon this man then surely he must be happy to have me."

6.

Days passed as usual and the town went about its business according to custom. Summer was summer and winter was winter, and as time went on some matches were arranged and some weddings took place. Moshe Pinchas still had not found his intended bride. There are those who say it was because he was so devoted to his studies that his heart wasn't open to matters of matchmaking. Others say that it was on account of his mother, who hindered every match by consulting with sorceresses. Every time a potential mate was suggested to her son these women would insist that she was not his intended. Afterwards, it became apparent that all of this was simply nonsense and when the spirit moved him to take a wife he would take a wife. And so Moshe Pinchas remained unmarried and did not yet don a tallit.

And we have yet more to tell. That same year, when Reb Shlomo's elderly father-in-law was called to the Torah as Hatan Bereishit, he offered a certain sum of money to the building fund of the synagogue, in addition to which he also donated the wood for heating, inasmuch as the custom in our town is for the Hatan Bereishit to contribute the wood to heat his study house. And here we must share that the donation was a timely one because the study house was truly in need of repair. And in the manner of God-fearing wealthy men, he did not put off his donation. And the gabbai didn't even hold onto the dedicated money to use it for trade, but rather immediately hired a craftsman and purchased stones and girders. The craftsman however, dragged his feet, like those craftsmen who chase after work their whole lives and once work is available for them they don't attend to it and instead go courting after other work. In the meantime the days of snow and extreme cold had arrived. And when the cold comes to our town all builders cease their labors. That winter was a particularly difficult one and many took ill from the cold. And the old man, who was elderly and delicate and whose set place in the study house was in the alcove by the window, was seized by a chill and caught cold and was beset by his illness from the Sabbath of Hanukah until Passover. The old man, knowing full well that he was sick only because they had been negligent in making the building improvements, increased the craftsman's pay so that he would get going with his work and ordered him to seal off the alcove in front of the window where the drafts gust in, bringing with them the chill. They fixed up the building and closed up the alcove. When the story was told at the Kloyz, one scholar stood up and said, "I'm astonished that they were allowed to do that, because they obviously diminished the amount of holy space." Reb Shlomo came in. That same scholar said, "Let us hear the opinion of Reb Shlomo." Moshe Pinchas jumped up and declared, "It is forbidden to alter the interior space of a synagogue by reducing it even by one finger's length, for this would violate a Biblical prohibition." Reb Shlomo tried to quiet him gently and tell him, "I also said the same thing, but what's done is already done." But when he saw the aging bachelor leaping about and shouting, heaping proof upon proof in defense of his position, he dismissed him with a wave of his hand and said jokingly, "*A bukher makht kidesh af a groyp.*"

7.

I have no idea where that saying comes from, but in our town it was commonly used to dismissively tease young unmarried men who tried to insinuate themselves into the company of their married elders, as equals. Moshe Pinchas, who had already attained a third of a man's normal lifespan but remained a bachelor only because he hadn't yet found a suitable match, recoiled and returned to his place where he sat tugging at the clumps of his beard in distress. From that point on he did not speak to Reb Shlomo, and if Reb Shlomo asked how he was, he would respond reluctantly. At first, no one noticed anything. And when they did begin to notice, they were incredulous. Why would

Reb Shlomo, who showed respect even to the lowliest ones, humiliate one of the most erudite scholars? And they were even more critical of Moshe Pinchas for being so vengeful and bearing a grudge. Reb Shlomo went to Moshe Pinchas and said, "I beg you, forgive me for the words that unintentionally escaped from my mouth." But Moshe Pinchas just glared at him and did not respond.

That very day a bookseller brought the book *Ketzot HaHoshen* to the Kloyz. The conversation got around to the book's author, the Ba'al HaKetzot, who had labored in matters of Torah while living in deprivation and poverty. A plank over a barrel served as his table, and in winter he had no wood to light his stove and was forced to stay in bed and write his book there. And sometimes the ink would even freeze from the extreme cold and he would put it under his pillow to thaw out. When he had finished the first part of his book, he went to see the master sage, our Rabbi Meshulam Igra. And when the Ba'al HaKetzot began to present a Talmudic disputation to him, Reb Meshulam interjected, "Sir, you must be intending to say it this way." And the other responded, "No, not really." Reb Meshulam looked at him briefly and said, "Then undoubtedly the gentleman must be intending to say it this way or that way," and this went on until the author had completely run out of innovative ideas, for Reb Meshulam had a knack of understanding each and every sage's way of analyzing things and had honed in on the Ba'al HaKetzot's precise thinking on every innovation the latter could present on any given issue. The Ba'al HaKetzot then said to Reb Meshulam, "Look, as we speak I'm already busy composing the second volume, and I am wondering if there is any point in my continuing to toil on it? Tell me, Sir, what could I possibly add now by way of commentary to the Shulhan Arukh's finance code from chapter 200 on?" At that point Reb Meshulam realized that he had disheartened a very gifted man and was filled with remorse. It is said that when this story was relayed, Reb Shlomo added that from this point on Reb Meshulam had fasted every Monday and Thursday for the rest of his life because of having aggrieved that sage. And people say that when this story was told, Reb Shlomo groaned and said, "I don't come close to Reb Meshulam's level of righteousness." Those around him had a sense of where things were going and said to him, "And Moshe Pinchas doesn't come close to Ba'al HaKetzot's level of Torah scholarship!" Reb Shlomo replied, "Reb Moshe Pinchas is a great scholar and learns Torah for its own sake." When this was relayed to Moshe Pinchas, he just shrugged and said, "Leave me be. I don't even want to hear that man's name." A short while later, Moshe Pinchas arose from his studies, collected his Gemara and left. When a day or two had passed and he still hadn't come back, people assumed that he'd gone to his mother's in the village, even though it wasn't his custom to go there on weekdays. A few days later, a voice was heard emanating from the Tailors' Synagogue and they recognized it as belonging to Moshe Pinchas.

The Tailors' Synagogue was located above our old study house, opposite the bathhouse, and it was somewhat similar to the Great Synagogue, resplendent with paintings of the Chariot and of the musical instruments of the Temple and also with depictions of the animals and birds in the teaching of Yehudah ben Teimah in tractate Avot, with the words of the Mishnah underneath each of the illustrations. Under the leopard it said, "Be bold as a leopard," under the eagle, "Light as an eagle," under the deer, "swift as a deer" and under the lion, "strong as a lion." And under all of them it was written, "To do the will of our Father in heaven." And why do I mention all of this? To demonstrate to you that a wise man learns from everything around him and, by gazing at the drawings he devotes his heart to the Torah. They say that when the women used to go to the mikveh and would hear Reb Moshe Pinchas's voice, they would bless themselves and say, "May we be worthy to have sons like him."

8.

Here it should be told that at that time his mother's income from leasing the mill had run out. And with the end of the mother's income came the end of the son's sustenance. However, relief and deliverance came from another place. Residents of the town began bringing him their sons and paying him tutoring fees. It's been said that Reb Shlomo had dropped a hint that people ought to seek wisdom from such a scholar. Reb Moshe Pinchas selected three or four talented pupils and taught them Talmud and its commentaries, earning enough for his own needs and even enough to give to his mother. From this time on he no longer had to go to the village and didn't have to waste time on traveling back and forth. And where did his mother hear Kiddush and Havdalah? Thank God, even in villages there are Jews, and a Jew's door is always open to all who want to hear hallowed words.

Moshe Pinchas found lodging in a certain tailor's house, and the tailor even made him a new suit, not of fine silk like that of Reb Shlomo, but nonetheless sufficiently respectable. The other artisans saw this and were envious of the tailor. The milliner went and made him a new hat and the cobbler made him shoes. One Sabbath eve, when Moshe Pinchas went to the bathhouse, they took his hat and shoes and replaced them with the new ones they'd made. Moshe Pinchas was dressed in new clothes, new shoes and a new hat so that his entire appearance was transformed. His pupils, who recognized his erudition in Torah, began to referring to him as Rabbi Moshe Pinchas, and it goes without saying that the tailors and the rest of the artisans were very proud of this great scholar who had ensconced himself in their house of prayer. And every artisan who had a daughter used to gaze upon him and say "May it be God's will that he become my son-in-law." Mercifully, one affluent man beat them to it. Reb Meirtche, the son of Shaindele the Righteous. Reb Meirtche had a fabric store and an only daughter. He lavished upon his daughter a dowry of one hundred and fifty coins of pure silver, thereby landing Moshe Pinchas. And from this we can learn that all the idle talk of the gossip mongers was unfounded, because when the time comes for a man to marry. his match will surely be found.

Once Reb Moshe Pinchas was married he was able to stand with the great ones and discourse with the Torah elders like all the other tallit wearers. And yet he didn't leave his place or alter his customary behavior. Since his father-in-law took care of his every need, he dismissed his pupils and returned to solitary study, and didn't budge from his studies except on Sabbath eve. And even on the eve of the Sabbath he didn't stay home all night. Even before the sun rose, he would return to his place of study. In summertime he would study in the Tailors' Synagogue and in the winter, when there was no lit stove there, he would move himself over to the old study house. The simple folk and even some of the students began to refer to him as Rabbi Moshe Pinchas even when not addressing him. Reb Moshe Pinchas didn't pay attention to this honorific. His entire sense of worth derived from sating himself on Talmud and rabbinical Codes.

9.

About Reb Moshe Pinchas there isn't much to tell for the moment. He was invested heart and soul in the Talmud, its commentators, and the commentaries on the commentators. He would complete one Tractate and immediately embark upon another.

But about Reb Shlomo there is what to tell. The Emperor's troops arrived in the town's environs for training exercises, with the Archduke in command. It occurred to the community elders that should the Archduke come to town he would surely visit the Great Synagogue to bestow honor on the Jews. And here there was no one who knew how to give a proper sermon, particularly not in the vernacular. For in those days our town languished without a rabbi, with an aged instructor serving in place of a rabbi. Moreover, that instructor was not accustomed to delivering sermons, even on Shabbat Shuva or Shabbat HaGadol, and it goes without saying not in the vernacular. They considered bringing in a preacher from Ternopil, from among the students of Yossel ben Todrus, known as Joseph Perl. Reb Shlomo offered, "I will deliver the sermon and I am confident that the merit of my sacred ancestors, whose righteousness endures, will sustain me." All were delighted that there would be no need to engage a preacher devoid of Torah and mitzvot and they were astonished that Reb Shlomo was willing to undertake to sermonize in a language to which he was not accustomed, because if he erred or stumbled it could only be for the worse, not for the better. The entire town prayed that he wouldn't trip over his own tongue, and that his words would be pleasing to the Archduke. The prayers did their share and Reb Shlomo's talent took care of the rest, so that when Reb Shlomo stood by the Holy Ark and greeted the Archduke it was a truly holy moment, and everyone saw and recognized that if a man makes the Torah his lifeblood, all other forms of wisdom will come to him on their own. And yet it wasn't a miracle at all, inasmuch as Reb Shlomo knew the entire Book of Psalms as translated by Reb Moshe by heart and also most of the hymns that Reb Wolf had translated, and some things he had after all learned from his wife who was fluent in German. This sermon brought him fame throughout the land. Reb Shlomo, however, tried to downplay it, so that it shouldn't be said he gained acclaim by means of the German language and so as not to create an opening for the "new enlightened ones" to try and curry favor with him.

10.

At around that same time a certain town was bereft of its rabbi. The town sent for Reb Shlomo. They found him suitable and he accepted the rabbinical post. After taking his leave from all the elders of his town and his wife's family, he visited the grave of his ancestor the sage Reb Pinchas and after leaving his ancestor he went to Reb Moshe Pinchas and said to him, "Now that I'm going to another town, I appeal to you that we make peace." Reb Moshe Pinchas responded, "There will never be peace between us. Not in this world and not in the world to come." Reb Shlomo heaved a heavy sigh and departed.

It is a widely accepted custom that when a new rabbi is hired by a congregation, all the townsfolk gather in the Great Synagogue to hear his sermon. And if the rabbi is among the famous ones, they even come from other towns. The topic of the sermon is announced a few days in advance, in order to give the scholars time to hone their studies in the event that they want to engage in back-and-forth with him. Originally, anyone wanting to debate would just interject himself into the sermon and start arguing. When everyone realized this led to confusion, it was resolved that all questions must be held until the conclusion of the sermon.

Now that the breadth of knowledge has waned, and sermonizers know nothing more than what they have specifically prepared, it has become customary instead to ask questions of the rabbi at his house. If he has an answer, he gives it. And if not, he becomes evasive and feigns fatigue. But, at that time, they were still allowing questions immediately after the sermon in front of the entire public. And so the date was set and the topic of Reb Shlomo's sermon was promulgated, and the announcement was copied and distributed among several towns. This very announcement reached our town as well.

II.

One day Reb Moshe Pinchas said to his wife, "I'm leaving for a few days." His wife, who was in the habit of accepting his pronouncements without complaint or argument, asked neither where he was going nor why. She gave him provisions for the road and said, "Go in peace." He gathered his tallit and tefillin and set off for Reb Shlomo's town.

The entire town was filled with guests. Those who had come for the sake of Reb Shlomo and those who had come to see who else had come. There were those who were eager to see the new rabbi and others eager simply to report what they had seen. The erudite Torah scholars walked around hunched over and debating with themselves. One would say to himself, "If Reb Shlomo says this, I will ask that and if he responds this way, I will inquire that way." And the way one man strategized, so precisely did his colleague, and so the next and the next. Among those that came you would have also found Reb Moshe Pinchas, who was sitting in the study house, busily ruminating on the precise Talmudic discussion that Reb Shlomo had announced as the topic of his sermon.

The whole town assembled itself into the Great Synagogue, which was already packed with those who had remained after the morning prayers. And when Reb Shlomo entered with his father the sage to his right and his uncle the other great sage to his left, the eyes of most of the assembly welled with tears of joy at having been granted the privilege of beholding two such venerable sages who embodied Torah in human form. And so Reb Shlomo entered, and with him his father and his uncle, and with them several other rabbis and Torah learners, even the least of whom in our generation would have been considered a sage among sages. The entire congregation raised a mighty cheer in their honor and roared, "Welcome! May your arrival be blessed!" until the brass candelabras swayed from the clamor.

12.

Reb Shlomo ascended to the Holy Ark. He wrapped himself in a new prayer shawl and recited the *Sheheheyanu* blessing. He kissed the ark curtain and whispered several verses which are particularly suited for suppressing pride, and began to sermonize incisively and eruditely, argument and counter argument. Reb Shlomo was possessed of a gift of silver tongued eloquence, and even knew how to sermonize in the lingua franca and all the more so in the holy tongue which he had worked with his entire life. And once he had begun to speak all were filled with joy and they said, "What great fortune has been bestowed upon us to have this rabbi in our midst." And even the simple folk recognized that great words were being uttered by him. Reb Shlomo endeared himself to them deeply. It's been told that one butcher cried out in great wonder, "I am ready and willing to proffer my own neck for the slaughter on behalf of our new rabbi." All the self-proclaimed debaters who had come intending to debate with the rabbi, set aside their arguments and stood trembling and quaking in trepidation lest they miss even one word of his oratory.

Reb Shlomo stood there wrapped in his new prayer shawl crowned with silver ornamentation, his face full of humility, his voice going from the Babylonian Talmud to the Jerusalem Talmud, from the Jerusalem Talmud to the commentary of Rav Alfasi, from Rav Alfasi to Maimonides, and from Maimonides to the Rosh, from the early scholars to the later ones and back again. Torah elders are in the habit of telling that they had heard from several old rabbis that those rabbis had frequently struggled to reconcile the very same Talmudic query posed by Reb Shlomo, and when they heard Reb Shlomo's solution they realized that their thoughts compared to his were like vinegar compared to wine. They also tell that at the time of Reb Shlomo's sermon, tears were seen in the eyes of that venerable sage Reb Shlomo's father and they saw that at times Reb Shlomo would nod his head to his father and his father would then point towards the Holy Ark. The pundits commented that the son was nodding towards his father as if to say, "Father, all of this comes from you," and the father, in turn, was pointing to the ark as if to say, "Your learning, my son, derives from there."

13.

Reb Shlomo was standing and sermonizing and his voice was like that of the humble nightingale on a summer night. Suddenly a gruff voice was heard and a man was seen pushing and squeezing his way, squeezing and pushing until he arrived at the Holy Ark. And when he got to the ark, to the place where Reb Shlomo was standing, his voice began to grate and drone. Reb Shlomo stopped his sermon and cocked his head to listen. As the congregation noticed Reb Shlomo straining to listen, they all cocked their own heads and heard that this man was negating Reb Shlomo's entire sermon by way of an explicit Talmudic statement. Their faces fell and they were embarrassed that they themselves hadn't picked up on the discrepancy, and a few of them imagined that they had in fact discerned it but that Reb Shlomo's sweet voice had mesmerized them. Only the simple folk remained as devoted to their rabbi as at the start, and when they saw that a man had the audacity to contradict him they were ready to rip him to shreds. But he took notice neither of them nor of their wrath; he saw but one thing: that he had been given an opening to totally destroy all of the theories of that incisive and erudite one, and to demonstrate that there was neither insight nor erudition here, but rather his analysis was utter folly. And the simple folk were already reaching towards the insolent one to cast him out.

14.

Reb Shlomo rapped on the podium and said, "Calm down and let me hear what Rabbi Moshe Pinchas has to say." And he immediately gazed upon him with great affection and added, "Rabbi Moshe Pinchas, please repeat what you said and I shall listen; perhaps I didn't hear you well." Reb Moshe Pinchas recounted what he had said, throwing in some words of derision. And still, Reb Shlomo was gazing upon him warmly and it appeared that he was reveling in his own distress. After Reb Moshe Pinchas had finished, Reb Shlomo said, "Rabbi Moshe Pinchas, do you have anything else to add?" Reb Moshe Pinchas was filled with wrath and shouted at the top of his lungs, "Is it not enough for you that I've demonstrated that you built mounds upon mounds of nonsensical arguments in contravention of an explicit Gemara? I already have shaken out the sand particles with which you attempted to blind the people's eyes."

The entire congregation was distressed about the insult to Reb Shlomo and a few of the scholars wanted to respond to the words of the challenger, but did not know what to say since they saw that he was in the right, in that Reb Shlomo had erred about an explicit Gemara and that in any case his entire sermon had been built on a shaky foundation.

Reb Shlomo's uncle now rapped on the podium and offered, "I'll respond." His father then rapped and said, "I'll respond." Without a doubt, they would have succeeded in countering Reb Moshe Pinchas's counter-arguments, but it is doubtful that they would have satisfied the Gemara's own contradiction. They were blinded by their love for Reb Shlomo and did not pay mind to the Gemara, but instead chose to justify him by means of Talmudic argumentation. Reb Shlomo waved his hand once towards his father and once towards his uncle and said, "With your permission, I myself will respond." Reb Moshe Pinchas jeered and said, "Is it not enough that a man refuses to concede the truth, but now he intends to heap lies on top of it?"

Reb Shlomo fixed his two luminous eyes upon him and said, "It appears you have saddled me with an enormously difficult question from the Gemara, and it would also appear that nothing can be said in response, except that if you had scrutinized the text carefully you would have seen that this version of the text is inaccurate, and already two illustrious pillars, the Maharshal and the Bach, have amended the text of the Talmud in this spot with the version postulated by the Rav Alfasi, and everything I have put forth I based on the true version of the text relied upon by most commentators to determine the law." And here Reb Shlomo began to weave from commentator to commentator until he arrived at the legal ruling. At the same time Reb Moshe Pinchas's countenance darkened like the edges of a cauldron and he did not respond at all; after all what would there have been to say given that the law was on Reb Shlomo's side? Reb Moshe Pinchas stood like a stricken man, and Reb Shlomo returned to his sermon. Reb Moshe Pinchas stomped on the floor so forcefully that the stones underneath cried out. And he also cried out, "*Panie* Horowitz, how fortunate for you that all your silver and gold have enabled you to purchase proofread books. Even so, your new conclusions are nonsense and your homilies mere folly." And immediately Reb Moshe Pinchas began to refute Reb Shlomo's words one after the other, to the point where the great Torah scholars were astounded by the sheer power of the man's intellect and the minds of these eminent ones were totally confounded. Reb Shlomo raised his right hand and said pleasantly, "Rabbi Moshe Pinchas, how vast is your erudition and how abundant your acuity, but tell me is it really fitting for a true scholar to use the Torah deceitfully? Surely, you and I both know full well that there is no substance to the refutations with which you are trying to undermine my position." And here Reb Shlomo chipped away, argument after argument, and did not omit responding to any of Reb Moshe Pinchas's refutations. Reb Moshe Pinchas turned apoplectic with rage and, leaping up and down, and bellowed, "In that case, I'll confront you from another angle." And right away he began attacking a different point in the lecture and to squawk about each of Reb Shlomo's findings until there was not one conclusion that he had not shattered. Reb Shlomo's face clouded over and he heaved a bitter sigh, like a warrior dealt a fatal blow, and stripped of his weapons.

By this point everyone was under the impression that Reb Shlomo was drained of all his strength and that he no longer had it in him to stand up to someone more forceful than himself. And once again Reb Shlomo sighed deeply and looked at Reb Moshe Pinchas with neither anger nor animosity. On the contrary, it was apparent that he pitied him, even though he was really the one in need of mercy, Reb Moshe Pinchas having humiliated him in front of the entire gathering on his very first day as rabbi. Reb Shlomo passed his hand over his forehead and said in a sad voice, "There is no limit to what a skillful man can accomplish by the force of his cunning, but what will you answer on Judgment Day?" Reb Moshe Pinchas sneered at him and said, "Can you believe how consumed this man is with his own piety, that I deliver him actual words of Torah and he responds with words about the fear of Heaven? If you are able to reply to me from Torah do so, and if not, confess in front of the whole congregation that your whole sermon is chaff and straw." Most of the congregants began to holler at Reb Moshe Pinchas, but a certain elderly and assertive scholar rebuked them. He said to them, "If scholars battle over Jewish law, who are you to interfere?" Reb Shlomo turned back towards the Holy Ark and laid his head on the curtain. Everyone assumed he was withdrawing and about to step down. Suddenly he turned back towards the people and the whole crowd noted that he seemed to have gotten taller by a whole head. Reb Shlomo said, "With your permission, gentlemen, I will repeat the essence of my sermon and you will determine the veracity of my words." Reb Shlomo succinctly recapped the crux of his presentation and reinforced it with new proofs, until the faces of the scholars lit up and they called out, "Hear, hear!," having been completely distracted from Reb Moshe Pinchas and all his argumentation. At the same time the simple folk glared at Reb Moshe Pinchas with daggers in their eyes and were just about ready to beat him up. Reb Moshe Pinchas dismissed them as the dust of the earth, even though he was consumed with a desire to show them that their rabbi was a poor scholar. And when he attempted to say something they started yelling and saying, "Enough already! We don't want to hear what you have to say." And when he raised his voice they silenced him and shouted, "Let's get him out of here and may his face no longer be seen in this place."

Already from the outset of the exchange, when Reb Moshe Pinchas had addressed Reb Shlomo "*Panie* Horowitz," the whole assembly had been shocked, as they had never before heard a learned Jew address a Torah scholar using a secular title, especially not in a holy place. The elderly sage jumped up from his place and admonished him harshly, "Show some common decency!" And the rest shouted, "You audacious lout!" Reb Moshe Pinchas paid heed neither to them nor their shouting, instead fixing his eyes on Reb Shlomo in order to relish in his humiliation. And if not for Reb Shlomo, they would have thrown him out of the synagogue. Now even Reb Shlomo could not quiet the congregation down. And since Reb Moshe Pinchas realized that they weren't going to let him speak, and all the more so since he was in a dangerous situation, he twisted his neck and started threading himself out of the congregation. And had it not been for Reb Shlomo's kindly eyes he would have had his limbs crushed on his way out. Reb Shlomo resumed his sermon, and Reb Moshe Pinchas returned to his hometown. And even greater than his regret over not being able to contradict Reb Shlomo's presentation was his regret that Reb Shlomo had attained even greater stature for showing him boundless affection from beginning to end.

15.

Upon Reb Moshe Pinchas's return to his town he entered the study house and gathered a pile of books and each and every book demonstrated to him that the law was in Reb Shlomo's favor. And even when he chanced upon a treatise which seemed to lean towards his interpretations it failed to ease his mind, since he was not inclined towards the kind of semantic splitting of hairs engaged in by hairsplitters, who push elephants through the eyes of needles with their sophistry. Reb Moshe Pinchas was consumed with regret for having attempted to delude himself, all the while having known the truth. He was overcome by sadness and fell into a dark melancholy. And when he managed to rise above his gloominess enough to return to his studies, he had lost the joy of learning. He ruminated, "What does it matter if I study or if I don't, if I derive no gratification from my studies?" He began to examine his deeds. He remembered his mother. He started rebuking himself and said, "Now that I don't need her, I've forgotten her." He sighed and said, "I shall go and see her." He gathered his tallit and tefillin and went to fulfill the commandment of honoring one's mother.

The old woman had aged considerably but was still going about her way as always. Each morning with the crow of the rooster she would arise from her bed and wash her hands and face in the water troughs at the old mill; then she would feed and water the fowl and check their roosts to see if any hens had laid eggs. After that she would feed the cat. After that she would fluff up the straw in her bed while saying, "Yesterday you were light, today you are dense; today you are sprawled on my bed and I'm sprawled upon you, but tomorrow you will be used to stoke the hellfire that torments my soul." Once she had made her bed she would sit and pray. When done praying she would perform the ritual hand washing and soak her bread in water so as not to trouble the last two tooth stumps remaining in her mouth, which she would need to eat the obligatory bit of matzah on the nights of Passover. Once she had eaten and then said the blessing over her food, she would sit and contemplate what else needed to be done. If there were people in need of help in the village, she would go to help them. If there were none needing help, she would go to her neighbor to trade an egg for a cup of milk or a spoonful of grain for her evening meal, which she would eat while there was still daylight since from the time her husband had died and Moshe Pinchas had gone off to reside in town she would not light candles except on Sabbath eve and the festivals. After she had eaten and blessed, she would take out her burial shrouds, lay them next to her bed and recite the Shema.

16.

When the son arrived at his mother's she was sitting on the ground in front of the house, cutting up apples and pears to dry them in the sun. Seeing her son approach she put down the knife, smoothed her apron, raised herself up from the ground and said, "I don't know how I got myself so caught up with these fruits. Have I not already eaten too much in this world? Oy, Moshe Pinchas, how many days, how many weeks, how many months have I not seen you?" Moshe Pinchas shook his head and said, "And as if I've seen you?" His mother saw that he was sad and said, "Heaven forbid, has trouble befallen you?" Reb Moshe Pinchas said, "To me, no." She said, "If I had a mirror in the house, I would show you your face which is as dark as the plague in Egypt. Perhaps you have problems with your wife or your father-in-law or mother-in-law?" He responded, "I have neither sorrow nor travails, not from my wife, not from my in-laws." His mother said, "This kind of face your father, may he intercede on our behalf, had when a certain good–for–nothing from the town wanted to build a steam powered mill. When you get to the river, take a look into the water and you will see your own face. Do you have an enemy, my son? Tell me his name and his mother's name." Reb Moshe Pinchas said, "His name and his mother's name, what do you need them for?" The old one said, "My son, do you remember Mikita, who stole a grindstone from the mill? That uncircumcised one went to prostrate himself on the graves of their saints and returned all fire and brimstone, and when he curses a man in his name and that of his mother he turns him into dust and ashes. So, tell me my son, the name of the one who hates you and his mother's name and I will go to Mikita." Reb Moshe Pinchas heard this and shuddered. As his mother began to pester him he told her, "This same man whom I hate seeks only my welfare." His mother said, "He seeks your welfare? Why then do you hate him?" Reb Moshe Pinchas said, "I hate him because he brings out in me this deplorable quality of hatred." The old woman said, "I don't understand a word you're saying." He told her, "Even I don't understand, except that this is the way it is and I can't explain it. Don't fret, Mother, the Holy One blessed be He will help me." The old one said, "The Holy One blessed be He will surely help you, for whom will He help if not for you? Don't you study His Torah?" Moshe Pinchas's face fell and he said, "Is it truly Torah that I learn? I'm worthless and I speak worthless words. Let me be, Mother, and I shall return to the study house. Perhaps the Merciful One will show mercy."

After he ate, he returned to his town and to his studies. From this time forward, he did not budge from the study house and they would bring him his meals there. And if it was not for the beadle, who would remind him that it was time to say Kiddush and eat the festive meal, he would not have returned home even on Sabbath eves, so engrossed was he in his studies. The elders of the study house would say, "If you have not yet seen a man prepared to kill himself for his studies, just take a look at Rabbi Moshe Pinchas."

17.

One day Reb Moshe Pinchas vanished from the town. People assumed he had gone to his mother, but finally it was discovered that he he had gone to see his first teacher, our renowned scholar Rabbi Gabriel Reinush, the author of *Horeh Gaver*, a commentary on Yoreh De'ah. For what reason did he go to his teacher? Let us listen and find out: he came to his teacher and found him lying on his bed reading a book. He said to him, "Is my teacher ill?" He responded, "Why?" And he said, "Because I see him laid out on his bed." He responded, "I am an old man and it no longer pays for me to get new clothes made, so I lie in my bed in order not to wear out my clothes from sitting. Turn away and I'll get dressed." The old man donned his clothing and stood up straight. Before long he had begun to hold forth to his pupil awesome and wondrous new insights, from the mere tip of which the rabbis of today's generation would compile voluminous books. Finally, he began to direct the conversation to the name of the town where he had attempted to obtain a rabbinical post and had raised, in his astute expertise, some doubts about whether it was permissible to arrange divorces there. In the midst of speaking, the teacher looked at his pupil and noticed that he was not happy, but how could that be when "God's precepts are straight and good, making our hearts rejoice." The teacher said to him, "You're sitting there as if you're listening to something insignificant. You know, Moshe Pinchas, we may need to send you back to primary school." Reb Moshe Pinchas lowered his head and said, "It is for that reason that I came." The teacher was moved by compassion for his pupil and said to him, "My son, what has brought you here?" Reb Moshe Pinchas whispered and said, "Woe is me, my teacher, for I have strayed from the path of righteousness." The old one responded, "The Torah protects and the Torah rescues." Reb Moshe Pinchas said, "This refers to someone who learns Torah for the sake of Torah." The old one said,

"God Forbid that a man who learned Torah from me did not learn Torah for its own sake."

Reb Moshe Pinchas heaved a sigh. "What can I possibly say?" he said. "There are things I know to be true and yet I twist them around so as to remove them from their truth." His teacher said to him, "You have to set your heart straight by delving into ethical literature, such as *Kav HaYashar* and *Shevet Musar*. Reb Moshe Pinchas said, "The Holy One blessed be He does not bother with the minor books." The old one smiled and said, "In that case, we shall turn to the major books." And he immediately began discoursing on the various halakhic midrashim, and Tosefta and the entire Talmud until the house expanded like the foyer of a grand hall and yet there remained not one item that Reb Moshe Pinchas could not complete from memory, nor one legal ruling from which Reb Moshe Pinchas had not drawn a genuinely true outcome. At the end of three days when Moshe Pinchas was about to take leave of his teacher, the latter said, "Here I am a man of seventy three years, and I have never before had the privilege of spending three days as joyful as these. Come sit down and I shall sign your rabbinic ordination, authorizing you to issue halakhic decisions. Though I am a small town rabbi, I am widely known and it is also known that my ordination is reliable since I was ordained by the Rav of Buczacz, the renowned sage Rabbi Hershele Kra, about whom our Rabbi Meshulam Igra said, "He is an ironclad rabbi!" The old man took a sheet of paper and wrote: "He shall teach! He may judge!" – the ancient formula for rabbinical ordination. He placed the paper in his pupil's hand and said to him, "Here you have a talisman against melancholy." The old one gazed upon Reb Moshe Pinchas and said to his household, "This pupil will not shame me when I appear before the authority of the heavenly court." Reb Moshe Pinchas returned to his town and to his studies.

18.

What more can we tell that we have not already told? Reb Moshe Pinchas returned to his town and to his studies and tried diligently to put these matters out of his mind. And once again he was studying the way he had been taught. The renowned sage, author of *Horeh Gaver*, who was fond of his pupil and was proud of him, used to tell anyone and everyone that he had ordained Reb Moshe Pinchas as an authorized rabbi. And in that generation, the rabbis would not grant ordination to anyone other than an accomplished scholar. Word had reached Reb Moshe Pinchas's father-in-law. His father-in-law said to him: "For the time being, you sit at my table and you share my food, but what will you do after my days on this earth are over? Perhaps it would be worthwhile to consider a rabbinic profession." Reb Moshe Pinchas shrugged his shoulders by way of refusal. When his father-in-law tried to bring up the subject again, Reb Moshe Pinchas said, "If my father-in-law keeps me from my studies with idle conversation, I will end up being a complete ignoramus." Reb Meirtche walked away from him, sighing and dejected.

19.

The Lord giveth and he taketh away, dethrones kings and installs others in their place. At that time, Reb Shlomo's father departed to his final resting place. After they had returned the expired sage to the earth and eulogized him, the entire holy congregation stood and anointed Reb Shlomo in place of his father. After the seven days of mourning, Reb Shlomo went to his town to collect his wife and children. The town leaders asked him, "Rabbi, whom should we appoint to your chair?" He said to them, "Remember the day that I delivered my first sermon and that young scholar tried to trip me up with the law? I tell you that there is no one more worthy of being a rabbi than he." The town leaders heard this and were astounded; here was a man who had publicly embarrassed him and had attempted to dishonor him and yet here he was advocating on his behalf. Reb Shlomo clutched his beard and said, "Know this, gentlemen, this Rabbi Moshe Pinchas is as great in Torah knowledge as the ancient sages, and even in a subject in which he attempted to trip me up his greatness was evident; I was saved only by the merit of my ancestors in that Moshe Pinchas was forced to study from a defective book and thus came to err, and when a man falls into error that error leads him to further error. And certainly by now he has recognized his mistakes. Go to his town and accept him as your Rabbi. And you, my beloved brethren, are bound to be happy with him, because the rabbinate suits him and he is suited to the rabbinate. And even the holy Torah is destined to be happy that one of her worthy sons is sitting at her throne."

20.

Not too many days had passed before two men arrived at our town and in their hands the rabbinical appointment for "Our teacher, the erudite and astute rabbi, great scholar excelling in the entirety of Torah, etc., etc., and so on and so forth, may his name be of blessed glory, the sage, Rabbi Moshe Pinchas, a just and upright man of Israel." They parked their carriage at the inn and entered, washed their hands, changed their clothes and went to see Reb Moshe Pinchas. At that same time, his wife Shaindel was sitting in the nursing chair, suckling her small son. Next to her stood her mother Elka, looking at the baby who was small for his years and yet melancholy for his age. Shaindel herself was also melancholy both on her own account and on account of her children, since as soon as one arose from his sick bed his brother was already laid up sick. And because she was immersed in gloom she flung it in the face of the entire world that it had been created only to oppress her in suffering. By her feet lay the cat, grooming itself. Elka observed this and remarked, "Your cat is washing itself." Shaindel grumbled and said, "What have you come to tell me?" Said Elka, "If the cat is licking its fur, it's a sign that guests are getting ready to arrive." Shaindel said, "A house in which the head of the household is not found, is not likely to have guests found in it. God forbid that I should say anything against Moshe Pinchas, who doesn't move from the study house. And where else would he sit? In this garbage heap? But this much I'll tell you, Mother, my strength has ebbed and I don't know why the Angel of Death tarries and doesn't just come and take me from this world. It would better for him to kill me a thousand times a day. Why is it that all day long my eyelashes twitch and don't stop twitching?" Elka asked, "Is it the right or the left eyelid?" Shaindel said. "You are a strange woman,

Mother, what's the difference whether it's the right one or the left one?" Said Elka, "There is a big difference in it. If it's the left, it's a sign the guests are coming." Shaindel said, "You see, Mother, it just so happens that it's the lashes of the right one that are twitching. That being the case, there are no guests or anything else, only drivel. Now I'm going to fix the lunch meal. The fire is burning and the pot is boiling and I am sitting here babbling as if it's Shabbat afternoon after the noodle pudding."

21.

Meanwhile, the two dignitaries entered the town. They came across a little girl and asked her, "Whereabouts here is the house of Rabbi Moshe Pinchas?" The little one ran to her mother and in a loud excited voice exclaimed, "Two Jews are asking after Father. Mother, had you seen their garments, you would have thought they were going to a wedding!" Shaindel scolded her daughter and said, "Why are you hollering? What, am I deaf? If they're asking, let them ask." The little one said, "Mother, Mother, on my life, on my life, I'm not lying! Two important Jews dressed like fathers-of-the-bride came and asked me, Whereabouts here is Rabbi Moshe Pinchas's house?" Shaindel said to her mother, "Go outside and see what this child is jabbering about, screaming non-stop like a crow." Tears flowed from the child's eyes and she said while crying, "I'm not screaming! I'm not screaming! I'm telling the truth! I'm telling the truth!" Said Shaindel, "Either you stop or get away from here. I will not tolerate yelling and crying. Oy, if only I had a place to escape to from here. How can one live in a house with incessant crying?"

Elka stepped outside and saw two important personages elegantly dressed. Guests like these, dressed in this manner, are not normally found in our town. She said to them, "Come in, honored guests, come in. This is the home of Rabbi Moshe Pinchas. Rabbi Moshe Pinchas is not at home right now. If you would be so kind as to wait a moment, I shall send the little one to bring him." The dignitaries came inside and sat down. Said Shaindel to her mother, "Mother, watch the baby and I'll go and get him, for if the little one goes to call him he will not heed her." She wrapped herself and went to his study house. She was gone for as long as she was gone and returned with her husband. Reb Moshe Pinchas greeted the guests and sat down. He took the salt box that was on the table and fidgeted with it, while wondering why these people had come and what they wanted of him. One of them stood up from his chair and said, "Rabbi, we have come for the purpose of..." He did not finish his sentence before taking out the rabbinical appointment, handing it to Reb Moshe Pinchas. Reb Moshe Pinchas read it and accepted their proposal. His mother-in-law heard and sent for her husband. He heard and came over. They fetched fresh water from the spring and brought rose petal preserves so that the guests could refresh themselves.

The emissaries sat with their rabbi until the time for the afternoon prayers had arrived. In the meantime, a few of the town dignitaries gathered and came to greet the visitors and congratulate Reb Moshe Pinchas on having been elevated to the standing of rabbi. Elka prepared a meal for the guests, as well as for the next day's luncheon and evening meal. And at every meal new faces came to pay homage to the Torah, and at every meal Reb Moshe Pinchas shared wondrous new insights, something he had not been in the habit of doing up to this point, as he was not one to converse with just anyone and if he did converse he did so only in truncated conversations. And when the dignitaries had left for the inn, his father-in-law Reb Meirtche summoned the tailor and the shoemaker to make clothing and shoes for Reb Moshe Pinchas, since the clothing and shoes that had been made for his wedding were worn out. The tailor labored at his craft as did the shoemaker, for they knew that so long as their work was not complete Reb Moshe Pinchas would be detained from leaving and an entire congregation would be left in limbo, like an abandoned wife without a divorce forever chained to her husband. And as such, they hastened to finish and did justice to their craft. And when Reb Moshe Pinchas donned his new clothes, his appearance truly was transformed into that of a rabbi. While all this was going on, his mother-in-law prepared everything that was needed for the journey. And when all was ready, Reb Moshe Pinchas boarded the coach and half the town came to escort him, all being jubilant that this talented scholar who had toiled in Torah was so esteemed by the Torah itself that people had come from another town to secure him for a great honor. And even his mother came to part from her only son, leaning on her cane, and in her hands a really large loaf like the ones she used to give him in the early days. She gazed upon her son and said, "My son, you look a rabbi. If only your father had been fortunate enough to see you this way, he would still be alive. The miller mills all his days, mills and mills endlessly, and in the end he mills his own bones until he dies. And I too shall die, and I don't know where I will be taken. Remember, my son, and don't forget that I carried you and gave birth to you and nursed you, and I implore you now to admonish the evil angels lest they vilify me."

And thus Reb Moshe Pinchas boarded the coach, dressed in his new finery that had that very day left the hands of the tailor, with the two dignitaries, emissaries of their town, sitting one to his right and the other to his left. After he had completed the traveler's prayer he lit upon two peculiar questions that all the rabbis had wrestled with: why does Maimonides never mention the traveler's prayer and why would the Maharam of Rothenburg recite the prayer in his house upon departing on a journey? In the heat of the events which transpired later on his observations on that issue were forgotten, and it is a shame that such a fine pearl of wisdom was lost to us.

22.

And so the carriage left town and arrived at a crossroads, where Reb Moshe Pinchas looked down the road leading to the town that had hired him as Rabbi. He recalled the day on which he had gone there on foot and he remembered everything that had befallen him in that town. He mused to himself, "Here I am, traveling by carriage to the very place where the residents rose up to swallow me whole because I sought to undermine their shepherd." He suppressed the anger in his heart with words of Torah and began to expound on the verse, "Do not come to anger on the road," the text of which the Gemara interpreted to mean, "When on the road, do not engage in matters of law." And, therefore, he began discussing other matters. The two emissaries were reminded of Reb Shlomo, their rabbi, who had left their town and encouraged them to take on Reb Moshe Pinchas as their next rabbi. And since they remembered their rabbi, they also remembered his righteousness. One of them said to Reb Moshe Pinchas, "I'm wondering, Rabbi, why you haven't asked us how it came to be that we selected you as our new rabbi." Reb Moshe Pinchas said, "I was also wondering, but was preoccupied with matters of Torah law and forgot to ask you." The dignitary said, "In that case, I will tell you. When our great rabbi the sage Rabbi Shlomo, may he live long, was elevated to the seat of his father the sage, of blessed memory, the town elders asked him, 'Our rabbi, whom shall we put in your place and who is worthy to sit in your chair?' He said to them, 'If you want to bestow joy on our hallowed Torah, select Rabbi Moshe Pinchas as your rabbi, for he is a genuine scholar among the true scions of the Torah.' And inasmuch as our great rabbi was much beloved by us, we hastened to do his bidding." Reb Moshe Pinchas's expression began to undergo a transformation. After a short while, he said to the coachman, "Stop!" They assumed that he had to attend to a call of nature and stopped the carriage. He stepped down and took his bags. They asked him, "What's this?" He said to them, "Any kindness that comes to me from that man – I don't want it!" They said to him, "Rabbi, please relent and don't embarrass a leading Jewish town." He waved them away and said to them, "Go safely and in peace."

What more can we add and what more is there to tell? There is nothing more to add and nothing further to tell, except that once he had parted from them he did an about-face and began walking towards his hometown. The dignitaries chased him after him and called out, "Rabbi, Rabbi!" Since they saw that he was not listening to them they said, "Please come back into the carriage and we'll bring you home." He shooed them away with his hand and did not return. They stood there unable to decide whether to pursue him or to go on their way. And while they were standing there, he had covered so much distance that they could no longer see him. They lost their resolve and re-boarded the carriage. They returned to their town, and he to his.

Reb Moshe Pinchas returned to his town and entered the study house. His wife and all her father's household got word and rushed over, and with them his sons and daughters. They asked him, "Why did you come back?" He responded to them in the same words he had used with the two dignitaries. Shaindel wept and cried out, "Oy, what have you done to us?" He sat there in silence. And when his father-in-law reminded him of the expense he had gone to for the clothing, etc., he stood up, removed his top coat, and said to him, "Take it and leave me be."

And what took place after that? There was no difference between before and after, none at all. Reb Moshe Pinchas would sit and study, his sons and daughters grew up, and his father-in-law fell ill and passed on. When he died, Reb Moshe Pinchas was deprived of his means of support and forced once again to take on students for a fee. And since he was burdened with sons and daughters he was not afforded the ability to be selective and say, "This pupil suits me and this one does not." And from to time, he even had to take on an unworthy student.

23.

And now we shall lament the fickleness of time. Three or four generations back nothing had been more beloved than Torah, but two to three generations ago Torah began a gradual decline. (God forbid that Torah should decline, rather despisers of Israel should decline!) The study houses remained full, but the students studied for their own gain, in order to be called "Rabbi" and be seated in places of honor. Albeit, the decline was not like that in our own generation, but the beginning of a decline is still a decline. Not many days had passed before Reb Moshe Pinchas had grown to detest his students and his students to detest him, for they sought wit without substance and he had studied for the sake of true Torah. They say that he did not find even one worthy student, and if he did find a worthy student he was one of the poor ones who were unable to pay tuition. The elders of that generation, who would act according to their custom and vie with one another in matters of law, might have mistakenly assumed that all was as it should be. And yet in truth the world was not the same and norms were not normal. And as the number of dedicated hearts dwindled, the number of books proliferated, and anyone who could rub his fingers together would write "innovative works" and bring them to the print house. However, in contrast to those basketfuls of hollow gourds there were found some truly sharp analyses, such as the book of the true scholar Rabbi Shlomo HaLevi Horowitz, which clarified a number of laws in matters that had resurfaced in recent generations and had not been addressed by the books of the earlier scholars. About Reb Moshe Pinchas, we have nothing to relay. Reb Moshe Pinchas was involved with nothing but Torah. And when they would mention him in praise, they would add, "He's like a mountain palm – perseveres in difficult conditions, but his fruit is so meager." He had already despaired of the rabbinate and, needless to say, no town in need of a rabbi ever approached him. The story of what he had done to a leading Jewish town had spread throughout the land. And towns that needed an instructor found themselves a scholar more agreeable than he.

24.

When Reb Shlomo had advised the people of his town to appoint Reb Moshe Pinchas to succeed him, tears had streamed from their eyes. After all the ill will that this man had aimed at him, their rabbi was still striving to help him even though several members of the rabbi's own family were seeking to take over his position. Could there be in this generation a person so righteous that he was able to overcome human nature, relinquish his honor and bestow kindness upon his affronter? As a result, the townspeople had not hesitated and had sent a letter of appointment to Reb Moshe Pinchas, as we have recounted. Now we shall relate a little something concerning what happened to Reb Shlomo after Reb Moshe Pinchas had sent the town away empty-handed.

When news reached Reb Shlomo that Reb Moshe Pinchas had withdrawn from the rabbinate because he had not wanted to receive any benefit from him, Reb Shlomo's countenance darkened like the edges of a cauldron and the matter gnawed relentlessly at his heart. Reb Moshe Pinchas had so begrudged him that he had shamed a town of Jewish eminence and was willing to live impoverished. Reb Shlomo remembered the days when the two of them had been ensconced in the same town. One sitting at the height of honor and the other living a life of sorrow without joy, without good fortune and without a wife, exhausting himself over Torah study, and in the end when Reb Moshe Pinchas had cited the law accurately, he hadn't told him, "Well said!" but rather had belittled him and thrown in his face that he still remained a bachelor. And it is said that from that time on mirth had never again graced Reb Shlomo's face. One day discussion began to revolve around the sermon incident. Reb Shlomo said, "Perhaps I should have let him triumph over me, but then again did I prevail only for the sake of my own pride? Surely it was for the sake of the Torah that I beat him and saved him from stumbling." Nonetheless, Reb Shlomo's mind would not rest.

25.

We must once again mention that which we are inclined to forget, namely the grim one, who reaps without having sown. In those days the elderly teacher passed away, the one who was not a rabbi but had occupied the teaching post in our town as an instructor. When the previous rabbi had gone to meet his Maker, our town remained unable to find a suitable replacement. They had brought in a rabbi from one of the small towns and appointed him as an instructor until they could find a rabbi commensurate with their prestige, and one worthy of the exceptional sages who by tradition had served as rabbis in our town. A year passed, then two, and ten, and twenty, until forty years had gone by and in all those years they had not approved any rabbi. At first, because for every rabbi who had sought the rabbinate in our town the town elders had said, "The post is bigger than he." After that, it was out of habit. And after that, it was out of respect for the old instructor. When he died, many rabbis had come to eulogize him, some of them intending from the outset to seek the rabbinate. However, the town leaders had already focused their attention on Reb Shlomo. And even though Reb Shlomo's town was bigger than ours, and was the town of his father the great sage, yet our town was superior since it was one of the long-established communities, and even before the year 1648 had been famously praiseworthy, having been mentioned in a responsum of the Maharshal. There's even been speculation that several great rabbis had begun their service in our town. And after all, if it was his wish to serve in a place of his ancestors the sage Rabbi Pinchas, Reb Shlomo's great-grandfather, had served in our town and prior to his passing had predicted that one of his descendants would someday reside in our midst. And because of this, he had decreed that no one should be buried next to him before the passage of a hundred years, and that the deceased must be of his seed.

26.

Several of the prominent men of our town journeyed to Reb Shlomo and brought him a letter of appointment. Reb Shlomo received them with great honor and reminisced with them about the good years he had spent in our town and he spoke of the praiseworthiness of our town and its inhabitants, and the highest praise he heaped upon the mighty Torah sages, the most eminent in the land, who had led the town. And he added that it would be an honor for a rabbi to be ensconced in a holy and splendid assembly where great rabbis had served, and that it was a great privilege for him to be offered the rabbinate of our town. The emissaries heard this and were filled with joy and said, "And it will be a privilege for us that our Rabbi Shlomo will be residing in our midst. And even our sagacious rabbis, who rest in peace, will derive contentment that he sits in their place." The noble wife of the rabbi rejoiced immensely, for since the day she had left the town of her birth she had longingly yearned to return, and now that she had heard he was being offered the rabbinate of our town she said, "This is the day I had been hoping for." A deep sigh was wrought from the heart of Reb Shlomo, he pondered briefly, and finally he said, "For my own private reasons, I cannot accept this rabbinate." His wife swooned and began to weep. And he, who forever had honored her more than life itself, was now unmoved by her tears, and it was evident that nothing in the world could move him to his change his mind. The emissaries said, "Rabbi, is there a town on this earth as fine as ours, are there people on this earth as pleasant as ours, are there on this earth lovers of Torah and peace as we have in our town – and not only that, but they all love you, our Rabbi, and you, our Rabbi, love our town and it goes without saying also your wife. We will give you time to reconsider, and we implore you not to turn us away." Reb Shlomo gazed upon them with unfettered affection and took the hand of one of them, as one shakes hands with his friend in agreement. And he repeated, "I have already told you, for reasons that are sealed up within me, that I am unable to accept." The emissaries understood on their own that the hidden reason was that Reb Moshe Pinchas had not been among the signatories on the letter of appointment. But they reasoned that if they appointed Reb Moshe Pinchas to a judgeship in town, Reb Shlomo would acquiesce to take the rabbinate. They said to Reb Shlomo, "Rabbi, we are going back to our town and will return another time. And we trust that meanwhile the Rabbi will relent and not reject our town." And when the emissaries returned to our town it was agreed in the presence of the entire congregation to take on Reb Moshe Pinchas as a religious judge, on the condition that Reb Shlomo be installed as rabbi. Reb Moshe Pinchas said, "I already told him that I do not want to be anywhere near him, neither in this life nor in the world to come." So Reb Shlomo did not accept the rabbinate in our town because of Reb Moshe Pinchas and our town did not obtain Reb Moshe Pinchas as a judge because of the grudge.

27.

Reb Moshe Pinchas remained without any source of livelihood. A little merchandise remained from his father-in-law's inheritance. Once this had been sold off and the widow's portion distributed, not even one meal's worth was left for Reb Moshe Pinchas. Well-to-do Jewish householders support themselves and their children, so long as they are still alive; when they die their sustenance dies with them. Rabbi Moshe Pinchas was willing to make due with a slice of bread dipped in salt. Before long, even his bread and salt became scarce. And now his children went begging for bread and a piece of cloth to cover their nakedness. And at home there was neither bread nor garment.

The Holy One blessed be He did not leave him long to suffer. One day Reb Moshe Pinchas took ill. The second day word got around that he was seriously ill. The third day word spread in town that he was dangerously ill. When Reb Moshe Pinchas sensed that they were preparing for his demise, he raised himself upon his bed and said, "The time has not yet come for this man to die; there still remain some pages of Talmud that he has not studied sufficiently well." Not many days passed before he had arisen from his sickbed. And naturally, upon leaving his bed he entered the study house and did not budge from there until he had learned those very pages and completed studying the entire Talmud. Had he postponed the conclusion of his studies he would have lived, but could a man whose entire life had been Torah survive even one day without Torah? As he completed the Talmud, his life also ended. The Kaddish prayer, customarily recited upon completing Talmud study was recited instead by his son at his gravesite.

28.

Reb Moshe Pinchas was raised on Torah, labored on Torah, acquired a good name and passed on from the world with a good name. At his burial, his eulogizer got excited while giving the tribute and proclaimed, "Happy is he who arrives in the next world with his learning in hand. At this funeral it is as if we have just buried all of the major works of Torah interpretation." His mother who had aged greatly, stood at her son's grave, leaning on her cane and rubbing her eyes dimmed with age saying, "Would you have ever imagined that my little Pinchas would do this to me, that he would go off to the Garden of Eden and leave his mother behind in a world that is worse than hell? And wouldn't it have been more fitting that I should die and he should live? I implore you, good people, look and see, I haven't even the eyes with which to cry." And so, Reb Moshe Pinchas parted from this world. And after the snows had melted and the ground had firmed up, they placed a monument on his grave, like those of the great rabbis who had served in the rabbinate of our town.

29.

About Reb Moshe Pinchas we will presently add not a word more. However, about Reb Shlomo we will tell, for about him there is what to tell. Reb Shlomo was a man of high stature. He had married off his sons and daughters and with each passing year his prominence soared. His teachings were recognized throughout the land and all the most difficult questions were brought before him. And it goes without saying that our town, which had no rabbi, made no move either large or small without consulting him. And although besieged with burdensome inquiries, his responses were never tardy. The majority of them began thus: "To my beloved soul mates," and other such words of endearment. And at times at the end of his response he would add new insights gained during the course of his studies. He would also respond to insights sent to him by students, in order to strengthen their devotion to Torah.

30.

In the meantime the rabbinical post in our town stood vacant, and every time a wealthy householder from our town was invited to Reb Shlomo's town he would say to him, "Rabbi, when will you finally come to us? The rabbinical seat still awaits you." A few of those in the community, who feared that the matter would drag on and that our town would remain without a rabbi as it had until now, entered into discussions with a sage from one of the nearby towns. This sage, seeing that most of the people were leaning towards Reb Shlomo, got out of it by way of a jest. He said, "After all, I am already a rabbi in your town, as most of the householders who are in my town reside in yours." And here we must explain the words of the sage. "Reside" meant reside in the jails, in that some of the householders of his town would be caught conducting fraudulent business and would be incarcerated in the jails of our town, as the jails in our town serviced the entire region.

31.

Reb Shlomo occupied the seat of his father and led his congregation peacefully and equitably. He issued several rulings which were good for the rich as well as for the poor, for the mighty as well as for the meek, for the men as well as for the women. How so for the rich? Among the wealthy are those who avert their eyes from the poor and do not give charity. When the needy die, even if their debts are paid off, they are not permitted to be buried until their heirs pay a certain amount for plot fees. And at times this would delay the deceased from burial so long that the body emitted a stench. Reb Shlomo ruled that every rich person had to purchase a burial plot in the cemetery and donate annually to the poor fund an amount equal to the interest he would have earned had he loaned the same amount that the land had cost him. And the result was that the rich and poor benefited equally. And how so for the mighty and the meek? There were some people who could not afford to pay tuition for private tutors and were embarrassed to bring their children to the local schoolhouse, for that is where the children of the poor study and it would become known that they were poor. Reb Shlomo appointed good teachers at the school and personally tended to the pupils. Some of the wealthy householders envied them and began to bring their boys there as well, so that one could no longer distinguish between the poor and the rich. For men and women, how so? It was customary in town that when an important person died his remains would be purified in the ritual bath. As this caused some women to fear going to that mikveh, Reb Shlomo decreed that it was prohibited to bring the dead for immersion.

32.

And thus Reb Shlomo sat in peace and led his congregation equitably. He issued many rulings and received everyone graciously. But anywhere he detected even a hint of desecrating God and His Holy Torah he wouldn't stand for it, even from the upstanding. In the town there was a certain wealthy Enlightenment scholar, one of those about whom scripture says, "Can an Enlightened one seek after God?" Once during the life of the old scholar of blessed memory, this man was seen riding in a steam-powered wagon, which today is called a train, on the second day of the festival, a holy day. And when he was chastised instead of saying, "I was forced to," he rather attempted to prove that travel by this type of wagon is permitted even on the Sabbath. Back in those days, transgressors used to seek a lenient interpretation of the rules of law, the very same kind of interpretation that the later medieval rabbis had decreed to be without foundation. When Reb Shlomo had been appointed as rabbi of the town, that same Enlightenment scholar had tried to get close to him, mistakenly thinking that he had found someone of like mind, inasmuch as the rabbi was familiar with German. Reb Shlomo, who embraced everyone, detested those scholars who used their knowledge perversely, uncovering ways to interpret the Torah in contravention of religious law, all the more so with respect to Sabbath observance upon which the redemption of Israel depends. And the more this man tried to get close to him, the more he would keep him at a distance. He started griping about the rabbi, and once he started griping about the rabbi, he discovered other gripers like himself.

There was an elderly money-lender in the town, scholarly and observant of the commandments, named Reb Asher. Reb Asher had authored a book and named it "His Bread Shall be Fat" so named for the verse "Out of Asher his bread shall be fat." The old man began pestering the rabbi, seeking an endorsement of his book. One time when the old man was harassing the rabbi, the rabbi said to him, "And who's going to endorse your other book, your book of usurious loans?" The old man stormed out fuming and began griping about the rabbi. And once he started griping, he discovered other gripers like himself.

In the town there was a "Clothing of the Naked" welfare society. One time, the treasurer used money from the society's funds to buy tefillin for a young pauper, relying on the verse, "It is the only covering for his skin," which had been interpreted by an important mystical text to mean that tefillin are to be regarded as clothing. The rabbi heard about this and required the treasurer to pay for it out of own pocket. He started griping about the rabbi. And once he started griping about the rabbi, he found other gripers like himself.

The grandson of a Hassidic Rebbe had lived in the town. When he passed on, the Hassidim sought to immerse his body in the ritual bath. The Rabbi would not permit it. They began to bad-mouth the rabbi. And once they began to bad-mouth the rabbi, they discovered many other gripers like themselves.

There was an old judge in Reb Shlomo's religious court, whose son-in-law, Reb Fischel Toen, was a certified instructor, and used to counsel litigants and issue legal rulings in his neighborhood. When the old judge passed on, Reb Fischel sought to be appointed in place of his father-in-law. The rabbi knew him to be a quarrel monger and schemer who, when he saw that the law was leaning in favor of the deserving party, would counsel the culpable party on how to prevail. The rabbi said to him, "Refrain from pursuing this matter; I will not consent to your appointment as a judge." Reb Fischel left disappointed and began to gripe about the rabbi. And once he began to gripe about the rabbi, he discovered other gripers like himself.

All the gripers banded together as one, each one for a different reason, and composed a slanderous letter to the town's officials accusing the rabbi of being a fanatic, an unenlightened zealot. The town officials and government bureaucrats, who knew the Rabbi, tore up the letter and rebuked the rabble-rousers. How did they react? The Hassidim amongst them said, "Because he studies the languages of the Gentiles, they side with him." The Enlightenment followers among them said, "Because the Gentiles like him, he hastens to be strict even when there is room for leniency, in order to capture the hearts of the most religious."

And yet the dispute had not progressed beyond being just an ordinary dispute, until Reb Fischel was widowed and remarried a woman from the Feivush family. This is the same Feivush family that was named after its leader Reb Uri Veibush the Provider, who used to rule the town with an iron fist, and the fruit of his loins had emulated his qualities and maintained a firm grip on the town. The head of the community, Reb Feivush the Great, was a member of the Feivush family. The congregational scribe, Feivush the Lesser, was his sister's son. Reb Feivushel the Elder was the treasurer of the holy burial society. Feivush the Hoarse, the religious supervisor of the slaughterhouse, was from the family of Feivush. The Feivush who was nicknamed Fabius was in charge of the registry of births and deaths. Fabius, whom everyone called Feivki, and Feivki who called himself Febus, together controlled the tobacco market and its branches. The distillery was leased to the husband of Reb Feivush the Great's sister. The fields belonging to the town's Baron were leased to the father-in-law of the husband of Feivush the Great's sister. And all of them together were partners in leasing the liquor authority. In short, there was not even one office of importance or monetary value that was not in the hands of the House of Feivush. Even the appraisers and tax assessors and the one in charge of the charitable consecrations were from this same family. Since Reb Fischel had married a woman from the family of the House of Feivush, the Feivushes said, "Why not nominate him for a judgeship? Surely he is entitled to it by rights of his first father-in-law and surely by his own right he is worthy to be a judge." Those who were dependent on the Feivushes, tagged along behind them. Those who were not dependent on the Feivushes leaned at times in one direction and at times in the other. And so the peace was stripped away and the conflict had begun.

33.

From time to time wealthy people from our town from would visit Reb Shlomo's town for trade and commerce or to conduct some other business. And when someone from our town would visit Reb Shlomo's town, he would go to meet him and deliver tidings to the rabbi's wife from her brothers and other relatives. On days that she received visitors from our town the rabbi's wife would make it a holiday for them because she liked her hometown folk, the vast majority of whom were fine and well-mannered people, and needless to say she liked the town itself which was worthy of affection. As the conflict had intensified and Reb Moshe Pinchas had already passed on, the rabbi's wife went back to her wishful thinking that her husband the rabbi would return to our town. And she used to prepare large feasts for the guests to avail them the opportunity to speak with the rabbi and hear about new developments in our town. While there were not terribly many new developments in our town, still there is no town without something new. One development, from which you can learn how much our town loves peace and distances itself from conflict, is worth mentioning. When a member of one the new Hassidic sects, Vovi Zeinvil Fleshkidrige, broke the rules and wore a festive fur hat on the Sabbath immediately preceding the mournful fast day of Tisha B'Av, the entire town ridiculed him but it did not deteriorate into a brawl.

And here it must be said, as we've already said before, that all our townsfolk were scholars. And whenever they used to sit around at a feast anywhere, it seemed as if the Divine table was actually standing in our town due to the plethora of Torah discussions that could be heard around it. From Torah discussions they would arrive at matters close to the Torah and it goes without saying to the matter of the rabbinate in our town. Reb Shlomo showed no indication that he was leaning towards accepting the rabbinate in our town. To the contrary, in those days he was urging the visiting dignitaries to seek another rabbi for themselves, as it is not right to leave an important Jewish town without a leader. One time Reb Shimon Eliyah, Reb Shlomo's brother-in-law arrived with three of the best of our town, amongst them the distinguished Reb Yehudah, the father-in-law of my grandfather Reb Yehudah. After the evening prayers, during the meal, conversation got around to the conflict with the Feibushes and their entire clan. Reb Shimon Eliyah said to his brother-in-law, "Flee this town of quarrelsome people and come to our town." The distinguished Reb Yehudah, father-in-law of my grandfather Reb Yehudah, added, "It is brought forth in Maimonides's 'Laws of Temperaments' that if a man resides in a country whose leadership is malevolent and whose people fail to follow the just path, it behooves him to move to a place whose people are righteous and conduct themselves in the ways of virtue." Reb Shlomo shut his eyes like a man who was contemplating his advisor's advice. When some time had passed and he had said nothing, all the dignitaries said as one, "Rabbi, what will you reply to us?" The rabbi opened his eyes and said, "You know that

I am not a man of conflict and I am neither obstinate nor fond of polemics, neither am I dependent on rabbinical compensation. But what shall those rabbis do whose wives did not bring them a dowry and whose fathers-in-law did not bequeath them wealth and assets? Heaven forbid that they should make the Torah a doormat to be trampled by all. If a rabbi is poor and dependent on people, he is not given enough to make a living and not only that but he is also insulted and derided. And if he is rich, they come to him with complaints because of his wealth. The edges of the robe of the sage Rabbi Gabriel Reinush were worn out from age and he had to shorten it and the entire town raised a hue and cry that he was wearing short clothing, German-style. The sage Rabbi Abraham Teomim who was very wealthy and would allocate all of his earnings towards the needs of the town, was forced from his hometown because the town's bigwigs claimed that he was depriving them of their livelihood because they were lending money to the local nobility at an interest rate of twenty percent, while he was satisfied with only eight percent. And did they not gripe about me that I was lending my money with interest and cutting into their livelihood? And surely you know that I entrusted the funds left to me by my father-in-law, may he rest in peace, to reliable people so that they would give loans from the earned interest to marketplace merchants, from whom the lenders take twenty to twenty-five percent from the principal and deduct the interest up front, then charging them as if they had loaned them the full amount. And I tell you further, my dear friends, that I have spent the majority of my days tranquilly; now that they have sent some troubles my way should I be more demanding and issue a challenge? I am a decent man and deserve to live my life in peace. I am reminded that there was a great scholar in your town who practically killed himself for the sake of Torah study and when he died he didn't leave his wife and children even enough for one meal. And I, Blessed be God – my livelihood is assured and my burial clothes are ready for me. Therefore, what do I need to worry about? They will not carry me out in a garbage wagon like the people of Belz did to their rabbi, the Bach of blessed memory, who was ushered out of the town on the eve of the Sabbath after noon. I beseech you, my brothers, please do not wound me; rather take for yourselves a rabbi." The dignitaries said to him, "We already have a rabbi." "Who is it?" asked Reb Shlomo. The dignitaries smiled and answered coyly, "Why, of course, it is you Reb Shlomo, may you live long!" Reb Shlomo rose from his chair and said to them, "Take note, gentlemen, I have already told you that I will not accept the rabbinate in your town, and I am not changing what I have said." Reb Shimon, his brother-in-law, said, "We've already been assured by your grandfather, the great Rabbi Pinchas – may his merit protect us– that one of his descendants is destined to reside in our town." Reb Shlomo responded, "Rabbi Pinchas, my grandfather, was a great and righteous man. And when a righteous man says something, it is bound to come true. But after all, my grandfather, of blessed memory, left many children who also have borne children devoted to Torah. Since they are my kinsfolk, it is not proper for me to recommend them. And you, if it is your desire to fulfill my grandfather's words, chose for yourselves from among his progeny one who is worthy of that responsibility." All the dignitaries responded in unison, "That righteous man clearly said, 'a singularly special one from among my seed.' And there is no one in this generation greater than our rabbi, Rabbi Shlomo, may he live long." Reb Shlomo responded, "Even though you are mistaken to think of me as being unique in this generation, my grandfather never said that I would sit in his chair; he said only that one of his seed would come to dwell among you. And who knows what that righteous one meant to infer?"

The whole time that this had been going on, the rabbi's wife had been gazing upon her husband the rabbi and praying in her heart that the words of the dignitaries would have an impact on him. But the rabbi took no notice of his wife and apparently even the Holy One blessed be He did not heed her prayers. And when they had finished the meal and chanted the grace after meals, the rabbi arose from the table and said, "Sit for a while with my wife while I briefly visit my study." When he had gone, the rabbi's wife said, "Did you see him? He's only forty seven and already he's gone grey. All of his troubles come from nowhere else but the mother of that lad from the village. I heard the old woman involves herself with practitioners of witchcraft." In the middle of this she heard her husband's footsteps and stopped talking. The rabbi returned with a book in his hand as was his custom whenever he had visitors over, so that in case they rose in his honor, they rather would be standing in honor of the book in his hand. He looked and observed their despondency and the unhappiness on their faces. He smiled and said, "I had expected that my wife would bring you something hot to drink." The rabbi's wife got up and brought over tea with Assyrian apples, which we call lemons. The dignitaries sat and drank, and never again mentioned anything from all of those discussions.

34.

Now let us leave aside Reb Shlomo's town and return to our town and dissipate a bit of the anguish of the conflict by recounting the virtue of the charitable souls of our town.

Prior to his death one of our town's wealthy people allocated a specific sum for charity to go towards a perpetual fund to purchase houses, yards and fields and distribute annually on the anniversary of his death the revenue from the houses, etc., to the poor Jews of the town under the supervision of the town's rabbi, to be managed by three trustees appointed by him during his lifetime, as they saw fit. However, in his will he set a precondition that the poor within his family would take precedence to other poor folk in benefiting from his bequest. The brother of the honorable deceased came accompanied by other relatives who did not reside in our town, demanding a significant portion from the perpetual fund. And a doubt arose as to whether the brother of the deceased had a right, inasmuch as he had not been poor at the time of the endowment. And further, as to how far to extend the priority of kinship. And the appointed trustees of the bequest were concerned about the commentary of our sages of blessed memory as follows: "The apportionment of charity to the poor of a town cannot be overseen by that town's own authorities." Therefore, as they were wont to do, they turned to the sage Reb Shlomo for a legal ruling.

Several weeks passed without an answer. And here the anniversary of the death of the benefactor was fast approaching. The poor relatives were expecting to get their share, and even the rest of the poor were pounding on the doors of the trustees. And the trustees were at a total loss as to what to do. And the days were days of winter, and the mail was unreliable due to the snows and the cold. And even the wagon masters, who are in the habit of endangering themselves even for small wages, went out very infrequently during that time, inasmuch as due to the heavy snows the roads were covered and the horses would get mired in the snow, unable to free themselves. At the end of several such days, a letter arrived from Reb Shlomo that he was going to attend his sister's daughter's wedding in some other town and since it so happened that the town was close to our town, he intended to drop in at our town and provide an oral ruling for the trustees of the bequest. The town abounded with joy and prepared itself to greet him. And here we must recount a wondrous event. There was an old man in town, who must have been about a hundred years old, for he was born the same year that the great sage Reb Pinchas (Reb Shlomo's grandfather) had passed and he had been named after him. For a long while he had been wishing to die, because he was very old and terribly weakened by the burden of the years. And yet in those days he began to pray rather that he would live in order to behold the grandson of that pious one.

Meanwhile, Reb Shlomo Eliyah cleared a special room for his brother-in-law, the rabbi, and he ordered that the furnace be fixed. And when the furnace had been repaired, they would fire it up twice daily, even though many were doubtful whether the rabbi would come since the roads were impassable and every journey life threatening. The distinguished rabbi Reb Yehudah, father-in-law of my grandfather Reb Yehudah, said "I have no doubt that he will come. As it is not Reb Shlomo's way to go back on his word."

35·

One day, close to the time for the afternoon prayers, a winter carriage arrived in our town and on it a man dressed like one of the high officials, in an enormous winter fur cloak. The carriage rolled in and stopped by the store of Reb Shimon Eliyah. The store's clerks jumped up and ran out to greet the carriage, and all the trade agents

of the town surrounded it assuming that a high official was coming to procure merchandise. They had not realized that it was Reb
Shlomo, a high official in Torah, which surpasses any merchandise.
Reb Shimon Eliyah came out accompanied by his two sons, and
with them the charity fund treasurer, and helped the rabbi alight
from the carriage. The lady of the house, Reb Shimon Eliyah's wife,
overheard the commotion and ordered the servants to add logs to
the furnace. They brought Reb Shlomo to the house, removed his
heavy cloak and leather boots and sat him down in a soft chair, his
feet facing the furnace, and they covered his knees with a fur mantle
and observed him closely to see what else would suit him and what
more they could do for him. He was spent from the hardship of the
journey. And when the snow in his beard melted they realized that
the snow was not melting, in other words that his hair had gone
white, and not due to the passage of time but rather due to grief
and suffering. And even though he was completely worn out, he
sent for the trustees so as not to not delay justice to the poor. And
meanwhile he instructed that his bags be opened and he took out a
variety of sweets that he had brought from the wedding feast of his
sister's daughter. He gave some to his relatives, and to the servants and
maids he gave first choice, and he asked them to eat them in front of
him and said Amen after the blessings. After they had tasted them, he
asked if they were good. He probably had a particular motive, since
the bride had been orphaned from her father and her uncle the great
sage was concerned that perhaps they had not bothered to prepare
fine delicacies for her.

While this had been taking place, half the town had arrived to
greet the rabbi and with them came the distinguished trustees. Due to
the great number of guests, they were unable to get around to discussing the matter of the bequest. But the next day, immediately after the
morning prayers before he even ate or drank, the rabbi sat down with
the trustees until he had arrived at a true and just ruling. That is, to
give half to the poor relatives and half to the poor townsfolk. As to
the half for the poor of the town, equal shares would be distributed
to all. But the half portion for the relatives would be divided giving
priority to the closest kin, and the brother of the deceased, who was

the closest of all, would be given a third of that half, the remaining two thirds to be divided without differentiating between those who resided here and those who resided elsewhere. In the presence of the distinguished trustees the rabbi wrote these things down in clear language and substantiated his reasoning on the basis of the Gemara and the great commentators. Since he wrote the response without books in front of him, he left blank spaces, which he circled until he would be able to check further and add citations. The ones who had the book published filled in some of the blanks.

After he had handed over the response to the trustees, he rested his head on the pillow. Later he got up from his bed and ate a little something and received every visitor, until the day and most of the night had passed. In the morning he wanted to go and pray in the Kloyz, but his legs would not oblige him and he was forced to pray in his room. A prayer quorum of ten men was found to pray with him, for many had come with the intent to pray with the rabbi wherever he prayed. After prayers his sister-in-law, the lady of the house, brought him coffee and something sweet. He drank the coffee and left the sweets. The matron saw this and said, "Rabbi, you shame my handiwork." He tore off a small bit and ate. Some say that from the time he had learned of the matter of Reb Moshe Pinchas rejecting the rabbinate he hadn't allowed himself so much as a taste of anything indulgent. While still sitting there, he raised his skullcap and wiped his forehead. This he did several times. The distinguished Reb Yehudah, father-in-law of my grandfather Reb Yehudah, observed him and hinted that they needed to let the rabbi rest. They began to leave. And Reb Yehudah also tried to leave, but the rabbi gestured to him with his hand to detain him.

The rabbi sat and said the grace after meals, while his brother-in-law and the rabbi Reb Yehudah and two other gentlemen who had arrived after everyone else had left were standing there and gazing upon him affectionately. He took out his handkerchief, wiped his forehead, and rose from his chair as if intending to leave. Where was he intending to go and who was worthy of the rabbi coming to see him? Out of an abundance of courtesy, no one dared ask. Finally, he came back, sat down and said, "I have been meaning to ask

you. What is the state of affairs with Reb Moshe Pinchas's widow?"
Reb Shimon Eliyah responded, "Like the situation with every poor
widow, so it is with this widow. She receives a little sustenance from
heavenly mercy and a little from the mercy of people." Reb Shlomo
glanced over at the distinguished Reb Yehudah, father-in-law of my
grandfather Reb Yehudah. Reb Yehudah said, "I give so that she and
her children should not die of starvation." Reb Shlomo said, "And
who gives to them so that they should live?" The great sage looked
over at his brother-in-law, who was very wealthy, perhaps worth ten
thousand pieces of pure silver.

Rabbi Shimon said cleverly, "It is told that Sir Rabbi Moses
Montefiore always used to say 'It's better to be a poor man among
Israel than to be a rich man among Israel.'" The great sage grasped
his beard, obviously suppressing his anger with difficulty, and said,
"It is one thing to talk about a time when there were such generously charitable souls as Rabbi Moses Montefiore. But at a time…"
He hadn't finished what he was saying before he stood up from
his chair and asked, "Where does she live?" They realized that he
intended to call on her. They said to him, "Better you shouldn't
go, as she lives in a squalid, cold hovel." The rabbi sighed and
said, "She lives in squalor, the furnace is not kindled and people
know this and yet are indifferent!" When they saw that he was
going, they wanted to accompany him. He waved them off with
his hand and said, "You have no interest in kindling her furnace,
so why trouble yourselves? I also shall not kindle her furnace since
you can see I am dressed nicely, and wouldn't it be a pity for one's
clothes to get soiled."

36.

It was exceedingly cold that day, and as cold as it was outside, inside
the house it was colder still. The furnace was lit, but not enough to
warm the house. The woman and her children sat wrapped in tattered clothing, vapor rising from the ground, and from the corner
of the house there arose the sweet, pleasing voice of the eldest son
of Reb Moshe Pinchas, sitting and studying at home because he had

no shoes to wear to the study house. Because he was so engrossed in his studies, he had not noticed the rabbi enter. But the rabbi noticed him: that he was studying very nicely. And he immediately began to discuss Torah with him and was aware neither of the chill in the house nor of the heat of the fever within his body. The people in our town are in the habit of telling that upon his return from there he had said, "Had I not already married off my sons and daughters, I would marry them off to the sons and daughters of Reb Moshe Pinchas." And he also had said, "For what reason has the significance of Torah waned in this generation? It is because the rabbis marry off their sons to daughters of the wealthy. The grooms are dependent on the riches of their fathers-in-law who buy them rabbinic posts, and they fail to toil wholeheartedly in Torah. Having secured for themselves rabbinic posts and exhausted their dowries, they naturally look to the wealthy householders for hand-outs in order to satisfy the needs of their wives, because the daughters of the rich cannot tolerate the pain of poverty, and as a result of that these rabbis are prone to obsequiousness and other unsavory traits. This is in stark contrast to one who marries the daughter of a poor scholar who all of her days had been accustomed to scarcity and deprivation, and her husband does not need to demean himself before boorish ignoramuses, and does not diminish the power of Torah." Regarding the sage Reb Shlomo, it cannot be said that he was harmed on account of his wealthy wife, in that the merit of her ancestor our rabbi Ba'al HaLevushim enabled him to serve the Torah from a place of wealth and to perform good deeds of charity and kindness. But it has been said in his name that he used to say, "I doubt that it is appropriate for a rabbi to deal in money lending, even to do a good deed."

He went to visit the widow once again. They say that he went to ask if there remained any writings of her husband and to bring her a dowry for her daughters. This time he did not linger at her home and did not discuss Torah with her son, because speaking had become difficult as a result of the severity of his cough, so he invited the boy to come to him. And when the boy did come, he dispensed with the town leaders and spoke with him.

37.

That day happened to be the twentieth day of the Jewish month of
Tevet, and it was the sage Reb Shlomo's practice to devote that whole
day to the works of Maimonides inasmuch as it was the anniversary
of the death of Maimonides, of blessed memory, and in the evening
he would share any new insights that he had gleaned from his studies. Due to the onslaught of visitors, he had not had a chance that
day to study and at any rate had not gleaned any new insights. And
when the town leaders arrived and with them the great scholars, he
told them, "Today is the anniversary of the death of Maimonides, of
blessed memory, and it would be fitting for us to speak about him, but
because of the infirmity of my body I have not studied today. Yet I will
tell you a fine elucidation about Maimonides which I heard attributed
to the sage and pious Reb Elazar of Amsterdam, of blessed memory,
which he told before the great ones of his time when he came to our
country to bless his family prior to going up to the Holy Land."

"In the book Fundamentals of Torah, chapter 7, Maimonides,
of blessed memory, says the following: 'Prophetic insight does not
alight upon anyone other than a great Torah scholar who is also a man
of great principle.' The commentary Kessef Mishneh raised the following quandary: 'Why did Maimonides not write that he should be
powerful, wealthy and humble, as in the opinion of Rabbi Yonatan in
Tractate Nedarim, page 87'? In addition to Kessef Mishneh, the Lehem
Mishneh raised the question, 'Why didn't Maimonides think of what
was indicated in the tenth chapter of Tractate Sabbath, page 84, that
the Divine Presence does not come to rest upon anyone other than
one who is wise, wealthy, humble and tall?' Except that our rabbis do
give us a way to reconcile Maimonides. For after all, we have found in
the Gemara that the Divine Presence rests even upon a total pauper,
and even upon someone who is not tall. And if so, Rabbi Yonatan's
principle must be rejected, as it is told in Tractate Sanhedrin, page
11, "One time, the great rabbis were assembled in an attic in Yavneh
and a heavenly voice came to them and said, There is one present here
who is worthy of the Divine Presence resting upon him, except that
his generation does not merit it." The scholars cast their eyes upon

Samuel the Small. Yet another time they were assembled in an attic in Yavneh and a heavenly voice called out and said, "There is one present here who is worthy of the Divine Presence resting upon him, except that his generation does not merit it." The scholars cast their eyes upon Hillel the Elder.' We conclude from this that the Divine Presence can rest upon a pauper, for after all it is said in Tractate Yoma, page 37, that Hillel the Elder was the greatest of paupers and that he was a woodchopper. And we conclude also that the Divine Presence can rest upon one who is not tall, for after all the scholars had gazed upon Samuel the Small. Indeed, Tosfot Yom Tov says in his Mishnah commentary, chapter four of the tractate Ethics of the Fathers, 'Why was he called Samuel the Small? Because he used to belittle himself, except that according to the literal interpretation it appears that he really was quite short.'"

38.

Our story is approaching its end and what is more the end of our rabbi is fast approaching. On the Sabbath he had it announced that he would be giving a eulogy for Reb Moshe Pinchas on the anniversary of his death. And when the beadle announced that the sage would be delivering a eulogy for Reb Moshe Pinchas, the entire town prepared itself to hear it, both on account of the one being eulogized and the one giving the eulogy. Back in those days, two or three generations ago, people were not yet awash in sermons. If a scholar came and offered to sermonize, everyone wanted to hear. Due to the cold weather, the sage agreed to give the eulogy in the old study house because in the large synagogue there was no furnace. And all who came to pray there were in the habit of donning their tefillin in the old study house for they could not expose their arms because of the cold. And because the study house could not accommodate all of the people, it was announced those who had warm clothes would stand in the courtyard, and those who didn't have warm clothes would stand inside. And the whole matter was a bit peculiar - could it be that the rich and the mighty would end up standing outside at a distance, while the paupers and beggars would be close up?

Meanwhile the sage had taken ill and his cough was ripping up the walls of his chest. His blue eyes had reddened and his beautiful face had puffed up. But he consoled them and said, "It's merely an illness and I will get over it." The anniversary of the death Reb Moshe Pinchas arrived. However, when the sage arose from his sickbed his strength abandoned him, his head spun and his throat was hoarse. Also, he had no strength in his legs. When he had completed his prayers, some while sitting and some while in bed, he looked at the timepiece and said, "The day is still young and the mercy of God, may He be blessed, has still not waned." He began to gargle and to imbibe honey and sweet tea, and allowed himself to utilize some of the curatives mentioned in the Gemara, although one does not use the curatives in the Gemara any longer because the nature of the body has since changed. He poured himself a concoction consisting of one-third wine, one-third vinegar and one-third oil and drank it. And when he drank it, it seemed that he was returning to health. And as the time for the afternoon prayers drew near, he rose from his bed, pulled on a fur cloak over his clothing and on top of that the same overcoat he had worn on his journey. Reb Shimon Eliyah and his wife, the lady of the house, tried to prevail upon him not to go, for the doctor had said that if he went outside he would be endangering himself. The sage nodded his head as if to agree with them, but he went anyway. He had not arrived at the study house before having to return. And he did not return on his own two feet; rather they carried him in their arms.

That whole night long he mumbled feverishly. It is told that many times they heard his lips whispering, "*A bukher makht kidesh af a groyp.*" The town's nobleman, who was very fond of the Scheiner family, sent his own personal physician. The doctor examined him and said, "There is nothing to worry about here. After three or four days the patient will recover, but he needs to be watched as this illness tends to recur. And if the patient isn't careful enough, he is liable to endanger himself."

In addition to all of the physiological treatment, they also undertook spiritual healing. In all of the synagogues and study houses they recited Psalms, in addition to eighteen psalms selected by the sage

Noda BeYehudah, which are tried and true healing remedies. Even the tranquil women neither rested nor were calm and they drifted from one holy place to another and opened the Holy Ark to pray for the ill one. And on Thursday when the Torah was being read, they added to his name the name Moses, for the act of adding the name Moses to that of a true scholar who is ill was capable of healing him, as we had seen when the glorious sage Reb Meshulam Igra had fallen ill and they had added the name Moses to his, and a few days later he had returned to health. After that they gave charity in the ritual for the redemption of the soul, and said what they had to say. And there's no need here to list every single word, because it is all spelled out in the book Tikkun HaNefesh.

39.

And now let us recount the end of the righteous one. When he realized that the hour of his passing from the world was drawing near he said to those responsible for seeing to his burial, "Bury me next to Reb Moshe Pinchas." And then he instructed them to hand him the second volume of the Shulhan Arukh Law Code and he studied the rules relating to the process of dying. After that he blessed those close to him, including the male and female servants who attended him. Afterwards he blessed the townsfolk. And then he performed the ritual hand washing and recited the final confession prayers. After which he uttered the "Hear O Israel" prayer. Once he had arrived at the verse "And you shall love..." his pure soul departed.

I have already related how in those days the snow was falling nonstop. In our town, when the snow starts to fall it doesn't stop falling until the beginning of Passover. And so the snow falls and falls, and all of the roads are covered with snow, especially those roads where no one comes and no one goes. Like heaps upon heaps the snows remain piled there, snow on top of snow. But the two head gravediggers, may they be remembered for good, tall Chaim who was nicknamed Long Life, and short Kaddish Leib, who was called Half Kaddish, went up to the cemetery and trudged through the deep snows to dig a grave for our rabbi the sage, may his memory be blessed.

We had hoped that he would guide us in the ways of life, but instead God took him suddenly to the bright light in the prime of his life. All that remained to us from the righteous one were his holy remains, which were laid out on the ground. Until it was time to give him over to the earth, they stood over him and recited verses, hymns and entreaties. Suddenly a frail, bird-like voice was heard and Reb Pinchas the Elder was seen leaning over the deceased reciting the Song of Songs. Immediately everyone present began to chant the Song of Songs, verse by verse, the same way they had when the sage Reb Pinchas Ba'al Mofet had been laid out on the ground before being brought over to his resting place. It has been the legend in our town from the time of our ancestors, who rest in Eden, that when our rabbi's forefather, the sage Reb Pinchas Ba'al Mofet, had been laid to rest, the whole town had stood before the deceased and recited the Song of Songs. All that night not a soul went to bed and from the edges of town came the sound of old men and women lamenting for the righteous one. The snow came down and a pure light illuminated the night. The snow by its very nature is pure, and that night it was purer than pure. We heard from reliable sources that snow like that had not been seen before, or since. And yet, every heart was filled with darkness and gloom.

When daylight dawned the entire town came out, the young and the elderly, children and women, to escort our rabbi to his eternal resting place. No man kindled his furnace, no woman cooked her meals, not an infant remained in its crib, no sick person stayed in his bed. Rather, all came out to follow the coffin with eyes overflowing with tears, the tears freezing then melting then freezing once again. And not a person complained, "I'm cold," and not a sound was uttered, except by the beadle who was walking and reciting, "Righteousness shall walk before him." And so they walked on behind the bier of the righteous one until they arrived at the great synagogue. And when they got there, they set the bier on the ground and circled it seven times according to custom, and all those who had been involved in the purification of the body and in the circling of the coffin immersed themselves in a pure ritual bath. Afterwards, they proceeded to the cemetery and buried him in the grave that they had dug for him. When the snows had melted and the esteemed wife of the great sage, may his memory be blessed, came to weep over his grave and a few prayer quorums of ten men accompanied her, they observed that he had been laid next to his ancestor Reb Pinchas. Perhaps you are thinking that the gravediggers had erred, but in reality the elder sage had claimed the younger for himself. How great righteous ones are even in their death, inasmuch as on the our rabbi was buried a hundred years and one day had passed since the death of his righteous ancestor, who had stipulated with the town that no one be buried next to him until after the passage of one hundred years and that the deceased be of his own seed. And verily Reb Moshe Pinchas had also had a hand in this, because he had never made peace with Reb Shlomo and had not wanted him as a neighbor. And just as our Reb Shlomo had been a lover of peace and had always given in during his lifetime, so too did he acquiesce in death.

In recounting all of this, I did not intend to give an example of an exemplary man or to tell about the zeal of Reb Moshe Pinchas. Rather, I have merely told the tales of two scholars who were in our town two or three generations ago, at a time when Torah was the glory of Israel and all of Israel walked in the paths of Torah, which is the delight of the Lord our Fortress until the coming of the Redeemer at the end of days. At which time we will be privileged to hear God's Torah directly from the lips of our righteous Messiah, who will sit and study Torah with all those of Israel who have studied Torah with love.

Translated by Paul Pinchas Bashan & Rhonna Weber Rogol
Annotated by the Translators with Jeffrey Saks

Annotations to "Two Scholars Who Were in Our Town"

1. Title: Two Scholars Who Were in Our Town / Cf. Sota 49a: "Two scholars who reside in one town, yet cannot abide each other in matters of Torah law – one will die and the other will go out to exile."
3. Enhanced wisdom / Cf. Isaiah 28:29.
3. Wisdom calls aloud… / Proverbs 1:20.
3. Hoshen Mishpat / The essential work of Jewish financial law, codified in R. Yosef Karo's 16th century *Shulhan Arukh* code of law.
3. Kloyz / A small house of study and prayer.
3. Fifteenth of the month of Av… / The Kloyz, in other words, was open for study and prayer around the clock, with the exception only of the month-long period of mourning (in mid-summer) for the Temple, from the fast day of the 17th of the month Tammuz until the 15th day of the following month of Av, when study did not take place in the evenings.
3. Joy of the Lord… / Cf. Nehemiah 8:10.
4. Gemara / Rabbinical analysis and commentary on the Mishnah, together the two comprise the Talmud.
4. Not a birthright… / Cf. Mishnah Avot 2:12.
5. Kosher for Passover / Since there can be no trace of leavened bread on Passover, the rabbi would have to ensure that the millstones were properly cleaned before the Passover flour for baking matzah could be ground.
5. *Horeh Gaver* on Yoreh De'ah / Reinush and his *Horeh Gaver* are fictitious, but cf. Job 3:3 from which Agnon takes the name of this rabbinic work, purported to be a commentary on a section of the *Shulhan Arukh*.
5. Kiddush and Havdalah / Kiddush is the benediction over the wine at the onset of the Sabbath; Havdalah is the ceremony at the end of the Sabbath separating it from the secular week.
5. Three parsas / A Talmudic measure of itinerant distance: one parsa is about four kilometers, approximately the distance a man can walk in 72 minutes.
5. Mikveh / A bath used for the purpose of ritual immersion to obtain purification.

6. Shemoneh Esreh / "The Eighteen" blessings, so called in reference to the original number of constituent blessings (there are now nineteen), is the central prayer of the Jewish liturgy, recited three times a day. It is also known as the Amidah (or, "Standing" prayer).
6. "Myriad are the needs of your people"/ Opening line of a short prayer recited during times of imminent danger or extreme stress; see Berakhot 29b.
7. Reb Mordechai Yafeh / Called "Ba'al (author of) HaLevushim" after the series of halakhic (religious law) works he authored, an important scholar and posek (legal arbiter) (1530-1612, Poland).
7. Horowitz the Holy Shelah / A Hebrew acronym for Shnei Luhot HaBrit ("The Two Tablets of the Covenant"), a book written by the revered rabbi and kabbalist R. Yesha'ayahu Horowitz (1560-1630), usually referred to as the "Shelah HaKadosh (the Holy)."
7. Ba'al Mofet / A saintly man or man of wonders.
8. Reb Moshe / Moses Mendelssohn (1729-1786), German Jewish philosopher, considered the father of the Haskalah (Jewish Enlightenment), had translated the Hebrew Bible into German.
8. Rabbi Wolf / R. Binyamin Zev Wolf Hindenheim (1757-1832), a grammarian and translator of the siddur to German.
8. Samuel II 6:16 / "And [as] the ark of the Lord came [into] the city of David, Michal the daughter of Saul peered through the window, and she saw the king David hopping and dancing before the Lord; and she loathed him in her heart." – for her criticism of her husband King David, it is implied that Michal died childless (compare v. 23)
9. Tallit / Prayer shawl traditionally worn only by married men.
9. *Hatan Bereishit* / The "groom" of the Book of Bereishit (Genesis), is the term used for the person called up for the first reading from the Book of Genesis on the holiday of Simhat Torah. This high honor is reserved for a respected member of the community.
9. Gabbai / Treasurer.
10. Forbidden to alter the interior space… / See Deuteronomy 12:4: "You will not do likewise to the Lord Your God," which prescribes the destruction of idolatrous spaces, but proscribes doing the same to Holy space such as the Temple, and by extension synagogues (cf. Megilla 29a). The specific case, boarding up a space in the

synagogue to block a draft, which does then reduce the "volume" of "holy" synagogue space, is discussed in the rabbinic commentaries, and is left as a difference of opinions between various authorities. The sources under question are outlined in E.E. Urbach's important Hebrew essay on this story, "*Shnei Talmidei Hakhamim Shehayu Be'Irenu – Mekorot uFerush*" in *LeAgnon Shai*, Urbach and D. Sadan, eds. (Jerusalem: Jewish Agency Press, 1959), pp. 9-25.

10. *A bukher makht kidesh af a groyp* / Yiddish: "An unmarried boy makes kiddush on barley grain."

11. *Ketzot HaHoshen* / Important commentary on Jewish financial law authored by Rabbi Aryeh Leib HaCohen (1745-1812).

11. Rabbi Meshulam Igra / A master sage who became the Chief Rabbi and Rosh Yeshiva of Pressburg, Hungary (1742-1801). R. Igra was a native of Buczacz, Agnon's Galician hometown, which is never named explicitly as the "our town" of this story, although this seems apparent.

11. Chapter 200 / Volume 1 of the Ketzot HaHoshen is a commentary on the first two hundred chapters (simanim) the Shuhan Arukh's 427-chapter section on financial law, the Hoshen Mishpat.

12. Chariot / As depicted in the vision related in Ezekiel, chapter 1.

12. Yehudah ben Teimah in tractate Avot / Mishnah Avot 5:23: "Yehudah son of Teimah said, Be bold as a leopard, light as an eagle, swift as a deer, and strong as a lion to do the will of your Father in heaven."

12. Deliverance came from another place / Esther 4:14.

14. Shabbat Shuva or Shabbat HaGadol / The Sabbaths before Yom Kippur and Passover, respectively, on which rabbis traditionally deliver the major sermons of the year.

14. Ternopil / Major city of Eastern Galicia (today, Western Ukraine), about 70 km. north of Buczacz.

14. Perl / (1773-1839), major figure of the Galician Haskalah.

17. *Sheheheyanu* ("Who has given us life and sustained us") / A blessing said to celebrate special occasions, especially in thankfulness for new and unusual experiences.

17. Rav Alfasi, Maimonides, Rosh / The major medieval commentaries on the Talmud and halakhah.

19. Reveling in his own distress / Cf. Prov. 17:5.

19. Maharshal, Bach, Rav Alfasi / R. Shlomo Luria (1510-1573); Bach – R. Joel ben Samuel Sirkis (1561-1640); Rav Alfasi - Isaac ben Jacob Alfasi (1013-1103) of Fes – all three engaged in determining the accuracy of the Talmudic text. Unable to access these rarer editions of these volumes (on which Reb Shlomo based his lecture), Reb Moshe Pinchas launched his attack on the incorrect text from the commonly available volumes.

20. Panie / Polish meaning "Mister"; i.e. Reb Moshe Pinchas is calling him "Mister" instead of "Rabbi" Horowitz.

21. If scholars battle / Cf. Bava Metzia 59b.

23. Shema / Recitation of the Shema ("Hear O Israel") prayer, traditionally recited twice daily, as well as upon going to sleep.

25. Permissible to arrange divorces there / In Gittin (Jewish divorce documents) the name of the town has to be spelled out in Hebrew characters, a cause of dispute about the proper spelling of certain town names in Europe, and subsequently the ability of divorces to be executed in those towns.

25. God's precepts are straight / Psalms 19:8

25. Torah protects and the Torah rescues / Cf. Sotah 21a.

26. Kav HaYashar / "The Just Measure") authored by Rabbi Tzvi Hirsch Kaidanover, first published in 1705. Shevet Mussar – "The Rod of Admonition", authored in Ladino by Rabbi Elijah HaCohen, in 1863.

26. Tosefta / A compilation of the Jewish oral law from the period of the Mishnah.

26. Kra / R. Zvi Hirsch Kra (1740-1814), served as rabbi in Buczacz from the departure of R. Igra in 1794 until his death.

31. Maharam of Rothenburg / Meir of Rothenburg (c. 1215-1293) was a noted German rabbi, poet, and author of Tosafot commentary on the Talmud.

31. When on the road / Gen. 45:24 as interpreted in Taanit 10b.

36. 1648 / The year of the calamitous Khmelnytsky pogroms, wherein Cossacks decimated eastern European Jewry.

36. Maharshal / Rabbi Shlomo ben Yehiel Luria (1510-1573) of Lublin. The citation is to Responsa (Shut) Maharshal #101, dealing with a 1572 case of evidence in a case of marital engagement.

37. Bread dipped in salt / Cf. Mishnah Avot 6:4 ("bread in salt" is a rabbinic metaphor for minimum sustenance; akin to "living on bread and water" in English).
38. As he completed the Talmud, his life also ended / The theme of the Angel of Death waiting for his victim's completion of a portion of study, or performance of some *mitzvah*, is found in Mo'ed Katan 28a, Ketubot 77b, and elsewhere.
38. Happy is he who arrives... / Moed Katan 28a.
41. Can an Enlightened one... / Cf. Psalms 14:2 (translated here out of context and ironically according to the narrator's intention, the word "maskil" in the Biblical verse means "wise one" but here is applied to a follower of the secularizing Jewish Enlightenment movement).
41. Out of Asher / Genesis 49:20.
41. It is the only covering... / Exodus 22:25-26.
44. The Divine table /Cf. Mishnah Avot 3:3, "Rabbi Shimon says: Three who ate at one table, without saying words of Torah while upon it, are considered to have eaten from sacrifices to the dead [i.e., idols] as it is written (Isaiah 28:8): 'All their tables are full of vomit and excrement, without a clean place'. But three who ate at one table and said upon it words of Torah are considered to have eaten from the table of God, as it is written (Ezek. 41:22): 'And he said to me: This is the table which is in the presence of God'."
44. Maimonides's 'Laws of Temperaments' / Maimonides, Mishneh Torah, Hilkhot De'ot 6:2.
45. Teomim / (1814-1868) served as rabbi in Buczacz from 1853 until his death.
45. Bach / R. Joel ben Samuel Sirkis (1561-1640); a prominent halakhist who was known for various clashes with lay leaders.
47. The apportionment of charity... / Bava Batra 43a.
51. Sir Moses Montefiore / (1784-1885) English Baronet, financier and banker, advocate of social reform and great philanthropist.
53. Rabbi Elazar Rokeach / (1685-1741) Galician rabbi who was appointed to the Amsterdam rabbinate late in life, prior to emigrating to the Holy Land. This particular insight is found in his *Arba'ah Turei Even* commentary to Maimonides.

53. Fundamentals of Torah, chapter 7 / Maimonides, *Hilkhot Yesodei HaTorah* 7:1.
53. Kessef Mishneh / A commentary on Maimonides's Mishneh Torah, written by R. Joseph Karo (1488-1575).
53. Lehem Mishneh / A commentary on Maimonides's Mishneh Torah by Abraham Hiyya de Boton (c. 1560 - c. 1605).
53. Yavneh / The seat of the High Court after the destruction of the Second Temple in 70 CE.
54. Tractate Yoma, page 37 / Three of the Talmudic citations in this passage are incorrect. The correct page numbers are: Nedarim 38a, Shabbat 92a, and Yoma 35b. Urbach, op. cit., p. 22, n. 16, insists that these were intentional errors inserted by Agnon, mimicking the common phenomenon of a sage mis-citing a specific page number when referencing from memory, as would have been this case in the learned discourse presented by Reb Shlomo. Urbach further points out that the thrust of Reb Shlomo's presentation of the sources, and resolution of the question on Maimonides's teaching, is that even Reb Moshe Pinchas, with all of his flaws, would have been worthy of receiving prophecy.
54. Tosfot Yom Tov / An important commentary on the Mishnah by Yom-Tov Lipmann Heller (1578-1654, Cracow).
56. Noda BeYehudah / Yehezkel ben Yehudah Landau (1713-1793), rabbi of Prague. His work, *Tikkun HaNefesh* (Healing of the Soul) prescribes 18 specific chapters of Psalms to be recited as merit for the healing of the sick.
56. Even the tranquil women / Cf. Isaiah 32:9.
56. And you shall love… / Deuteronomy 6:5.
56. Half Kaddish / Used to punctuate divisions within the prayer service. The nicknames of the gravediggers are plays on the meanings of their names – Chaim means life, since he was tall he was called "Long Life"; Kaddish was a name sometimes given to a child born to a couple in old age, as he would be the one to recite the mourner's Kaddish when they die. Agnon is being playful in assigning these names to gravediggers.
57. Righteousness shall walk / Psalms 85:14.

In the Heart of the Seas

A Story of a Journey to the Land of Israel

"So he took the lamp and all the other vessels for light in the House of Study, and mixed sand and water, and went and sat him down behind the stove, and rubbed them and polished them until they shone like new. That day people said, the lamps in our House of Study are worthy of lighting before Him who hath light in Zion."

Illustration by T. Herzl Rome for the 1948 edition

Chapter one

Dust of the Roads

J ust before the first of the hasidim went up to the Land of Israel, a certain man named Hananiah found his way to their House of Study. His clothes were torn, rags were wound around his legs, and he wore no boots on his feet; his hair and beard were covered with the dust of the roads, and all his worldly goods were tied up in a little bundle which he carried with him in his kerchief.

Ye sons of the living God, said Hananiah to the comrades, I have heard that you are about to go up to the Land of Israel. I beg you to inscribe me in your register.

He Who will bring us up to the Land, said they to him, will bring you up as well. And they wrote his name in their list and assigned him a place to rest in the House of Study. He rejoiced in them because he would go up to the Land of Israel with them; while they rejoiced in him because he would complete the quorum, and they could pray as a congregation on their journey.

It can clearly be seen, said the comrades to Hananiah, that you have walked far.

True indeed, said he to them. It is not a short distance I have come.

Where were you? they asked.

Where was I? he answered. And where was I not?

Whereupon they began to question him on every side, until at last he recounted all his travels.

At first, said Hananiah, I went from my town to another town, and from that town to yet another. In that way I went from place to place until I reached the frontier of a country where no man is permitted to pass unless he pays a tax to the king. They took my money from me and stripped me naked, and left me nothing but a kerchief with which to cover myself. But the people of that town took pity on me, and clothed me and gave me all I needed, a tallit and tefillin and tzitzit.

Now in that country it is cold for the greater part of the year. At the Festival of Shavuot their houses stand in snow though it is May, while at the Feast of Sukkot a man cannot even hold the *lulav* to shake it on account of the cold; and they have no citrons for the blessing. So what they do is, all the congregations share a single citron, a slice for each congregation. They hallow the Sabbath over black bread instead of white wheaten loaves, and they mark the Sabbath's end by drinking milk, for they have no wine. When I told them where I was going, they took me for an exaggerator, because they had never in all their days heard of any man who really and truly went up to the Land of Israel.

By that time I myself was beginning to doubt whether the Land of Israel actually existed; so I decided I had better leave them to themselves and went away. Better, said I to myself, that I should perish on the way and not lose my faith in the Land of Israel.

I do not remember how long a time I had been journeying or the places to which I came, but at length I reached a robbers' den. The robbers allowed me to stay among them and did not do anything to me; but every time they went off on their business they would say to me, Pray on our behalf that we may not be caught. And most of them had their good qualities, and were merciful, and were a stay and prop to the poor in their need, and believed in the Creator; and once they took an oath by the Everlasting they would never go back on their word even if they were to lose their lives. And they were not robbers to begin with, but lords and nobles whose oppressors compelled them to give up their fields; and so they came to try their hands at robbery and pillage.

One of them I saw putting on tefillin. I made the mistake of thinking that he was a Jew, though he was not one; but the robber chief before him had worn tefillin, and when he was killed, his successor put them on.

Now this was the story of how that robber chief of theirs had been killed. He used to leave his booty with a certain Greek priest. But once the priest denied that anything had been left with him. The robber chief threatened to take vengeance on him; whereupon the priest went and denounced him to the king; the king at once ordered him to be killed.

When they took the robber chief off to be executed, they said to him, If you tell us where your comrades are, we shall let you go.

You do what you have to do, said he to them.

Well, they tied the rope around his neck and sent his soul on its way. When he died, he said, Alas for you, O my wife, and alas for my children, whom I leave behind to be orphans.

Once, continued Hananiah, the new robber chief wished to lead me to the Land of Israel through a certain cave. But the idea entered my heart that maybe it would not be His blessed will for a robber to be my groomsman. And since I was possessed by this idea, I did not go with him, for if it had been His blessed will that I should go with him, would He ever have let such a thought enter my mind? But I felt ashamed because I did not accept his favor, and so I went on to another country.

Now in this other country all their days are toil, so that they have neither Sabbath nor festivals; so that at last I forgot when it was the Sabbath. So whenever I went from one place to another, I never went farther than a Sabbath journey of two thousand ells for fear that that day might be a Sabbath or festival.

Once a gentleman met me on the way and said, Where are you going?

To town, I answered.

He invited me up into his carriage. When he saw that I was not getting up, he raised his voice and shouted, Shadai. Now he was speaking Polish and in Polish *shadai* means sit down, but I did not know it and thought that he was using the Holy Name of Shaddai; so up I jumped into his carriage.

It was the Yom Kippur; but I never knew it until we reached town at the time they were praying the Closing Prayer. At once I flung myself off the carriage, and took off my shoes, and entered the synagogue, and lay outstretched, and wept all that night and all of the day following. There I heard the Land of Israel being mentioned. So I gave ear and heard people telling one another how the men of Buczacz had decided to go up to the Land. At once I started off and came here to you; and since I went barefoot, my legs became swollen and it took a long time.

They went and fetched him boots, but he would not accept them. Rabbi Akiva, they reminded him, ordained seven things, and one of them was to be careful to wear shoes. To which Hananiah replied, These feet did not feel the sanctity of Yom Kippur; let them remain bare.

After Hananiah had told all this, he untied his kerchief, took out a Book of Psalms, and read until the time arrived for the Afternoon Prayer. Following the prayer, he took a candle and went on reading. Seeing that the lamp had grown rusty, he took his kerchief and made a knot in it. Next morning, when he took out his tallit and tefillin from that kerchief, he said to himself, What is this knot for? To remember that rusty lamp.

So he took the lamp and all the other vessels for light in the House of Study, and mixed sand and water, and went and sat him down behind the stove, and rubbed them and polished them until they shone like new. That day people said, the lamps in our House of Study are worthy of lighting before Him who hath light in Zion.

And Hananiah did something else; he made little hollow dishes for the lamps; for in the lands of Edom tallow candles are lit and thrust upright into the candlestick, but in the Land of Beauty it is the custom to light oil lamps, a dish being filled with oil and the wick placed within it. Therefore Hananiah went and set dishes under the candlesticks, that they might fill them with oil.

But it was not only the illuminating vessels that Hananiah rubbed and polished. He also took the washing basin and the pitcher and the holy vessels and all those vessels and implements within which the *Shekhinah,* the Divine Presence, conceals herself; and made them all shine. He likewise repaired the torn books, setting them in fresh boards and wrapping them up in fine skins. The day before, they had been torn and sooty, but that day they rejoiced as on the day they had been given to the children of Israel on Mount Sinai.

Are you a coppersmith? Hananiah was asked.

No coppersmith am I, said he to those who asked, nor yet a bookbinder; but when I see a defective vessel, I feel pity for it and I say, This vessel seeks its completion. Then the Holy One, blessed be he, says to me, Do this or do that, and I do it.

Here is a simple man, said the comrades. Yet every word he utters teaches a virtue. Wherever such a man may wander, God will be with him.

Perhaps, one of them asked Hananiah, you know how to make a box for carrying goods?

Perhaps I do, answered he.

After all, said this man, we are going a long way and we require things for the journey. Perhaps you can make me a box or trunk.

I can try, said he.

How do you try? said the other to him.

Hananiah went out to the forest and brought lumber, and sawed it into planks which he squared and planed and joined, and made into a box and painted red, which is a good color for utensils to be.

The other men who were going up to the Land saw how fine the box was and asked Hananiah to make boxes for them as well. So out he went to the forest, brought lumber and made the same sort of boxes for them. He also made a Holy Ark for the Torah Scroll which they were going to take up to the Land of Israel. He used iron nails to join all the boxes except the Holy Ark, which he joined with wooden pegs; so that if, God forbid, they should come to magnetic mountains which draw iron from vessels, this Ark would not fall apart.

Hananiah made boxes for all the travelers, but as for himself he remained satisfied with his kerchief.

Chapter two
Those Who Prepared

The greater part of Adar had already passed. The clouds which had been obscuring the sun's course began to shrink, while the sun grew gradually larger. What only yesterday had been the time for the Evening Prayer became the time for Afternoon Prayer today; while yesterday's getting-up time became the time to start saying the Morning Prayer today.

The snow warmed up and began to melt, and the trees of the field grew black. One day they were black as earth; the next, they would be putting forth leaves and blossoming like the Lebanon. The pools and marshes were covered by a film, and the birds began to chirp. Every day a different kind of bird would come around and there began a cheeping on every roof. Our men of good heart started going out and asking when the road would be fit for travel; they meant the month, of course, when the road would be fit for wayfarers.

Never in all their lives had these good folk so feared death as at that particular period. How great is the sanctity of the Land of Israel though it be in ruins! And what is the body's strength even at its height? For after all, suppose a man wishes to go up to the Land of Israel and does not go up, what if his soul should suddenly depart from his body and he be left lying like a dumb stone without having gone up; what would become of all his hopes?

Those who knew enough to study the Bible sat and studied the Bible; those who knew enough to study the Mishnah sat and studied the Mishnah in order to strengthen their hearts with the study of the Torah. Throughout those days neither the sun nor the moon ever saw a single one of them sitting idle. Although they were busy selling their houses and casting up their money accounts, they nevertheless crowned their days with Torah and prayer.

The Passover festival came to an end. The sun pitched its camp in the sky, and all the water in the swamps and marshes dried up. Even the big swamps had no water in them. The roads fairly asked to be put to use, and the wagoners set out on their ways. Horses began posting from one end of the world to the other, their bells jingling as they went; and the wagoners tugged at the reins and shouted, Geeup! Whoa there!

Those who were to go up to the Land gathered together at their House of Study. In came old Rabbi Shelomo, a well-disposed *kohen* who had dealt in commerce all his life, but had finally given up the estates of this world and set his heart on going up to the Land of Israel. Rabbi Shelomo used to say, If a king is angry with his servants they ought never to go far away from him. Instead, let them stand at the king's gate and lament their misfortune until he sees their distress and takes pity on them.

And then in came Rabbi Alter, the slaughterer-and-inspector, who had handed over his butcher's knife to his son-in-law; and together with him came Rabbi Alter the teacher, who was his brother-in-law's son and who had spent all his days in the tent of the Torah, studying keenly and casuistically with his students. Once while he sat studying in the tractate Ketuvot about marriage contracts, it occurred to him that after all the Land of Israel is a marriage contract between Israel and the Holy One, blessed be he; and it is an accepted principle that a man must never be without his marriage contract. Whereupon he felt that as long as he continued to dwell outside the Land he would have no rest. So he ceased his studies, and dispersed his students, and sold his house and his set of the Talmud and the commentary of Alfasi, and went and inscribed himself in the list of those who were going up to the Land.

And in came Rabbi Pesach, the warden of the House of Study, who was going to the Land with his wife Tzirel, for their benefit and advantage in the hope that the merits of the Land of Israel might give them the merit of children.

And in came Rabbi Yosef Meir, who had divorced his wife because she refused to go up to the Land of Israel. Her father had sent to him, saying, If you wish to take back my daughter and dwell with her in Buczacz as before, I shall double her dowry.

Said Rabbi Yosef Meir, I have already contracted with another bride and I cannot shame her.

And in came Rabbi Moshe, the brother of Rabbi Gershon, may he rest in peace, the same Rabbi Gershon whose soul departed while he was reciting the verse, 'The King hath brought me into his chambers,' as is told elsewhere in my story, 'The Rejected One.' For love of the Land of Israel Rabbi Moshe was leaving his two daughters behind and had inscribed his name and that of his wife in the register among those who were going up to the Land.

And in came Rabbi Yehudah Mendel, one of the last of the followers of Rabbi Uriel, whose soul is treasured on high. As long as Rabbi Uriel had been alive, a bond had extended all the way to his home from the Land of Israel. Once he passed away, nothing in the whole world had any value for Rabbi Yehudah Mendel until God put it in his heart to go up to the Land of Israel.

Then in came someone else whose name we have forgotten.

And in came Leibush the butcher, whom the Land of Israel afterwards spewed forth because he spoke in its disfavor, saying, Have you ever seen a country where you can find nothing but mutton?

And in came Rabbi Shmuel Yosef, the son of Rabbi Shalom Mordekhai ha-Levi of blessed memory, who was versed in the legends of the Land of Israel, those legends in which the name of the Holy One, blessed be he, is hallowed; and when he commenced lauding the Land, people could see as it were the name of the living God engraved on the tip of his tongue.

And when they all came together, Hananiah stood at the entrance, holding in his hand the kerchief containing his prayer shawl and phylacteries and other baggage, like a man who is prepared to set off at once.

The women stood in the Women's Section, while the men were sitting in the House of Study. There was Mistress Milka the coral-seller, who had entered into a second marriage on condition that her husband go up to the Land of Israel with her, and who had received a divorce from him because he would not go; and near her Feiga, her kinswoman, the widow of Rabbi Yudel of Stryi, may he rest in peace, a descendant of gentry and trustees who used to send money to the poor of the Land of Israel; and near her Hinda, the wife of Rabbi Alter the slaughterer; and near her Tzirel, the wife of Rabbi Pesach the warden; and near her Esther, the wife of Rabbi Shmuel Yosef, the son of Shalom Mordekhai ha-Levi; and near her Sarah, the wife of Rabbi Moshe, grandson of Rabbi Avigdor the communal president, of blessed memory; and near her Pessel, the daughter of Rabbi Shelomo ha-Kohen, who had just been widowed at that time and joined her father on the journey in order to bear her suffering in the Land of Israel.

Then up rose Rabbi Shelomo ha-Kohen to his feet, and set his two hands on the table, and bowed his head, and said to them, Why do you wish to go up to the Land of Israel? Surely you know that many sufferings come upon wayfarers besides their being pressed for food, and they fear evil beasts and robbers, particularly upon the sea.

To this our men of good heart responded, saying, We are not afraid. If we are deserving in His eyes, may he be blessed, he will fetch us to the Land of Israel; and if we are not deserving (God forfend!), then we are deserving of all the troubles that may befall us.

What Rabbi Shelomo said to the men he said to the women as well, and as the men answered so answered they.

Whereupon Rabbi Shelomo said, Happy are ye who cleave to the Land of Israel, for the Land of Israel was created only for Israel, and none can remain in the Land of Israel save Israel. All the things I said, I said only in order to increase your reward.

Thereupon Rabbi Alter the slaughterer put his hand on the shoulder of Rabbi Alter the teacher, and Rabbi Alter the teacher put his hand on the shoulder of Rabbi Alter the slaughterer, and they began dancing and singing:

'Oh that the salvation of Israel were come out of Zion! When the Lord turneth the captivity of his people, Let Jacob rejoice, let Israel be glad.'

Rabbi Shmuel Yosef, the son of Rabbi Shalom Mordekhai ha-Levi asked Rabbi Moshe, Perhaps you know the tune to which your brother, Rabbi Gershon of blessed memory, sang the verse, 'The King hath brought me into his chambers'?

That tune, said he, it is not our practice to sing because my brother departed from the world therewith; but I know the tune to which he sang the verse, 'Draw me, we will run after thee.' If you wish to hear it, I shall sing it for you.

All those assembled lowered their heads, and Rabbi Moshe began singing, 'Draw me, we will run after thee.'

Then Rabbi Yosef Meir rose and said, Would that we might merit to sing the verse, 'The King hath brought me into his chambers' in Jerusalem, the holy city. Those assembled responded, Amen, and they proceeded to their homes in peace.

When they left the House of Study, the whole town was already deep in slumber. The houses lay in the secret place of night, concealed by the darkness. The moon was still hidden in the skies, and only stars lit up the summits of the mountains. Buczacz lies on a mountain, and it seemed as though the stars were bound to her rooftops. Suddenly the moon came out and lit up all the town. The river Strypa, which had previously been covered by darkness, suddenly gleamed silver, and the market fountain overflowed in two silver rivulets. One of the company said, I never in all my life knew that this town was so pleasant. It seems to me that there is nowhere in the world a town as pleasant as ours.

That, responded his companion, is just what occurred to me this very moment.

Every city, remarked Rabbi Alter the slaughterer, in which decent and pleasant people live is decent and pleasant.

And now, added Rabbi Alter the teacher, those decent and pleasant people are going to go up to a truly pleasant place.

At that very moment one of the women was saying to another, I don't know what has come over me: for first I think that I have never seen such a lovely night, and then it seems to me, on the contrary, I have already seen such a night, and the very things I hear now I have heard before. I know that is not so, yet I cannot be certain it is not so.

To which her companion replied, Perhaps we have already journeyed once before to the Land of Israel, and everything we have heard and seen here we heard and saw before on some other night.

In that case, said the first, why are we here and not in the Land of Israel?

My friend, said the other, we have already been there.

If we have already been there, said the first, how is it we are here?

My friend, said the other, ere you go asking how we come to be here, I shall ask you how we came to be exiled from the Land of Israel and how we came to be scattered among the nations.

I cannot make out what you are talking about, said the first.

My friend, said the other, didn't you tell me that it suddenly seemed to you that you had seen such a very night as this before?

Well, they hired themselves two long, high wagons covered with a kind of booth, and turned their household goods into money except for those utensils which they would require for the way; and they packed away their money in their clothes. They filled their boxes with pots and pans, and glasses and ladles and plates, and smoked meat, and fine pellets of baked dough that last a long time without going bad; and then they went to request permission from the dead to depart.

Some went to the graves of their fathers and their kindred, while others went to the graves of great pious folk, the constant props of the world, who had accepted burial outside the Land, entailing the pangs of having to make their way to the Land of Israel by rolling through caves and tunnels at the End of Days, all in order that meanwhile they might protect the town from evil decrees. At the graves our company burst out weeping, for they were very moved; the graves of the pious always arouse people to repentance. And they went on weeping until they reached the threshold of the cemetery. There they turned their faces back to the graves and looked at them.

Then came Rabbi Abraham the circumciser, who had inducted more than half the town into the covenant of our Father Abraham, may he rest in peace. He took a circumcision knife and passed it under the soles of each and every one of the company, saying, Children, I make this blade to cut under you in order that the dust of your city may not hold you. And he likewise passed the knife under his own feet.

Thereupon they all burst out weeping and went back home. They put on big boots especially prepared for the journey, with heavy iron nails on the soles to make them last a long time; the boots could be heard from one end of the town to the other when they walked. And that is why people in Buczacz say of noisy folk, They make as much noise in town as if they were going up to the Land of Israel.

They made the rounds of all the synagogues and Houses of Study in the town and passed through all the streets, discoursing about the Torah, praying and giving charity, so that they might never have to return to those places to make amends for any blemishes which they had been the cause of. Then they went from house to house to take leave of the living; and they asked each and every person separately, Perhaps you have something against me, or perhaps I owe you some money? Then they opened the charity boxes of Rabbi Meir the Miracle Worker and made bundles of the money to take it to their brethren in the Land of Israel; and they kissed each and every mezuzah on each and every doorpost, until they reached the river Strypa.

When they reached the Strypa, they paused to beg indulgence of the waters, saying, All the rivers run into the sea. We pray you, waters of the Strypa, do not be angry with us on our way. Finally they entered their own House of Study and prayed. At length they mounted their wagons, the men in one wagon and the women in another. The wagoner took the men's wagon and entrusted that of the women to Hananiah, whom he had appointed his assistant, as is the practice of wagoners who have two wagons and entrust one to one of the travelers and do not charge him any fare.

All the town went out to speed them on their journey, except the rabbi. For the rabbi used to say, Those who proceed to the Land of Israel before the coming of the Messiah remind me of the boys who run ahead of the bridegroom and bride on the way to the bridal canopy.

Chapter three

The Departure

They departed the town and entrusted themselves to the horses. The horses lowered their heads and sniffed the way they were required to take. The wagoner mounted one wagon and Hananiah the other. Then the wagoner tugged at the horses' reins and urged them on. The horses raised their heads and prepared for the way, but still delayed their going, lest anyone had forgotten something and had to return. But nothing was to be heard save the sound of people weeping at leave-taking; so the horses lifted their legs and started off.

Hananiah took the whip in his right hand and cracked it over the heads of the horses, who turned their heads, looked at him, and went on. Those of the women who were accustomed to travel to markets and fairs said, Never in our lives have we had such an easy journey as this.

Are you a wagoner?, the women then asked Hananiah.

No, said he, I am not a wagoner, but horses are horses and know what is required of them, so they go.

Are you telling me, said the wagoner to Hananiah, that you are not a wagoner? The very way you crack your whip shows that you are one.

Never did I drive a wagon and horses in my life, said Hananiah, except for the time when I saw a Jew and his horses drowning
in the river and got them out and took him back to his home.
In this way they journeyed for nearly two hours through fields
and forests and villages until they reached the Holy Congregation of
Yaslovitz. Here the wagoner whistled to his horses and stopped the
wagon, for it had been agreed in advance that the wayfarers would
make a pause there in order to see their kinsfolk in the town before
their departure.

There is no town so close to Buczacz as Yaslovitz. The head of
one lies, as you might say, alongside the tail of the other; nevertheless, there is no peace and good will between them. Why? Because,
when the old rabbi of Buczacz died, the town elders set their eyes on
his brother-in-law who was rabbi in Yaslovitz, and desired to appoint
him their head. They went and proposed the post to him, but he was
not prepared to accept it.

Could it be, said he, that I should leave Yaslovitz, which is a
small town where nobody disturbs me in my study, and go to a large
town full of sages and merchants who give the rabbi no rest, the first
with their casuistics, the second with their business?

Well, what did the Buczacz folk do but take a carriage and
horses, and go into his house one night and seat him on the carriage
and run off with him to Buczacz. It had barely grown light, when the
whole of Buczacz shone with his honor and glory, while the light of
Yaslovitz grew dim. Thereafter, whenever anyone from Buczacz went
to Yaslovitz, the folk of Yaslovitz would quarrel with him and try to
pull his hat off since Buczacz had taken away their crown.

Now however, since our company had left Buczacz behind
them and were about to proceed to the Land of Israel, all the hatred
of the Yaslovitz folk vanished; the whole town gathered together to
honor them and received them with brandy and cakes and confec-
tionery and fresh water which they brought from the well.

Even the Gentiles showed them respect on account of the honor
in which the Land of Israel is held. Never was so much honor and
respect shown in those parts. People actually prostrated themselves
before the wayfarers, and kissed their garments, and gave fodder to

their horses, on account of their affection for the Land of Israel; with
the exception of the Armenians, who did not share in all this, since
they are descended from Amalek and Amalek is the foe of Israel. The
Armenians dwell all over the country and do business with the Ori-
entals in peppers and spices and scents, thus competing with Israel;
and their country is near the river Sambation, beyond which lie the
lands of the Ten Tribes of Israel; and they wage war with the pious
King Daniel who slays a thousand of them together, and who dwells
in Armenia in the community called The Blood of the Chick; and
he is a great and mighty king, tall as a giant, and thirty-one kings
pay homage to him.

It is the custom among the Armenians, if one of them should
smite and kill another, for the murderer to pay three hundred and
sixty-five gold dinars corresponding to the three hundred and sixty-
five veins and sinews of the human body; but they cannot do anything to Israel, because they were overcome long ago by Joshua.

After the men of good heart had refreshed themselves from the
journey, they entered the Great Synagogue, which was the one that
school children had found hidden in the hill and had cleaned out.
There the Baal Shem Tov of blessed memory used to hide in an attic
to study Kabbalah; and there his soul had been exalted unto heaven.
Prayers said in the Great Synagogue are never in danger of idolatry,
but all of them reach the Gates of Mercy entire.

There the men of good heart prayed that they might go up
to the Land in peace and not be harmed on the way by packs of
beasts or brigands, neither by land nor by sea. Then they went back
and climbed into their wagons, and all the townsfolk accompanied
them as far as the limits of a Sabbath day's journey. If you did not
see the way the Yaslovitz folk gripped the hands of the Buczacz
folk, you never have seen what affection is like in Israel. While the
grown-ups stood shaking hands and embracing one another, the
children patted the horses' tails, since their hands could not reach
up to those of the folk in the wagons. And that is why they say in
Yaslovitz when a little fellow tries to pretend to be grown-up, Go
and stroke the horses.

Chapter four

Temptation on the Road

The company traveled for several hours until they reached the Holy Congregation of Yagolnitzi, where they spent the night. In the morning they started out and came near Lashkovitz, that Lashkovitz where there is a great fair whose like is not to be found in the whole world; for more than a hundred thousand merchants come there year after year to do business with one another. At that particular time the fair was taking place, and they met small groups of merchants and wagons laden with all kinds of goods, so that the very earth groaned beneath them.

There it was that Satan came along and stood in their way and asked them, Where are you traveling?

To the Land of Israel, they answered him.

And how are you going to make your living over there? said he.

Some of us, said they, have sold houses, and others have other resources.

Don't you know, said Satan, that journeys eat up money?

We know it well, they answered. So each one of us has labored to lay up money for the expenses of travel, for inns and the ship's fare.

And how about stuffing the pockets of the frontier guards? he asked. And who is going to pay ransom tax for you to the King of the Ishmaelites?

How much does he ask? said they to him.

May you have the good luck, he answered, to have him leave you food enough for a single meal. Well then, what you must do is go to Lashkovitz and earn money. Happy is the man who dwells in the Land of Israel and does not need to be supported by the Holy Cities. How people toil to reach Lashkovitz! And now that you have come this far, will you go away without doing business?

Busy as he was with the men, Satan certainly did not ignore the women. Kerchiefs and headcloths and dresses he showed them, until their hearts were near bursting after the fashion of women who see fine clothes and covet them.

When your mother Rebecca, said Satan to the womenfolk, reached the Land of Israel, what did she do, according to the Holy Writ? Why, she took her veil and decked herself to show her loveliness in her fine things. And now you propose to go to the matriarchs and yet you don't behave as they did! Why, is Lashkovitz so far away? Why, it's in front of your noses. If a man sneezes here, people will say good health to him in Lashkovitz. Even the horses are turning towards it. The very beasts know where the road leads.

But Rabbi Shelomo took out his pouch and filled his pipe with tobacco, and struck iron against a flint, and lit the pipe, and half closed his eyes, and began puffing out smoke fast, like a man who wants to get rid of a thought. He saw that the horses were gadding about in an unusual way, wanting to go on in one direction but actually going in another. Whereupon he touched the wagoner with the long stem of his pipe and said, Take yourself towards Borsztszow. And he urged him to hurry, since folks who proceed to the Land of Israel are like they who go to synagogue, and are duty-bound to run.

The wagoner cracked his whip, and tugged the reins one way and the other, and whistled to the horses, and turned them towards Borsztszow. The horses tossed their heads and dashed on until the dust rose from under their feet. At once the wagons with the goods in them vanished, and the whole countryside filled up with the lame, the halt, the blind, and every other kind of cripple carrying waxen models of limbs, models of hands and legs. For it is their custom to take these to the graves of the holy, there to set them up as candles in order that the holy men might see their deformities and remedy them.

Thereupon the men of good heart understood that all those enticements had come their way only to delay them, so that while they engaged in business to make money with which to live comfortably in the Land of Israel, their souls would depart from them outside the Land.

Like the king who invited his friends to a feast. The wise ones came at once, saying, Does the king lack anything in his palace? But the foolish friends delayed until they had filled their bellies with their own food so as not to require the food of the king. The result was that the wise friends were seated with the king and ate and drank of his best food and wished him well, while the others stayed at home and became drunk on their own wine and besmirched their garments, so that they could not even show themselves in the presence of the king. The king rejoiced at his wise friends and held them dearer than all the others, and was angry at the fools and introduced confusion in their midst.

In just the same way the King over all kings, the Holy One, blessed be He, invites those who love Him to ascend to the Land of Israel. Is there anything lacking in the house of the King? say the wise ones, and proceed there at once and bless His great Name by the study of the Torah, with songs and praise; and the Holy One, blessed be He, rejoices to see them and does them honor. But the fools tarry at home until they fill their pockets with money, in order, as one might suppose, not to require anything of Him, blessed be He, in the Land of Israel. And at the last they grow drunk with their wine, that is, with money, and besmirch their garments, that is, the body, when buried in earth outside the Land.

Rabbi Alter the teacher spoke first and said, I hate the evil inclination, which brings people to sin.

Rabbi Moshe responded in turn, The inclination to evil deserves to be hated, but I do not hate it; for all the merits I may have, come to me from the evil inclination. But it is only just that the wicked should hate it, since it always leads them into evil; in spite of which, not only do they not hate it but they pursue it as though it were their own true love.

Well said, said Rabbi Shelomo.

But the wagoner said, Here are these people journeying to the Land of Israel and wanting to live on good terms with their evil inclination. I should not wonder if they take it along with them up to the Land of Israel.

Don't worry about us, said Leibush the butcher to him. Instead, just touch up your horses with the whip a bit, so that Satan will not overtake you on the road.

The wagoner turned his face to him angrily and said, And could I touch them up more if I had two whips?

Rabbi Yehuda Mendel looked with friendly eyes at Leibush the butcher, whose words amused him, and put his hands into his sleeves; for the day was already declining and the heat of the sun had diminished.

The wagoner took the reins and urged his horses on. They dashed ahead till they reached the village near Borsztszow where all wayfarers make a halt. The horses betook themselves towards the inn and pulled up at the stable door. The wagoner got down and unharnessed them, gave them their oats and watered them, while Hananiah aided our men of good heart and took down the pillows and cushions and all their other goods.

Then the travelers stretched their limbs and entered the inn to give rest to their bodies and to say the Afternoon and Evening Prayers.

Chapter five
Welfare and Wayfarers

When the innkeeper saw them, he stared in astonishment. Here they were, coming along to his place at the very time when the whole world, as you might say, was off to the fair. He put it to Rabbi Shelomo, who answered, That's how it is, you see. The whole world goes faring downward, but we are faring upward.

To which Rabbi Alter the teacher added, You see, all the world is going to the fair, but we are leaving the fair aside and going up to the Land of Israel.

Well, the innkeeper was happy enough to have them since that was the case; and he went and fetched two bottles of brandy that they might wash away the dust of the road.

Which do you prefer? he asked them. The strong or the sweet?

Whereupon Rabbi Moshe clapped his hands with delight and cried, Oh, I love both the strong and the sweet.

The innkeeper supposed that Rabbi Moshe was talking about the liquor, but he was really referring to his Father in Heaven. And they said their blessings, and drank to long life, and said the Afternoon and Evening Prayers, the men inside the house and the womenfolk in the outer room.

Now several days had gone by in that house without a word of prayer being heard, and suddenly there was a whole quorum. The innkeeper and his wife had already been thinking of packing up and moving to the town where you can hear and take part in congregational prayer every day and all day long if you want to; but once a zaddik had stayed with them.

And how do you know, he had said to them, that the Holy One, blessed be he, requires your congregational prayers? Maybe what he wants of you is a glass of brandy and a dish of buckwheat groats. I assure you, this fine meal you serve wayfarers is as sweet to Him, as you might say, as any of the fine hymns of praise they chant to Him in the town. So, on account of the words of that zaddik, they did not remove but did their best to serve wayfarers with food and drink.

While the company were standing and praying, the innkeeper's wife stood over her pots and pans preparing the evening meal. Happy the woman whose good fortune it is to have such guests come her way! Why, the very fire in the grate recognized the worth of the guests. Scarce had they finished their prayers when they found their supper ready, buckwheat groats boiled in milk which had come from the cow just before the Afternoon Prayer.

The company sat at the table, the men separate from the women. Rabbi Shmuel Yosef, the son of Rabbi Shalom Mordekhai ha-Levi, sweetened the meal with tales and legends recounting the praises of the Land of Israel. Desolate the Land might be, yet she remained as holy as ever, and Prophet Elijah, may he be remembered to good effect, still offers daily sacrifice in the Temple. Desolate though it be, the Temple is as holy as ever it was. The Patriarchs everlastingly stand at Elijah's side as witnesses and Heman and Asaph and Jeduthun are the choir. And from the skins of the offerings Elijah makes many a scroll on which he inscribes the many merits of Israel.

Well, having eaten and drunk and said grace, the men took books out of their sacks and sat down to study, while the women took out needles and wool and sat down to knit. The wagoner sent his horses to graze in the meadow but hobbled their legs that they might not stray off to the forest and be eaten by wild beasts. Hananiah prepared the straw in the wagons and under the seats that there might be no delay when the time came for them to start out. Then he sat down in his own wagon and took out the Book of Psalms from his bundle and read by the light of the moon.

Gentiles from the village came to the door of the inn and took off their hats out of respect for the guests, saying, When there are guests in the house, God is in the house. The men of good heart sat silent, staring at these lofty countryfolk, who were tall as giants and whose hair was black as pitch and grew thick at the back of their necks, while it was cut short and shone over their foreheads. For they have no combs, and they grease their hair with lard and that is why it shines. And their beards are shaved and they clip their mustaches on either side; and their eyes are dark and gloomy with the servitude imposed upon them by their masters.

The chief of the villagers came over to the table and said, Spit into our eyes, O ye wayfarers to the Land of Israel. At that Milka took out one of the honey cakes she had brought with her for the journey and shared it out among them. They lifted up their pieces to the level of their eyes and said, God's gift, God's gift. And then each man kissed his piece and put it in his bosom next to his heart. After that they took their leave and went.

Meanwhile Rabbi Alter the slaughterer saw Rabbi Leibush the butcher sitting in amazement. What are you amazed at? he asked.

Those Gentiles, answered Rabbi Leibush, have neither share nor inheritance in the Land of Israel and still they hold the Land of Israel so dear!

The reason, answered Rabbi Alter, is because of the head of Esau which lies buried in the Cave of Machpelah.

Then the one whose name we have forgotten asked Rabbi Yehudah Mendel, who is always known as the pious Rabbi Yehudah Mendel, Why did Esau merit having his head buried in the Cave of Machpelah?

The reason, replied the pious Rabbi Yehudah Mendel, is because Hushim, the son of Dan, took a stick and hit Esau over the head so that his head fell off and fell on the feet of Jacob; and they buried it with him.

That of course, said Rabbi Alter the teacher, is the plain meaning; but there is a great and mystic secret behind it as well. For during all the years that Jacob was outside the Land of Israel, Esau was in the Land of Israel, and its merits stood him in good stead. Indeed, Jacob had already begun to fear that Esau and his sons might gain the right to the Land of Israel; but then the Holy Writ came and informed him that Israel are 'a nation one in the Land,' and not Esau and his sons. Then of course, you might argue that Ishmael had a claim; but Writ has provided even for that in the verse saying, 'The son of this bondwoman shall not be heir with my son, even with Isaac. Said the Holy One, blessed be he: The Land is dear to me and so is Israel, therefore I am going to bring Israel who is dear to me into the Land which is dear to me.

Rabbi Shelomo brought out his long pipe and filled the bowl with tobacco, and twisted himself a spool of paper, and lit it, and began smoking, and looked in friendly fashion at the company sitting and discussing the Torah. How they had toiled before they left their town; and how thoroughly weary and tired they are yet to be. He raised his eyes aloft and meditated in his heart: We cannot know what to beseech of Thee; but as Thou hast done with us until now, so mayest Thou continue to do unto us forever.

The innkeeper's wife sat quietly gazing in front of her. There was a lighted candle on the table and the voice of Torah was heard continually in the whole house. Here in this inn which had been parched for words of Torah, those same words could now be heard rising on high.

While she was sitting there, a moth came and fell into the flame. How long had it lived? A moment. Just a few moments earlier it had been flying through the house, then for a little while it had gone circling round the flame, and at the last the flame had just licked it and turned it into so much cinder.

So it was with her. For a little while the Omnipresent had given her ample room; for a little while He had lit a great light for her; for a little while she had sat in this contentment, listening to the words of the living God; the next morning the guests would go their way and she would be left again without Torah, without prayer, and without life.

But while she was communing with herself, a number of countrywomen came in and curtsied to the pilgrims; they took a pile of pine cones from their aprons to place under the pillows of the way-farers to the Holy Land, that they might sleep sweetly.

But the men of good heart were in no haste to sleep. Instead they sat studying and meditating on the Torah, while the women sat knitting socks and stockings for the journey. Sarah turned her head towards her husband Rabbi Moshe, as he sat with his head resting on his arm, holding a book in his hand. Her mind turned back to her two daughters whom she had left behind in Buczacz; now, she thought to herself, their husbands are just coming to eat their suppers, and maybe they too have boiled buckwheat in milk and are shaking fine sugar over the porridge to sweeten the food; but the men do not even notice the women's labor, but sit down at table and look into a book; sons-in-law like father-in-law.

While she was communing with herself, the woman next to her jogged her and said, Just take a look at Tzirel gazing at her hus-band Pesach as if they were all alone in the world. And Sarah, sigh-ing, said, She who leaves nothing behind can be happy even when she leaves her town forever.

Well, the folk of good heart sat as long as they wished, until the wagoner came and advised them, You had better rest your limbs before the combs of the cocks turn white and you have to get up.

Sleep is fine for wayfarers, especially on Iyar nights in a vil-lage, when the whole world is still and the grass and the trees are silent and the beasts graze in the meadow and have no complaints against human beings. A gentle breeze is blowing outside and wind-ing around the roof and rolling in the flower-cups of the straw which rustle, whispering with the breeze, making a man's sleep pleasant and sweetening his limbs.

But the men of good heart remembered that sleep was created only in order to strengthen the body that a man may rise fit and well for His blessed service. Before the third watch was over, they had all risen. At the same time the Holy One, blessed be he, brought up the morning star; and the other stars and the planets began to fade.

The clouds grew red and sailed away hither and thither. The grasses and greenery began to drip and the trees glistened with dew. The sun was about to appear, and the birds clapped their wings and opened their eyes to utter song. The horses whinnied and stamped their hoofs and lifted their tails. The men of good heart rose, and prayed, and ate the morning meal, and climbed up on their wagons, the men on one wagon and the women on the other. And they took their leave of the inn and set out on their way.

Chapter six

Through the Land of Poland and Moldavia

T he wagons went on and on, the horses vanishing and then reappearing in all manner of grasses, tall and short. Pleasant breezes blew, rousing the spirit. The grasses began to move to and fro in the fields and made their utterances before the Holy One, blessed be he. Many a village peeped out from the midst of the fields, and vineyards and forests and lakes stood silent. The sun shone on the rivers and on the riverbanks; and white clouds bore the folk of good heart company from the heavens.

And so they journeyed across the land of Poland until they crossed the border and reached a spot called Okup, where they safely crossed the river Dniester and spent a night. From Okup they made their way to Hutin, which lies on the right bank of the Dniester, and where there are several Jewish householders dwelling in the shadow of the powers that be and managing to bear up under the Exile. These were engaged in commerce and handicrafts with great honor. When there were riots, the nobles would conceal them in their own homes and no harm would befall them.

It was their tradition that they and their forefathers had been dwelling in that place since the days of the Second Temple; except of course for those Jews who had come from Poland. For when the Tartars made forays into the Kingdom of Poland, they would take away captives whom they transported to the Land of Ishmael, which is Turkey, to sell them; and the kings of Poland used to send Jews to redeem them. Those Jews saw that it was a good land and thinly inhabited and that commodities were far cheaper than in other lands, and that the Jews who dwelt there lived on good terms with their neighbors and had no reason to fear them and merely paid a small amount to the king; so they came and settled there. At the old fort of Hutin a coin had been found dating from the time of the Royal House of the Hasmoneans, on which were engraved the name of Jerusalem and the figures of a bunch of grapes, a myrtle bough, and a citron.

Furthermore, living there were many women who did not know what had befallen their husbands, but there was no authority to deliver them from their fate, and they could not remarry as they remained 'chained' to their missing husbands, some of whom had gone to do business in Europe or Turkey and had not come back, while others had been slain on the way and their burial place was unknown.

One of these 'chained' women joined our comrades to make the journey with them. This was her sad story: Formerly she had dwelt with her husband and had borne him sons and daughters, never hearing a harsh word from his lips. His business had been dealing in horses which he bought for the nobles, who all trusted him and gave him money on account. He had never broken faith, neither in those matters which lie between one man and another nor in those that lie between a man and his God. But once he set out to buy horses with a lot of money in his possession and he never came back. It was plain when he never came back that he must have been slain on the road. His disappearance created a great commotion among the rest of the Jews and they set out in search of his body, asking many wayfarers whether they had seen such and such a Jew named Zusha, the horse dealer. Nobody admitted to having seen him, but some had heard that robbers had attacked a Jew and there was little chance that he had escaped alive from their hands. What was more, the same was said by an old wise Gentile woman who was versed in the stars. There is no sense in the Jews being excited, said she. That man has already left the world. The same was said in slightly different words by a Gentile who trafficked in witchcraft. The way he put it was, The Jews are not smart. They are spending their money for a tiny heap of bones. More than that he did not say, it being the practice of witches not to say what they do not know. But when they entreated him to take pity on the woman and her children and to interpret his words, he said, The Jews are not smart. They are looking above-ground for what has already been put underground.

Now there was an old judge who was present and he said, If he is referring to that Jewish robber chief who was hanged in the Land of the Ukraine, I can promise that they will not find him any more.

Now why should they have suspected that robber of having been Zusha? Well, several years earlier some Jews of that town had come and said that they had seen Zusha standing at the crossroads as a highwayman.

Here your wife and children, said they to him, are moving heaven and earth for your sake, and you...

Before ever they finished, other robbers arrived. But Zusha said, They are my townsmen. So they let them be.

Well, the Government heard about it and sent to capture him, but he was not to be found because he had already moved on to another country. Before long there came news that a robber chief had been caught in the Ukraine and there hanged; and the good name of the Jews was desecrated among the nations, because he was found to have a pair of tefillin and thus identified as a Jew. And that was the last news to have been heard about Zusha.

But his wife took her children and went from one zaddik to another, weeping in their presence; but they had nothing to answer her. At last she came to the renowned Rabbi Meir of Primishlan, who told her, If you wish to weep, go to the place where the sea and the Danube weep for each other, and weep there. Meir has no love of tears. So she and her children were proceeding to the spot where the river Danube empties into the sea in order to seek her husband there.

The women sat knitting, tears falling from their eyes for this poor woman left 'chained,' and for her husband who had died a sinner and left his children orphans. Yet the woman did not despair of her husband and was still searching for him; for, she argued to herself, could Zusha, who had lived at peace with every man and had always done his business so honestly, have joined a band of robbers and highwaymen? She was sure it was all a false charge.

The wagoner stopped his wagon and called to Hananiah, who came up level with him and stopped. Hananiah, said the wagoner, did you hear the story of the poor woman?

I heard it, Hananiah answered.

What do you think, Hananiah? went on the wagoner. Who is the robber they hanged?

It's my opinion as well, said Hananiah, that the fellow can have been nobody but Zusha.

The sun sank, sank again, and then sank once more. The women dropped their knitting needles, and wiped the tears from their eyes. Hananiah took out his kerchief and knotted it for a sign. In silence they rolled along the riverbank until they arrived at Lipkani, where they halted. From Lipkani they made their way towards Radiaitz, where the wagoner took off the horses' bells so that robbers and highwaymen might not hear them jingling. From there they made their way to Shtepenasht, a small town on the Basha river not far from the river Pruth. The folks of Shtepenasht are heavy in flesh and light in Torah; a fist-sized bite of food to them is like a mere olive-sized bite of food for others.

From Shtepenasht they made their way to Jassy, where they arrived at dusk on the Sabbath eve. There are twenty-one large synagogues in Jassy, apart from one hundred and twenty Houses of Study and small synagogues and prayer rooms; yet when they came to Jassy, they did not pray in a single one of them but stayed at their inn and constituted a prayer quorum for themselves, as the Sabbath had begun ere they had time to change their clothes.

But next day they hastened to the Great Synagogue, dressed in their Sabbath clothing and wearing their prayer shawls. By the time they reached the synagogue the congregation was already deep in prayer, since the folk of Jassy start early and leave early. Anyone who has never seen Jassy at her ease never saw a contented city in his life. More than twenty thousand Jews lived there, eating, drinking, rejoicing, and enjoying life. Among them, indeed, were some for whom the eating of cookies in the shape of Haman's ears at Purim was more important than eating matzah at Passover. The holy men of the age labored greatly to make them stand erect instead of wallowing in the dust.

In brief, our men of good heart arrived in the midst of the prayers at a time when no man greets another. They stood where they were and nobody paid any attention to them. But when the time came to read the Torah, the sexton summoned them to the reading. What was more, the sexton summoned each one of them by his own name and the name of his father—except for Hananiah, whom he did not summon. It is the general custom that when a man comes to a place where he is not known and the warden wishes to summon him to the Torah, the man is asked for his name and the name of his father and then summoned; but this fellow summoned them without first asking any questions. If he was not a prophet, he was an angel or more than an angel; since even an angel has to ask, as we find in the case of Jacob, whom the angel asked, 'What is thy name?'

After the prayer was ended, the sexton arranged a fine repast in their honor, and while they sat together he asked each one of them about his affairs. They were astonished, for he told them everything that went on in their homes and their town. Yet from the way he ate and drank there was no sign that he was on a high spiritual level.

But once the wine went in, his secret came out.

Don't you recognize me? he asked them.

We have not the honor, they answered.

Then he said, Do you remember Yoshke Cossack, who once sold himself to the king's army for a skullcap full of money?

We remember, they replied, that they used to feed him on all kinds of dainties. If he wanted raisins and currants, they gave them to him. If he asked for Hungarian wine, he received it. If he wanted a bed with pillows and cushions, they had one prepared for him. When they took him off to serve the king, he asked for his pay to be doubled and they doubled it; and then, after all that, he ran away and deserted.

Would you suppose, said he to them, that he ran away to the Garden of Eden?

His actions, they responded, were not such as to indicate that there would be any place prepared for him in the Garden of Eden.

Well, said he, if you want to see him, just lift up your eyes and take a look at me. So then they stared at him and sure enough they recognized him.

There was another great marvel which our men of good heart saw in Jassy. This was a man with hair growing from the palm of his hand. On one occasion when folk had been talking of the coming of the Messiah, he held out his hand and said, There is as much chance for the Messiah to come as there is for hair to grow on the palm of my hand. Before he even had a chance to drop his hand to his side, there the hair was. He always wore a bandage around that hand and would take it off only to prove that we must never despair of the Redemption. Of course, the wiseacres who know everything had already tried pulling out the hair, for, they said, he must have it fixed on with paste; but by the next day the hair would have grown again.

On the day after the Sabbath they left Jassy and arrived at Vaslavi, a town on the river Vasli, which joins the river Barlad. In that town there is a great market for honey and wax, from which five hundred householders make a comfortable living. They spent the night there and next morning proceeded to the Holy Congregation of Barlad, so called after the river running through its midst. In this town there are two graveyards, one new, and the other old, in which people are no longer buried. It stands in the middle of the town and in it are the graves of martyrs killed for the sanctification of the Name; graves that are black as soot and face the east. They spent one night there and in the morning made their way to Tikotsh, a large town containing between five and six prayer quorums. There they spent a night and went on next morning to Avitshi, whence they journeyed to a large town called Galatz on the river Danube, where you take ship for the Black Sea, which the ships must cross in order to reach Stambul.

All the time that our comrades were journeying through this country, the wagons followed one another through villages surrounded by meadows and vineyards and cucumber fields; flocks of sheep were scattered over the whole countryside, grazing in the meadows and drinking from the water troughs next to the wells; and shepherds sat piping pleasant tunes to them, tunes that were sweet and sad and sounded like the tunes that are sung in the House of Prayer on Yom

Kippur. How do Gentiles who tend sheep merit such holy music? This was once explained by Rabbi Israel Baal Shem Tov of blessed memory, who said that this people have suffered a great deal but never denied their God, and therefore they merit piping the very music that Israel, who are holy, sing on a holy day and in a holy place before the Holy One, blessed be he.

So the wagons went their way with the horses pacing ahead, neighing and with their tails raised; other horses which they could not see answered them from the meadows, at which they would twitch their ears and pause. Countless sheep went by, crowding and thrusting one against the other, with their wool all in curls; and a cloud of dust rose all around the sheep as they walked, while a little shepherd strode behind them with a whistle in his mouth, playing to himself. Tall hills rose above the ground, now to the east and now to the west. Water ran down from the hills and the hills themselves came together, as if they did not want to let the wagons pass. But the handiness and skill of the wagoner and of Hananiah, who drove their horses expertly, got them out of the narrow pass. They entered one town and left another, and wherever they arrived the men of good heart were received with great affection. Beds were made ready for them and tables were set with food and drink: with *mamaliga* floating in butter, and with sheep cheese, and with wine; and when they departed the town, the cantor would accompany them singing the Sabbath verse, 'Happy in their departure.'

When our comrades arrived at Galatz, the party broke up. All the travelers awaited a ship which would take them to the Black Sea, while the wagoner went around looking for other wayfarers. The comrades sat in their inn and wrote letters to their brethren in Buczacz. They had much to write and they wrote much. This is the proper place to mention the good quill pens of the men of Galatz, which do not scratch or pierce the paper and do not splutter and scatter ink while writing; for since their geese are fat, the quills are soft.

The wagoner went to the market and hired out one wagon to the merchants of Leshkovitz, where the fair was still going on, since it sometimes lasted for four weeks and sometimes longer. The other wagon he loaded with sheepskins to take with him to Buczacz, trusting to the Lord that he would do good business with them.

But on the way he began to think, and his thoughts were disturbing. He thought to himself, What kind of fool am I to be going back to Buczacz, when those folk are going up to the Land of Israel? Here I have to water my horses and feed them hay, and do today what I did yesterday, and so every other day, until my time comes, and they lay me away in the ground with my teeth up, and the worms eat me. But why should I slip into thoughts of this kind? Has mine been a case of being able to go up to the Land and not wanting to? Rabbi Abraham the circumciser was certainly worthy of going up, but if the Name, be blessed, did not want him to go up, he did not.

The sun was about to set and its rays gradually faded. The hills were covered over, and the moon came up and lit the way. Everything was silent. All that could be heard was the sound of the wells of the murderers; for it is a custom of the people of those parts when they kill somebody to dig a well to atone for their sin, and put a creaky pump on top.

The horses twitched their tails and their hoofs began slipping. The wagoner looked around him and saw that they had left the right path. He tugged at the reins and cracked his whip, shouting, Where are you dragging me to, you beasts? I'll show you the way to behave.

The horses lowered their heads and went the way they were required to go. And the wagoner wound the reins around his wrist and went back to thinking, now of himself, and now of Hananiah. This Hananiah fellow bundles his tallit and tefillin in his kerchief, and winds rags around his legs, and goes off to the Land of Israel, while all I do is go back to Buczacz. And why do I go back to Buczacz instead of going up to the Land of Israel? Because I am not prepared for the way. And when the Angel of Death comes, is he going to ask me whether I am ready?

While the wagoner was speaking to himself, his head sank on his chest. The horses turned their heads and saw that he was asleep. So they went ahead on their own accord, till suddenly they stopped. Whereupon the wagoner started up and took his whip and beat them until their flanks began to steam with sweat. And he yelled, Oh, you beasts, you always have to be sent off in a different direction from the way you want to go. By your lives, I shall thrash you until you forget that you are horses.

Chapter seven
Many Waters

When the company arrived at Galatz they paid the tax required by the king of Ishmael, the Sultan of Turkey, and entered the town. There they found a market place full of food and drink, with all manner of delicacies and fruits whose names will not be found even in the chapter on blessings to be said over fruit in the *Shulhan Arukh* code of law. They bought provisions for the way, bread and wine and fruits and other things which sustain the heart. As for the people of Galatz, they showed their affection by giving them all kinds of preserves, to restore them while on the sea. Then the comrades shaved their heads and went to the bathhouse. The warm water drew the weariness out of their bodies, so that they really felt like new beings. After coming out, they hired themselves a ship and set sail on the river Danube until they reached a certain spot called Wilkup, where the river falls into the Black Sea and whence the ships go off to Constantinople. There they waited several days for the rage of the sea to die down, so that they might embark on a big ship.

When they arrived at Wilkup, it was already twilight. They set up a camp, said the Afternoon and Evening Prayers, and then repeated Psalm Sixty-nine which begins, 'Save me, O God, for the waters are come in even unto the soul,' and which finishes joyfully, 'For God will save Zion... and they that love His name shall dwell therein.'

The sea was silent and the waters were still. The men took out the cushions and pillows and the pots and pans, while the women gathered wood, kindled a fire, and cooked the supper. Every day during their stay at that place Hananiah used to go out with the women and gather branches which dripped resin. These give off a fine smell when they burn and add a spice to the meal.

They sat on their boxes and ate their meal in the moonlight. The trees and plants smelled sweetly and the night too gave off many goodly odors; the water moved to and fro in the sea, the stars and planets gave light on high, and the earth whispered to itself below, restoring their souls. The good folk got up, spread out a place to sleep on the ground, and prepared to sleep, reciting the 'Hear O Israel' and praying for protection against demons, and evil and harmful spirits, and evil sins, and evil dreams, reminding God that they were dust and ashes and worms and corruption, and beseeching Him to forgive all their transgressions, as it is written, 'for with thee there is forgiveness.'

Suddenly they were pounced upon by every kind of mosquitoe, big as frogs, which bit them so that their faces swelled up. Never had they spent nights as bad as these. They could not sit, they could not lie, and they could not read any books. They could not sit up because of the mosquitoes, they could not lie down because of their sores, and they could not read any books because the mosquitoes covered the light.

This is the proper place to mention Rabbi Shmuel Yosef, the son of Rabbi Shalom Mordekhai ha-Levi, who sweetened their sufferings with tales of the Land of the Sons of Moses and the Four Tribes who dwell beyond the river Sambation in large houses made of precious stones and pearls, and who need no lamps or candles at night, since the stones of their houses shine sevenfold brighter than any candle; furthermore, they live for a hundred and twenty years, and no son dies during the lifetime of his father, nor daughter during the lifetime of her mother. They are forty times as many as the numbers of those who left Egypt and possess all the good things of the world as a reward for their study of His blessed Torah and observance of His Commandments. There is nothing impure in all their borders, neither an impure domestic beast nor an impure beast of prey, nor impure birds, nor vermin, nor reptiles, nor flies, nor mosquitoes. And every day they hear a Divine Voice proclaim, 'Woe is me for I have destroyed my house, and burnt my mansion, and sent my children into exile.' And they wait for the Omnipresent to return them to the Land of Israel.

Great are the works of his Name, be blessed. Happy the man who devotes his heart to them and knows how to explain them to others. Happy is Rabbi Shmuel Yosef, who at all times can relate the good deeds which the Holy One, blessed be he, does for Israel. Every night that they were upon the sea Rabbi Shmuel Yosef cheered them with his words and told them tales of salvation and comfort; such as the tale of Rabbi Gad of Jerusalem, and the tale of Malkiel the Hero, and the tale of the letters which the Sons of Moses sent to the men of Jerusalem.

When day broke and the sea could be seen, the women began crying, Oh, we are afraid to set out on the sea, we are afraid to sail by ship; when a man dies on board ship they don't bury him but they tie him to a plank of wood and let him down into the sea! And then all kinds of big fish come, and some of them eat the soles of his feet while some eat his nose and lips. Last of all a big fish comes and swallows the corpse together with the plank which he is tied to, or else the sea spews him out on the sand, and all kinds of unclean birds come and peck out his eyes and pull the flesh off his bones. Whatever happens, the poor fellow never gets to a Jewish grave!

It was at that time that the women all made up their minds to go back to Buczacz, and screamed and cried for divorces. So they went off to the town and asked where a rabbi was to be found. But the folk of the town could not make out what they were talking about, for in those parts they do not have a rabbi, but a *hakham* who spends his time in the Yeshivah teaching the congregation Torah and right conduct. So the women asked, Then where is the judge?

We don't go in much for quarreling, said the people of the town, and so we do not need anyone to judge us.

But at last they found an ordained rabbi from the lands of His Imperial Majesty, the Emperor of Austria, who happened to live in that town; and he arranged the divorces for the womenfolk. Then of course, after they had been divorced, the women remembered how folk buried outside the Holy Land must suffer by having to roll their corpses through caves and tunnels underground to reach the Holy Land. And they began wailing aloud at the top of their voices. Each and every one of them flung herself at the feet of the man who had been her husband and wept before him and entreated him, until the husbands arranged to take them under the bridal canopy and marry them all over again.

Then Rabbi Moshe said to Rabbi Yosef Meir, What a happy fellow you are, Rabbi Yosef Meir, to have given your wife her divorce before you started out, so that you no longer have to worry about divorces and marriages. Now here you have a Jew who wishes to prepare himself on the way in order to enter the Land of Israel with a clear mind. Suddenly his wife turns on him in a fury, wanting a divorce or demanding a bridal canopy. It is not good for a man to be alone; and when his wife is with him it is no good either. God forbid that I should complain about my virtuous paragon; but if you wish to study or if you wish to think some pure thoughts, up she comes with her talk and you have to devote your heart to what is a waste of time.

But Rabbi Yosef Meir only sighed and said nothing. He had never thought anything wrong with his wife, until the business of journeying to the Land of Israel came up, and then he had divorced her because she did not wish to go along; and once he had divorced her he had put her out of his mind. But now when the women were so disturbed at the sight of the sea, his divorced wife appeared before his mind's eye. Rabbi Yosef Meir said, Tomorrow the Holy One, blessed be He, will send us a good wind and I shall set off to the Land of Israel, while she, poor thing, remains forsaken outside the Land.

Within a few days the sea became calm and peace was restored upon the waters. The waves that had thought to rise up and flood the whole world now flattened out when they reached the sand, and went back. The captain ordered the men and goods to come aboard. Thereupon each of the comrades took his goods in hand and went aboard, with his wife holding on to his tails and going up with him. Once they were on board, the sailors took oars in hand to make their way through the sea and began shouting, Hoya! Hoya! Within a very short while the wind began blowing on the masts and sails of the ships, and the ship began to move.

Chapter eight
On the Sea

The ship reached the point at sea where the waters move, and sailed along calmly. Our comrades stood reciting the Prayer of the Sea and the eight verses which Jonah had recited in the belly of the fish. Then, weeping, they sang Psalm One hundred and seven, which considers the kindness of the Lord and his wonders by land and sea, how he shall redeem his redeemed ones, and gather them together from all the lands, and lead them on the straight way, and satisfy the souls of those who hunger and thirst, and fill them with all good things; even if they reach the very gates of death, God forbid, He saves them by his mercies, and delivers them from their distress, and brings them to their desired haven; so that at the last they relate his deeds in song. Even if he raises the sea against them and brings up a stormy wind, he quiets the sea at once and silences the waves; and then they rejoice and give thanks to the Holy One, blessed be he, and rise from their affliction, having seen that all that comes from the Lord is loving-kindness, but that it is necessary to consider wisely in order to see and rejoice in the mercies of the Lord.

After they finished reciting the entire Psalm, they sat down on their belongings, and took their books in hand, and read verses from the Pentateuch, the Prophets, and the Writings. When a man forsakes his home and reaches another place and finds a vessel which he had used at home, how he rejoices! How much pleasure he derives from the vessel! This is far truer of books, which are read and studied and engaged in every day. Thus Rabbi Moshe sits reading: 'The Land must be exceedingly good if the Lord desires us and brings us unto it and gives it unto us, a land which is flowing with milk and honey.' And Rabbi Yosef Meir sits reading, 'I have forsaken my house, I have cast off my heritage'; and both of them finished by reading together: 'Afterwards the Children of Israel will return and entreat the Lord their God and David their king, and they will fear the Lord and hope for His goodness.' Finally, they put the books down and rose, and each one placed his hand on the other's shoulder, and they sang:

'Oh that the salvation of Israel were come out of Zion!
When the Lord turneth the captivity of his people,
Let Jacob rejoice, let Israel be glad.'

The ship made her way quietly and a pleasant smell came up out of the sea. The waters moved after their fashion and the waves dwelt together in peace; while birds of some kind flew above the ship and beat their wings and shrieked. The sun sank below the horizon, the face of the sea turned black, and the Holy One, blessed be He, brought forth the moon and stars and set them to give light in the heavens.

One of the company looked out and saw a kind of light shining on the sea. Brother, said he to one of the comrades, perhaps you know what that is? But he did not know, and so he asked another of the company and that one asked still another.

Then they all turned their eyes and gazed at the sea and said, If that be the lower fire which comes from hell, then where is the smoke? And if it be the eye socket of Leviathan, then no eye has ever seen it.

Suppose, said Rabbi Alter the teacher, that it is one of the evil husks of the sea.

But Rabbi Shelomo said, It is time to say the Evening Prayer. Then they promptly rose and prepared to pray, since there is no evil husk or demon that has any power or authority over a full prayer quorum.

When they stood up to pray they saw that they were lacking one for a minyan. Hananiah, who had made the journey with them, had vanished. In the morning he had gone down to the market to buy his food, but he had never come back.

Then they began to beat their heads and to wail: Woe and alas, is that the way to treat a companion! It would have been better if we had gone back and been lost. We should have held one another's hands and come up into the ship all together, but we did not. When we came aboard, each one carried his own baggage and said, 'All is well, my soul!'

How hard Hananiah had toiled until he reached them! He had gone halfway round the world, and had been stripped naked, and had fallen among thieves, and had forgotten when Sabbaths and festivals occurred, and had profaned Yom Kippur, and had made his way barefoot, without boots. And then when he had reached them he had gone to all kinds of trouble for their sakes. He had rebound the books, and made cups for the oil lamps and boxes for their goods, and had not asked for any payment. All the trouble with the horses had been left to him on the way; they had been happy to have him because he would complete the minyan. But now that they had embarked on the ship and were on the way to the Land of Israel, he had been left behind. So they stood miserable and unhappy, lamenting at heart because an unobtrusive vessel had been in their midst and had been taken away from them for their sins.

So everyone prayed separately, and while praying they beat their heads against the sides of the ship in order to divert their thoughts. Finally, everyone returned to his own place and sat down as though he were in mourning. Gradually the night grew darker and the ship went its accustomed way. The sailors tightened the masts and sails and sat down to eat and drink, while facing them our comrades sat, distress eating at their hearts. Who knew where Hananiah could be? Maybe he had been taken captive, God forbid, and sold as a slave.

The darkness grew thicker and thicker. Rats and mice were scurrying around in the lower parts of the ship and were gnawing at utensils and foodstuffs.

Where there is great anxiety, sleep helps to put it right. But who could enjoy sleep when one of their number had left them, and they had no way of knowing whether he was alive or dead. How much Hananiah had wandered about! How much trouble he had gone through! He had put himself in danger and disregarded his own life and had had no fear for his body, desiring only to go up to the Land of Israel; and yet now that his time had come to go up, something had gone wrong and he had not come aboard!

At the midnight hour the comrades sat on their baggage and uttered songs and prayers in honor of the great Name of Him who dwells in Zion. The stars moved in the sky, while the moon was now covered, now uncovered. The ship went on, the waters moved as usual, and a still small voice rose from the ship. It was the sound of song and praise rising from one firmament to another, till they reached the Gateway of White Sapphire where the prayers of Israel gather and join together until such time as the dawn comes to the Land of Israel. Corresponding to the prayers of Israel, praises of the Holy One, blessed be he, rise up from the waters.

Is it possible for water which has neither utterance nor speech so to praise the Holy One, blessed be He? But these sounds are the voices of the boys and girls who once flung themselves into the sea. After the wicked Titus destroyed Jerusalem, he brought three thousand ships and filled them with boys and girls. When they were out to sea, they said to one another, Was it not enough for us to have angered the Holy One, blessed be he, in his house, and now are we to be required to anger him in the land of Edom? Thereupon they all leaped into the sea together. What did the Holy One, blessed be he, do? He took them in his right hand and brought them to a great island planted with all manner of fine trees, and surrounded them with all kinds of beautifully colored waves, blue and marble and alabaster, looking like the stones of the Temple; and the plants from which the Temple incense was made grow there. And all those who saw that plant would weep and laugh. They would weep because they remembered the glory of the House, and they would laugh because the Holy One, blessed be he, is destined to bring that glory back.

And the boys and girls still remain as innocent as ever, fenced about from all iniquity, their faces like the rosebud, just as we learn in the tale about the rose garden which was once to be found in Jerusalem. And the brightness of their faces gives light like the planet Venus, whose light comes from the shining of the Beasts that are before God's throne.

And the children have no wrinkles either on their brows or their faces, apart from two wrinkles under the eyes from which their tears run down into the Great Sea and cool the Gehenna of those sinners of Israel who never lost their faith in the Land of Israel. These children are not subject to any prince or ruler, neither to the king of Edom nor to the king of Ishmael, nor to any flesh-and-blood monarch; but they stand in the shadow of the Holy One, blessed be He, and call him Father and He calls them my children. And all their lives long they speak of the glory of Jerusalem and the glory of the House, and the glory of the High Priests and the altar, and of those who offered the sacrifices and those who prepared the incense and those who made the shewbread.

And whenever the Holy One, blessed be he, remembers his sons who have been exiled among the nations, who have neither Temple nor altar of atonement, nor High Priests nor Levites at their stations, nor kings and princes, he at once is filled with pity and takes those boys and girls in his arm and holds them to his heart and says to them, Sons and daughters mine, do you remember the glory of Jerusalem and the glory of Israel when the Temple still stood and Israel still possessed its splendor?

They at once begin telling Him what they saw in their childhood, and go on interpreting like Daniel, the beloved man, and Jonathan ben Uziel. The only difference is that Daniel and Jonathan wrote in Aramaic, while these children speak the Holy Tongue, which is the tongue the Holy One, blessed be He, uses. And at such times the Holy One, blessed be He, laughs with them; and you might say that at no other times does he laugh and smile as he does when he hears the praises of his House and the praises of those who came to his House. At such times he says, 'This is the people which I formed for Myself that they might tell of My praise.' And he also says, 'Comfort ye,' for in the future Jerusalem will be builded a thousand thousand times more great than she was, and the Temple will reach from one end of the world to the other and be as lofty as the stars of the heavens and the wheels of my divine Chariot; and the Divine Presence will rest upon each and every one of Israel; and each and every one of them will speak in the Holy Spirit.

Furthermore, all the years that those boys and girls have dwelt in the midst of the sea they have constantly awaited salvation, and there is no ship sailing to the Land of Israel which these boys and girls do not follow. For when they see a ship at sea, one says to the other, The time has come for the Gathering of the Exiles. Thereupon, each of them takes one of the great sea waves and mounts it as a rider mounts his horse and rides until he comes near the ship.

And as they ride they sing, 'I will bring them back from Bashan, I will bring them back from the depths of the sea.' And their voices are as golden bells in the skirts of a garment, and they are heard by those who go down to the sea. Indeed we have heard a tale from such as tell only the truth, of how they were sailing to the Land of Israel on the Great Sea and heard a voice so sweet they wished to leap into the sea and follow that voice; but the sailors tied them up with their belts until the ship had sailed a distance away from the voice.

The moon sank, the stars went in, and the planets went their way. The Holy One, blessed be He, brought forth the dawn and lit up the world. As the dawn grew bright the travelers saw the likeness of a man on the sea. They stared and saw that he had a full beard, earlocks on either cheek and a book in his hand; and a kerchief was spread out under him and on it he sat as a man who sits at his ease. No wave of the sea rose to drown him, nor did any sea beast swallow him.

And what did the Gentiles say when they saw a man sitting on his kerchief and floating in the sea? Some of them said, Such things are often seen by seafarers and desert-farers. Others said, Whoever he is, he has a curse hanging over him so that nevermore can he rest. That is why he wanders from place to place, appearing yesterday on the dry land and today on the sea.

On that ship there were representatives of each of the seventy nations of the world, and each of them was overwhelmed and terrified at this apparition. So Israel stood on one side and the nations of the world on the other, fearful and staring, until their eyelashes became scorched by the sun. Then Rabbi Shmuel Yosef, the son of Rabbi Shalom Mordekhai ha-Levi, said, It is the Divine Presence, which is bringing back the people of Israel to their own place.

And Rabbi Moshe wept and said, 'The counsel of the Lord is with them that fear Him, and his covenant to make them know it.'

Chapter nine
Eternal Secrets

The ship went on after her fashion and a pleasant odor rose from the water. Clear clouds floated in the sky and the waves kissed. The air was damp and had a salty tang. The fish thrust out their lips and amused the people, and the birds which fly about hither and thither not recognizing the authority of any man, nor associating with human beings, nor being fed by them, flew through the air and fluttered close to that shape out at sea. The waves went on rolling and the ship moved gently, not disturbing those in it overmuch. Our comrades sat, some of them conversing about the new souls that Israel, who are holy, receive in the Holy Land, while others were engaged in the secret questions of the universe, such as why the Land of Israel was first given to Canaan when it was actually intended for Israel. The reason being, of course, to instruct coming generations that although the nations rule over the Land of Israel and Israel is given into their hands, into the hands of Sennacherib and Nebuchadnezzar and the wicked Titus, the nations are not resident there but are driven out, nation after nation, unsuccessful there and achieving nothing but destruction until they are expelled; but Israel are established in the Land for ever. Similarly, we find that the Holy One, blessed be He, gave Bathsheba to Uriah, the Hittite, although she had been intended for David ever since the six days of Creation. Uriah died without children, but an entire dynasty of kings and princes came from David.

The sun began to give way and returned to its place in order to make room for the moon and the stars. Stars and planets came and took up their posts in the sky, and the light shone back at them from the waves, and a sweet sound rose from the sea like the sound of song and praise.

One of the men said to another, Brother, do you hear that voice? What is it?

And the other said to him, The fish in the sea, brother mine, are uttering song. The same we find recorded in the special Section of Song in the Prayer Book, where it says, 'The fish in the sea utter song.' And the song they utter is, 'The voice of the Lord is upon the waters, the God of glory thundereth, even the Lord upon many waters.'

But his comrade said to him, No indeed, for I clearly heard a voice saying, 'My help cometh from the Lord, who made heaven and earth.'

That verse, answered the other, is uttered by the seagull; for that too we find in the Section of Song: 'The seagull says, "My help cometh from the Lord, who made heaven and earth."'

Let us also sing, said our comrades to one another. And thereupon one of them began singing:

'For a small moment have I forsaken thee,
But with great compassion will I gather thee.'

And his companions joined in the chorus, singing:

'And the ransomed of the Lord shall return,
And come with singing into Zion.'

The Holy One, blessed be he, has an excellent gift whose name is Sabbath, and because of his love and pity for Israel, he gave it to them. Great is the Sabbath, whose holiness shines even on ordinary people; for when the Sabbath comes, the Holy One, blessed be he, makes his blessed light to shine, and all created things shine with the higher illumination and yearn to cleave to his holiness. All the more is this true of pious hasidim and men of miraculous deeds, who reduce their own requirements and seek nothing but the pleasure and satisfaction of the Divine Presence.

When the Friday morning arrived, our men of good heart rose early and began to prepare for the Sabbath. Rabbi Alter the slaughterer slew a fowl in honor of the Sabbath and burnt a garment and covered the blood with its ashes. Feiga kindled the fire and boiled the bird, while the other women engaged in cooking for the Sabbath. The captain passed them and looked at them with friendly eyes. Seeing this, the sailors brought them fish they had caught in the sea, and taught them to bake bread after the fashion of the Holy Land, where coals are spread out on the ground and the dough is poured onto them. And so the women were able to fulfill the commandment of setting aside part of the Sabbath loaf, and they made loaves for the feast of the Sabbath night and the feast of Sabbath morning and the third feast of Sabbath afternoon; and ere noon everything was prepared for the Sabbath day.

Our men of good heart hastened to wash their faces and hands in hot water. They trimmed their nails, changed their clothes, and put on fine garments in honor of the Sabbath, an undergarment, an overgarment, a girdle, and a long coat. Then they sat down together and considered the deeds they had done during the six week days, and in their hearts considered the hidden purposes underlying the deeds of his Name, blessed be he, who had distinguished them for good from all the other folk in their town and given them the strength and courage to uproot themselves from their former home and to follow the right and clearly-marked way which goes up to the Land of Israel.

But their hearts bled and suffered for Hananiah, who had gone along with them all the time and had willingly taken upon himself all manner of suffering and anguish so long as he could go up to the Land of Israel; and then when he should have taken the boat, he had missed his opportunity and was left behind in the lands of the nations. Could the Holy One, blessed be he, still be angry with him for having forgotten when it was Sabbath and when the Day of Atonement? Was it his will not to admit Hananiah into his portion? Or was there some other purpose at work here, such as ordinary thought could not comprehend? At that moment a great awe took possession of their hearts, and they recognized that it had not been their righteousness which had allowed them to proceed to the Land of Israel but his blessed mercies. They were aroused to correct all the errors which they had made, in deed, in word, or in thought; in order that they should meet with no obstacle, God forbid, such as might delay the Higher Providence from bringing them to the Land of Israel. They also concentrated on elevating all the divisions of the soul and adding additional spirit to it. In this way the men of good heart sat together with their Maker until their ecstatic souls were awakened and an additional Sabbath soul was added to their own. They took their Bibles and completed the study of the section of the week, reading it twice in the original Scripture and once in the Aramaic version, together with the explanations of Rashi; and they also recited the Song of Songs.

As for the women, they took out of their sacks the book of *Tehinnot,* which contains in Yiddish the prayers for the lighting of the Sabbath candles. They also brought out for study the volume called, *Come Ye Forth and See,* which explains the Torah for women and ignorant people.

The sun descended into the sea to dip itself in honor of the Sabbath and stayed as long as was fitting. Sabbath is never ushered in on high until it has been ushered in below on earth. The women quickly removed the victuals from the coals, prepared the table with bread and wine, and lit the candles. The sun arrayed itself in a garb of many colors and entered the Mansion of Silence in order to usher in the Sabbath in the Assembly on High.

Our men of good heart stood and recited the Afternoon Prayer. The man who says the prayer beginning, 'Give thanks unto the Lord' with devotion assuredly feels the loving kindness of his Name, blessed be he, towards human beings; all the more so they that go down to the sea in ships, who see actually and with all their senses, the words and wonders of his Name, blessed be he.

They who recite the prayers with devotion and say the prayer beginning, 'And mayest Thou return to Jerusalem Thy City in mercy,' assuredly draw near in spirit to Jerusalem. This is particularly true of those who sail on the sea; for when they pray, the Holy One, blessed be he, moves the boat and brings it closer to Jerusalem.

Since the six days of work were over and the profane week was at an end, our men of good heart stood singing the Psalm and song for the Sabbath day, until the whole world began to shine with the light of those crowns which had been taken from Israel because of the sin of the golden calf, and given to Moses, and which Moses returns to Israel every Sabbath eve.

After they had finished the Sabbath eve prayers, they hallowed the wine and bread, and broke bread, and ate and sang until the light of the candles came to an end and the light of the stars was doubled. When flesh and blood kindle a light it is doubtful whether it will take fire or not; and even if it does take fire it will go out. But the Holy One, blessed be he, kindles any number of lights in his heavens and not one of them goes out.

Great is the Sabbath, for then the body rests. Even greater is the Sabbath on board ship, when in any case a man does not toil all the week long and it follows that all the restfulness that is in a man can be kept solely and entirely for Sabbath.

Our men of good heart sat with their hands in their sleeves and looked out at the sea. When a man sits silent, it is assuredly a very good thing, since he is not sinning. This is particularly true when he is sitting in a ship that is going to the Land of Israel. Not only is he not sinning but he is actually fulfilling a commandment, since he is going up to the Land of Israel; and that is a deed which is accounted as equal to the fulfillment of all the other commandments.

All the commandments to be found in the Torah engage only part of the body. Thus the tefillin occupy the head and the arm, and the fringes of the tallit occupy the heart. Furthermore, they are fulfilled only during the daytime, and men are required to perform them while women are exempt. We are required to dwell in booths only at the Feast of Sukkot, and again men are required to do this but women are exempt. Matzah is enjoined upon us only at Passover, and the absolute requirement to eat it applies only to the first night. Furthermore, once a person is dead he is free from the fulfillment of the commandments. But dwelling in the Land of Israel encompasses a man's whole body and applies equally to men, women, and children, and it is required both by day and by night, and never under any conditions becomes null or void. Furthermore, if a person dies and is buried in the Land, its soil makes atonement for him, as it is written: 'And his Land doth make expiation for him.' Also this commandment is as weighty as all the others put together. So it is that when a Jew wishes to go up to the Land of Israel, Satan immediately gets in his way and does not permit him to do so.

Rabbi Alter the teacher began and said, When I was about to go up to the Land of Israel, Satan met me and asked, Where are you going?

To the Land of Israel, said I to him.

Why, he answered, I have just come back from halfway there because of the ants in the ship which got into all the food.

Indeed, said I to him, on the contrary, we can learn from them, as is written in the Book of Proverbs: 'Go to the ant, thou sluggard, consider her ways and be wise.' The ant, this little creature which is not one of those that have intelligence, still prepares its food in the summer. Then should not a man in Israel make preparations?

Then Rabbi Moshe began, When I got on to the wagon to go to the Land of Israel, Satan was already there. Where are you going? said he to me.

To the Land of Israel, I answered.

It would be better for you, said he, if you were to stay in your place and serve your Creator with all the other decent householders, until the time comes for you to go up together with all Israel.

When I sold my house, I answered him, you were the one who whispered to me, Raise the price, go on, raise the price, because you are going up to the Holy Land! And now that I have sold my house, do you come and advise me not to go? I shall not listen to you.

Then Rabbi Shelomo began and said, When I set my mind on going up to the Land of Israel, Satan came along and said to me, Is an old man like you really prepared to go and lose the money he earned with so much toil and weariness?

Fine accounts you keep, I said to him. But then I also know how to balance the loss resulting from not keeping a commandment against the profit that comes from keeping it.

Then Rabbi Shmuel Yosef, the son of Rabbi Shalom Mordekhai ha-Levi took up the tale. When I was about to go to the Land of Israel, said he, Satan came to me and said, Where do you propose to go?

To the Land of Israel, I answered.

Why, said he to me, have you such a desire to go to the Land of Israel? Because so many of the commandments enjoined on Israel can only be fulfilled in the Land of Israel? By your life, there are still any number of commandments waiting for you to fulfill them outside the Land.

Wasn't it you, said I to him, who came to one of the zaddikim and advised him to fulfill all the commandments if only he did not fulfill one particular one? Surely you remember the answer you got from that zaddik. He told you, I am prepared to transgress against all the commandments, provided I fulfill this particular commandment in its entirety. And at that he let me be.

As for me, said Rabbi Yehudah Mendel the pious, Satan did not have to expend much effort on me, for he and I dwell together like two neighbors. When the idea occurred to me of going up to the Land of Israel, I said to myself, Why are people so afraid of going up to the Land of Israel? Because there is no food and drink? Because there are no human beings there like ourselves? Well, anybody who lives here can live there as well. After all, the Land of Israel was not given to the ministering angels; so why should I not go as well? Once Satan heard this argument he stopped trying to delay me.

That, said Rabbi Pesach the warden, is exactly what I said to my wife Tzirel. What do you suppose, Tzirel, said I to her, that the Land of Israel is made of bits of paper on which holy names are inscribed? There as well as here you will find houses to live in, and there as well as here fat soups are not made from the juice of Hosannah willows.

In that case, said Leibush the butcher, why do they make the Land of Israel such a great affair?

Why, answered Rabbi Alter the slaughterer, in order that nothing wrong should be done in those same houses.

But Rabbi Yosef Meir sighed and said, It would be shameful indeed if all those houses were nothing more than what they seem to the eyes to be.

On still another occasion our men of good heart sat discussing the Evil Inclination which busies itself with Israel to prevent them from going up to the Land of Israel, since everyone who goes up to the Land of Israel there receives a new soul. Happy is he who goes up to the Land and has the merit of dwelling there, and alas for him who goes up to the Land and has not that merit; for angels surround the Land of Israel and permit none who are unfit to enter the Land, according to the tale told by Rabbi Shmuel Yosef, the son of Rabbi Shalom Mordekhai ha-Levi.

His tale concerns two old men who journeyed until they reached the frontier of the Land. At night they heard the sound of joy on the one side and of howling on the other. They raised their eyes and saw a troop of ministering angels, carrying harps and violins and all manner of musical instruments in their hands, leading one old man with great honor and singing before him; while in the other direction another troop of angels of wrath was dragging an old man and abusing him most shamefully.

By your charity, said the two old men to the angels, why did you make music before one and treat the other so shamefully?

He who is worthy to go up to the Land, said the ministering angels, him we accompany joyfully and precede with music.

But he, said the angels of wrath, who is not sufficiently worthy to go up to the Land but still goes up, him we drive away.

Perhaps, Rabbi Moshe asked Rabbi Shmuel Yosef, the son of Rabbi Shalom Mordekhai ha-Levi, you have heard why Rabbi Abraham the circumciser was never worthy to go up with us to the Land of Israel, seeing that he is a fit and proper man, God-fearing and greatly occupied with the fulfillments of the commandments and above all with the commandment of circumcision, in virtue of which we were given the Covenant of the Land?

Why, said Rabbi Shmuel Yosef, the son of Rabbi Shalom Mordekhai ha-Levi, the reason is that he put our Father Abraham to the trouble of leaving the Land of Israel and going forth outside the Land. For once there was a students' riot in town and all Israel hid themselves in their houses. Now on that very day Rabbi Abraham went to circumcise a baby whose father had just been slain on that same evil occasion. When he came in, he found nobody there to hold the baby, not even a chair on which to sit.

Can I, said he, be both godfather and circumciser?

Well, he looked out of the window and saw an old man walking along the street with a little stool in his hand. Rabbi Abraham knocked on the window to attract the old man's attention. In he came, sat down on the stool and took the baby on his knees. Then Rabbi Abraham circumcised the baby and said the blessing with the phrase, 'Who has hallowed the friend from the belly.' After Rabbi Abraham had completed the blessings, the unknown godfather vanished. Everyone thought that Elijah, the Angel of the Covenant, had been revealed to him, but in truth it was our Father Abraham who came to show his affection for his son on the day of his introduction into the covenant of Abraham.

All the countless heavens on high grew dark and the stars and moon were covered. The air was damp and had a salty tang. The whole world was still. Nothing was to be heard but the sound of the sea waves kissing. The company broke up and went to their sleeping places. The moon sank, the stars went in, and the planets went on their way.

The ship sailed on and on, while the Holy One, blessed be he, rolled the light away before the darkness and the darkness before the light, and sent a wind which moved the ship. Every day the sun grew stronger, so that no one could gaze at it, while at night each separate star gave as much light as the moon. And the sea waves swayed and moved and sparkled with light, and a kerchief floated upon the waves like a ship in the heart of the sea; and a man sat on the kerchief, his face turned to the east. Not a great wave of the sea rose to drown him, no sea beast approached to swallow him, but the seagulls soared and flew around him in the air. How long the comrades had been on board ship you can judge for yourselves; for before they went aboard they had shaved their heads, and now the head tefillin sank into the hair. Yet whenever they looked out to sea, facing them they could see the light sparkling on the waters, the kerchief floating like a ship in the heart of the sea, and a man sitting upon the kerchief with his face turned to the east.

Chapter ten
Stambul

In due course the ship reached Kushta the Great, which is Constantinople, which is Stambul. There the comrades took a small boat and entered the town to wait for the ship which is hired by the congregation of Stambul every year; for every God-fearing Sephardic Jew who has the means goes up to the Land of Israel to prostrate himself upon the graves of the Fathers or to settle there.

Now Stambul is a great city whose like is not to be found anywhere in all the world, having many quarters in which representatives of all the peoples dwell and the king of Ishmael, the Great Turk, rules over them. Himself he lies on a bed of ivory which lulls him to sleep. Sometimes he sleeps half a year and sometimes a whole year. There is a box full of snuff beside him, with a gold bird resting upon it. When the time comes for the king to awaken, the bird opens the box and goes to the king and places the snuff in his nostrils; then the king sneezes and the bird says, Your good health!

Thereupon all the princes and pashas come along with all the dukes and ask the king how he is. And he has three hundred and sixty-five princes, one for each day of the year; and as soon as each of the princes has done his day's duty, the king gives him a golden thread, whereupon he knows that his time is come to depart from the world; he goes home and strangles himself, while the king, watching from his window, claps his hands and rejoices.

Then there is a clock in the king's palace, made of human bones, and on the hour it can be heard tolling from one end of the city to the other. Even babes still in their mother's wombs quiver at the sound. And the city has many gardens and orchards and bathhouses and places of amusement, each more beautiful than the next —beautiful within but filthy without. Numberless dogs roam the streets; nowhere in the entire world are there so many dogs as in Stambul. And unclean birds stroll about at their ease, gorging on the filth and the carrion. There are also rats as large as geese; and these dwell even in the mansions of the princes.

Furthermore, there are many fires in Stambul, and when a fire begins in one house, the licking flames consume all the houses in the whole street, since their houses are made of wood. Sometimes these fires burn three hundred or four hundred houses together, and sometimes even more. They take no steps to stop the fire; only, the watchmen of the city stand shouting, Allah is God and Mohammed is his Prophet.

The synagogues in Stambul are many, numbering a hundred and more, with rugs and carpets woven of gold and silver thread, on which great sages recline and teach the revealed and the secret Torah. They have many books in their possession and happy is the eye that has seen them all. Why, they even have that rare and precious volume, 'Desire of the Days,' which is a wonder, as the well-informed know. They exercise their authority by permission of the state and do not understand our own Yiddish tongue. So when anyone wishes to talk to them, he must speak in the Holy Tongue. They are clean in thought, and cleanly in dress, and pleasant in speech, and all their deeds are done gently, and their figures are princely.

Their customs differ from our own, and they put on their tefillin while seated, in accordance with the view of the sage Rabbi Joseph Karo. Some of them indeed put on two pairs of tefillin at the same time. They have no fondness for casuistry when they study the Talmud, their great strength being rather in erudition. But the love of the Land of Israel burns in their hearts, and when they go up to the Land of Israel they take with them the carpets on which they have studied Torah and burn them on the grave of Rabbi Simeon bar Yohai on the thirty-third day of the Counting of the Omer.

There are Karaites to be found in Stambul who do not believe in the words of our rabbis of blessed memory but they are versed in Scripture and are as familiar with the twenty-four books of the Bible as an ordinary Jew is with his prayers; and they have synagogues of their own. They do not wear fringes as our own Jews do, but hang them up in the synagogue and look upon them in order to fulfill the injunction, 'that ye may look upon it'; and they do the same with the palm fronds at the Feast of Booths. They have sages of their own who produce fresh interpretations and commentaries on the Torah every day; but they have no quarrel with our own Jews, since they must have recourse to us. For inasmuch as they still observe all the biblical laws of ritual purity and impurity and do not defile themselves by attending to the dead when any of their own community dies, they must hire poor rabbinist Jews to perform the last offices of burial. In former times they used to sit in the dark on the Sabbath eve and kindled no light, until the light of our teachers was revealed to them. The Land of Israel is precious to them; they mourn over its destruction and donate vessels and money to their own House of Study in Jerusalem and find all kinds of excuses in order to go up and increase their number in the Holy City.

But they are not successful, for they behaved shamefully towards the works of our master, Rabbi Moshe ben Maimon of blessed memory. For it happened on one occasion that the sages of Jerusalem had to take counsel in secret on account of impending evil decrees and events. So they gathered in the synagogue of the Karaites, whose synagogue lies lower than the other houses, so that no word said within it is heard outside. When they entered they saw that one step in the staircase differed from all the others. They investigated and found underneath that step a copy of Rabbi Moshe ben Maimon's book, 'The Mighty Hand,' which had been placed there by the Karaites to be trodden upon and belittled.

Now the Kabbalist Rabbi Hayyim ben Attar of Morocco, who is known as the 'Light of Life' after his book of that name, was present on that occasion and he cursed the Karaites, saying, May their settlement never increase and may they never be worthy to pray with a full quorum. Since then no new Karaite has ever arrived in Jerusalem without another Karaite being carried out dead. Once a great number of Karaites went up to the Land together and were all carried off by the pestilence, may the Merciful One deliver us.

Well, our comrades stayed in Stambul waiting for a ship. One day they went to the grave of Job, and another they went to the grave of the author of 'The Ordination of the Sages,' who died there on his way to the Land of Israel; and yet another day they went to the port to see if a ship had arrived bringing Hananiah, of whom they did not yet despair. Was it possible that this Hananiah who had wandered over half the world and had overcome so many trials could have given way to despair when his ship went off without him? Assuredly he must have possessed his soul in patience and waited for another ship.

During those days Rabbi Shmuel Yosef, the son of Rabbi Shalom Mordekhai ha-Levi, sat before the sages of Constantinople and read all those books, great and small, good and upright, which are full of the fear of Heaven and of wisdom; and he increased in reverence and wisdom of the revealed and secret Torah, in grammar and in style, in the ways of the holy language and its secrets. There has come unto our hands a letter which he wrote to the society of the comrades, the hasidim who dwell in the city of Buczacz, may it increase. It runs thus:

We hereby inform you that we have reached in peace that glorious city Kushta, which is hinted at in the mystical work, 'The Additions to the Zohar'; and blessed be his Name, for the way before us was good. Rain did not detain us on land nor storm terrify us on sea. Indeed it were fit and proper to inscribe all our journeyings and all the good deeds done unto us on the way by our brethren, the Children of Israel, in respect to food, drink, and lodging, and in respect to good counsel and proper guidance, by our brethren in the country of the Turk no less than those in the Land of His Imperial Majesty, the Emperor of Austria. However, by reason of our sorrow at heart, we are deprived of the strength to continue with this account at length, for the upright Rabbi Hananiah, who is known unto you, did vanish of a sudden on the way. We do not know what has happened to him; but pray you to give notice of this to the Rabbi, long life to him. Indeed, we are aware that Rabbi Hananiah did not leave any wife behind him. Yet it may be there is a woman who is waiting for him to marry or reject her, according to the Law. Pray inform us how goes it with the learned, pious, etc., Rabbi Abraham the circumciser, may he increase in strength, and all that has befallen him; and pray transmit our regards to all our friends and those beloved of our soul who are forever engraved on our hearts; and so on and so forth.

In the inn where the comrades lodged there was a certain Sephardic sage, who had gone forth from the Holy Land as an emissary to rouse the cities of the Exile to remember the distress of the men of Jerusalem. He was an understanding and scholarly man, a Kabbalist whose figure was kingly and whose eyes had grown dim on account of the tears he shed, mourning that every city stands firm on its foundations, but the city of God is abased to the nether Sheol.

This emissary asked our friends, Whither do you go and where do you wish to establish yourselves? In Jerusalem, or in Hebron, or in Safed, or in Tiberias? He told them the advantages and qualities of each of the cities and the virtues of its particular climate, also the holy places to be found in each.

As for Safed, he who dwells in Safed and is buried in its soil, since it is loftier and has pleasanter air than all the other cities of the Land of Israel, his soul soars off at once to the Cave of Machpelah, whence it passes to the Garden of Eden. In Safed, Israel are at peace with the Gentiles, so that even a woman can go about alone in the town and the field. There are many dwellings to be found in Safed, and everything can be bought cheaply. The synagogue of the Kabbalist Rabbi Isaac Luria is in Safed, together with the platform to which he used to summon the Fathers of the World, of blessed memory, to the reading of the Torah; summoning Aaron first as Priest, then Moses as Levite, Abraham as third reader, and so on. Most of the men of Safed are observant of the Torah, and scholarly, and God-fearing, and merciful.

Two hours distant from Safed is a place called Meron, where the cave of Rabbi Simeon ben Yohai is to be found. From all the cities of the Land of Israel men come to Meron three times a year to prostrate themselves on his grave, where they spend a night and a day and study the holy book Zohar; these three times being in Elul, before the New Year, at the end of the month of Adar between Purim and Passover, and on the thirty-third day of the Counting of the Omer after Passover. Furthermore, on the thirty-third day of the Omer people come to Meron even from as far away as Damascus and Aram Zoba, which is Aleppo, as well as from Egypt; and in Meron they set beautiful silken kerchiefs on fire in barrels of olive oil and they make great feasts and banquets and dance to the drum and the pipe and utter all manner of song and praise. That is the day of the Rejoicing of Rabbi Simeon bar Yohai, when the Divine Presence comes to frolic with the saintly in the Holy Assembly.

Even greater is Hebron, whose dust the Patriarchs esteemed. They lie in the Cave of Machpelah, above which is a great building builded by King David, peace be upon him; although by reason of our sins Israel are not permitted to enter the Cave. But there is a small hole outside the gate which opens on the graves of the Fathers and the Mothers, and there candles are lit and prayers are said. Outside the Cave of Machpelah is the nearby grave of Rabbi Moshe ben Nahman of blessed memory; as he wrote at the end of his book, 'The Law of Men,' where he said that he was going to hew himself a grave there near the Fathers. Facing it is the grave of Jesse, the father of David, as well as the grave of the judge Othniel, the son of Kenaz. Below are caves where other pious men are buried.

The householders of Hebron are men of might with many fine qualities, above all hospitality, a virtue for which our Father Abraham, peace be upon him, was renowned. And the whole town is surrounded by vineyards and groves, and you can see the oaks of Mamre, and the bathing pool of our Mother Sarah, peace be upon her, and the tent of our Father Abraham, peace be upon him; the tent which is fenced about with blocks of hewn stone. There is a cistern of hewn stone within the tent, and fresh living water sweet as honey and very pleasant to drink flows within the cistern.

But how good it is to dwell in Tiberias, which is Rakkath—where even the most worthless are as full of fulfilled commandments as a pomegranate is of seeds, and where they are more nimble about their affairs than in any of the other cities of the Land of Israel. As our rabbis of blessed memory said: 'May it be my lot to be among those who welcome the Sabbath in Tiberias.'

The four species of plants for the Sukkot lulav are plenteous in Tiberias, particularly the date palms, whose fronds are used to cover the booths for the Feast of Booths. And the Sea of Kinnereth, which the Holy One, blessed be he, loves more than every other sea surrounds Tiberias; and concealed in that sea is the well of Miriam, which is destined to be revealed in due course by the holy Rabbi Isaac Luria of blessed memory; for it heals the soul. Corresponding to the well of Miriam, the baths of Tiberias make the body hale and hearty and cure all manner of sickness. And in the future the revival of the dead will commence at Tiberias, where the redemption will likewise begin, as is written in the tractate Rosh ha-Shanah.

Yet in spite of all this, who would exchange the sanctity of Jerusalem, the place of our Temple, for any of these? For Jerusalem faces towards the Gate of Heaven.

Chapter eleven

A Great Storm at Sea

In due course the time came for the ship to set sail on the sea. The comrades went aboard together with a vast congregation of Sephardic Jews from Stambul, Smyrna, and all the other cities belonging to the Turk, both men and women; not to mention uncircumcised Christians and circumcised Moslems of all nationalities; more than a thousand folk in all, apart from the servants of the ships and the servants of the servants.

They put down their goods and prayed that they might arrive in peace in the Land of Israel, and that they might not be injured on the way by earthquakes or convulsions or by any of the creatures that are in the sea. When they had ended their prayer, they split into two parties. One party went to see where the sweet water was drawn from and where wood was got for cooking, while the other went off to look at the ship and watch the sailors at work, standing high upon the masts or rolling up the ropes or spreading the sails. Meanwhile, our Sephardic brethren settled in their places, and calmly opened their sacks, and arranged their belongings, and took out fine volumes bound in red and green leather, covered with papers of many colors, like the picture tapestries hanging in the king's palace. They sat down crossing their legs beneath them, and prayed that they might be worthy to walk before the Lord in the Land of Life and be buried in Jerusalem.

How pleasant it was to see them sitting in fine garments, with their measured movements and princely appearance, their beards resting on their books as they read in awe and fear and humility, their lips moving and their attention fixed, rejoicing in the study of those things that are befitting persons proceeding to the Land of Israel. Their wives sat facing them, holding in their mouths pipes which were fixed in round glass bottles through which they inhaled tobacco. Whenever they heard the name of Jerusalem uttered by their husbands, they would raise their hands to their eyes and joyously repeat the word aloud, kissing their fingertips as though the name of Jerusalem were there engraved.

Meanwhile, the sky threw the sun over its shoulder, and the water began to grow darker and darker. The ship's officers examined the ropes and spars, lit lamps, sat down to eat and drink, and began to sing songs about wine and about the women of the sea who turn their eyes on human beings and steal their souls away with their singing. The Jews (mark the distinction) said the Evening Prayer and restored their souls with refreshments, reading the Song of Songs and the section in 'The Book of Zohar' concerning the Complete Unity which the Holy One, blessed be he, will achieve with the Congregation of Israel in days to come. Feiga and Tzirel, the housewives and stewardesses of the group, arranged pleasant sleeping places for themselves and their companions. They lay down to sleep and rested their bodies until they arose for the Midnight Mourning.

The stars gave light and then were hidden, but others came and took up their posts. Our men of good heart rose for the Midnight Mourning, while their Sephardic brethren ground beans and boiled *kahava,* a kind of drink which rouses the heart and causes sleep to depart, and which is not known in the Land of Poland, although it is mentioned in the *Shulhan Arukh* codes of law. They also behaved generously towards their Ashkenazic brethren, giving them likewise to drink; and they did the same with their wine and books. And when it became necessary, the Sephardic brethren spoke well of them to the

ship's officers and men, the sages of the Sephardim being well versed
in the languages of the peoples, some among them even knowing the
seventy tongues, like the members of the Sanhedrin in days of old.

Three weeks passed peacefully. The ship's crew subdued the
waters, the ship moved gently and our men of good heart sat studying
Scripture and Talmud or else relating the praises of the Land of Israel.
Rabbi Shmuel Yosef, the son of Rabbi Shalom Mordekhai ha-Levi,
made the time pass sweetly with those praiseworthy legends wherein
the Land of Israel is praised. As a king who spreads a curtain over the
entrance to his palace for whoever is wise to roll back and enter, so
did Rabbi Shmuel Yosef roll back the gates of Jerusalem before them
and enter with them to discover all that lay innermost.

Facing them sat our Sephardic brethren, who are not versed in
the Yiddish tongue of the men of Poland; but they saw the joy of their
brethren and asked, Why are you so happy? and were answered in the
Holy Tongue: Thus and thus did Rabbi Shmuel Yosef relate to us.

Then they also wanted to listen, and Rabbi Shmuel Yosef immediately opened his mouth and began to speak in the Holy Tongue like
unto the ministering angels, relating the praises of Jerusalem and the
joy with which the Divine Presence would rejoice in them. For ever
since the day when the Temple was destroyed, there is no day without its vexation, the Holy One, blessed be He, having long sworn
that He would not enter the Jerusalem on high until such time as
Israel would enter the Jerusalem below. And our Sephardic brethren,
listening, could have kissed him on the mouth for those words.

Three weeks passed peacefully. The ship sailed along quietly.
The sun gave light by day and the moon by night. The sky was full
of stars and the sea behaved after its fashion, while the waves went
along as one who goes to a festivity. But on the bed of the sea the
waters began grumbling, and the wind began slapping at the masts
of the ship. At last a great storm arose and the ship rocked this way
and that, sometimes to the right and sometimes to the left, sometimes
sinking and sometimes rising and rearing up, the waves wrestling
angrily with the ship, ready to swallow the ship and all who dwelt
therein. The whole sea was covered with foam as though the Great
Sea had been transformed into a Sea of Foam.

Happy is he who rests on such a night in the shadow of his own house, and the four walls of his house surround him and his roof protects him from the rain so that he can lie on his bed and cover himself with a warm blanket and listen to the sound of the footsteps of the night watchman passing in front of his house. Then in the morning he can put on his prayer shawl, and crown himself with tefillin, and say his prayers in the House of Prayer, and calmly eat his meal, and go out to the market place, and engage in business honestly, spending his days and his years honorably and passing away with a good name, worthy of burial with his fathers.

But on that night the eyes of the comrades were deprived of sleep and their body of rest. All their bedding was soaked with salt water. There were sixty myriads of waves spitting in their faces and roaring. Where was the river Strypa where they used to dip themselves on Sabbath eve on sunny days, and where they would cast away their sins on the New Year's Day? Why, the river Strypa was hundreds of leagues away. Now they were in the midst of the sea, and waves as huge as mountains were rising to the sky, and the ship was being slung about like a stone from a sling. And the sailors were growing too weak to steer the rudder much longer and subdue the waters.

All those on board were thrown against the sides of the ship, and screamed and wept and wailed. A chill salt sweat appeared on their faces, drops of salt dripped from their hair and rolled down into their mouths. Some of the comrades brought up their mother's milk, while others felt their bellies near bursting. I do not wish you such a passage, all ye seafarers!

At midnight the storm grew worse, and breached the walls of the ship. The ropes began to part and the noise grew ever greater. No one could be heard above the sound of the waters. There arose a great tumult among the people on board the ship. One man raised his hands and cried for aid, while another tore his hair. There was no one to subdue the waters and no one to aid a comrade in the hour of his distress. Yet mention must be made of the captain, who remained at his post and encouraged the sailors not to despair of mercy and not to slacken their labor.

In a little while the ship started and shook more than ever, as though it had struck a reef and were about to break. All the gear was tossed high into the air, and falling struck the people down. When our men of good heart saw that they were indeed in danger, they said: When our holy rabbis of blessed memory went to the Land of Israel, namely, Rabbi Nahman of Horodanki and Rabbi Mendele of Primishlan and all the other pious men like them, they were in such distress as this on the sea. Then Rabbi Nahman took the Torah Scroll on his arm and said, Even if, God forbid, the Court on High has decreed that we must pass from this world, nevertheless, we, a court on earth, together with the Holy One, blessed be he, and his Divine Presence, do not concur in that decree. And all those present responded, Amen.

At that moment a sailor mounted to the masthead and said, Looking through my glass I espy the cities of the Land of Israel.

Those, said our men of good heart to themselves, were indeed great pious men, mighty heroes. May it be His will that we may be delivered from this distress, on account of their merits and the merits of the Land of Israel.

Their prayers achieved one half and the ship's men achieved the other half, and the Holy One, blessed be he, in his blessed mercy achieved the whole. Within a few moments the fury of the Prince of the Sea died down, and the face of the waters changed for the better. That day passed without mishap, nor did any evil befall them at night. The moon came out and gave light, and the ship proceeded peacefully. The sick gradually regained their health.

Gradually the moon turned pale. It was already time for the sun to rise. In the twilight of dawn the waters of the sea grew silent and a kind of reddish veil spread over the face of the waters. The ship stood still in the midst of the sea, powerless to move, and a mood of relief passed through everyone.

Brethren, said one of our comrades, do you know what I say to you? I am like a person who is shown the king's treasure house. The attendants go down into the cellars with him and his feet stumble, but since he knows where they are taking him and that it is to the king's treasure house, he rejoices.

'Who shall ascend into the mountain of the Lord,' responded Rabbi Yosef Meir, 'and who shall stand in His holy place?'

When the sea burst forth, said Rabbi Shmuel Yosef, the son of Rabbi Shalom Mordekhai ha-Levi, and was about to flood the ship, what was I thinking of at that time but the story of the holy Rabbi Shmelke, may his merits shield us.

Once upon a time a very harsh decree was to be imposed on the men of the Holy Congregation of Nikolsburg, but the king had not yet set his seal to it. So the holy sage journeyed to Vienna to the king. It happened to be the season when the ice was melting, and at that time the river cannot be crossed by ship. Go, said Rabbi Shmelke to his holy disciple Rabbi Moshe Leib of Sasov, and fetch me a trough. He went and fetched a trough and put it in the river. They got into the trough and stood erect. The holy rabbi chanted the Song of the Red Sea and his holy disciple responded, until they reached Vienna safely. The folk of Vienna stood staring at two Jews crossing the river in a small trough at a time when it cannot be crossed even by a ship, because chunks of ice as large as hills float about in the river, crashing together with great fury and roaring like thunder.

The king heard what had happened. He came out together with his lords and princes and saw two Jews standing upright in a trough and chanting, while huge chunks of ice as big as hills were crashing together in the river, not touching the trough, but parting and making way for it to pass safely through. No sooner did that zaddik reach the king when the king said to him, I shall certainly listen to you, holy man of God, and he annulled the decree.

Well, said Rabbi Alter the teacher, what do you think of that story?

Ahh, said Rabbi Alter the slaughterer, where shall we find such a trough today!

Feiga sighed and said, We are traveling in a big ship, not to a king of flesh and blood but to the King who is King over all kings, the Holy One, blessed be he, and we see no signs of betterment.

And Tzirel said, That is just what I was about to say: here we are on our way to the Land of Israel and not as much as the smell of a miracle.

But Milka silenced them, saying, Women, you are ungrateful, for is the Holy One, blessed be he, showing us so few signs and wonders? He put the understanding in our hearts to go to the Land of Israel, and led us peacefully and safely across the land and set us on a good way with no obstacles or mishaps, and provided us with a ship to set sail on the sea, and took a wind out of his treasury to set the ship going. Then when the sea began quaking round us, He silenced it and ordered the Prince of the Sea to control his anger, which he did, so that the water began moving gently again, and in a day's time he will be fetching us to the Land of Israel. And *you* say that He is not showing us any sign of His goodness! Lord of the Universe, what ought Hananiah to have said? How that Hananiah toiled! He went on foot from town to town and from country to country, and the frontier guards took away his money and stripped him naked, and he was taken captive by robbers, and forgot when the Sabbath occurs and profaned the Holy Day, and wandered about many days, all in order to go up to the Land of Israel! And then when the time came for him to embark, the ship set off and left him behind.

Yes, said Rabbi Alter the teacher, that's the way to talk, the way Milka talks. By your lives, while she was speaking every limb of mine could feel the miracles that have been done for us!

But once they came to talk about Hananiah, their faces twisted with grief on account of the poor fellow who had actually thrown away everything for the sake of the Land of Israel; and then when his time came to go aboard ship and proceed to the Land of Israel, the ship had gone off and left him behind, and nobody knew whether, God forbid, he was dead. Yet in spite of the grief in their hearts, their eyes shone as the eyes of good people shine when they talk about a good man.

Then Rabbi Pesach the warden said, Do you remember Hananiah's kerchief in which he kept all his goods? When he would stand up to pray he would take out his things and tie the kerchief round his loins as a prayer girdle. On one occasion I said to him, Hananiah, here is a girdle for you so that you needn't shift your things about, in and out and out and in; but he wouldn't take it. And what answer do you think he gave me?

You have to treat a vessel respectfully, said he, and even if you find a better, you mustn't put your first vessel out of use. And he gave the same answer to Milka. On the way Milka gave him a sack for his belongings, but next day she found him with his bundle tied up in his kerchief again. Didn't I give you a sack for your belongings? said she to him.

You did, said he.

And still you go on using your kerchief, said she.

And do you think, he said, that just because a kerchief hasn't any mouth, I have the right to treat it disrespectfully?

At that point Rabbi Alter the teacher interrupted and said, Now that the Omnipresent has made things easier and the sea has quieted down, it is proper for us to say the Morning Prayer.

But after they had prayed they could not eat anything because the sea water had spoiled their food. The Holy One, blessed be he, salted the Leviathan for the end of days when it will be eaten, and the sea has been left full of salt. But who needs food and drink when he is going to reach the Land of Israel in a day's time? The comrades had already heard that the ship was approaching the port and promptly forgot all the toil of the journey and the difficulties of living on board ship and the storm at sea. Legs that had been heavy as stone suddenly became light, while eyes that had been sore with weeping now shone like the dawn.

They all put on their Sabbath garments and adorned themselves in honor of the Land, taking great care that none of the dust of Exile should be upon their clothing, that they might enter the Land pure.

Rabbi Moshe had a little bag suspended round his neck containing earth from the Land of Israel, to be buried with him. Now when they were expecting to enter the Land, he opened the sack and emptied the earth into the sea.

Our sages of blessed memory, remarked Rabbi Moshe, said that in days to come the Land of Israel will expand all over the world. For that reason I fling this earth from the Land of Israel into the sea, in order that an island may grow up from it whereon shall be built a great city of the Land of Israel.

Then they all began singing and uttering praise because it was their merit to be approaching the Land of Israel. And they arranged their belongings and tied them around with ropes, not to be delayed when the time came to go ashore.

But it was not yet their appointed time to stand in the Royal Palace. When the sailors climbed the masthead to see where they were, they gazed and saw the likeness of a large city; it was neither Jaffa nor Acre nor Tyre nor Sidon, nor any other of the coastal cities of the Land of Israel, but the city of Stambul! Then the hands of 'them that handled the oar' grew weak and they were seized with trembling. Here they had spent three weeks and more trying to reach the shores of the Land of Israel and at the end the winds had taken hold of the ship and brought it back to Stambul! The Holy One, blessed be he, had perhaps wished to test his invited guests and to see whether they were fit to serve in his legion; so he had brought a stormwind upon them and taken them back to their starting place. Those who wished to go up to the Land of Israel could remain on board, while those who wished to return to the lands of Ishmael and Edom might so return. But they all responded as one, We shall go up at once! We shall not go back!

The captain sent the sailors to fetch food from the city, since all the food they had on board had gone bad; and the sailors took their oars and got into ramshackle boats and went to town and fetched back all the good things from the land of Ishmael. The ship spread its sails, the captain took up anchor and the Holy One, blessed be He, promptly drew out a wind from his treasury and broke its force, saying to it, Be careful not to injure my friends. And the ship started off and ran joyously ahead, as one who joins in a dance.

Lightning does not strike twice in the same place. Blessed be He who led them on the right way by sea and by land, and by sea again. The ship proceeded quietly for five days and nights and arrived safely near Jaffa. When the morning star rose on the sixth day, the last day of their journeying, Jaffa rose from the sea like the round sun floating up from the River of Fire to light up the world. That was Jaffa before them, Jaffa which is the gateway to the City of God, into which the exiles of Israel come in order to go up to Jerusalem.

The morning star rose higher and higher, the sun shone more and more brightly, and it began to be really hot on board ship. The fire from on high branched out and it became burning hot. The sailors took off most of their clothes, for they were sweating like bears. And the Jews (mark the difference!) likewise took off their upper garments, and removed the hats they wore over their skullcaps and fanned their faces with them; but they continued to simmer in their sweat and the sun, simmering the sweat again, dried their bodies to the very marrow of their bones.

While they were sitting fanning themselves, Leibush the butcher asked Rabbi Alter the slaughterer, Tell me, Rabbi Alter, what need is there for this sun?

Why, he answered, the Holy One, blessed be He, is roasting the Leviathan for the great feast of the righteous at the end of days, and that is why he has heated the sun to the boiling point.

What is happening to me? said one of the women to another. My eyes are growing dim!

Do you think, answered the other, that my eyes are made of glass? I feel as though they were being pierced with white-hot spits.

That's not the sun in the sky, said Tzirel, but a fiery oven.

But Rabbi Moshe overheard them and said, No, your eyes are growing dim because of the radiance of the Divine Presence.

Even Feiga, who had made the journey for love of the Land of Israel, could not feel satisfied with what she saw. Where were those pleasant breezes which, people said, blew all day long among pleasant gardens and groves of myrtles and palms and citrons? And all the mountains of spices and odors like those in the Garden of Eden? Here the fires of hell were descending and burning the very marrow of their bones. Had the ship lost its way and strayed, God forbid, into a desolate wilderness of fiery serpents and scorpions, and were all manner of fresh woes about to descend upon them? The womenfolk knew that the Land of Israel is in ruins and that many troubles dog a person's heels; but they preferred to remember what suited them and to forget what did not suit them.

Milka sat across the way, smiling.

Are you grinning at me? said Feiga to Milka.

It's not you I am grinning at, answered Milka, but myself. In my dreams I saw a long and beautiful mantle at Lashkowitz to wrap one's whole body in, and I wanted to buy it. And now do you know what I am thinking? If I had bought it, what could I have done with it? Why, wrap up the sun in it so that it should not catch a chill.

In my dreams, I too, answered Feiga, was sitting in a wagon and a fur coat appeared to me and I heard someone or other whisper, Just you go along to the fair at Lashkowitz, for there are all kinds of bargains waiting for you there.

And did you suppose that Satan had our good in mind? said Milka. All he wanted was to hold us up on the road.

The sun stood in the middle of the sky, heating up the ship, which became as hot as a pot resting on coals. Yet he in whose heart the love of the Land of Israel is fixed gathers strength from the sanctity of the Land, where the Higher Light still flows freely and without any hindrance, though the Land is in ruins.

Meanwhile the men of good heart withdrew their attention from the toils and troubles of their wayfaring and from all the devils who had hindered them, and their faces were aflame with the force of their perfect will. Rabbi Alter the teacher stretched out his hands and began tapping the box before him with his fingers and singing the mystical hymn beginning, 'Sons of the Heavenly Hall, who yearn,' and Rabbi Alter the slaughterer accompanied him with, 'May they be with us...'

Ere the day was over, the ship reached the Jaffa shore and fired a loud cannon. Arabs came out of the town, wearing miserable clothing, short and dirty shirts reaching only to their knees and tied round with a thick rope, and the soles of their stockingless feet were covered only with slippers. They spoke noisily as though they were quarreling, and nobody could make head or tail of their language. Up they came on board, yelling at the top of their voices. They dragged the folk away like captives, and took their goods and flung them down into their ramshackle boats. They took their fee, yet even that was not enough for them, and they wanted to beat our comrades; but the Holy One, blessed be he, rescued them from the Arabs' hands and brought them safe and sound to shore.

Chapter twelve
Holy Soil

As soon as our men of good heart reached the shore they flung themselves on the ground, kissed the earth, and burst into loud weeping, until their eyes streamed like wells. How is it possible for children who return to their father's home and find it ruined not to weep? Yet even in their mourning they rejoiced because they had been worthy to return home. They took one another by the hand and sang, 'I rejoiced when they said unto me, Let us go up unto the house of the Lord.' Furthermore they sang, 'The Lord loveth the gates of Zion more than all the dwellings of Jacob.' And the Ishmaelites stood in the distance staring.

And so they went their way singing until they were brought to a certain courtyard known as the Courtyard of the Jews. There they found chambers, one for prayer with the congregation when they were ten together, and two more known as the Holy Chambers where there were beds for the use of the sick people coming from the journey; one chamber for men and the other for women. And there was another chamber there which was the chamber of the beasts, where the beasts on which people rode up to Jerusalem were stabled.

When a caravan that has been on a journey reaches its destination, the travelers assuredly rejoice, particularly if they have been in great distress and have come forth from it; for then indeed they have good reason to rejoice. But when one of the group is missing and nobody knows whether he is alive or dead, the thought of him is bound to come up no matter how much they rejoice and to disturb their joy. So it was with our comrades. For Hananiah had gone through so much together with them and had passed through so many adventures on his own in order to go up to the Land of Israel. And then when his time had come to go up to the Land he had not done so, and they did not know whether he was alive or dead; so how could their joy be complete? They vowed to have his name commemorated in Jerusalem and to pray for him at the Holy Places.

And now it is fitting to find out what happened to him—to Hananiah, that is. When his comrades went to fetch victuals for the journey, he went along with them. But on the way he parted from them and went in a different direction, but they did not notice it. After a while he came back and did not find them. Off he went to the port. When he came there, he saw that their ship had already set sail. How the poor fellow had toiled and labored in order to go up to the Land of Israel! And now when his time had actually come, the ship had started off and left him behind, and he stood watching and could not go with it!

Now Hananiah was always quick and nimble; so what had held him up on the way? Well, while he was standing in the market, a Gentile came along.

Aren't you the fellow, said Hananiah to him, who wished to lead me to the Land of Israel through some cave or other?

Yes, said he, I am the man.

And what are you doing here? asked Hananiah.

I don't know any more than you, said the other. Every day when I put on the tefillin of our former robber chief, I hear him weeping for his wife and children, and now I am wandering through the world in search of them.

May you live a hundred years, said Hananiah to him. You are earning your share of the world-to-come. Come along with me.

They went to a certain house, and Hananiah knocked on the window. The householder opened the window and asked, What do you want?

Where is the woman, answered Hananiah, who came here from Hutin?

I do not know, said the other. She went out with her children this morning and has not come back. Perhaps she has already gone off to Hutin.

On hearing this, Hananiah sighed and said nothing.

What do you need that woman for? asked the householder.

Hananiah pointed to the Gentile and said, This fellow can bear witness as to where he last saw her husband.

It would be a good thing, said the householder, if he were able to give his evidence before a rabbi.

While Hananiah was talking to the householder, the Gentile went to one side to put on his tefillin. No sooner had he done so when the woman came along and shrieked, Oh, those are my husband's tefillin!

If Zusha is your husband's name, said the Gentile, then these are his tefillin; and he promptly handed them over to her and told her the whole story of Zusha. And that was what caused Hananiah to be delayed.

There are ever so many tales about salvation, each finer than the next; like the story of the man who was lost in the desert. Suddenly a huge bird appeared and lifted him on its wings and in a single hour flew with him to his house, a distance it would have taken several years to journey. But no bird came to Hananiah. An even greater wonder was the mantle of King Solomon, peace be upon him, for he would sit on it and the wind would bear it away, so that King Solomon could eat his breakfast in Damascus and his supper in Media, though the one is in the East and the other is in the West. But that mantle has vanished since the day that King Solomon, peace be upon him, passed away, and nobody knows where it is concealed. And even if Hananiah were to find it, he would not be able to do anything with it, since nobody in the world ever knew how to sit upon it except Solomon and his four princes: one the prince of humanity, and one the prince of the demons, and one the prince of the beasts, and one the prince of the birds. Likewise, even in the generation before our own miracles were performed upon the water, such as that of the holy

sage Rabbi Shmelke of Nikolsburg and his holy disciple Rabbi Moshe
Leib of Sasov, who crossed the river Danube in a trough in a dangerous season. But where is such a trough to be found nowadays?

So Hananiah, seeing that he was indeed in distress, raised his
eyes to the sky and said, Lord of the Universe, I have nothing on
which to depend except on your many mercies.

Thereupon the Holy One, blessed be he, gave Hananiah the
idea of spreading out his kerchief on the sea and sitting upon it. So he
spread his kerchief upon the sea and sat down upon it. The kerchief
promptly floated off to sea, carrying him upon it all the way to the
Land of Israel. Nor was that all. For he actually got there before his
comrades, who were first delayed at Stambul waiting for a ship, and
then found themselves in distress during the storm at sea; whereas
he crossed the sea peacefully.

Now let us return to all our other comrades. In brief, they
reached the sea of Jaffa, that same sea of Jaffa which is kept in store
for the pious in days to come. For at Jaffa the Great Sea brings up
all the ships that are lost anywhere upon it, together with their gold,
and silver, and jewels and pearls, and glassware, and valuable vessels,
and in time to come the Messiah King will give each of the righteous
his share of the wealth.

They got off the ship and into a ramshackle Arab boat. The
sailors took their oars and shouted, Yoho and Oho, and subdued the
waters and made passage through the sea, and led the boat between
sharp rocks which have been there ever since the Creation. For before
any of the waves in any of the seas and rivers start out on their journey, they come to prostrate themselves before the sea of the Land of
Israel; and if the sharp edges of the sea did not break their force, never
a ship would be able to reach Jaffa on account of all the waves.

They came safely forth from the sea and from its sharp teeth,
and received all their goods intact, and came up on the shore at Jaffa,
the threshold of the gate of the City of God. There they flung themselves on the ground, kissed the earth, wept over the ruin of the Land,
and rejoiced that they had been worthy to arrive.

Then came two wardens and led them to the Court of the
Jews, which was a hostelry for the Exiles of Israel. This court was

surrounded by a wall, and fine trees were planted in it, and it had its own well of water in the center of it. They stood and prayed according to the usage of their own land and restored their souls after the journey. There they stayed until they obtained animals for proceeding to Jerusalem. They went out knowing that all was good, on the day whereon God twice saw that his handiwork was good, namely the third day of the week; and they traveled until evening, when the air grew chill.

Then they got down from their donkeys, opened their sacks, took out their cushions and pillows and covered themselves; but still they felt cold. So they got back on their animals and went on until they reached a certain spot called Ramleh, which is the city of Gath that David captured from the Philistines. There they descended from their donkeys and made themselves a resting place, arranging their sacks and lying down there all night long until the morning star arose.

When the morning star arose, they said their prayers, and ate the morning meal, and mounted their donkeys and resumed their journey. At nightfall they reached a well. They got down from their donkeys, made themselves a resting place there, lay down to rest on their sacks, and slept until the morning star arose.

When the morning star arose, they said their prayers, and ate the morning meal, and then got on their donkeys and journeyed until they reached a certain spot called Motza, from which in ancient times willow boughs were brought to the altar, as we learn: 'There is a place below Jerusalem called Motza, to which people go down to gather willow boughs which they afterwards set up beside the altar.' And willows are still to be found there.

There they made a resting place and stopped over. All these ways are desolate because of robbers, and even the Ishmaelites themselves dare not pass on these ways unless they go out in a caravan together. But God took pity on our comrades, so that no mishap occurred to them on the road except that their sacks fell from the backs of the animals once or twice. There are chains of high and lofty mountains all along the way, with all manner of clouds covering them, clouds of blue and purple, clouds radiant and gently bright, with the radiance of the jewels and blossoms of the Garden of Eden.

Every hour a new light made its appearance, and none of the lights resembled one another; and goodly odors there were on every side, issuing from all manner of fragrant plants. And castles, and palaces whose beauty was once the glory of the country now stand desolate, and there is no settled place, nothing but the black tents of Kedar dispersed and forsaken among the mountains, and goats trailing down the mountainsides, sustaining themselves on the thorns and thistles and brambles and briars mentioned in the Scriptures; and half-naked men sit there, wearing nothing but a shirt and girdle and a black kerchief bound by a woolen rope on their heads. And fine springs and streams of water run down into the valleys from the mountains, and they taste like the springs in the Garden of Eden. Our comrades drank of those waters, and in those waters washed their hands before the prayer, and rinsed their eyes because of their tears over the destruction of the Land, and hallowed their hands in honor of the Holy City.

This they did for three days, until the Sabbath eve arrived, and the Holy City, the joy of the whole world, appeared before them in the distance. At once they descended from their asses and rent their garments, weeping bitterly, and proceeded on foot until they reached the gates of Jerusalem. They kissed the stones of her walls and rent their garments a second time in memory of the Temple. May it be His will that it shall be rebuilt speedily and in our own days. Amen.

Chapter thirteen
They Stand Within Jerusalem

Within a very short while their arrival became known throughout the city. All Jerusalem came forth to meet them, both the pious and the devoted scholars; and they wished them peace, greatly rejoicing in them and offering them every manner of honor, and saying to them, Happy you are to have come hither without considering your bodies and your wealth, but thinking only of your souls; so that you have been found worthy to stand in the Temple of the King who is King over all kings, the Holy One, blessed be he.

And the rabbi of the hasidim, the chief of the Seph-ardic sages in the Holy City, showed his great love for the men of 'Turkey' and brought them to his own House of Study, where every day and every night they held soul-satisfying gatherings.

These they continued for four weeks corresponding to the four periods in a man's life: the first week being for the week of birth, when the infant grows and is not yet completed, for which reason he is not subject to punishment in the Assembly on High, until he has reached the age of twenty years; then a second week corresponding to his best years which last until he is forty, these being the choice years of a man's life when a man's strength is on the increase; the third week corresponding to middle age, when he gradually grows weaker; and a last week corresponding to old age, when a man runs the course of his days and years to their completion until he passes away.

But the dead of the Land of Israel are not thought of as dead, but are described as being stationed beneath the Seat of Glory, where they enjoy the light of the Messiah and see the happy state of Israel and all those fine things which the Holy One, blessed be he, will in time to come do for Israel. And on those occasions when the day grows dark, the dead do not become startled or cry out, for they know that the darkness is due to the clouds which go forth to carry Israel and bring them back to Jerusalem; as was expounded by our rabbis, who said that the time will come when Jerusalem will be like unto the Land of Israel and the Land of Israel will be like unto the whole wide world, and the clouds will carry Israel from the ends of the world and will bring them to Jerusalem; this being why the prophet praises them, saying, 'Who are these that fly as a cloud?' And every Sabbath they enter into the Assembly on High where they study the portion of the week as expounded by Adam, by Enoch, by Noah, by Shem and Eber, by Melchizedek, by Abraham, Isaac, and Jacob, and by Moses, Aaron, and the seventy elders; in addition of course to the story of the Creation as far as the completion of Heaven and earth and the resting of God on the seventh day, and in addition to the whole of Jacob's blessing to his sons at the close of the Book of Genesis, which they learn from the very mouth of the Almighty. And at the Sabbath Afternoon Prayer, all the prophets come and teach them the section from the prophets, and Rabbi Abraham ibn Ezra, of blessed memory, interprets the difficult passages, since often when the prophets prophesied they themselves did not know what they were prophesying. Of all Rabbi Abraham ibn Ezra's interpretations the most highly thought of is the one of the verse beginning, 'And he [Jacob] bought the parcel of land,' which Rabbi Abraham ibn Ezra explains as indicating what a great virtue is in the Land of Israel, for a portion in the Land of Israel is reckoned as though it were a share in the world-to-come.

But now let us return to our comrades. In brief, they were welcomed by the Holy Congregation of Jerusalem with every manner of honor and respect, and the people of the city showed their affection by taking our comrades to their homes, and fetching them food and drink, and preparing them beds with pillows and cushions. They refreshed themselves and rested their weary bones until noon, when they went to the bath to purify themselves in honor of the Sabbath and in honor of the city. And the bath of Jerusalem is the most praiseworthy of baths, because it has inner and outer rooms. In the outer rooms people take off their clothes, in the inner they wash naked. And there is a room in which attendants rub down the bathers after they have finished their baths. And they have an oven there under the ground, which is stoked with animal droppings and manure. All the rooms are hot, some hot and some hotter; there are reservoirs of water and a perennial pool of fresh water, which is neither hot nor cold, but lukewarm. The bather pays two pennies to the bathing master and one to the attendant and receives a sheet for modesty's sake.

Well, they went down and dipped themselves in the ritual bath. Then they went up and sweated and afterwards proceeded to the room where the attendant rubbed them down and poured cold water over them. They went and dipped once again, came up and dried themselves, put on white garments, and came out like newborn creatures. And when they came out they gave the attendant a penny, and he wished them good health. Back they went to their homes, put on Sabbath garments, and proceeded to the Western Wall.

Now the Western Wall is all we have left of our beloved Temple since ancient times. It has been left by the Holy One, blessed be he, by reason of his great pity for us, and is twelve times as tall as a man, corresponding to the Twelve Tribes, in order that each man in Israel should devote his heart and will to prayer in accordance with his height and his tribe. It is built of great stones, each stone being five ells by six, and their like is not to be found in any building in the world; and they stand without pitch or mortar or lime between them, in spite of which they are as firmly united as if they were one stone, like the Assembly of Israel which has not even the slightest sovereign power to hold it together, yet is, nonetheless, one unit throughout the world. Facing the Wall on both sides are courtyards belonging to Arabs, who dwell there with their beasts and do not disturb Israel in their prayers.

Our men of good heart kneeled, and prostrated themselves, and kneeled, and took off their shoes, and washed their hands, and walked with bowed head until they reached the Wall, and weeping kissed each and every stone. Then they opened their prayer books and recited the Song of Songs with great passion and devotion, their souls being aroused more and more with every verse. Rabbi Moshe rested his head against the Wall and remembered that he was standing at a spot from which the Divine Presence itself had never moved. He began reciting the Song of Songs with awesome fervor and with the very chant with which his brother, Rabbi Gershon, may he rest in peace, had recited it at the time his soul departed from him, until he reached the verse beginning, 'The King hath brought me into his chambers,' saying which Rabbi Gershon, his brother, had departed from the world. But here Rabbi Moshe managed to complete the entire verse, the joy of the Land of Israel entered into him, together with a fresh vitality.

After they had completed the Song of Songs, they recited a number of psalms and said the Afternoon Prayer. And they added a special prayer for their brethren in exile, and for Hananiah who had vanished. Much had they wept for him upon the sea and much had they wept for him upon the dry land; yet all those tears together were but as a single drop in the sea against the tears they shed for his sake before the Western Wall; for they felt the sanctity of the Place, and he was not there with them.

This can be compared to a story about a king's friends who came to visit him and the king showed them his treasures. While they were standing before the king, they remembered that a certain person whom the king loved above all others had not come with them. So they began to grieve on his account, because he was not there to see what the king was showing them; they grieved all the more as he had been far more zealous on the journey than all of them, and the king would assuredly have been pleased and contented with him. Hananiah was worthy of standing at their head, and now at the end he had to be far away from all this beneficence!

Finally they ushered in the Sabbath with song and praise and then proceeded to their homes, said the prayer of Sanctification, broke the Sabbath loaf, ate the Sabbath feast, and drew the sanctity of the Sabbath into their very limbs. And many of the most precious folk of Jerusalem came to visit them, as people go to the Sabbath eve feast before a circumcision; since each person who goes up to the Land of Israel is like a new-born child, having taken upon himself the Covenant of the Land. So they sat all night long, reciting tales and legends and uttering song and praise, until the sun rose and they proceeded to the synagogue.

Having come to the synagogue, they prayed sweetly with full hearts. Who shall describe the great virtue of prayer in the Land of Israel, and all the more in Jerusalem, where once the Temple rose of which it is written, 'Mine eyes and My heart shall be there perpetually.' Rabbi Shelomo went up twice to recite the priestly blessing, since in Jerusalem the priests raise their hands in blessing every day and not merely at festivals as is the practice throughout by far the greater part of the Exile; and on days when the Additional Prayer is said, they raise their hands in blessing both at the Morning and Additional Prayers. And Rabbi Shmuel Yosef, the son of Rabbi Shalom Mordekhai ha-Levi, poured water on the hands of the priests from a silver pitcher which Rabbi Moshe had brought from the home of his grandfather, Rabbi Avigdor. Rabbi Shmuel Yosef used to fulfill with fervor every injunction which came his way and all the more so those which served as a commemoration of the Temple. While pouring the water, his hands trembled so for joy that the pitcher beat against the basin and it gave forth a sound like the musical instruments of the Levites of old. The Priests went up to their platform, turned their faces to the people, parted their bent fingers on which the blessings are engraved, raised their hands on high, blessed the congregation in a voice like the voice of the wings of the cherubim in the Garden of Eden, and prolonged the blessings until the congregation had said the Thanksgiving, which they then closed with Amen. Great was the joy of Rabbi Shelomo, and great indeed the love with which he chanted his blessing when he first had the merit of going up to the priest's stage, to recite the blessing in Jerusalem, the Holy City. The blessings fairly tripped over themselves in their haste.

To the reading of the Torah they summoned Rabbi Shelomo first as Priest, after him Rabbi Shmuel Yosef as Levite, then Rabbi Pesach as third reader, followed by Rabbi Yosef Meir as fourth, by Rabbi Alter the teacher as fifth, Rabbi Alter the slaughterer as sixth, then Rabbi Yehudah Mendel as seventh, and Rabbi Moshe for the closing passage and the reading from the Prophets. Leibush the butcher was honored with the raising of the Torah on high for all the congregation to see, and the man whose name we have forgotten was honored with the rolling up of the Torah Scroll. They recited the blessings before and after the reading and also the blessing of thanks to God as befits seafarers who have come up from the sea. The congregation responded Amen after them, and wished them to be worthy to remain in the Palace of the King until such time as the Messiah King is revealed, may it be speedily and in our days. Amen.

All of a sudden a fine voice was heard, finer than all the voices there and like to that voice which we heard upon the sea. Our comrades looked up and saw Hana-niah before them, his face bright with joy and radiant as the waves of the sea when the moon shines upon them. He was taller than he had been and wore shoes upon his feet. He greeted them and rejoiced with them exceedingly, saying, Sons of the living God, happy are you that you have come hither.

But who brought you up here? they asked him.

I spread my kerchief out upon the sea, he answered, and I sat upon it until I reached the Land of Israel.

Then they knew that the figure they had seen floating upon the sea had been Hananiah.

And they uttered praise and thanksgiving to the One who is worthy of all praise, yet unto whom all praise is as nothing, and in whom all those who hope need never be shamed; as it is written, 'I am the Lord, for they shall not be ashamed that wait for me,' and they said, 'The Lord is good unto them that wait for Him.' And of Hananiah they said, 'But he that trusteth in the Lord, mercy compasseth him about.'

After the prayer the Holy Congregation of Jerusalem celebrated with a fine repast in their honor, with grape wine and brandy wine, which each man makes for himself at the time of the vintage shortly before the Sukkot holiday. Householders from all over town sent them preserves of citron, of figs, and of other fine fruits for which the Land of Israel is famous; and they showed them every manner of affection. But above all they showed their affection for Hananiah, who had accepted the covenant of suffering and the Covenant of the Land. Indeed, they wished to place him at their head, but he belittled himself and took the lowest place next to the door. When our righteous Messiah comes, said he, we shall not be able to push too close to him, and then he will have to invite me higher up if he wants me. And then I shall know that I have some slight degree of importance as far as he is concerned. And if I have not, then who am I anyway to be seated at the head?

Thus they sat and drank of all the wines and many times blessed the One who is good and who does good, and they studied the passage dealing with the ten sanctities whereby the Land of Israel is sanctified more than all other lands. A vegetable was brought to our comrades which tasted like fowl fried in goose fat. How remarkable is the Land of Israel! Here is a vegetable which you can buy in the market two for a penny. Take and fry it in sesame oil, and it tastes like fowl fried in goose fat. Then they said the grace for wine and food, and washed their hands for the feast.

Chapter fourteen

In the Presence of the Divine Presence

After the Sabbath our comrades hired themselves a dwelling near the Western Wall, the windows of which directly faced the site of the Temple; and so they found themselves in the presence of the Divine Presence. The women purchased themselves garments of white wool and the choicest food and drink of the Land, and of its fruits. They cooked and baked and conducted their households with wisdom. They lacked for nothing, even having goat's milk for the Shavuot holiday.

Our comrades resided before the Lord in the Land of Life, in Jerusalem, devoting themselves to Torah and prayer and good deeds and the practice of charity, and to love and to fear and to humility. And on the eve of the New Moon and the other days on which the Prayers of Supplication are said, they would go out to the Holy Places and pray for themselves and their brethren in exile.

All hours are not the same. It is widely known that every righteous man who comes up from outside the Land to the Land of Israel must begin by falling from his original level. For the air of the Land of Israel is holy and retreat needs precede and advance. But God came to their aid and gave them the strength to accept submissively all that befell them, until they were worthy to receive a fresh mindset, namely the intelligence of the Land of Israel. Day after day they were tried and tested, by insults and by curses, by loss of money and injury to their persons. For Jerusalem is not as the places that are outside the Land, since never has a man gone to sleep in Jerusalem bearing unrequited sins. For day after day the Holy One, blessed be He, settles that day's accounts, in order that the spiritual debts of Jerusalem might not increase and multiply. Like a judge of flesh and blood, who considers and reconsiders the cases of those brought before him that they might be found innocent; so the Holy One, blessed be He, turns, as one might say, His eyes on Jerusalem and chastises its inhabitants that they might be cleansed of every iniquity.

Pessel, the daughter of Rabbi Shelomo, perished from the kick of a mule, and Feiga perished from the blows of Ishmael. For once a water carrier brought water to Feiga on a day when it was raining heavily and all the cisterns and wells were full, so that she did not need his water. Thereupon he emptied his water-skins over her, and she caught a chill and died.

But our men of good heart lovingly accepted everything that befell them, not rebelling at their sufferings or making claims against God. Instead they bore all their losses and comforted themselves, saying that on the morrow the Holy One, blessed be He, would redeem them and then all their troubles and distress would be over. And when the common people used to ask why the Holy One, blessed be He, did not exact vengeance upon the wicked nations who treated his children like captives, they would reply, Our answer is in the words of your question: Once there was a king whose son was attacked by enemies. Thereupon the king said, Why should I go to the trouble of sending soldiers to avenge myself on them? I shall immediately go forth myself with all my army to expel and sentence them for making my son suffer; and I shall bring my son back home with much joy and honor.

All trouble is hard to bear, but hardest of all is the trouble of making a living. When a man becomes poor, hunger irks him every day. There seemed to be a hole in our comrades' pockets and their money ran out. Before the end of the year they felt the hardships of making a living, since the Land of Israel has been purged of all vanities and there is no source of money save the money that a man brings with him from abroad. And so at length they were compelled to obtain their sustenance from the Exile.

When that time came, Leibush the butcher separated from the group and made up his mind to return to Buczacz. For Leibush said, Have you ever seen a country where nothing is to be had but mutton? From the very beginning he had not been pleased with Jerusalem. What he sought he did not find, while with what he did find his body was not satisfied. On the other hand, Rabbi Yosef Meir also had to prepare to leave. He wished to dwell in the Land of Israel but was not permitted to, on account of an ancient ordinance that no man may dwell in Jerusalem without a wife for more than a single year.

But the Holy One, blessed be he, will use one and the same means for chastising the unrighteous and for doing good to the righteous. The ship on which Leibush returned to the Exile had brought with it the divorced wife of Rabbi Yosef Meir. On her arrival he sent her greetings and afterwards brought her under the bridal canopy, and Rabbi Yosef Meir lived to see a generation of upright, God-fearing and God-loving descendants. Rabbi Pesach and Tzirel were likewise found worthy in the course of their residence in the Holy City, and their house was built by sons and by daughters who in due course of time were enlisted in the legions of the Lord of the Universe.

And so our redeemed brethren dwelled together within the Holy Congregation of the Holy City, joyously fulfilling the commandment to dwell in the Land of Israel; until their end came and they passed away, returning their souls unto Him to whom all souls belong, and leaving their bodies to the bosom of their mother; for they were found worthy to be buried in the soil of the Holy Land on the Mount of Olives at Jerusalem, facing the Temple of the Lord, at the feet of the Holy One, blessed be he; until the time comes for them to awaken to everlasting life, on the day of which it is written: 'And His feet shall stand in that day upon the mount of Olives.'

But Hananiah lived many long years, strength and energy accruing to him year by year. When he was a hundred years old, he was like a lad of twenty in his fulfillment of the commandments and performance of good deeds; and neither weakness nor weariness could be recognized in him. Many fanciful tales are told about that same Hananiah, such as the tale that when our men of good heart arrived on shore at Jaffa, they found Hananiah drying his kerchief in the sun. But this is not the truth, as Hananiah was already in Jerusalem ere his comrades had arrived in the Land. All kinds of fanciful tales are likewise told about his kerchief; for instance, that the Emperor Napoleon saw it and made a flag out of it and was victorious in his wars. But that is not the truth either, since, when Hananiah had passed away, they covered his eyes with his kerchief.

The day on which Hananiah died was the first day of the month of Nisan. He had tied his kerchief round his loins and was about to proceed to the synagogue. Suddenly he felt his legs failing. This fellow's legs, said he, are entreating him not to bother them; so I shall pray at home.

And when he came to the words, 'The heavens are the heavens of the Lord; but the earth hath He given to the sons of man,' his soul departed from him in purity. They came and closed his eyes and covered them with his kerchief. Then with much difficulty they took his prayer book out of his hands, purified his body, and brought him to his eternal home.

Many accompanied him to the cemetery, and many spoke his praises. One praised him for his simplicity, another for his whole-heartedness, a third for his nim-bleness in fulfilling commandments, a fourth for his love of the Land of Israel, a fifth for his faith, and a sixth for all of these qualities together. For all the good and upright qualities which were given to Israel to glorify God's blessed world were to be found together in Hananiah, peace be upon him.

The sages and rabbis of Jerusalem have long desired that all that befell Hananiah should be put on record in a book. But by reason of harshness of servitude and the urgency of livelihood, as well as because of strife and contention, the matter was deferred from day to day and from year to year; until I came and wrote all the adventures of Hananiah in a book which I have called 'In the Heart of the Seas.' This name I have given this book in memory of Hananiah, peace be upon him, who went down into the heart of the sea and came forth peacefully. I have not left out anything I have heard and I have added nothing more than my soul advised.

Some will read my book as a man reads legends, while others will read it and derive benefit for themselves. With regard to the former I quote the words of the Book of Proverbs: 'But a good word maketh the heart glad'; a good word maketh the soul to rejoice and delivereth from care. But of the latter I say in the words of the Psalmist: 'But those who wait for the Lord, they shall inherit the land.'

Translated by I.M. Lask
Revised and Annotated by Jeffrey Saks

Annotations to "In the Heart of the Seas"

65. Title / Cf. Jonah 2:4.
67. Register / To join the group who will be travelling to the Land of Israel.
67. Quorum / Minyan; group of 10 men for communal prayer service.
67. Kerchief / The kerchief – a central symbol throughout this tale – is revisited by Agnon most famously in his story, "The Kerchief", in *A Book That Was Lost*.
68. Lulav and citron / The palm-branch and citron (*etrog*) used as part of the Sukkot celebration (cf. Lev. 23:40).
69. Robber chief / This element is taken from the legends of the Ba'al Shem Tov.
69. A certain cave / Cf. Agnon's "Fable of the Goat", in *A Book That Was Lost*.
69. Two thousand ells / The Sabbath boundary outside of which one is forbidden to travel.
70. Shaddai / Playing off the homonym: *Shaddai* (Hebrew for "The Almighty") being one of God's Holy names and the Polish *siadaj*, meaning: Sit!
70. Took off my shoes / One is forbidden to wear leather shoes on Yom Kippur.
70. Buczacz / Agnon's hometown in Eastern Galicia, today Western Ukraine, and the setting for this story's opening.
70. Rabbi Akiva / cf. Pesachim 112a.
70. Him who hath light in Zion / Isaiah 31:9.
72. Adar / Hebrew month corresponding to February-March.
73. Kohen / Descendent of the priestly caste.
73. Slaughterer-and-inspector / Responsible for the production of kosher meat.
73. Ketuvot / Talmudic tractate dealing with laws of marriage contracts.
74. Alfasi / R. Isaac Alfasi of Fes, known as Rif (1013-1103), medieval Talmudic commentator.
74. The King hath brought… / Song of Songs 1:4. Rabbi Gershon is the central character of Agnon's earlier story *HaNidach* ("The Banished"), which is set around 1815. Based on this fact we can

speculate that "In the Heart of the Seas" is set around 20-30 years later.

74. Rabbi Shmuel Yosef / Agnon's own name; the author has retrojected himself as a character into his own story.

75. Stryi / A town about 135 km. west of Buczacz.

75. Esther / Agnon's own wife, Esther *née* Marx (1889-1973), similarly retrojected into the story.

75. Rabbi Avigdor / One of the protagonists of the earlier mentioned story *HaNidach*.

76. Oh that the salvation… / Ps. 53:7.

76. Draw me… / Song of Songs 1:4.

76. Strypa / A left tributary of the Dniester River, runs through Buczacz.

78. Rabbi Meir the Miracle Worker / A charity fund to support residents of the Holy land, named for the 2nd century C.E. rabbi of the Mishnah.

78. All the rivers… / Ecclesiastes 1:7.

81. Rabbi in Yaslovitz / Da'at Kedoshim – Based on actual case of R. Avraham David Wahrman (1770-1840), who left the Yaslovitz rabbinate to take up a position in Bucazacz in 1813. The tale is related in Agnon's story *"Da'at Kedoshim"* in his volume *Ir uMelo'ah*.

82. Sambation / According to ancient Jewish legend the Sambation River marked the place beyond which the Ten Lost Tribes were exiled.

82. Baal Shem Tov / R. Yisral ben Eliezer (d. 1760), called the "Master of the Good Name", mystic and founder of Hassidut.

85. Buried in earth outside the Land / cf. Shabbat 153a.

88. Zaddik / Lit. "righteous one", title used to designate a Hassidic Rabbi.

88. Heman and Asaph and Jeduthun / I Chron 25:1; Bava Batra 14b names them as among the authors of Psalms.

89. Head of Esau / Esua was the brother of the biblical Jacob. According to legend (Targum Yonatan to Gen. 50:13) his decapitated head was buried in the Cave of Machpelah, i.e., the Tomb of the Patriarchs in Hebron.

91. Iyar / Hebrew month corresponding to April-May.

94. Chained / An *agunah* is a woman unable to obtain a halakhic divorce, in this case as her husband has gone missing with no

evidence of his death or whereabouts, leaving her "chained" to him and unable to remarry.

95. Rabbi Meir of Primishlan / Hassidic rabbi (1783-1850).
97. What is thy name? / Gen. 32:28.
97. But once the wine went in / Sanhedrin 38a.
98. Stambul / i.e., Istanbul.
99. Mămăligă / A porridge made out of yellow maize flour, traditional in Romania and Moldova. It is similar to the Italian *polenta*.
101. Shulhan Arukh / 16th century Code of Jewish law by R. Yosef Karo.
102. Hear O Israel / *Shema Yisrael* (Deut. 6:4), central declaration of faith and a twice-daily Jewish prayer.
102. For with thee… / Psalm 130:4.
103. Hakham / Sage; title amongst Sephardic Jews for a scholar or rabbi.
105. Eight verses / Jonah 2:3-10.
106. The Land must be exceedingly good / Numbers 14:7-8.
106. I have forsaken my house / Jeremiah 12:7.
106. Afterwards the Children of Israel / Hosea 3:5.
106. Oh that the salvation / Psalm 53.
106. Evil husks / Kabbalistic idea of the *kellipot* (shells or husks) represent evil and impure forces within our non-redeemed world.
107. Minyan / Prayer quorum of 10. Careful readers will note that even without Hananiah they were ten men, a mystery planted by Agnon into the story.
108. Boys and girls who flung themselves into the sea / Gittin 57b.
109. Jonathan ben Uziel / Mishnaic rabbi and author of translation of the Prophets into Aramaic.
109. This is the people… / Isaiah 43:21.
110. I will bring them back… / Psalms 38:23.
111. The counsel of the Lord… / Psalms 25:14.
112. Sennacherib and Nebuchadnezzar and the wicked Titus / Non-Jewish rulers responsible for the destructions of the First and Second temple in Jerusalem, and exiles of the Jewish people.
113. Section of Song / *Perek Shira* is a poem-like collection of Biblical and Talmudic verses of praise to God placed in the figurative mouths of the heavenly bodies, the elements of the natural world, the various members of the vegetable, animal, bird, marine and

insect kingdoms. The text appears in authoritative editions of the prayerbook, but is not part of the liturgy. Author and date are unknown but the work may go back to Talmudic times.

113. The voice of the Lord... / Psalms 29:3.

113. My help cometh... / Psalms 212:2.

113. For a small moment... / Isaiah 54:7.

113. And the ransomed... / Isaiah 35:10.

114. Burnt a garment and covered the blood / The blood of a slaughtered animal or fowl must be covered over with earth or ash, cf. Lev 17:13.

114. Setting aside part of the Sabbath loaf / Numbers 15:20.

115. *Come Ye Forth and See / Tze'nah u-Re'nah*, late 16th century Yiddish anthology of Jewish writings organized around the weekly Torah portion. Written for women, the work was immensely popular and widely distributed.

116. Song for the Sabbath Day / Psalm 92; central passage in the prayers for welcoming the Sabbath.

117. And his Land doth make... / Deut. 33:42.

117. Go to the ant... / Prov. 6:6.

118. Hosannah willows / Willow branches used as part of the rituals of the concluding day of the Sukkot festival; the meaning here is – in the Land of Israel they, too, have actual this-worldly food to eat.

119. Students' riot / *Schiller gileif*, anti-Semitic riot led by Jesuit seminary students.

120. Godfather / *Sandek*; the one who holds the baby on his lap during the circumcision.

120. Who has hallowed... / Blessing recited at circumcision.

120. Rolled the light away... / From the evening prayer.

121. Stambul / Istanbul, then the capital of the the Ottoman Empire.

122. Desire of the Days / *Hemdat Yamim*, kabbalistic work detailing various customs and laws of the holidays.

122. Holy Tongue / Hebrew.

122. Rabbi Joseph Karo / Renowned halakhist and mystic (1488-1575), author of the *Shulhan Arukh*.

123. Rabbi Simeon bar Yohai / 1st century mishnaic rabbi and mystic, purported author of the Zohar. The 33rd day of the Omer

(Lag BaOmer), the anniversary of his death, is marked by pilgrimages to his grave in the Galilee region of northern Israel.

123. Karaites / Sectarian movement which broke from Rabbinic Judaism, rejecting the Oral interpretation of the Torah.

123. Moses ben Maimon / Maimonides (1135-1205), gretaets medieval rabbinic figure, author of the encyclopedic Mishenh Torah, also known as the Yad HaHazakah ('The Mighty Hand').

124. Rabbi Hayyim ben Attar / Talmudist, kabbalist and author of the popular Torah commentary Or HaHayyim ('Light of Life') (1696, Morocco – 1742, Jerusalem).

124. Grave of Job / The Eyüp Sultan Mosque in Istanbul, holds the tomb of Abu Ayyub al-Ansari, not the Biblical Job, a 7th century figure whose tomb was mistakenly conflated with that of the Biblical Job.

124. Ordination of the Sages / R Naftali ben Yitzhak HaKohen Katz of Ostrowo, Ukraine (1660-1719), rabbi and kabbalist, died in Istanbul en route to the Land of Israel.

124. The Additions to the Zohar / Tikkunei Zohar, a collection of mystical hymns, part of the collection of early kabbalistic literature.

125. Woman who is waiting for him to marry… / Cf. Deut. 25:9.

125. Isaac Luria / Known by the acronym Arizal (1534-1572), preeminent medieval kabbalist.

126. Moshe ben Nahman / Nahmanides or Ramban (1194-1270), leading Spanish rabbi, philosopher, halakhist and exegete. Arrrived in the Holy Land in 1267.

127. Rakkath / Cf. Josh. 19:35.

127. May it be my lot… / Shabbat 118b.

127. Sea of Kinnereth / Sea of Galilee.

127. Revival of the dead will commence at Tiberias / Rosh HaShanah 31b.

129. Midnight Mourning / *Tikkun Hatzot*. Elegies of kabbalistic orientation recited at midnight in mourning for the destroyed Temple and in hopes of Redemption from exile.

131. Cast away their sins / The *Tashlich* ritual prayer recited on the first day of Rosh HaShanah near a body of water, symbolizing the casting away of sins.

132. Rabbi Nahman of Horodanki / Disciple of the Baal Shem Tov and grandfather of Rabbi Nahman of Breslov; arrived in the land of Israel in 1764.
133. Who shall ascend… / Psalms 24:3.
133. Rabbi Shmelke / Shmuel Horowitz (d. 1778), rabbi in Nickolsburg.
133. Song of the Red Sea / Exodus 15.
135. Leviathan / According to rabbinic legend this will be the meal served to the righteous at the feast of the End of Days.
136. We shall go up at once! / cf. Numbers 13:30.
136. River of Fire / Rabbinic metaphor for the Milky Way, cf. Hagigah 14a.
138. Sons of the Heavenly Hall / *Bnei heikhala* – Aramaic hymn composed by Isaac Luria, about the longings for revelation. Commonly sung at the final Sabbath meal.
139. I rejoiced when they said… / Psalms 122:1.
139. The Lord loveth the gates of Zion… / Psalms 87:2.
143. The third day of the week / Gen 1:10 and 1:12 – Tuesday (third day of creation) is only day twice indicated as "good".
143. Place below Jerusalem called Motza… / Mishnah Sukkah 4:5.
146. Who are these that fly as a cloud? / Isaiah 60:8.
146. Abraham ibn Ezra / 1089-1164, Spanish exegete, philosopher and poet.
146. Bought the parcel of land / Genesis 33:19.
149. Sabbath eve feast before a circumcision / Custom of *Shalom Zakhar*, visiting with the newborn on the Friday evening prior to circumcision.
149. Mine eyes and My heart… / Chronicles II 7:16.
149. Priestly blessing / Numbers 6:24-26.
150. I am the Lord… / Isaiah 49:23.
150. The Lord is good… / Lam. 3:25.
151. Ten sanctities whereby the Land of Israel is sanctified / Mishnah Kelim 1:6.
154. And His feet shall stand… / Zach. 14:4.
155. The heavens are the heavens… / Psalms 115:16, from the Hallel prayer recited on the first of the New Month.
156. But a good word… / Prov. 12:25.
156. But those who wait for the Lord… / Psalms 37:9.

In the Prime of Her Life

"My father sighed. We walked on and skirted the town, and my father placed his hand in my own and said, This way. As we approached the outer limits of the town we suddenly came upon an old woman digging in her yard. My father greeted her and said, Please tell us, good lady, is Mr. Mazal home?"

Illustration of Szybusz by Yosl Bergner for *A Simple Story*

My mother died in the prime of her life. She was barely thirty-one years old. Few and harsh were the days of her life. She sat at home the entire day and never stirred from within. Her friends and neighbors did not visit, nor did my father welcome guests. Our house stood hushed in sorrow, its doors did not open to a stranger. Lying on her bed my mother spoke scarcely a word. But when she did speak it was as though limpid wings had spread forth and led me to the hall of blessing. How I loved her voice. Often I would open her door just to hear her ask, Who's there? I was still a child. Sometimes she rose from her bed to sit by the window. She would sit by the window dressed in white. She always wore white. Once a relative of my father's was called into town and seeing my mother, took her for a nurse, for her clothes misled him and he did not realize it was she who was unwell.

Her illness, a heart ailment, bowed her life down. Every summer the doctors would send her to the hot springs, but she would turn back shortly after leaving, for she said her longing gave her no peace, and once again she would sit by the window or lie on her bed.

My father began to ply his trade less and less. He no longer left for Germany where, as a bean merchant, he had traveled year after year to deal with his clients. In those days and at that time he forgot the ways of the world. Returning home at dusk he would sit by my mother's side, his left hand tucked behind his head and her right hand held in his own. And every so often she would lean forward and kiss his hand.

The winter my mother died our home fell silent seven times over. My mother forsook her bed only when Kaila went in to tidy up. A carpet was placed in the hallway to absorb the sound of each and every footfall, and the odor of medicine wafted from one room to another. Every room was encumbered with grief.

The doctors arrived unsummoned and refused to leave, and whenever we asked whether her health had improved all they said was, With God's help. Meaning all hope was lost—there was no cure. But my mother didn't sigh or complain, nor did she shed any tears. She lay quietly on her bed and her strength fled like a shadow.

But there were days when hope tugged at our hearts and we believed that she would live. Winter had come and gone and the earth was arrayed in the first days of spring. My mother seemed to forget her pain and we saw with our own eyes how her illness abated. Even the doctors consoled us, claiming there was hope: spring was drawing near and the sun's rays would soon reinvigorate her body.

Passover was at our doorstep and Kaila made the necessary preparations for the holiday, while as mistress of the house my mother attended to her duties and ensured nothing was amiss. She even made herself a new dress.

Several days before the holiday my mother, having left her bed, stood before the looking-glass and put on her new dress. Shadows glimmered over her body in the mirror and the light of the living illumined her face. My heart beat with joy. How beautiful was her face in that dress. And yet the new dress was not that different from the old one. Both were white and the dress she now discarded was good as new, for being bedridden all winter she had had little use for clothes. I'm not sure in what I discerned a sign of hope. Perhaps a scent of hope blossomed from the spring bloom she pinned above her heart—or was it that the medicinal odors had faded away? A new fragrance freshened our home. I was familiar with a variety of perfumes but had never before come across one so delicate. Once though, I inhaled the scent of such sweetness in a dream. Where could this fragrance have come from? For my mother did not dab herself with feminine perfumes.

My mother rose from her bed and sat by the window where there was a small table with a drawer. The drawer was locked and the key to the drawer hung from my mother's neck. My mother opened the drawer without making a sound and removed a bundle of letters which she then spent the rest of the day reading. She read until evening. The door opened twice, three times, but she did not ask who was there, and when I spoke to her she did not answer. When she was reminded to drink her medicine she swallowed the contents of the spoon without making a face or uttering a word. It was as though their bitterness had vanished. And no sooner had she drained her medicine than she returned to her letters.

The letters were written on thin paper in a clear, immaculate hand. They were written in short and long lines. Seeing my mother reading I told myself she would never relinquish the letters, for she was bound to them and the drawer by the string around her neck. Later that afternoon she took the bundle, secured it with the string hanging around her neck, kissed the letters and the key and tossed them into the wood stove. The flue, however, was blocked and only one ember flickered in the stove. The ember gnawed through the thin paper, the letters burned in the fire and the house filled with smoke. Kaila hastened to open the window, but my mother forbade her to do so. The letters burned and the house filled with smoke. And my mother sat by the open drawer and inhaled the smoke from the letters until evening.

That night Mintshi Gottlieb came to inquire about my mother's health. Mintshi was her close friend. As young girls they had studied together under Akaviah Mazal. For close to three hours Mintshi sat by my mother's bedside. "Mintshi," my mother said, "this will be the last time I see you." Drying her tears, Mintshi said, "Leah, take heart, you will soon regain your strength." My mother remained silent, a solemn smile playing over her feverish lips. Suddenly she clasped Mintshi's right hand in her own and said, "Go home, Mintshi, and prepare for the Sabbath. Tomorrow afternoon you will accompany me to my resting place." This occurred on a Thursday night, which is the dawn of Friday, the Sabbath eve. Taking hold of my mother's right hand, Mrs. Gottlieb spread out her fingers and said, "Leah." A stifled sob held back her words. Our spirits sank.

My father returned from work at the store and sat by the bed. My mother's solemn lips hovered over his face like a shadow as she bent forward and kissed him. Mrs. Gottlieb rose, wrapped herself in her coat, and left. My mother got out of bed and Kaila entered to change the sheets. The hem of the white dress rustled in the semi-darkness of the room.

My mother returned to her bed and swallowed the medicinal syrup my father offered her. And she took his hand and placed it above her heart, and said, "Thank you." The drops of syrup trickled one by one on his hand like tears. My mother took a deep breath. "Rise now," she said, "go and have some dinner." "I cannot eat," he replied. Again she urged him to eat until he finally withdrew to the dining-room. And he ate the bread of tears and returned to my mother's bedside.

Regaining some of her strength, my mother sat up and held his hand a second time. She then had the nurse sent home and instructed my father to inform her not to return. And she lowered the wick in the lamp and lay still. "If only I could sleep," my father said, "I would do so. But since God has deprived me of sleep, I will sit, if I may, by your side. Should you ask for me I will be here, and if not I will know that all is well with you." But my mother would not hear of it. So he returned to his room and lay down. He had not slept for many nights and as soon as his head touched the pillow he fell asleep. I too lay down and slept. But suddenly I awoke in alarm. I leapt out of bed to tend to my mother. She lay peacefully in bed, but, ah, she had ceased to breathe. I woke my father up and he cried with a great and exceedingly bitter cry, "Leah!"

My mother rested peacefully on her bed, for her soul had returned to the Almighty. My mother yielded up her soul and on the Sabbath eve at twilight she was borne to the cemetery. She died a righteous woman, on the Sabbath eve.

Throughout the seven days of mourning my father sat in silence. In front of him was my mother's footstool, and on it lay the book of Job and the Laws of Mourning. People I had never seen came to comfort us. Not until the days of mourning had I known there were so many people in our town. Those who came to comfort us suggested my father prepare the headstone. My father, however, remained silent, he didn't say a thing. On the third day, Mr. Gottlieb arrived. "Here," he said, "I have brought the epitaph for the headstone." Everyone stared in surprise, for my mother's name was formed out of the first letter of each verse and the year of her death was inscribed in every line. Gottlieb then spoke to my father about the stone, but my father barely listened to his words. And so the days of mourning passed.

The days of mourning passed and the year of mourning drew to an end. A somber grief hung over us and lingered that entire year. My father resumed his work, and when he returned from his store he ate his food without uttering a word. And in my misery I said to myself, My father has forgotten me; he has forgotten his daughter is alive.

Around that time my father stopped reciting the Kaddish, and approaching me he said, "Come, let us go and choose a headstone for our mother." I put on my hat and gloves. "Here I am, Father," I answered. My father drew back in surprise, as though noticing for the first time that I was wearing mourning. He opened the door and we left the house.

Once on our way, my father stopped in his tracks and said, "Spring has arrived early." And he passed his hand over his brow as he spoke. "If spring had not been late a year ago she would still be alive." My father sighed. We walked on and skirted the town, and my father placed his hand in my own and said, "This way."

As we approached the outer limits of the town we suddenly came upon an old woman digging in her yard. My father greeted her and said, "Please tell us, good lady, is Mr. Mazal home?" The woman set aside the spade she had been digging with and answered, "Yes, Mr. Mazal is at home." My father grasped my hand firmly. "Come, my daughter, let us go in."

A man in his mid-thirties opened the door. The room was small and pleasant-looking and sheaves of paper were piled on the table. The man's face was veiled in sorrow. "I have come to ask you to write the epitaph for the headstone," my father said. And it suddenly dawned on him who we were, and he covered the sheaves of paper and welcomed us, and he stroked my cheek and said, "You have grown a great deal." Looking at him I was reminded of my mother, for the way he moved his hands resembled my mother's gestures. And my father stood before the man; each facing his brother. "Who knew then," my father said, "that Leah would leave us." The man's face brightened for a moment as my father appeared to encompass him in his grief, but little did he know that my father had directed his words at me. The man extracted a sheaf from under the heap of papers and handed it to my father. My father took the sheaf and as he read his tears blotted the tearstains on the page. I stared at the sheaf and the script and was astonished. I had seen such a page and such writing before. Even so, upon seeing something, I often feel that I have already seen that very same thing before. Nor were the tearstains foreign to me.

My father read the poem to its end without saying a thing, for his words were held back in his mouth. And he put on his hat and we departed. We walked into town and arrived home just as Kaila was lighting the lamp. I prepared my lessons and my father read the epitaph for the headstone.

The stonecutter arrived and carved the headstone according to my father's wishes. And he copied down Akaviah Mazal's epitaph on large sheets of paper. And my father and I stood on either side of the stonecutter in order to choose the lettering for the headstone. But none of the letters seemed right to my father. And there was a bookshelf in our home, and one day, after sifting in vain through the sheaves of paper, my father went to fetch a book from the shelf and his eyes lit up as he leafed through his books. In those days our home was shrouded in a merciful melancholy. And at that time, as my father searched for the right lettering for the headstone, he all but forgot my mother. And he never grew weary, as a bird collecting twigs for its nest never tires in flight.

And the stone engraver arrived and thumbing through the books and letters, he found a script for the headstone. That was during the first days of spring. The stone engraver set about his work outside. As he struck the stone the letters clustered into rhymes, like bees drawn to the sound of their companions swarming among field-stones. The headstone was made of marble. And the stone engraver filled in the letters in black. In this way he shaped the letters on the headstone. And he coated the heading in gold. And once the work was completed the headstone stood over her grave on the appointed day. My father then rose and went to the cemetery along with the townsfolk to recite the Kaddish. He rested his head against the stone and grasped Mazal's hand. And since the time we went to the cemetery to raise the headstone, my father and I have visited her grave daily—apart from the Passover holidays, for one must not enter a graveyard on the holy days.

"Shall we go for a walk," my father said one day during the intermediate days of Passover. I put on my festive dress and approached him. "You have a new dress," he said. "It is for special occasions," I answered as we set out.

Once on our way, I thought to myself, What have I done, for I have made myself a new dress. Suddenly I felt God stirring my conscience and I stood still. "Why have you stopped?" my father asked. "I couldn't help thinking, why have I put on my holiday dress," I replied. "It doesn't matter," he said. "Come." I removed my gloves and rejoiced as a gust of cold air enveloped my hands. We continued on our way.

As we reached the outskirts of town, my father turned off the road in the direction of Mazal's home. Mazal hurried towards us as we entered. Removing his hat, my father said, "I have searched through all her belongings." After falling silent for a moment he sighed and conceded, "I have labored in vain, I sought, but did not find."

My father saw that Mazal did not grasp the meaning of his words. "I thought to publish your poems and I looked through all her drawers, but I could not find a thing." Mazal shuddered. His shoulders shook, and he didn't say a word. Shifting from one foot to the other, my father stretched out his hand and asked, "Do you have a copy?" "There is no copy," Mazal answered. My father drew back, frightened. "I wrote the poems for her, that is why I did not make any copies for myself," Mazal added. My father sighed and raised his palm to his head. Mazal then grasped the corners of the table and said, "She is dead." "Dead," my father answered, and fell silent. The day waned. The servant entered and lit the lamp. My father bade Mazal good day. And as we left, Mazal extinguished the lamp.

>❦ >❦ >❦

In those days classes resumed at school and I applied myself to my lessons all day long. In the evening my father returned from his work at the store and we supped together. We sat hushed over our food and neither spoke a word.

"Tirtza, what are you doing?" my father asked one spring evening as we sat by the table. "I am preparing my lessons," I replied. "And have you forgotten your Hebrew?" he asked. "I haven't forgotten." And he said, "I will find you a teacher and you will learn Hebrew." My father then found me a teacher to his liking and brought him home. The teacher, at my father's urging, taught me grammar, for as with most of our people, my father believed grammar was the soul of the Hebrew language. The teacher taught me the Hebrew tongue, the rules of logic, and the meaning of "What profit hath man." I was left breathless. And in addition to grammar, a *melamed*—a teacher for beginners—instructed me in the Bible and prayerbook. For my father had me study under the teacher's guidance subjects that other young girls did not know, while the *melamed* came and taught me all that they did know. He appeared daily and Kaila would bring him a glass of tea and cream cake. If the evil eye had taken hold of her she would approach the *melamed* and he would whisper into her ear. And when he spoke, a smile in the depth of his beard glimmered as in a mirror.

How tired I grew of grammar and its endless rules. I could not make head or tails of the meaning of such words as *Bedingungs-Buchstaben* and *Sprach-Werkzeuge*. Like a parrot I chattered a string of meaningless names. Once the teacher exclaimed, "I have labored in vain, I have spent my strength for nothing and vanity." On another occasion he was approving as I parroted whatever he said word for word. I commanded my brain: Onwards! I cried out to my memory: Help me!

One day the teacher arrived while the *melamed* was still in the house. The teacher waited and waited for the *melamed* to leave. He, however, did not go. Kaila came from the kitchen as they sat and said to the *melamed*, "I dreamt a dream and my spirit has been shaken." "What did you see, Kaila?" he asked. "I saw a small Ashkenazi with a red wool cap on his head." "What did the Ashkenazi do?" he asked. "He hiccupped and yawned," she answered, "and since I woke up that morning I can't stop sneezing." The *melamed* stood up, closed his eyes, and spat three times in front of the teacher. Then, all in a whisper, he cast his spell. But before he could finish the teacher leapt to his feet in anger and exclaimed, "Wickedness and fraud! Are you throwing sand in the eyes of an innocent woman?" And the *melamed* called after him, "Heretic! Are you belittling the customs of Israel?" And in his rage the teacher spun on his heel and stomped out. From that day on, the *melamed* stayed vigilant for the sound of the teacher's footsteps. But the teacher stopped coming and the *melamed* taught me the weekly portions, which we hadn't studied yet and which we set out to learn now that the teacher came no more. And I remembered his pleasant voice, for a spirit of grace and supplication swept over me.

Summer arrived and the golden grasshopper took to the air. Its strains swelled about us as it spread its thin wings and its coppery belly gleamed in the daylight. Sometimes we heard from within the muffled sound of the house-grasshopper striking its jaws against the woodwork. My heart would then beat feebly, fearing death; for such a sound heralds death.

And in those days I read from the Book of Joshua and Judges, and at that time I found a book among my mother's books, may she rest in peace. I read two chapters, for I told myself, I will repeat the words my mother read, may she rest in peace. I was dumbfounded, seeing as I understood what was before me. I read on and the stories were familiar to me. Reading my mother's books, I felt like a little child who in hearing his mother chuckle and chirp suddenly recognizes his own name.

School recessed for the summer holidays. And I sat at home and altered my dresses, for they had last been worn before my year of mourning and no longer fitted me. One day, while my father was at home, the doctor called on us. My father was delighted by his visit, for he had lived in the company of doctors during my mother's lifetime, may she rest in peace. The doctor told my father, "Look at you both sitting indoors while summer beckons." He grasped my hand and felt my pulse as he spoke, and when he leaned over me I recognized the odor of his clothes. It was just like my mother's odor when she was ill. "How you've grown," the doctor said. "In a few months I won't be able to call you child any more." And he asked me my age and I answered, "I am fourteen." Then, noticing my dress, he asked, "You also know how to sew?" "Let another man praise thee, and not thine own mouth," I replied. The doctor smoothed his mustache with two fingers as he laughed, "A bold girl, and looking for compliments." Turning to my father, he added, "Her face is the very likeness of her mother's, may she rest in peace." My father turned and gazed at me. Kaila then came from the kitchen with marmalade and a pitcher of water. "My, it's hot today," the doctor exclaimed, and he opened a window. The streets were silent for want of passersby. We lowered our voices as people do when all about them it is very quiet. The doctor drained his glass of water, covered the marmalade with a bowl, and said, "You have been sitting here in town long enough, now you must find yourselves a place for the summer." My father nodded, a sign that he would follow the doctor's advice, even though it seemed his heart was not in the matter.

At that time Mrs. Gottlieb invited me to spend the remaining days of my vacation at her home. My father agreed, saying, "Go now." But I answered, "How can I go alone?" And he said, "I will come and visit." Kaila stood dusting by the mirror and winked at me as she overheard my father's words. I saw her move her lips and grimace in the mirror, and I laughed to myself. Noticing how my face lit up my father said, "I knew you would listen to me." Then he left.

Once my father had gone I told Kaila, "How strangely you behaved, making faces in the mirror." Kaila appeared angry. "What's wrong, Kaila?" I asked. "Have you lost the use of your eyes?" she retorted. "Kaila," I cried out, "May God be with you, but do speak up, please—and stop tormenting me with all sorts of riddles." Kaila wiped her mouth angrily and said, "If you do not know, my dove, then just take a good look at your father. Why, he's nothing but skin and bones and creeps around like a shadow on the face of the earth. When I was polishing his shoes I thought to myself, Where did he collect such mud, and it suddenly dawned on me that his shoes were caked with earth from the cemetery. I also recognized his footprints by her grave, which he visits seven times a day."

Only then did I fathom Kaila's thoughts and the meaning of her insinuations in the mirror: if I stayed with the Gottliebs my father would feel obliged to come and see me and would no longer visit the cemetery. I gathered my dresses and folded them in my trunk. And

I filled the iron with coals to press two or three blouses before leaving for the Gottliebs. The following day, my father sent my clothes ahead with the young servant, and at noon we ate together, and then rose and departed.

The Gottliebs' home is on the edge of town, a short distance from the road leading to the train station. A large tract of land lies between it and the rest of the town. The building is a cosmetics factory and its rooms are large and empty. For in constructing the plant, Gottlieb had told himself, I will build my factory large enough to house all my employees, and my factory will be renowned throughout the country. We crossed the town and arrived at the Gottliebs. Mintshi emerged from the garden where she had been picking cherries, and hurried toward us and welcomed us and led us back into the garden. Partchi then came at her summons, carrying two bowls of cherries and Mintshi invited us to sample the freshly-picked fruit.

The day waned and Gottlieb returned from the factory. Partchi set a table out in the garden. The pale blue night cloaked us in its pleasing warmth. The moon stood in a heaven swarming with stars. A songbird fluted its purest song and the train's whistle sounded from the station. After the meal Gottlieb asked my father, "Would you care for a smoke?" "In the dark?" I interjected in astonishment. "And why shouldn't he smoke in the dark?" Gottlieb asked. "I once read that every smoker longs to gaze at the red ashes and the plume of incense rising from his cigarette," I replied and added, "That is why the blind do not smoke, for being blind they see neither ash nor smoke" "Haven't you learned yet that books and all their profundities are of little use?" Gottlieb said, laughing. "In my case I first learned to smoke in the dark. Lying on my bed at night, I treated myself to a cigarette as soon as my father fell asleep. You see, I chose to smoke at night because I feared doing so in front of my father during the day. Partchi, bring the cigarettes and cigars, and don't forget the matches and ashtray." "If my husband smokes today then it is indeed a good sign," Mrs. Gottlieb said to my father. Mr. Gottlieb, however, pretended not to hear her words. "Now I will tell you what I have read. In bygone days, if a man smoked a pipe they hung it from his nose, for they said that there was death in the tobacco, and the government dealt harshly with anyone who sold tobacco in the country. Even now, my friends, a worker from my own factory was put behind bars for importing tobacco from a foreign land, for our government, you see, has monopolized the tobacco industry." Gottlieb was always grumbling about the actions of the government and he had little patience for government employees of any kind.

That night my father did not prolong his visit, for he said, "Tirtza must learn to stay in your company without me." Mrs. Gottlieb then led me to a small room and kissed me on the forehead and left. The room contained an iron bed, a table, a closet and mirror. I lay on the bed by the window and as a breeze blew through the trees, I fancied I was being cradled in a hammock in the garden. At daybreak fresh rays of light lit up my window. The sun graced the wings of birds trilling from their heights. I jumped out of bed and ran outside to the well, where I splashed my face with spring water. Partchi then called me to the table.

There was no joy in the Gottliebs' home; he would criticize his wife after each meal she prepared. "What's this I'm eating – straw?" he would exclaim. Since her husband dealt in perfumes, Mrs. Gottlieb went to pains to preserve his sense of smell and avoided cooking anything too spicy. Moreover Partchi, the daughter of Gottlieb's deceased sister, was not made welcome in their home. Mrs. Gottlieb gave the girl no peace. Mintshi and the girl's mother had quarreled, and now the daughter was being punished for her mother's iniquities. And Gottlieb was cross with her, lest it be said his sister's daughter walked barefoot. Few visitors called on the Gottliebs. Mr. Gottlieb met with his business associates in his office at the factory, and Mintshi refrained from befriending other women from town. In this she resembled my mother, may she rest in peace. When together they had been like the two Austrians who meet outside of town and one says to the other, "Where are you going?" and the other replies, "I'm off to the forest to be alone." "Why, I also want to be alone," exclaims the first. "Let's go together." Thus I sat by Mrs. Gottlieb's side, her only companion.

Mrs. Gottlieb was a diligent woman. Yet she never appeared to be busy, whether working at home or in the garden. And even when she paused in the midst of her chores it seemed as though she had just arrived to admire the job done. I sought her out at least seven times a day, yet I never felt I was intruding upon her affairs. During my stay with the Gottliebs we evoked the memory of my mother, may she rest in peace. And at that time Mintshi told me how Mazal had loved my mother, may she rest in peace, and how she had loved him in return, but her father had opposed their union for he had already promised her hand in marriage to my father.

I lay on my bed at night, asking myself, What if my mother had married Mazal? What would have become of me? I knew such speculations to be fruitless, and yet I did not abandon them. When the trembling that accompanied my musings finally ceased, I said: Mazal has been wronged. He seemed to me to be like a man bereft of his wife and yet she was not his wife.

Summer dragged on. All day long I lounged under the oak and birch trees and stared into the blue sky. Sometimes I strolled to the factory and chatted with the herb gatherers. They were as carefree as the birds of the field and their spirits never seemed to dip even for a single day. I will wander in the woods with them and forget my sorrows, I told myself. But I did not join them, nor did I escape into the woods, and I lay idle for hours on end. "Look, our friend is boring a hole through the heavens," Mr. Gottlieb said laughing as he saw me staring up at the sky. And I laughed along with him, though with a heavy heart.

How I loathed myself. I burned with shame without knowing why. At times I pitied my father and at times I secretly grew angry at him. And I poured my wrath upon Mazal as well. I recalled the fluttering blows of the grasshopper against the walls of our home at the onset of spring, but death no longer frightened me. Sometimes I asked myself: Why did Mintshi Gottlieb upset me by telling me of bygone memories? A father and mother, are they not man and woman, and one flesh? Why then should I brood over secrets from before my time? Yet I thirsted to know more. I could not calm myself down, nor could I sit still for a moment. And so I told myself, If Mintshi knows what happened, surely she will tell me the truth. But how will I open my mouth to ask? For my face turns crimson at the mere thought of speaking. I gave up all hope—I would never know the rest.

One day, however, Gottlieb left for an long journey and Mint-shi asked me to sleep in her room. And again she began to speak of my mother and Mazal. And what I had least expected was told to me.

"Mazal was still a young man when he arrived here. He had left Vienna to travel around the rural townships and he came here as well. He came to see the town, and since coming to our town some seventeen years ago, he has never left." Mintshi spoke in a low voice and a cold gust of air rose from her words. It was the very chill I had felt upon touching my brow against the marble slab of my mother's headstone, may she rest in peace. Mintshi swept her left hand across her brow and exclaimed, "What more can I tell you that I haven't already said?" She then shut her eyes as though in a dream. Mintshi suddenly started awake and fetched a bound diary that was popular among educated girls a generation ago. "Read this," she said, "for I have copied Mazal's journals. I have copied all that he wrote in those days." I took the notebook that Mrs. Gottlieb had copied and slipped it into my bag. I never read in Mintshi's room at night since the light of a candle prevented her from falling asleep. And the following morning I read all that was written in the book:

How I love the rural townships during the summer months. The market is hushed, a town and its inhabitants, a pot with flowers that peer out and no one to admire them. Her sons are in hiding, the sun has driven them into their homes, and I walk solitary in a peaceful land. I am a student at the university and God has led me forth to one of the towns. As I stood in the street I saw a woman standing by a window and she placed a bowl of millet on its sunlit sill. I bowed to her and said, "Won't the birds feast on your millet?" I had barely finished my sentence when a young girl appeared at the window and she stared at me and mocked my words. I was nearly put to shame and lest the young girl sense my confusion I said to her, "May I have some water please?" The young girl then offered me a glass of water from the window. "Why have you not asked the man in to take a rest?" the woman said to the girl. "Does he not live in foreign parts?" And she said, "Come in, sir, come in." And I turned and entered the house.

The household appeared prosperous and a man in his prime sat over a volume of Talmud. He had dozed off over his books and he now awoke and greeted me and asked, "Who are you and what brings you to our town?" I returned his greeting and replied, "I am a student and have come to see the countryside during my vacation." They were struck with wonder at my words. "Look now and see for yourself," the man said to the girl. "The learned come from afar to admire our town, and all you ask is to leave us and our town. Now you can banish that thought." The young girl listened and remained silent. Her father asked me, "So you are studying medicine, you wish to become a doctor?" "No, sir," I replied, "I am studying philosophy." The man was surprised to hear this and said, "I always said philosophy wasn't to be learned in school, for the true philosopher is the man who broods over scholarly tomes and fathoms their meaning."

The day waned and the man told the girl, "Bring me my sash and I will recite the *minhah*. Don't feel embarrassed at my reciting the afternoon prayer." "I too will pray," I exclaimed. "Bring me the prayerbook," he said. She then hurried to fetch the prayerbook. And he took the prayerbook and showed me the passage we would read. "Sir," I said, "there is really no need, I know the prayer well." The man was surprised to hear that I knew the prayer by heart. He gestured toward the east where an embroidery hung on the wall, and I read all that was embroidered on the *mizrah*:

> *Blessed is he who shall not forsake Thee*
> *And he who shall cleave unto Thee.*
> *For those who seek Thee shall not fail*
> *Nor shall they be put to shame*
> *Those who seek and dwell within Thee.*

As soon as I had finished praying I extolled the *mizrah,* for indeed it was splendid. My words, though, were like the sun's dying rays at dusk, illuminating only the fringes of the east, while the whole is left in darkness, for I could utter but a fraction of the praise that swelled within me.

The woman set the table and bid me share their meal. The dishes were placed before us and we ate. Although the food was not abundant, consisting of just cornmeal with milk, we nevertheless lingered over our food as the man spoke of all that had happened to them, for he had once been wealthy, trading with the landed gentry and investing his money in field crops. Such was his way year after year. But riches are not everlasting. The owner of the estate did not keep to his end of the agreement. Money he took but produce he did not give. A bitter and prolonged quarrel ensued between the two men and what remained of the fruits of his labor was frittered away in legal fees. Though bribing is a criminal offence and it is forbidden to bribe a state judge—and even the gentile is subject to the laws of the land—the overlord offered the judge gifts so that the verdict would not go against him. "Eternity may well come to an end," he said, "and still I wouldbe far from ending my account of all that came to pass in those days. My adversary slandered me with false accusations and my eldest son, though disabled and exempt from serving the Emperor, was pressed into the army, and the same overlord was a high-ranking officer and my son died under the crush of his iron fist."

"But a man should not mourn the loss of imaginary possessions, blessed be the Holy Name for He has not taken His merciful eye from us. Even though the Almighty has not blessed me a second time with wealth and happiness, I thank the Lord daily, for we are not lacking in food. And yet whenever I call to mind the inflictions wrought upon my son, I am tempted to choose death over life."

The members of the household dried their tears and the woman asked her husband, "If he were alive today, how old would he be?" "What sort of woman-talk is this?" he answered. "Do not lay reproach on the Almighty; the Lord giveth and the Lord taketh, blessed be the name of the Lord. How splendid are the words of Malbim, blessed be his memory, concerning the verse, "*he shall shave his head over the loss of property*" – *for it is forbidden to do so over the dead.*

The oil in the lamp was nearly spent and I rose from the table and asked, "Tell me please, is there an inn in town, for I will not be able to continue on my way tonight." The man and woman conferred and said, "There are a number of inns but who knows if you will find comfort in any one of them. Ours is a small town and the inns are of the plainest sort, for respectable guests seldom come here and anyone who isn't accustomed to such conditions will not find such inns very restful." The man glanced at his wife and said, "A stranger shall not sleep outside. I will open my door to a guest."

The young girl then brought a candle and lit it and placed it on the table as the oil in the lamp was spent. We sat together for another hour. They did not tire of hearing about the wonders of Vienna where the Emperor lives. I felt deeply drawn to their way of life. Later that evening they prepared a bed for me in a corner of the house and I fell into a deep and peaceful sleep.

And I started awake at the sound of a man's footsteps. The master of the house stood by my bed, his prayer shawl and phylacteries under his arm and the Morning Prayer on his lips. "Ah, sir," I cried out, "you are on your way to pray while I lie in the lap of indolence." The man smiled. "I have already prayed," he said. "I am on my way back from the synagogue, but be at ease, my son." And seeing my discomfort, he added, "If you have slept soundly then lie back and rest; the time will come soon enough when there will be no sleep. But if you are awake then rise and we will breakfast together." After eating I made to pay for my food. The woman and her daughter drew back in shame and the man smiled and said, "Such are the ways of the city dweller, they do not know that an act of charity is honored and that it is a sacred duty to invite a guest into one's home." I thanked them for letting me stay in their home for the entire night and morning. "Blessed are you in the eyes of the Lord for your kindness," I exclaimed. And as

I turned to leave, the man inquired, "Where will you be going?" "I will walk the length and breadth of the town," I answered, "for that is why I have come." "Go then in peace," said the man. "But return to eat with us at noon." "I am unworthy of such kindness," I said. And I walked into town. Presently I arrived at the Great Synagogue which housed a rare prayerbook whose gilt letters were inscribed on deerskin parchment. But the gold was obscured by a film of smoke that had risen from those martyred in the name of the Holy One and had seeped through and blackened the pages. And I walked over to the *Beit Midrash*. The sun's rays beat against its walls. The pupils, seated before the altar, had removed their coats and were surprised to see me. They implored me to speak of other houses of learning, and visions of distant places lit up their eyes. And I left the House of Study and turned towards the forest. I was overwhelmed with grief as I approached the green and somber woods. And I fell to my knees and lay amid the scrub by the oak trees. The Lord's mercy did not leave me. Suddenly I remembered the invitation extended to me to share the midday meal and I rose and returned home.

The members of the household reproached me as I entered, "We waited for you and you did not come. We thought you had forgotten us and so we ate without you." "I went for a walk in the forest," I explained. "I am late and now I will be on my way." But the woman looked at me and said, "You will go nowhere before having eaten." And she fried me some eggs. "The cantor will pass before the Ark of the Law," said the master of the house, "he will pray in the synagogue. Eat something, and then come with me to the synagogue. The bed we prepared for you yesterday is still in its place. Stay with us another night and tomorrow you will be on your way."

I do not play an instrument nor can I carry a tune. And my knowledge of music is slight, nor do I understand it. When dragged to the opera I sit and count the windows. But I now told the master of the house, "Very well, I will accompany you." I will not describe the cantor's singing, nor will I speak of what was on my mind just then. Rather I will speak of what I did when we returned.

I returned with the man and after eating we sat on the doorsteps of his home. So, I told myself, have I not longed to travel the length and breadth of the countryside? If I stay here one more day I will surely use up all the days of my vacation. It is fine to explore the countryside, my heart cried out suddenly, but to sit here is even better. I was in the best of health and in those days the thought of taking time off never even crossed my mind. It was like one of those notions a man acquires without knowing how it might bear on his own life. Alas, those days have passed and are gone and whatever peace of mind I had has been swept away with them. The following morning I asked the members of the household, "Tell me, do you happen to have a spare room, as I wish to remain in your company for the rest of my vacation." So they led me to their *succah*, a festival booth that also served as a room. "Stay here as long as you wish," they said. And the woman prepared my meals, while I in turn instructed their daughter in language and reading skills.

I lodge in the home of these good people. They have vacated a special room for me—the festival booth built as a room. There is even a small stove in the booth. Some will say it has no use, but soon enough winter will come and we will warm ourselves by its heat. And I sit in my rooftop den and look down at the town. From my perch I can see the huge marketplace where women sit, their baskets laden with vegetables. They sell the rotten ones while they keep the good ones until they rot too. And there is a wellspring in the center of the market with water gushing from its two spouts, and the country girls draw from its source. A Jew suddenly approaches one of the young girls, desiring to drink from her pitcher. "Jew," I call out from my garret, "why do you drink drawn water? Don't you have the entire well in front of you? And spring water at that?" But the Jew does not hear me. For he is hunched over while I dwell in the heights.

And a new voice resounded in the house. The voice of a young woman. I folded my coat behind the windowpane to catch a glimpse of myself before descending to see the young woman. Leah introduced me to her friend Mintshi. I greeted her with a bow. Returning to my room I spent the rest of the day lost in delusions and fancied Mintshi lived in the capital, and while there she had witnessed the respect lavished on me when my poems were praised in public. When she returned home, her mother said that a man had lodged in her room. "And what's his name?" she asked. "Akaviah Mazal." Then her heart skipped a beat, for she had had the privilege of knowing me. My God, how I held my head high. And I buried myself in religious, ethical tracts; perhaps it would extinguish the glowing ember of lust burning within me. But I could not stamp it out and I sought comfort in moral precepts: You shall love the Lord your God, et cetera, with both inclinations—the good and the bad—taught the Sages of blessed memory. If only it were so.

The students at the *Beit Midrash* were delighted to see me. They sought to study the ways of Haskalah literature—and is there a better teacher than I? Today two boys came to see me and instead of reading the *Gemara* they pored over the contents of profane books. And in my presence one of the boys started to read a German poem, and the one chanted while the other read. My students sigh and ask only to be enlightened by the new literature. As for me? My only desire is to follow in the path of the Lord all the days of my life.

What is God's path? A man takes to the road and his strength fails him. His knees buckle and his tongue is parched. He stumbles seven times and rises without reaching his longed-for destination. The road is long and the illusions are myriad. The man will then say to himself: Perhaps I have strayed from the path, this is not the way. And he will turn off the path he first took. And turning off the path, he sees a light flickering in the distance. Although he does not know yet whether this is the right way, who will say that the man erred in choosing a path different from the first? Even though I am a teacher of the "Haskalah," I declined the boys' request. How will I provide for myself if the lining of my purse is empty? I am like a thief who stumbles upon a pouch of coins, returns the pouch to its owner, and then snatches the money back from the owner's pocket, for he is a thief and cannot live otherwise. I teach Leah and her friend Mintshi, as well as the sons of the rich. My friends mock me in their letters, and my father, seeing that I have abandoned my studies at the university, weeps for my fate daily. Summer swept by and my vacation drew to an end, but I did not return home.

How resplendent was my booth during the Feast of Tabernacles. We hung from its boughs red lanterns and assembled in it the finest of the household utensils. As Leah made to hand me the *mizrah,* a ring came undone and fell from one of its corners. Leah took the ring and slipped it on my finger. She then untied the crimson ribbon fastened to her locks and with it secured the *mizrah* to the wall, reading out loud, "Blessed is he who shall not forsake Thee." I read on, "And he who shall cleave unto Thee." Suddenly we both blushed, for her father and mother were peering in, their faces beaming with joy. They called me master of the house as we sat together in the booth, and they thought of themselves as my guests. Leah came to the booth at least seven times a day. Sometimes she brought food and other times she cleared the table. And we thanked God for bearing us aloft toward love. How resplendent was my booth during the Feast of the Tabernacles. But the festive booth is now stocked with beans and lentils for a bean merchant has rented the booth to store his merchandise. I have left my home, I have abandoned my booth, and I have rented a room on the outskirts of the town. My lodgings are small and peaceful. An old woman tends to my needs, she prepares my meals and washes my linen. I am surrounded by peace and quiet, yet my heart knows no peace. Mr. Mintz, who has rented the booth, is a wealthy man. His trade has spread throughout the land and Leah's father has promised him his daughter's hand in marriage.

And I am but a poor and unworthy teacher. They befriended me when I came from the city. Ah, they drew near me with their words while their hearts were elsewhere. How strange are the ways of my brethren.

In addition to instructing Leah in language and books I also taught her Hebrew. Her parents had been happy to see her learning the Holy Tongue. But her father came to envy her knowledge, and he drew us apart. Ah, sir, surely she will not forget all that I taught her. She will brood over the poems I have written, and though she has left me she will hold fast to my teachings.

One day I went into town and saw Leah's father and swiftly made to leave. But he ran after me and said, "Why have you run off, I must talk to you." My heart pounded. I knew he had nothing to say that could possibly calm me and yet I stood and listened. He is Leah's father, I thought, he will speak of Leah. He then glanced sideways and seeing no one in sight, continued, "My daughter is ill. She suffers from the same illness as her brother." I remained silent and he continued as he had begun, "She was not born for toil, physical labor will be the death of her. If I don't assure her complete rest she will die before my own time has come." He appeared suddenly to take fright at his own words. At last he raised his voice and blurted out, "Mintz is a wealthy man, her health will be restored under his care. That is why I have promised her to him. He will send her to the mineral springs and will provide for all her needs."

"Ah, sir, another illness altogether afflicts your daughter's heart, which all the spas cannot heal. And I said I would cure her, but you drew us apart."

As I moved away from the man I slipped off the ring Leah had given to me. For she is engaged to another man. And a sudden chill swept over my finger.

So ended the chronicles of Akaviah Mazal.

Twice, three times a week my father arrived at the Gottliebs and dined with us in the garden. A soothing dusk veiled the table and dishes. We ate by the light of the fireflies. The red lanterns by the tracks lit up the night, for the railroad was not far from the Gottliebs' home. Rarely was my mother's name mentioned. And when Mrs. Gottlieb did speak of her you could not tell that the name of the departed was on her lips. Only when I grew accustomed to her words did I understand that she acted out of good sense.

My father made every possible effort to turn the conversation to my mother, may she rest in peace, exclaiming, "We are the miserable widowers." How strange his words were—it was as if all of womankind had died and every man was a widower.

One day Mr. Gottlieb journeyed to see his brother. He was a wealthy man and Gottlieb hoped he might join his business and contribute to the factory's expansion. Mintshi, who normally did not like to interfere in her husband's affairs, let slip more than she wished. Suddenly she realized what she had done and seemed to ask me to forget what she had just recounted, and she told me of her first visit to her father-in-law's house when the groom had entered and welcomed her, and then had turned on his heel and left. Mintshi had been greatly distressed by his abrupt manner. But he was no sooner gone than he returned, and before she had time to recover he asked to kiss her and she had drawn back, offended. Mintshi had not known at the time that she had been greeted at first not by the groom, but by his brother, whose features were identical to the groom's.

The holidays were coming to an end. "Stay until Tuesday evening," my father said. "I will come Tuesday evening and we will return home together." He was suddenly seized by a spasm of coughing. Mintshi poured him a glass of water. "Have you caught a cold, Mr. Mintz?" she asked my father. "Indeed," he answered, "I have considered leaving my work." We listened in astonishment as he continued, "If not for my daughter I would wipe my hands clean of my trade." How strange a reply. Does a man leave his trade because of a slight cold? To wear a long face would only have led him to think that he was ill. And so Mrs. Gottlieb said, "What will you do then, write books?" We all laughed. He, the merchant, such a practical man, sitting down and writing books.

The train's whistle sounded. Mrs. Gottlieb exclaimed, "My husband should be here in ten minutes," and fell silent. Our conversation was cut short as we waited for Mr. Gottlieb to arrive. Mr. Gottlieb entered. Mintshi peered at him intently; her eyes ran over her spouse. Gottlieb rubbed the tip of his nose and chuckled like a man intending to amuse his listeners. He then spoke to us of his travels and what had happened at his brother's home. On arriving, he had found his brother's wife sitting with her son. And he lifted the boy up on his lap and leaped up and whirled him about. They had been surprised, for the boy followed him fearlessly even though he had never seen him before. Mr. Gottlieb's brother entered while they were playing and the boy stared first at his father and then at his father's brother—his eyes darting from one to the other in disbelief. All of a sudden he turned his face away, burst into tears and flung his small arms out to his mother, and she embraced him as he buried his face in her bosom.

⊱⊰⊱⊰

I returned home and to school. And my father found me a new Hebrew teacher, a Mr. Segal with whom I studied for many days. Mr. Segal came three times a week, and not liking to skip from subject to subject, divided my studies into three parts: one day of the week I studied the Bible, another, grammar, and on the third day I studied composition. Segal set out to explain the Holy Writings in a lucid manner, and he did not refrain from teaching me the commentaries of our Sages. Hours were spent over such commentaries and exegeses, leaving us little time for the Book. He spoke to me of all the splendors which until then I had not found in books. Wishing to revive our language, whenever I spoke he would say, "Please, say it in Hebrew." He spoke with a certain flourish, like an advocate, and delighted whenever he stumbled upon a passage that resonated in his heart, for a prophet had spoken, and the prophets, after all, knew Hebrew.

Of all the hours spent in study I cherished most those devoted to composition. Segal would relax and lean back, his left hand under his head and his eyes firmly shut. Ever so quietly he would read from the wellsprings of his heart without glancing even once at the book. Like a musician plying his instrument during the darkest hour of the night, his heart brimming to its banks, without a glance at his notes, playing only what God had placed in his heart—so was this man.

My father paid Segal three *gulden* a month for my studies. After clipping the notes together, I would quietly hand them over to Segal. Segal, however, counted the money openly, and exclaimed, "I am not a doctor and needn't be paid furtively. I'm a worker and am not ashamed to receive a salary for my labors."

And my father toiled ceaselessly at his work. Nor did he rest at night. When I went to sleep he would remain seated by the lamplight. Sometimes I rose in the morning to find the light still lit beside him, for being preoccupied with his accounts he would forget to extinguish the light. My mother's name no longer hovered on his lips.

On the eve of Yom Kippur my father bought two candles: one candle, the candle of the living, he lit in the house, and the other, the memorial candle, he took to the synagogue. My father brought the candle to the synagogue, and as I accompanied him, he said, "Don't forget, tomorrow is Remembrance Day for the souls of the dead." His voice shook as he spoke. I bent forward and kissed his hand.

We arrived at the synagogue. I peered through the lattice and saw one man greeting another in the midst of the assembly, asking forgiveness of the other. I then saw my father standing in front of a man without a prayer shawl, and I recognized Akaviah Mazal and my eyes misted with tears.

The cantor intoned *Kol Nidre* and his singing waxed from one moment to the next. The candles flickered and the building filled with light. The men swayed between the candles, their faces covered. How I loved the holiness of the day.

We returned home without speaking a word. The stars of silence in the firmament and the candles of the living in each home lit up our way. We took the path leading to the bridge, for my father said, "Let us rest by the water for a while, my throat is choked with dust." From within the rippling water the nocturnal stars peered out at the stars in the sky. The moon broke through the furrowed clouds and a low murmuring sound rose from the water. From his heavenly heights God sent forth silence. I shall never forget that night. The candle of the living bent its flame towards us as we arrived home. I read the *Shema* and slept till morning. I was roused from my sleep in the morning by my father's voice. We left for the house of prayer. The sky had veiled itself in white as was its custom in autumn. The trees cast their russet leaves earthward and the old womenfolk bestirred themselves to gather the leaves into their homes. From the surrounding farmhouses thin plumes of smoke rose where the dry leaves burned in the stoves. People wrapped in white garments swayed back and forth in the courtyards. We arrived at the synagogue and prayed, meeting in the courtyard between the morning prayer and the additional service, and then again between the additional service and the afternoon prayer. My father asked whether the fast was not too great a strain for me. How my father's voice confused me.

I barely saw my father during the holiday. I studied in a Polish school and we were not exempt from class during our own holidays. Returning from school at noon I would find my father and the neighbors crowded together in the *succah*. And I would eat by myself, as there was no place for women in the booth. But I was consoled by the coming of winter. Late in the evening we supped together and then bent over our work by the light of a single lamp. And the white oval shade cast its light over us as our heads merged into one black presence in the shadows. I prepared my lessons and my father put his accounts into order. At nine o'clock Kaila set before us three glasses of tea, two for my father and one for me. My father pushed aside ledger and pen, and reached for the glass of tea. One glass he drained steaming hot, and the second he drained cold after dropping into it a lump of sugar. We then resumed our work, I my lessons, and my father his accounts. At ten o'clock my father would rise, stroke my hair, and say, "And now go to sleep, Tirtza." How I loved his use of the conjunction "and". I always grew happy in its presence: it was as though all that my father told me was but the continuation of his innermost thoughts. That is, first he spoke to me from within his heart and then out loud. And so I would say to my father, "If you are not going to sleep I too will not sleep, I will stay up with you until you go to sleep." But my father did not pay attention to my words, so I would go to bed. And when I woke I would find my father still bent over his accounts, his ledgers crowding the table. Had he risen early or had he not slept the entire night? I did not ask nor did I ever find out. Late into the night I told myself: I will go now and appeal to his heart, perhaps he will listen to me and rest. But I would fall fast asleep before ever getting out of bed. I knew my father intended to leave his business, and that wishing to set his accounts in order, he now bent over his affairs with redoubled effort. I did not ask what he would do afterwards.

I turned sixteen and was no longer obliged by law to attend school. When the school year came to an end my father sent me to a teacher's college. He did not send me because of my talents. I had no talent for teaching, but I showed little enthusiasm for anything else as yet. I believed at the time that a person's future was determined by others. And I told myself so be it. My relatives and friends were baffled. How in the world will Mintz make a teacher out of his daughter?

To labor is our lot and therein lies all hope. We knew the teachers among the Hebrew women to be different from the Christian, for the former were sent to remote hamlets where, being Jewish, they were harassed by the cruel-hearted villagers. And one's earnings were quite spent by the time one arrived at the village, for all of it went on travel. And yet a great number of Hebrew women attended the college.

The college was a private institution and Mazal was employed there as a teacher. Once a year the principal traveled with his pupils to the district capital where the pupils were examined. The schoolgirls then applied themselves to their studies with redoubled effort. A girl was put to shame if she returned without a certificate in her hand, for the travel expenses were high. And she made herself a new dress before departing, and if she returned from the examination and had failed, her rival would say, "Why, you have a new dress. I don't believe I've ever seen it before." "It is not new," the girl would answer. And the other would say, "Didn't you sew it to wear for your examinations? But where is your certificate?" And if the girl happened not to be wearing her new dress, she was asked, "But where is your new dress, the one for your examinations?" That's how they would remind her of her shameful lack of a certificate. This is why the girls labored unceasingly at their studies. If the brain did not grasp then they drilled their lessons in by rote, for what the brain cannot do, memory shall.

I was surprised that Mazal gave no sign of recognizing me when I arrived at the college. I asked myself: do I not find favor in his eyes? Does he not know who I am? For days on end I could not keep myself from brooding over such feelings, and I studied twice as hard and was never idle.

In those days I loved to take solitary walks. No sooner had I finished my lessons than I would set forth to the open fields. If I happened to meet a friend on the way I did not call out a greeting, and when hailed I answered in a low voice, lest the person join me, when all I desired was to walk alone. Winter had arrived.

One evening I was out walking when I heard a dog barking and then the sound of a man's footsteps. I recognized the man: it was Mazal. And I wound my handkerchief around my hand and waved it before him in greeting. Mazal stopped in his tracks and asked, "What is wrong, Miss Mintz?" "The dog," I replied. "Did the dog bite you?" he asked, startled. "The dog bit me," I answered. "Show me your hand," he said, almost breathless. "Please," I said, "bind the handkerchief for me over my wound." Mazal took hold of my hand with shaking fingers, and as he held my hand I unwound the handkerchief and jumped up in the air, exclaiming as I laughed out loud, "There is nothing, sir! Neither a dog, nor a wound." Mazal was so taken aback by my words that for a moment he could only stand there frozen, knowing not whether to scold me or laugh. But he quickly recovered, and then he too laughed loudly and cheerfully, and said, "Ah, you are a bad girl. How you frightened me." He then accompanied me home, and before leaving he stared deep into my eyes. And I told myself: surely he now knows that I know he knows my secret. But I thought to myself, I will be grateful if you do not remind me of that which you do know.

That night I tossed and turned in my bed. I thrust my hand into my mouth and stared at the designs on my handkerchief. I regretted not having asked Mazal into the house. If Mazal had entered we would now be sitting in the room and I would not be nursing such delusions. The following morning I rose and gloomily paced about

overwrought with emotions. Now I stretched out on my bed and
now on the carpet, and I was beguiled by a fickle wind of delusions.
Only towards evening was I able to calm down. I was like someone
with a case of nerves who dozes off during the day and starts awake
at night. Calling to mind all that I had done the previous day I rose
and tied a red string around my wrist as a reminder.

The days of Hanukkah had arrived and geese were slaughtered.
One day Kaila left to ask the rabbi a question and a man well advanced
in age appeared. "When will your father be coming home?" he asked,
and I replied, "Sometimes he comes at eight and sometimes at seven-
thirty." "In that case I am early," he declared, "for it is now five-thirty."
I said, "Yes, it is five-thirty." And he said, "It doesn't matter."

I drew up a chair for him. "But why should I sit," he said.
"Bring me some water." And as I poured him tea into a glass, he
exclaimed, "He asked for water and she gave him tea." He then poured
some of the tea from the glass onto his hand and cried out, "Well,
well, and the *mizrah*?" Turning towards the wall he continued, "In
your grandfather's house a man didn't have to ask such questions, for
the *mizrah* hung on the wall." He then rose to his feet and prayed. I
took two, three large, dollops of goose fat and placed them in a bowl
on the table. The man finished praying and ate and drank and said, his
lips dripping with fat, "Schmaltz, my dear, schmaltz." "Here," I said,
"I will bring you a napkin to wipe your hands." "Rather bring me a
slice of cake," he said. "Do you have a cake that doesn't require hand
washing?" "Yes, and enough to spare," I said. "I will bring you some
cake at once." "Please don't hurry, you can bring the cake along with
the second helping. Will you not give me another helping?" "Why,
of course." "I knew you would, but you still don't know who I am. It
doesn't matter," the man said softly. "I'm Gotteskind. So your father
is indeed late today." I glanced at my watch. "It is a quarter after six,
my father will not arrive before half-past seven." "It doesn't matter,"
he repeated. "But do go on with your work. Don't let me disturb
you." I reached for a book. And he said, "What's that you have in
your hands?" "A book of geometry," I replied. Gotteskind seized the
book and asked, "And do you know how to play the piano as well?
No? Why didn't they teach you how to play the piano? Why, I've just

come from the pharmacy where the pharmacist told me he would never wed a woman who didn't know how to play the piano. 'Listen, Gotteskind,' the pharmacist said, 'I'm prepared to live in a small town since I can't afford to buy a pharmacy in the city.' But I failed to mention that he isn't really a pharmacist but the pharmacist's assistant. But what does it matter, assistant pharmacist, pharmacist, it's all one and the same. Surely you'll say: why, he doesn't even own a pharmacy. It doesn't matter, soon enough he'll purchase himself a pharmacy. 'And so, Gotteskind,' the pharmacist said to me, 'here I am about to settle down in a small town. If my wife doesn't play the piano she will surely die of boredom.' So, knowing how to play an instrument is a rare gift indeed, apart from the enjoyment of striking the keys, think of it also as a source of wisdom. But the hour of seven is about to strike and though I said I would go, will your father not be arriving soon?" Gotteskind stroked the wisps of his beard and continued, "Indeed, your father should realize that a faithful friend is waiting for him. And so, man knows least where his good fortune lies. The clock is striking two, three, four, five, six, seven. Let the clock be witness to the truth of my words." I grew weary, but Gotteskind prattled on, "Why, you didn't know who I was, nor did you hear mention of my name until today. And I knew you before you were formed, it was through my good services that your mother wedded your father."

He was still talking when Kaila arrived and we set the table. "You are also an accomplished housekeeper?" Gotteskind exclaimed with surprise. "And you said your father will soon return. If so, let us wait for him," Gotteskind said, as though having just made up his mind to wait.

My father arrived a little before eight. "We mentioned your name and here you are," Gotteskind said to my father. "Lo, the clock has struck. It will be witness to the truth of my words." And he winked at my father and went on, "I came to see you but behold the Almighty has also shown me your daughter."

That night I dreamt my father gave me away in marriage to the high chief of an Indian tribe. My entire body was impressed with tattoos of kissing lips and my husband sat opposite me on the sharp edge of a crag, combing his beard with the seven talons of an eagle.

I was struck with wonder, for I was certain that Indians shaved their heads and beards. How then had my husband acquired such a thick crop of hair?

Four days had lapsed since I met with Mazal. I did not go to school. And I feared lest my father would take notice and fret over me. I was of two minds whenever I thought of returning to school. Perhaps I would blush with shame upon seeing Mazal? And if Mazal was absent that day perhaps I'd shudder in anticipation of the sound of his footsteps? And what if I arrived after classes had begun, and what if he then suddenly cast his eyes upon me? In the end I did leave for the college, but only to find another man reading out our lessons. I asked one of the students, "Why hasn't Mazal arrived today?" "He didn't come yesterday either, nor the day before, and who knows if he will ever return to the college," she replied. "Your words don't make any sense," I said. "A woman's hand is in the matter," she replied. I shuddered at her words. The girl went on to tell me how Mazal had been forced to leave the school because of the teacher Kefirmilch who received from his grandmother an allowance earned as a servant in Mazal's home. One day she had slipped the money in an envelope taken from her master's letterbox. Kefirmilch unsealed the envelope and discovered a letter written to Mazal by one of the schoolgirls in the college. It so happened that the girl's father had lent Kefirmilch some money. Kefirmilch now told the man, "Forget my debt and I will give you your daughter's letter written to her lover Mazal." And hearing what had happened, Mazal, left the college lest the institution's name be tainted by his presence.

I returned home, relieved at not having seen Mazal at the college, and I did not tell myself: he has been stripped of his livelihood. From now on I will rarely see Mazal but neither will I blush in shame if I should happen to see him. And I suddenly loathed going to school. I stayed at home and helped Kaila with the housework. How I recoiled in horror whenever I thought of the aging schoolmistresses. Should I waste my life bent over books I couldn't understand and end up like one of them? Caught in such thoughts I forgot my own work and neglected the housework. I longed to leave the house, to fill my lungs with fresh air and stretch my legs. I rose, buttoned my coat, and went out. Once on my way I turned in the direction of the Gottliebs' home. Mintshi hastened towards me and took my hand and warmed it in her own, and she peered deep into my eyes, eager to know what tidings I brought. "No news," I said. "I went out for a walk and turned in your direction." Mintshi took my coat and seated me by the stove. After drinking a glass of tea I stood up and prepared to leave, for I had heard that the tax inspector was expected for dinner and I was afraid I would disturb Mr. Gottlieb in his business affairs with him.

The earth was drenched in rain and I remained at home. All day long I read books or else sat in the kitchen and helped Kaila with her chores. Desire no longer tugged at my heartstrings. I knew no wrong.

At eight o'clock my father returned home. He quietly removed his shoes and slipped on a pair of felt slippers. The faint shuffle of his slippers brought back to mind the stillness of the house. The table had been set before his arrival and when he arrived we sat and ate. After dinner my father returned to his accounts and I sat by his side until ten o'clock, when he rose and said, "Now, my daughter, to bed." Sometimes he would stroke my hair with his warm hand and I bowed my head. My happiness was too great to bear. So the rains came and went.

The sun rose over the town and the puddles were nearly dry. I lay wide awake in the morning, unable to sleep, as I sensed that something ominous had taken place. I turned towards the window where a faint bluish light shone. How could such a light have existed unbeknownst to me? Several moments passed before I realized I had been fooled by the curtain. And still my happiness did not leave me.

I leapt out of bed and dressed. Something had happened. I would go now and see what it was. I ventured out. And I stood spellbound whichever way I turned. I peered into the shop windows and the windows glowed in the daylight. And I told myself, I will enter and purchase something. I did not know what I would buy, but I insisted, I'll buy something and Kaila won't have to trouble herself. But I did not go into any of the shops and I turned and set out towards the bridge at the edge of town. And there was a cluster of dwellings under the bridge on both sides of the banks. Pigeons flitted from roof to roof and a man and woman stood on one of the rooftops mending its shingles. I called out good-morning to them and they returned my greeting. And as I made to walk on, I caught sight of an old woman waiting, or so it seemed, for me to ask her the way. But I did not ask. I returned home and gathered my books and left for the college. But the college had become alien to me. This house is a den of boredom. I realized there wasn't a soul to whom I could pour out my heart, and my disdain grew and I could not bear my studies. So I thought, I will speak to Mazal. I did not know how he could help, still, I welcomed and toyed with the thought all day long. But how was I to approach him? I dared not approach his home, nor would I find him outside. Winter passed, the snow melted and we did not meet.

At that time my father fell ill and Mr. Gottlieb came to inquire of his health, and he told my father that he was expanding his factory, for on becoming a partner in the factory his brother had given freely of his own money and the government had stopped putting any obstacles in their way since an important minister had sought his help after taking a bribe. "My dear sir," the minister had told Gottlieb, "all the bureaucrats, including the Emperor himself, hunger for money. There isn't a minister in this country who won't accept a bribe. Let me give you an example," said the minister. "When we ask, what makes Mr. So-and-so unique, are we not surprised when we are told, why the length of his nose is five centimeters. But five centimeters is indeed the length of every proboscis." "Heaven forbid I should condemn them," Gottlieb said to my father, "but their hypocrisy maddens me. Today you shower them with gifts and tomorrow you are a complete stranger to them. In this I admire the Russian bureaucrats; at least they accept a bribe without pretending to be honest."

As I accompanied Gottlieb to the door he exclaimed, "From one sickbed to another." "Who is sick?" I asked, concealing my confusion. "Mr. Mazal is ill," Gottlieb answered. For a second I longed to accompany him. And yet I restrained myself and did not go.

"Isn't it amazing, Tirtza," my father said, "Gottlieb has always been a hardworking man and hasn't ever complained at being childless.

So who will inherit the fruit of his labors when his final hour comes?" My father asked me to bring his ledger and he sat up in bed and worked until suppertime. The following morning he rose from his sickbed in good health, and that afternoon left for the store, while I set out to Mazal's home.

I knocked on the door, but there was no sound nor did anyone answer. I then said, thank God, the man is not home. Still I did not move. All at once, thinking that no one was at home, my hand grew bold and I knocked loudly.

Several moments passed and my heart beat feebly. Suddenly I heard someone stirring within the house and I took fright. Just as I meant to go, Mazal appeared. He greeted me buried in his overcoat. I lowered my eyes, and said: "Mr. Gottlieb dropped by yesterday and mentioned that sir was taken ill and I have come to inquire of his health." Mazal did not say anything. He beckoned me into his home with one hand as he clutched his collar with the other. I shuffled my feet in misery and he said, "Forgive me, Miss, for I cannot speak like this," and he vanished into the back room only to reappear several moments later dressed in his best clothes. Mazal coughed. The room suddenly grew silent and the two of us were alone in the room. "Please, sit down, Miss," he said, drawing a chair to the stove. "Has your hand healed from the dog bite?" he inquired. I stared into his face, my eyes filling with tears. Mazal took my hand into his own. "Forgive me," he said. His soft voice was warm and full of compassion. Little by little I grew less embarrassed. I stared at the room I had known as a child and suddenly it seemed new to me. The heat from the stove warmed my body and my spirits revived within me.

Mazal put a log into the stove and I hastened to help him. But in my haste I thrust my hand out and knocked a photograph off the table. I reached out for it and noticed it was a photograph of a woman. She bore the appearance of a woman who never lacked a thing, and yet her brows were knitted in worry, for her happiness was uncertain. "It is a photograph of my mother," Mazal said as he set it in place. "There exists only a single photograph of her, for only once in her youth was she photographed. Many years have since passed. Her face no longer resembles the face you see in the photograph, but

I will always cherish the likeness of her face as captured here. It is as if time passed and yet nothing changed." What prompted Mazal to speak? Was it the room's stillness, or was it my sitting by his side at dusk? Mazal spoke at length, and he told me of all that had happened to his kind mother. And he said:

"My mother is a member of the Bauden-Bach family and all the Bauden-Bachs are apostates. Her grandfather, Rabbi Israel, was wealthier than all his countrymen. He had a winery and fields and villages. He gave generously to scholars and he built centers of religious study. And at the time his name was lauded in print, for he dispensed freely of his money and gold in honor of the Torah and in pursuit of its study.

In those days it was decreed that all lands owned by Jews would be confiscated. Hearing this, Rabbi Israel spared no effort to protect his land, but all his efforts came to naught. So he changed his religion and returned to his home and estate where he found his wife reciting the morning prayer. 'I have converted,' he announced. 'Hurry now and take the children to the priest.' The woman recited the *Aleinu*, saying, 'Who has not made us as the heathen of the land,' and she spat three times and pressed her lips to her prayerbook, and she and all her sons went and changed their religion. Close upon that time she bore a son who was circumcised by my great-grandfather, Rabbi Israel, for they kept the Lord's commandments and only in the eyes of the gentiles did they behave as Christians. And they rose in their station and received the same respect accorded to nobles. The new generation, however, forgot their God, their creator, nor did they return to their religion when the decree was nullified, nor were they God-fearing, nor did they live by the commandments of the Torah. The only commandment they followed was to sell their leaven to the rabbi's emissary on the eve of Passover, for otherwise Jews would not touch their corn wine. Such is the law concerning leaven which is not sold to a gentile on the eve of Passover. My mother is the granddaughter of the youngest son. And she sat over the catechism yet all the priest's efforts came to naught. But time is too short to recount all that she suffered until the day the Lord took mercy on her and she found peace in his shadow. For she was also sent to a convent school and she was placed in the hands of harsh teachers. But she did not follow their ways. And she bent her mind over what was sealed and concealed from her. One day my mother found a picture of her grandfather and he looked like a rabbi. 'Who is he?' she asked. 'It is your grandfather,' they replied. My mother was stunned. 'What are those locks of hair falling over his cheeks, and what is that book he is reading?' 'He is reading the Talmud and he is twirling his earlocks,' they answered, and they told her grandfather's story. Thereafter she walked about like a shadow and she tossed in her sleep at night on account of her dreams. Once her grandfather appeared and took her on his knees and she combed his beard. Another time she saw her grandmother holding a prayerbook in her hands. She then taught her the holy letters, and when she awoke she wrote down the letters on a tablet. It was a miracle, for until that day my mother had never set eyes on a Hebrew book.

And there worked in her father's home a young Jewish clerk and she told him, 'Teach me the laws of the Lord.' And he said, 'Alas, I know them not.' Just then the rabbi's emissary arrived to buy leaven. The clerk urged her, 'Speak to him.' And my mother told the emissary all that I have recounted. 'Madam,' said the man, 'Pray come to my home today and celebrate with us the Passover holiday.' So that night she went forth to the man's home and she dined with him and his family and her heart inclined towards the God of Israel and she longed to follow His laws. That clerk was my father, may he rest in peace. He never studied the Torah or the commandments, but God created him pure of heart. My mother cleaved unto him and together they cleaved unto their faith in God. After their wedding they left for Vienna, and said, 'No one will recognize us there.' And he lived by the sweat of his brow and they did not turn to my mother's father for help. My mother gradually adjusted to her new station. My father toiled at his work. And he deprived himself of the fruits of his own labor, his one desire being that I study in the best of schools, gaining through knowledge and science a footing in the best of society, for he knew that he would be unable to leave me any money to speak of on the day of his death. In my father's eyes it was as if I had been barred from my own inheritance, for had my mother not married him, I would now be the son of a noble family. But my mother had no such designs upon the world. She loved me as a mother loves her son." It was getting late and Mazal finished his account, and said, "Forgive me, Miss, for I have spoken at great length today." "Why excuse yourself," I replied, "when you have done me nothing but good. I now know that you do not despise me, for you have opened your heart to me. Oh, don't hold back your words anymore!" Mazal passed his hand across his eyes, "Heaven forbid that I should despise you," he exclaimed. "I am glad to have spoken of my mother and to have found an attentive ear, for I miss her a great deal. But since you feel I have been sparing with my words I will go on and tell you more." Mazal then told me how he had come here, and yet he did not mention my mother and her father. He spoke of the hard times he had endured. He had yearned with all his heart to complete what his mother had set out to accomplish upon returning to the God of Israel, for he had returned to his people. Yet they did not understand him. He walked as a stranger in their midst—they drew him close, but when he was as one of them they divided their hearts from him.

I returned home in high spirits. I reeled like a drunkard and the moon poured its beams and shone upon my path.

As I walked I said, what will I tell my father? If I speak of all that happened between Mazal and myself he will listen and grow angry. But if I am silent a barrier will rise between us. Now I will go and speak to him, even if he is incensed he will see that I have not concealed my actions from him. I arrived home at the same time as the doctor who had come to pay us a visit upon hearing that my father was ill, and I clamped my mouth shut and did not say a thing, for how could I speak out in front of a stranger? And I did not regret doing so, as my secret consoled me.

I sat peacefully at home. I did not join the company of other young girls, nor did I send letters of greeting. One day, however, the postman arrived with a letter for me. And the letter was written in Hebrew by a young man called Landau. "As the errant wayfarer raises his eyes to the godly stars on a bleak night," its author wrote, "so do I now dispatch my letter to you, fair and resourceful maiden." My teacher Segal appeared for our lesson as I was reading the letter. "I have received a letter written in Hebrew," I said. "I knew you would," he replied. Segal then told me the young man was a pupil of his and that he was the son of one of the village tenants.

Eight days passed and I forgot the letter. One day I left for the college and caught sight of a woman and a young man. Seeing the young man I was certain that he was the author of the letter. Later in the day I told my father and he laughed, saying, "The son of villagers." But I thought to myself, Why has the young man behaved this way and why this strange encounter? Suddenly I pictured the young man. I imagined his discomfort and how he had blushed and I regretted not having answered his letter in case he had waited for my reply and had been offended. I would write to him the very next day, I resolved. Though I did not know what I would write. My body then grew numb under the balmy weight of sleep. This is the sweet slumber in which the blood runs smoothly in our arteries and the soul is soothed. Two, three days passed without my penning a reply to the young man and I told myself, It is too late to answer. But it so happened that while preparing my homework and innocently scribbling with my pen on paper, I suddenly found myself replying to the young man. I wrote only a few lines, and reading over my letter I thought that surely this was not the sort of answer that he hoped to receive. Nor did the paper earn my favor. Still, I sent the letter knowing I would not write another of its kind. I will not write any more letters to him, I told myself, for my mind is not intent on letter-writing. Several days passed without a letter from the young man, and I was sorry not to hear from him. But I gradually forgot the young man and his letters. It had been my duty to reply and I had done so. One day my father asked me, "Do you remember the woman and young man?" "I remember," I replied. "Well," he said, "the young man's father came to see me and he spoke of his son. The family is a good family and the young man is learned." "Will he come here?" I asked. "How can I know," he replied. "But I will do as you decide, for you have not kept your thoughts from me." I bowed my head. God, Thou hast known my heart. "So then," my father added, "we will not go to the stargazers and astrologers, nor will we ask them whether my daughter will find a groom." And he did not refer to the matter again.

One Sunday evening my father came home accompanied by a man. He asked us to set the kettle on the fire and light the large lamp, and he also looked to see whether the stove gave off a warm glow. Then they sat by the table and talked. The man did not take his eyes off me. I returned to my room to work. But as soon as I sat down at my desk a winter carriage drew to a halt under my window and Kaila came and announced, "Guests have arrived. Why not go straight to the living room." "I can't," I said, "for I have a great deal of work to finish today." But Kaila wouldn't leave me alone, and she said, "It is a night that calls for celebration, your father has ordered me to make blintzes." "In that case," I replied, "In that case I will help you prepare the meal." "No," Kaila insisted, "get you now into the living room. The man who has just arrived is a handsome lad." "Is Gotteskind also present?" I asked Kaila disdainfully. "Who?" she said. "Gotteskind," I replied. "Have you forgotten the man and all he had to tell us?" "Your memory is a marvel, Tirtza," Kaila replied, and left.

The food was ready to be served and I entered the living room and stared in astonishment, for the young man was now transformed into another person altogether. He no longer seemed ill at ease as when I had first seen him. And his black goatskin hat heightened the charm of his red cheeks.

Landau soon returned a second time. He arrived in a winter carriage wearing a wolfskin overcoat. And he smelled of a winter forest. No sooner had he sat down than he was up on his feet again. He was on his way to see the coppersmith and had passed by to ask whether I would join him on his journey. My father gave me his fur coat and we left.

We galloped under the moonlight along trails powdered with snow. The gleam of hooves mingled with the song of the horses' harness bells. I sat to the right of the young man and gazed out of the animal pelt. Buried in my overcoat I was unable to speak. Landau reined in the horses in front of the smith's house and alighted. He then lifted me out of the carriage and we entered. Our glasses were filled with brandy

and apples were baked in our honor. And Landau asked the smith to
come to our village the following day as the kegs in the winery needed
mending. The members of the household hung on his every word, for
he spoke with the authority of a prince. I too stared at Landau and
was astonished. Was this the young man whose letters were the outcry
of a solitary heart? On our way back I did not bury my face in the
folds of my overcoat, as I had grown used to the cold. And yet we did
not exchange a word, for my heart was girded in silence. Landau too
remained silent, only now and then speaking to his horses.

And my father said to me, "The old man Landau has spoken
to me of his son, for his heart is drawn to your heart, and now tell
me what I should say." Seeing my discomfort, however, he added,
"There is time for us to talk about the matter, after all, the young man
is not about to be conscripted into the army and you are still young."
Several days passed and Landau once again began writing me high-
flown letters filled with visions of Israel and its land. His roots were
in the village and since boyhood he had tilled its soil, and the land
did not cease to nourish him with dreams and visions. With time his
letters stopped arriving and he would occasionally come into town
on foot. He was constantly on edge lest he be found fit enough to
be pressed into the king's army. He would roam at night in the market and streets with the penitents. I shuddered in anguish whenever
I recalled their late-night melodies. And I thought of my uncle, my
mother's brother, who had come to an untimely end in the army. So
I told myself that if only I could accept Landau I would now be his
wedded wife. One day I ran into Landau on his way into town. His
eyes were sunken and his cheeks sallow and his clothes reeked of stale
tobacco. He had the appearance of a sick man. Returning home I
seized hold of a book, telling myself, I will study and soothe my grief.
But my throat hurt and I could not study. I then opened the book
of Psalms and read out loud. Perhaps God will think of him and the
young man will not perish.

And at the Gottliebs workers were busy constructing a left wing
to serve as a home for Gottlieb's brother who, as partner to the factory,
had come to live with him. Once the wing was completed Gottlieb
held a housewarming party. Until that day Gottlieb had never held

a housewarming party, for only then was the house built to his liking. Gottlieb was transformed. He even altered the cut of his beard. I saw the two brothers and laughed, remembering how Mintshi had been startled when she had first come to their father's home. During lunch Gottlieb removed a letter from his pocket and said to his wife, "I almost forgot, a letter has arrived from Vienna." And she asked, "Is there any news?" "No news," he said. "He sends his blessings for the housewarming. And his mother's condition hasn't changed—it's neither better nor worse." I realized they were speaking of Mazal, for I had heard his mother had taken ill and that he had left for Vienna to see to her health. And I recalled the day I had visited his home and the memory was a blessing to me.

After the meal Mintshi strolled with me into the garden. She had been restless while sitting with her sister-in-law and now she looked back on earlier times. "Screwy," she suddenly called out, and a small dog leaped towards her. I almost took fright. Mintshi fondly patted his head and said, "Screwy, Screwy, Screwy, my boy." Although I disliked dogs I stroked his coat and patted him. The dog looked at me warily and then barked in approval. I hugged Mintshi and she kissed me.

Their large home stood a short distance away. The clamor of children and the untiring sound of a woman's voice rose from within. The sun set and streaked the treetops red and a sudden gust of cold wind blew. "It has been a hot day," Mintshi said in a low voice. "Summer is almost over. Ah, I cannot bear all this commotion. Since the day they arrived even the birds in the garden have fallen silent." The dog barked a second time and Mintshi growled back, "What's wrong, Screwy?" She then turned to me and said, "Have you noticed, Tirtza, how a dog will bark whenever the postman approaches?" "We don't have a dog at home," I replied, "and no one writes me any letters." Paying no attention to my words, Mintshi continued, "The letter my sister-in-law sent after she left, telling me of her safe return, was delayed, for apparently it had slipped behind the gate and the postman had scribbled on the envelope, 'I have not delivered this letter to your door because of the dog.' Screwy, my clever one, come here!" Mintshi called out to the dog and resumed stroking his coat.

The evening twilight enveloped us and a light lit up the windows. "Let's go in, Tirtza, and prepare supper." As we walked back Mintshi said, "Mazal will soon return," and she embraced me. We entered the house. That evening the factory hands came to toast their masters, as they had not come during the day when the guests had been present. Mintshi set a table for them and when their hearts were merry with wine, they burst into song. And the worker who had been released from prison warmed our hearts with tales he had heard straight from the mouths of the prisoners. Gottlieb rubbed the tip of his nose, as was his way. I looked at Mintshi. Her face exuded verve and vigor and her sorrow was nowhere to be seen.

The holidays were over and the autumn skies lowered over the town. My father was preoccupied with his business and did not come home for lunch. I came to appreciate the autumn season and the splendor of its might. The sight of the russet woods and coppery leaves fortified the land far and wide.

My studies at the college resumed and grew more serious. That year our tutors ushered us into the classroom where we were expected to show our skills in teaching. I displayed little talent. Even so, I did as I was told.

Akaviah Mazal returned to town. He spoke to the local chroniclers and gathered material on the history of our town. When he unearthed ancient relics in the cemetery, Mazal's heart was so filled with joy in his work that he did not even heed the principal's summons to resume teaching at the college, for Kefirmilch had long been forgotten.

At that time my father's sister arrived, for her daughter's praises were being sung here and she had come to see the young man. This aunt of mine was quite unlike my father in the way she took pleasure in life. "I am glad, my daughter," my father said, "that you are fond of your aunt. She is a good woman and she is gracious and pleasant in every way. And yet I am not fond of her; perhaps it is because of you that I disapprove of her." And he fell silent.

My aunt returned to her home at the end of autumn. I cut across the open fields on my way back from the train station. The train's whistle faded in the air. Potatoes were unearthed from the bare fields that shimmered under the yellow sun and red currants gazed up. I remembered the tale of the currants and I walked in a daze.

I passed a farmhouse where I had bought fruit in the summer and the farmer gave me a bouquet of asters. I took the autumn flowers and continued on my way. Now as I walked home I noticed I was close to Mazal's home. I will go there and bid him good day, I thought to myself, for I have not seen him since he returned.

Mazal was not at home and the old servant sat by the doorway, waiting for him. Because of her grandson, Kefirmilch, she had had to leave her master's house, and she had gone to live in a neighboring village. And now, on her way into town with her harvest of wheat, she had stopped to see how he was faring. The old woman spoke of her master's good deeds. I was pleased to hear such words of praise, and as I turned to leave I scattered my flowers by the door.

Several days later we received a parcel from my aunt. She had also thought of Kaila and sent her a new dress. My father looked and said, "So, she has sent gifts. But she did not come to look after you when your mother passed away." Only then did I understand why my father resented his sister.

Autumn drew to an end. A tinge of leaden white obscured the eye of the heavens as swirls of mist were driven every which way and the rooftops shone under a thin drizzle of rain. A tainted melancholy spread over the land. The last shriveled leaves bent under the weight of the raindrops. Clouds, wind, rain, and cold. The raindrops chilled and froze and pricked like needles in the flesh. The stove was lit and Kaila spread thatches of hay on the windowsills. The stove blazed the entire day as Kaila cooked for winter. Soon snow began to fall and cover the lanes, and bells from the winter carriages jingled merrily. Leaving the college one day I caught sight of some girls with ice-skates slung over their shoulders. They were going to skate on the river, and they persuaded me to join them. I bought myself a pair of ice skates and slid along the ice with them. Snow drifts covered the frozen earth. The woodsmen chopped timber in the streets and the crisp winter air mingled with the fragrance of wood shavings and split wood. The days grew colder, the snow creaked under the soles of every passerby. And I raced along with my girlfriends, swallowing the river with our skates.

Those were fine times when I skated on the river. My body grew stronger and my eyes widened in their orbs and were no longer overcast with melancholy. My flesh and bones had found a cure. I ate heartily and when I sat down to read a book I lost all sense of myself. Twice on returning home I tiptoed up to Kaila as she bent over her work and suddenly lifted her into the air. Kaila cried out in vain, for I clashed my skates together and the din drowned out her voice.

But such times did not last for long. Although the sun was not to be seen, the snow melted. And when I went down to the river I found it deserted. The ice had almost thawed and crows perched on the loose floes of ice. It was then I felt sharp stabbing pains in my chest, and the doctor came and gave me medicine, and forbade me to exert myself over my lessons. "But sir," I said, "I have to complete my studies this year." "If that is so," he replied, "your turn to teach the villagers will come a year from now." And having gone that winter with the schoolgirls to skate on the ice I grew almost fond of the college. If the thing on which love depends ceases, love ceases.

Now the house was swept clean for the Passover holiday. And I fetched old books from the closet to give them a good airing. Whenever I found a book with a damaged binding I told myself, I will take it to the bookbinders. And rummaging through the closet I found the *mizrah* that had hung in the home of my mother's father, and I tucked it into my bag along with the books, intending to take it to the glazier, for its glass casing and gilt frame were cracked and scraped, and the crimson ribbon that my mother, may she rest in peace, had used to hang the *mizrah* was torn. And as I was about to leave, the seamstress arrived with my new spring dress. I quickly slipped on the dress, put on my hat and set out with the books and the *mizrah* for the bookbinder and the glazier. While at the bookbinder Mazal came in and stared at the books I had brought and then at the *mizrah* that was wrapped in broad sheets of paper, and he asked, "What is that book?" I removed the paper and said, "One moment, sir," and I unwound the string that I had twisted round my hand after running into Mazal and the dog, and I fastened the string to the *mizrah* and hung it on the wall. Mazal stared in disbelief. I read what was written on the *mizrah*: Blessed is he who shall not forsake Thee. Mazal bowed his head. I blushed and my eyes filled with tears. One moment I longed to cry out: You have brought upon me this shame! And the next moment I longed to prostrate myself before him. I made to leave, not wanting to linger at the bookbinder's.

But I stepped outside only to find Mazal standing on my right. I laughed and said loudly, "Now you know, sir." My throat burned and I could hardly bear the sound of my own voice. Mazal grasped my hand. His hand shook like his voice. He looked askance and said, "Soon we shall be seen." I dried my tears and tidied my hair. "Let them look," I said, still upset. "It's all the same to me." We walked on for a short while and, reaching the corner of my street, Mazal said, "Here is your father's house." I stared hard into his face. "I will not go home," I declared. Mazal remained silent. I was at a loss where to go. Many thoughts stirred within me and I feared lest Mazal abandon me without my having said a thing. Meanwhile we left the town behind and approached the edge of the woods. The verdant forest was about to burst into leaf. Birch trees opened their buds and a new sun rose over the woods. Mazal said, "Spring has arrived." And he gazed at my face and knew I was annoyed by his words. And he swept the palm of his hand over his head and sighed.

I sat on a tree trunk and Mazal was ill at ease and groped for words. He stared at my dress, my spring dress, and said, "The tree is still damp and you are wearing a light dress." I knew the tree was damp and that my dress was light. All the same I did not rise and I even took pleasure in my discomfort. Mazal turned pale, his eyes dimmed and an odd smile swept over his lips. I thought he would ask, Has your hand healed from the dog bite? My spirits weighed upon me. But I suddenly sensed a joy which until that moment I had never experienced, a wonderful warmth kindled within my heart. I quietly smoothed my soft dress. It seemed then that the man with whom I sat in the woods on that early spring day had already revealed to me all that was harbored in his heart. And I was startled to hear Mazal say, "I heard your voice at night. Was it you at my window?" "I was not by your window," I replied, "however I have called out to you from my bed at night. I think of you every day, and I looked for traces of you in the cemetery, by my mother's grave. Last summer I left some flowers and you came and went but you did not stop to smell my flowers." "Now let me tell you something," Mazal said, "such feelings will pass. You are still young. Another man has not captured your heart yet. That is why your heart is set upon mine. The men you have met were shallow, whereas you were not bored in my company and so you swore to yourself, It is he. But what will you do the day you find the man who will really capture your heart? As for me, I have come to the age when all I desire is some peace and quiet. Think of your future, Tirtza, and admit it is best we part before it is too late." I gripped the tree trunk and a stifled cry escaped from within me. "Let us remain good friends," Mazal said, placing his hand on my head. "Friends!" I cried out. How I loathed such romantic nonsense. Mazal stretched out his warm hand and I leaned forward and kissed his hand. And Mazal rested his head on my shoulder, which he then kissed.

The sun set and we made our way home. A spring chill, doubly potent after a sunlit day, settled in my bones. "We must talk again," Mazal said. "When, when?" I asked. Mazal repeated my words as though he did not grasp their meaning. "When? Tomorrow, before dusk, in the forest." "Fine." I looked at my watch and asked, "At what time?" "At what time?" Akaviah repeated, "At six o'clock." I bent over my watch and kissed the very same numeral on the face of the watch. And I relished the warmth of the watch that hung over my heart.

I made my way home and my body shook all over. My bones quaked from the cold as I walked, and I told myself: once home it will pass. But when I got home, rather than diminish the fever only grew worse. I lost all desire to eat and my throat burned. Kaila brewed me some tea and added sugar and a slice of lemon. I drank the tea and lay on my bed and pulled up the covers. But I was not warmed.

I awoke, my throat burning. And I lit a candle and then snuffed it out, for its flickering flame hurt my eyes. The wick's thin curl of smoke and my cold hands only increased my discomfort. The clock struck and I took fright, as I imagined that I was late in meeting Mazal in the forest. I counted the hours and prayed to God to keep the hour we'd arranged to meet from ever arriving. Three, four, five. Ah, I should get up, but I was overcome by sleep. Why couldn't I sleep until now? Soon I would meet Mazal, a restless night in my eyes. I must get out of bed and rid myself of any traces of sleep. But how can I wash when I have caught such a bad cold? I fumbled against the bedposts and finally managed to get out of bed. I shivered from cold and knew not where I stood. Here is the doorway, or is it the closet door? Where are the matches, and where the window? Why has Kaila drawn the curtains? I could slip and crack my skull against the table or stove—damn it! Where is the lamp? This time I won't find a thing, perhaps I've been struck blind. And now, just as I've lost all hope of finding myself a man, Akaviah Mazal will take me to be his wedded wife, and as one who leads the blind, so will Mr. Mazal lead me. Ah, why did I even dare talk to him? I have found my bed, thanks to a merciful God. I lay on the bed and covered myself, yet I fancied that I was still on my feet, walking. I tramped for a good many hours. Where to? An old woman stood by the road waiting for me to ask her the way. Wasn't she the old woman I first saw last month, when one bright day I ventured out of town? The old woman opened her mouth. "Here she is," she said. "I barely recognized you, aren't you Leah's daughter? Aren't you Leah's daughter," the old woman exclaimed, snuffing tobacco. And prattling on she did not allow me a word in edgewise. I nodded my head: Yes, I was Leah's daughter. The old woman said, "I said you were Leah's daughter didn't I, while you swept by me as if it did not matter a straw. The lambs are ignorant of the pastures where their mothers grazed." The old woman snuffed a second time, "Did I not nurse your mother with my own milk?" I knew this to be a dream, yet I was confused: my mother had never been nursed at the breast of a stranger, how dare the old woman claim she had nursed my mother. I hadn't seen the old woman for a great many days, nor had I thought of her, and this gave me further cause for surprise. So why had she suddenly accosted me in my dream? Wondrous are the ways of dreams and who knows their paths.

My father's footsteps woke me and I saw that he was sad. He gazed at me with tenderness through his bloodshot eyes. I felt ashamed of the mess in my room. My new dress and my stockings lay scattered on the floor. For a moment I forgot it was my father who stood before me, all I could think of was that a man was present in my room. I shut my eyes, filled with shame. I then heard my father's voice addressing Kaila, who stood by the door, "She's asleep." "Good morning, father," I called out, no longer ashamed. "Weren't you sleeping? So how are you my child?" "I'm fine," I replied, straining to speak in a clear voice, but a spasm of coughing took hold of me. "I caught a slight cold and now I will get up, for my cold is over." "Thank God!," my father said. "But I suggest that you stay in bed today my child." "No, I must get up," I cried out stubbornly, for I imagined my father would prevent me from going to my groom.

I knew that I had to throw myself on my father's mercy. Perhaps he would forgive me for having done that which is forbidden. My good father, my good father, I called out from within my heart, and I took courage and exclaimed, "Father, I was betrothed yesterday." My father stared at me. I longed to lower my eyes, yet took heart and called out, "Father, didn't you hear?" My father remained silent, thinking I had spoken out of my fever, and he whispered something to Kaila that I could not hear. He then went to the window to see if it was shut. Regaining my strength I sat up in bed and said to him "Although I caught a chill I am now better, sit by the bed, for I have something to tell you. Let Kaila come too, I have no secrets to hide." My father's eyes seemed to bulge out of their sockets and worry dimmed their light. He sat on the bed and I said, "Yesterday I met and spoke to Mazal. Father, what is wrong?" "You are a bad girl," Kaila exclaimed, frightened. "Hush, Kaila," I retorted. "I have opened my heart to Mazal. But why go on like this, I am betrothed to him." "Who ever heard of such a thing?" Kaila exclaimed, wringing her hands in despair. My father calmed Kaila down and asked, "When was this done?" "I do not remember," I replied, "even though I glanced at my watch I have forgotten the hour." "Have you ever heard of such a thing," my father said in embarrassment and laughed. "She doesn't know when it happened." I too laughed and all at once I heaved a deep sigh and my body shook. "Calm down, Tirtza," my father said in a worried voice. "Lie in bed for a while, later we will talk." And as he turned to go I called out after him, "Father, promise not to speak to Mazal until I tell you to do so." "What can I do," he exclaimed, and left the house.

As soon as he had gone, I took pen, ink and paper and wrote: *My dearly beloved, I won't be able to come today to the forest, for I have caught a cold. Several days hence I will come to you. In the meantime, be well. I am lying in bed and I am happy, for you dwell in my thoughts all day, undisturbed.* I then bade Kaila send the letter. "To whom have you written," she asked, letter in hand, "the teacher?" Knowing that Kaila did not know how to read or write, I replied in anger, "Read and find out for yourself." "Don't foam at the mouth, my bird," Kaila said. "The man is old while you are young and full of life. Why, you are just a child and barely weaned at that. If it weren't for my rheumatism I would carry you in my arms. But I have been thinking of your decision. Why fuss over a man?" "Good, good, good," I cried out laughing. "Hurry now and send the letter, for there is no time to waste." "But you haven't drunk your tea yet," Kaila said. "Let me bring you something hot to drink and water to wash your hands with." Kaila soon returned with the water. The chill subsided somewhat, my body grew warm under the bedcovers, and my weary bones seemed to melt into the sheets. Although my head burned, its heat was soothing. My eyes flamed in their sockets, and yet my heart was content and my thoughts had calmed. "Look, you've let the tea go cold," Kaila exclaimed, "and I've already brought you something hot to drink. It's all because of your endless brooding and soul-searching." I laughed and was overcome by a pleasant weariness. I barely managed to call out, "Don't forget the letter," before a welcome slumber settled over my eyes.

The day waned and Mintshi Gottlieb arrived. "I heard you were ill," she said, "and I have come to see how you are feeling." I knew my father had sent for her and so I concealed my thoughts and said, "I caught cold, but now I am well." Suddenly I seized hold of her hand and stared into her eyes, and said, "Why are you so quiet, Mrs. Gottlieb?" "But we haven't stopped talking," Mintshi replied. "Although we haven't stopped talking we haven't mentioned what is really important." "What's so important?" Mintshi exclaimed in surprise. And suddenly she added sourly, "Did you expect me to congratulate you?" I placed my right hand over my heart and thrust my left hand towards her, crying, "Indeed, why haven't you congratulated me?" Mintshi frowned. "Don't you know, Tirtza, that Mazal is very dear to me, and you are a young girl, while he is forty years old? Even though you are young, you can plainly see that a few years hence he will be like a withered tree whereas your youthful charm will only grow." I listened and then cried out, "I knew what you would say, but I will do what I must." "What you must?" exclaimed Mrs. Gottlieb in astonishment. "The obligations of a faithful woman who loves her husband," I replied, laying stress on my last words. Mrs. Gottlieb was silent for a moment and then opened her mouth and said, "When are you meeting?" I glanced at my watch. "If my letter has not reached him yet then he will now be waiting for me in the forest." "He will not wait for you in the forest," Mintshi said, "for he too has surely caught cold. Who knows if he isn't lying in bed? Why, you have behaved like schoolchildren. I can scarcely believe my ears." "Is he ill?" I asked, alarmed by her words. "How can I know if he is ill?" Mintshi replied. "It certainly is possible. Haven't you behaved like little children, sallying into the forest on a winter day in a summer dress?" "No!" I cried out. "I wore a spring dress on a spring day." "Heaven forbid," she said, "if I have offended your pride by saying you wore a summer dress on a winter day."

I was surprised that both Mintshi and my father spoke circumspectly. Still, my happiness did not leave me. While I was absorbed in my own thoughts Mrs. Gottlieb said, "My task is an odd one, my dear friend. I must play the bad aunt. But what can I do? I thought your folly was that of a young girl, but..." Mintshi did not complete her thought, nor did I ask her the meaning of the word "but." She sat by my side for another half hour and upon leaving kissed my forehead. And I savored in that kiss the tang of a new flavor. I embraced her. "Ah, little monster," she cried, "you've messed up my hair. Let go of me, I must tidy my hair." And picking up the mirror Mintshi laughed loudly. "Why are you laughing?" I asked, affronted. Mintshi gave me the mirror. And I saw that every inch of its surface was scratched, for I had etched into the silver the name Akaviah Mazal over and over.

A week passed and Mazal did not come to inquire about my health. At times I reproached him for fearing my father and acting in a cowardly fashion, and at times I feared that he too was ill. But I did not ask my father, nor did I have any desire to talk of the matter. Then I remembered the legend of the Baron's daughter who had loved a man from among the poor of the land. "It shall not come to pass," her father had decreed. Hearing her father's words the girl took ill and nearly died. And seeing how ill she was the doctors had said, "The wound is grievous, there is no healing of the fracture, for she is stricken by love." Her father had then gone forth to her suitor and implored him to marry his daughter. So I remained confined to my bed as sundry visions washed over me. And whenever the door turned on its hinges I asked, "Who's there?" My heart beat feebly and my voice was like my mother's voice at the time of her illness.

One day my father said, "The doctor tells me you have regained your strength." "Tomorrow I will go out," I replied. "Tomorrow," my father said, frowning. "Please wait another two or three days before going out, for who knows if the open air will, heaven forbid, not harm you. Three days hence and ours will be a different road. Stay here until the Memorial Day for your mother's death and we will visit her grave together. You will also find Mr. Mazal there." My father turned to go.

His words puzzled me, how did he know Mazal would come? Had they met? And if so, was it out of good will? And why had Akaviah not come to see me? And what was to happen? I was so excited that my teeth chattered and I feared I would fall ill again. Why had Akaviah not answered my letters? I cried out. And suddenly my heart was silenced, I ceased mulling over my thoughts, and I drew the covers over my hot flesh and shut my eyes. The day is still far off, I told myself, now I will sleep and the Lord will do what is good in His eyes.

What then happened to me I shall never know, for I lay on my sickbed for a great many days. And when I opened my eyes I beheld Akaviah seated in a chair, and his face lit up the room. I laughed in embarrassment and he too laughed, and it was the laugh of a good man. Just then my father entered and cried out, "Praised be God!"

He then strode towards me and kissed my brow. I stretched my arms out and embraced and kissed him, "Oh father, father, my dear father," I exclaimed. My father, however, forbade me to utter another word. "Calm down, my joy of joys, calm down, Tirtza, be patient for a few more days and then you will talk to your heart's content." Later that afternoon the old doctor arrived. And after examining me he stroked my cheek and said, "You are a courageous girl. This time you've come round, and now all the medicines in the world won't do you any harm either." "Blessed be the name of the Lord!" Kaila cried out from the doorway. Winter drew to an end and I was saved.

I was married on the eve of *Shabbat Nahamu*. A mere ten people were called to the bridal canopy. A mere ten and the entire town buzzed, for until that day such a simple wedding had never been witnessed in our town. And after the Sabbath we left our town for a summer resort and found lodgings in the home of a widow. The woman served us breakfast and dinner, but we lunched at the dairyman's house in the village. Three times a week a letter arrived from my father, and I too wrote regularly. Wherever I chanced upon a postcard I sent it to my father. Akaviah did not write other than enclosing his regards. And yet he gave a different shade of meaning to each of his greetings. And a letter arrived from Mintshi Gottlieb telling us that she had found us a place to live. And she drew a ground plan of the house and its rooms on a sheet of paper. Mintshi wished to know whether to rent the lodgings, thereby assuring us of a home on our return. Two days elapsed and we did not answer Mintshi's letter, and on the third day there were peals of thunder and flashes of lightning and all morning a hard rain poured down. The landlady came to ask whether to light the stove. "But it is not winter yet," I said laughing. And Akaviah told the woman, "If the sun has drawn in its flames then the heat from the stove will be sweeter sevenfold."

"Today," Akaviah said to me, "we will answer Mrs. Gottlieb's letter." "But what shall we say?" I asked. "I will teach you how to put reason to good use," my husband said, "and you will know what to answer. Mrs. Gottlieb has written us a letter to say she has found us lodgings, and this did not come as a surprise, for we are indeed in need of lodgings, and the rooms are agreeable and the woman is a woman of good taste as well as a friend, which gives us all the more reason to trust her words." "In that case I will write and say that the lodgings please us." "Wait," Akaviah said, "someone is knocking. The landlady is here to light the stove." And the woman kindled the fire with the wood she had brought. She then told us how she and her forefathers and her fathers' forefathers were born in this very village. She would never leave the village; here she was born, grew up and would die. It was beyond her why people left their birthplace and wandered to the far corners of the world. You have a home? Honor it and dwell in it. And if you say, 'I like my friend's garden,' well, why don't you plant a garden yourself? Why should the air stink in your own neighborhood, while it smells good in another part of town where your friend lives?" My husband laughed at her words and said, "Her words ring true."

The rain had stopped, but the soil hadn't dried yet. The fire blazed in the stove and we sat in our room and warmed ourselves. My husband said, "We have had such a good time that we nearly forgot about our future lodgings. But listen to what I propose and tell me whether it seems right in your eyes. You are familiar with my house, if it is too small we could add a room and live in it. Now we must write to Mintshi Gottlieb to thank her for her labors." We wrote Mintshi a letter of gratitude, and to my father we announced our decision to move into Akaviah's home. Our plans did not please my father, for Akaviah lived in a peasant's house. Yet my father did repairs on the house and he also built us a new room. A month passed and we returned. My home won over my heart. Although it was no different from the other farmhouses, a different spirit dwelled within it. And as we entered we were greeted by the sweet fragrance of potted flowers and a freshly baked cake prepared by Mintshi for our homecoming. The rooms were attractive and cozy, for the hands of a wise woman had adorned them. An adjoining servant's room had also been built. But there was no maidservant to serve the house. My father sent Kaila but I promptly sent her back, preferring to eat at my father's until we should find a young maidservant. And we would arrive at noon and return in the evening.

At the end of the holiday my father left for Germany to conclude his business affairs and consult with doctors. And the doctors directed my father to the city of Wiesbaden. Kaila then came to our home to help me with the household chores.

We soon found a young maidservant and Kaila returned to my father's home. The girl came for only two, three hours a day at the most. I then said, How will I manage all the housework by myself? But soon enough I realized it was far better to have the servant come for a few hours than for the entire day, for she would leave after completing her duties and then there was no one to keep me from talking to my husband as much as I pleased.

Winter came. Wood and potatoes were stored indoors. My husband labored over his book chronicling the history of the Jews in our town and I cooked fine and savory dishes. After the meal we would go out for a walk, or else we would stay at home and read. And Mrs. Gottlieb gave me an apron she had sewn for me. Akaviah caught sight of me in the large apron and called me mistress of the household. And I was happy being mistress of the house.

But times will change. I began to resent cooking. At night I would spread a thin layer of butter on a slice of bread and hand it to my husband. And if the maidservant did not cook lunch then we did not eat. Even preparing a light meal burdened me. One Sunday the servant did not come and I sat in my husband's room, for that day we had only one stove going. I was motionless as a stone. I knew my husband could not work if I sat with him in the room, as he was accustomed to working without anyone else present. But I did not rise and leave, nor did I stir from my place. I could not rise. I undressed in his room and bid him to arrange my clothes. And I shuddered in fear lest he approach me, for I was deeply ashamed. And Mrs. Gottlieb said, "The first three months will pass and you will be yourself again." My husband's misfortune shocked me and gave me no rest. Was he not born to be a bachelor? Why then had I robbed him of his peace? I longed to die, for I was a snare unto Akaviah. Night and day I prayed to God that I should give birth to a girl who would tend to all his needs after my death.

My father returned from Wiesbaden. He retired from his business, though not wanting to remain idle he would spend two or three hours a day with the man who bought his shop. And he comes to visit us at night, not counting those nights when it rains, for on such nights the doctor has forbidden him to venture out of the house. He arrives bearing apples or a bottle of wine or a book from his bookshelf—a gift for my husband. Then, being fond of reading the papers, he relates to us the news of the day. Sometimes he asks my husband about his work and grows confused as he speaks to him. Other times my father talks of the great cities he has seen while traveling on business. Akaviah listens like a village boy. Is this the student who came from Vienna and spoke to my mother and her parents about the wonders of the capital? How happy I am that they have something to talk about. Whenever they speak together I recall the exchange between Job and his friends, for they speak in a similar manner. One speaks and the other answers. Such is their way every night. And I stand vigilant, lest my father and my husband quarrel. The child within me grows from day to day. All day I think of nothing but him. I knit my child a shirt and have bought him a cradle. And the midwife comes every so often to see how I am faring. I am almost a mother.

A night chill envelopes the countryside. We sit in our rooms and our rooms are suffused with warmth and light. Akaviah sets his notebooks aside and comes up to me and embraces me. And he sings a lullaby. Suddenly his face clouds over and he falls silent. I do not ask what causes this, but am glad when my father comes home. My father takes out a pair of slippers and a red cap—presents for the child. "Thank you, grandfather," I say in a child's piping voice. At supper even my father agrees to eat from the dishes I prepared today. We speak of the child about to be born. Now I glance at my father's face and now at my husband's. I behold the two men and long to cry, to cry in my mother's bosom. Has my husband's sullen mood brought this about, or does a spirit dwell in womankind? My father and my husband sit at the table, their faces shining upon me. By dint of their love and compassion, each resembles the other. Evil has seventy faces and love has but one face.

I then thought of the son of Gottlieb's brother on the day Gottlieb came to his brother's home and his brother's wife sat with her son. Gottlieb lifted the boy up in the air and danced, but his brother entered and the boy glanced now at Gottlieb and now at his brother, and he turned his face away from them both and in a fit of tears he flung his arms out to his mother.

So end the chronicles of Tirtza.

In my room at night, as my husband bent over his work and I was afraid of disturbing him, I sat alone and wrote down all I had treasured up in memory. Sometimes I would ask myself, Why have I set my memories down, what new things have I seen and what do I wish to leave behind? Then I would say: It is to find solace in writing, and so I wrote all that is written in this book.

Translated by Gabriel Levin
Revised and Annotated by Jeffrey Saks

Annotations to "In the Prime of Her Life"

163. In the Prime of Her Life / Heb. *Bidmi Yamehah*, an adaptation of Isaiah 38:10, describing King Hezekiah's nearly being stricken down by illness in the prime of his life. The reference is doubly resonant with our story when we consider the Talmud's suggestion (Berakhot 10a) that the cause of his illness was an initial refusal to marry and father children; i.e., trampling upon a normal structure of family life.

169. Kaddish / Mourner's prayer, recited during the year of morning following the death of a close relative.

172. Melamed / Heb. teacher; a tutor hired to teach Jewish studies.

172. *Bedingungs-Buchstaben* and *Sprach-Werkzeuge* / "conditional phrases and linguistic methods"; i.e. German grammatical terms.

179. Sash / According to custom to wrap a ritual belt around the waist prior to prayer.

179. Minhah / Afternoon prayer.

179. Mizrah / Decorative sign indicating East and the direction toward Jerusalem in which prayers are recited; often embroidered with Biblical verses and the like.

179. Blessed is he who shall not forsake… / From the Musaf prayer of Rosh HaShanah.

180. Malbim / Meir Leibush ben Yehiel Michel Wisser (1809-79), better known by the acronym Malbim, was a Russian rabbi, Hebrew grammar, and Bible commentator.

181. He shall shave his head… / Job 1:20.

182. Beit Midrash / House of Study.

183. Succah / Festival booth used during the holiday of Succot; cf. Lev. 23:42-43.

184. Haskalah / The Jewish Enlightenment, 18th–19th century movement that advocated adopting values of the European Enlightenment, pressing for better integration into general society, and increasing education in secular studies.

184. Gemara / Talmud; main body of the Oral Law comprising a commentary on the Mishnah.

189. Kol Nidre / Solemn opening prayer of Yom Kippur.

190. Shema / "Hear O Israel" (Deut. 6:4), central declaration of faith and a twice-daily Jewish prayer; also recited at bedtime.

205. Screwy / In Hebrew the dog's name is *Me'uvat*, meaning broken, damaged, warped, bent (cf. Eccl. 1:15, "A *twisted thing* cannot be made straight...") – the translation cannot contain all the meanings contained in the name, including a mild hint of sexual perversion.

216. Shabbat Nahamu / "The Sabbath of Consolation", nickname for the Sabbath following the mournful three week Summer period commemorating the destruction of the Jerusalem Temple.

Tehilla

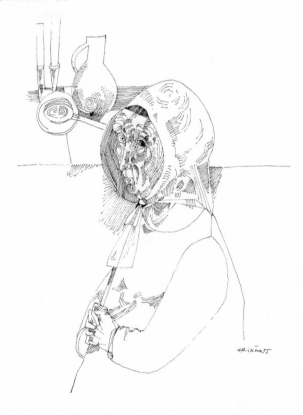

"Now there used to be in Jerusalem a certain old woman, as comely an old woman as you have seen in all your days. Righteous she was, and wise she was, and gracious and humble too: for kindness and mercy were the light of her eyes, and every wrinkle in her face told of blessing and peace."

Illustration by Avigdor Arikha

Now there used to be in Jerusalem a certain old woman, as comely an old woman as you have seen in all your days. Righteous she was, and wise she was, and gracious and humble too: for kindness and mercy were the light of her eyes, and every wrinkle in her face told of blessing and peace. I know that women should not be likened to angels: yet her would I liken to an angel of God. She had in her, moreover, the vigor of youth; so that she wore old age like a mantle, while in herself there was seen no trace of her years.

Until I had left Jerusalem she was quite unknown to me: only upon my return did I come to know her. If you ask why I never heard of her before, I shall answer: why have you not heard of her until now? It is appointed for every man to meet whom he shall meet, and the time for this, and the fitting occasion. It happened that I had gone to visit one of Jerusalem's celebrated men of learning, who lived near the Western Wall. Having failed to locate his house, I came upon a woman who was going by with a pail of water, and I asked her the way.

She said, Come with me, I will show you.

I replied, Do not trouble yourself: tell me the way, and I shall go on alone.

She answered, smiling: What is it to you if an old woman should earn herself a *mitzva?*

If it be a *mitzva,* said I, then gain it; but give me this pail that you carry.

She smiled again and said: If I do as you ask, it will make the *mitzva* but a small one.

It is only the trouble I wish to be small, and not the merit of your deed.

She answered, This is no trouble at all, but a privilege; since the Holy One has furnished His creatures with hands that they may supply all their needs.

We made our way amongst the stones and descended the alleys, avoiding the camels and the asses, the drawers of water and the idlers and the gossip-mongers, until she halted and said, Here is the house of him you seek. I said good-bye to her and entered the house.

I found the man of learning at home at his desk. Whether he recognized me at all is doubtful; for he had just made an important discovery – a Talmudic insight – which he immediately began to relate. As I took my leave I thought to ask him who that woman might be, whose face shone with such peace and whose voice was so gentle and calm. But there is no interrupting a scholar when he speaks of his latest discovery.

Some days later I went again to the City, this time to visit the aged widow of a rabbi; for I had promised her grandson before my return that I would visit her.

That day marked the beginning of the rainy season. Already the rain was falling, and the sun was obscured by clouds. In other lands this would have seemed like a normal day of spring; but here in Jerusalem, which is pampered with constant sunshine through seven or eight months of the year, we think it is winter should the sun once fail to shine with all its might, and we hide ourselves in houses and courtyards, or in any place that affords a sheltering roof.

I walked alone and free, smelling the good smell of the rains as they fell exultantly, wrapping themselves in mist, and heightening the tints of the stones, and beating at the walls of houses, and dancing on roofs, and making great puddles beneath, that were sometimes murky and sometimes gleamed in the sunbeams that intermittently broke through the clouds to view the work of the waters. For in Jerusalem even on a rainy day the sun yet seeks to perform its task.

Turning in between the shops with their arched doorways at the Street of the Smiths, I went on past the spice merchants, and the shoemakers, and the blanket-weavers, and the little stalls that sell hot broths, till I came to the Street of the Jews. Huddled in their tattered rags sat the beggars, not caring even to reach a hand from their cloaks, and glowering sullenly at each man who passed without giving them money. I had with me a purse of small coins, and went from beggar to beggar distributing them. Finally I asked for the house of the *rabbanit,* and they told me the way.

I entered a courtyard, one of those which to a casual passerby seems entirely deserted, and upon mounting six or seven broken stairs, came to a warped door. Outside I bumped into a cat, and within, a heap of rubbish stood in my way. Because of the mist I could not see anyone, but I heard a faint, apprehensive voice calling: Who is there? Looking up, I now made out a kind of iron bed submerged in a wave of pillows and blankets, and in its depths an alarmed and agitated old woman.

I introduced myself, saying that I was recently come from abroad with greetings from her grandson. She put out a hand from under the bedding to draw the coverlet up to her chin, saying: Tell me now, does he own many houses, and does he keep a maidservant, and has he fine carpets in every room? Then she sighed, This cold will be the death of me.

Seeing that she was so irked with the cold, it occurred to me that a kerosene heater might give her some ease: so I thought of a little stratagem.

Your grandson, I said, has entrusted me with a small sum of money to buy a stove: a portable stove that one fills with kerosene, with a wick that burns and gives off much heat. I took out my wallet and said, See, here is the money.

In a vexed tone she answered: And shall I go now to buy a stove, with these feet that are on me? Did I say feet? Blocks of ice I should say. This cold will drive me out of my wits if it won't drive me first to my grave, to the Mount of Olives. And look you, abroad they say that the Land of Israel is a hot land. Hot it is, yes, for the wicked in Hell.

Tomorrow, I said, the sun will shine out and make the cold pass away.

"Ere comfort comes, the soul succumbs."

In an hour or two, I said, I shall have sent you the stove.

She crouched down among her pillows and blankets, as if to show that she did not trust me in the part of benefactor.

I left her and walked out to Jaffa Road. There I went to a shop that sold household goods, bought a portable stove of the best make in stock, and sent it on to the old *rabbanit*. An hour later I returned to her, thinking that, if she was unfamiliar with stoves of this kind, it would be as well to show her the method of lighting it. On the way, I said to myself: Not a word of thanks, to be sure, will I get for my pains. How different is one old woman from another! For she who showed me the way to the scholar's house is evidently kind to all corners; and this other woman will not even show kindness to those who are prompt to secure her comfort.

But at this point I must insert a brief apology. My aim is not to praise one woman to the detriment of others; nor, indeed, do I aspire to tell the story of Jerusalem and all its inhabitants. The range of man's vision is narrow: shall it comprehend the City of the Holy One, blessed be He? If I speak of the *rabbanit* it is for this reason only, that at the entrance to her house it was again appointed for me to encounter the other old woman.

I bowed and made way for her; but she stood still and greeted me as warmly as one may greet one's closest relation. Momentarily I was puzzled as to who she might be. Could this be one of the old women I had known in Jerusalem before leaving the country? Yet most of these, if not all, had perished of hunger in the time of the war. Even if one or two survived, I myself was much changed; for I was only a young man when I left Jerusalem, and the years spent abroad had left their mark.

She saw that I was surprised, and smiled, saying: It seems you do not recognize me. Are you not the man who wished to carry my pail on the way to so-and-so's house?

And you are the woman, said I, who showed me the way. Yet now I stand here bewildered, and seem not to know you.

Again she smiled.—And are you obliged, then, to remember every old woman who lives in the City?

Yet, I said, you recognized me.

She answered: Because the eyes of Jerusalem look out upon all Israel, each man who comes to us is engraved on our heart; thus we never forget him.

It is a cold day, I said; a day of wind and rain; while here I stand, keeping you out of doors.

She answered, with love in her voice: I have seen worse cold than any we have in Jerusalem. As for wind and rain, are we not thankful? For daily we bless God as "He who causes the wind to blow and the rain to fall." You have done a great *mitzva:* you have put new life into old bones. The stove which you sent to the *rabbanit* is warming her, body and soul.

I hung my head, as a man does who is abashed at hearing his own praise. Perceiving this, she said:

The doing of a *mitzva* need not make a man bashful. Our fathers, it is true, performed so many that it was needless to publicize their deeds. But we, who do less, perform a *mitzva* even by letting the *mitzva* be known: then others will hear, and learn from our deeds what is their duty too. Now, my son, go to the *rabbanit,* and see how much warmth lies in your *mitzva.*

I went inside and found the stove lit, and the *rabbanit* seated beside it. Light flickered from the perforated holes, and the room was full of warmth. A scrawny cat lay in her lap, and she was gazing at the stove and talking to the cat, saying to it: It seems that you like this heat more than I do.

I said: I see that the stove burns well and gives off excellent heat. Are you satisfied?

And if I am satisfied, said the *rabbanit,* will that make it smell the less or warm me the more? A stove there was in my old home, that would burn from the last day of *Sukkot* to the first night of *Passover,* and give off heat like the sun in the dog-days of summer, a lasting joy it was, not like these bits of stove which burn for a short while. But nowadays one cannot expect good workmanship. Enough it is if folk make a show of working. Yes, that is what I said to the people of our town when my dear husband, the rabbi, passed away: may he watch over me from the world to come! When they got themselves a new rabbi, I said to them, What can you expect? Do you expect that he will be like your *old* rabbi? Enough it is if he starts no troubles. And so I said to the neighbors just now, when they came to see the stove that my grandson sent me through you. I said to them, This stove is like the times, and these times are like the stove. What did he write you, this grandson? Didn't write at all? Nor does he write to me, either. No doubt he thinks that by sending me this bit of a stove he has done his duty.

After leaving the *rabbanit,* I said to myself: I too think that by sending her this "bit of a stove" I have done my duty: surely there is no need to visit her again. Yet in the end I returned, and all because of that same gracious old woman; for this was not the last occasion that was appointed for me to see her.

Again I must say that I have no intention of recounting all that happened to me in those days. A man does many things, and if he were to describe them all he would never make an end to his story. Yet all that relates to that old woman deserves to be told.

At the eve of the New Moon I walked to the Western Wall, as we in Jerusalem are accustomed to do, praying at the Western Wall at the rising of each moon.

Already most of the winter had passed, and spring blossoms had begun to appear. Up above, the heavens were pure, and the earth had put off her grief. The sun smiled in the sky; the City shone in its light. And we too rejoiced, despite the troubles that beset us; for these troubles were many and evil, and before we had reckoned with one, yet another came in its wake.

From Jaffa Gate at far as the Western Wall, men and woman from all the communities of Jerusalem moved in a steady stream, together with those newcomers whom The Place had restored to their place, albeit their place had not yet been found. But in the open space before the Wall, at the guard booth of the Mandatory Police, sat the police of the Mandate, whose function was to see that no one guarded the worshippers save only they. Our adversaries, wishing to provoke us, perceived this and set about their provocations. Those who had come to pray were herded together and driven to seek shelter close up against the stones of the Wall, some weeping and some as if dazed. And still we say, How long, O Lord? How long? For we have trodden the lowest stair of degradation, yet You tarry to redeem us.

I found a place for myself at the Wall, standing at times amongst the worshippers, at times amongst the bewildered bystanders. I was amazed at the peoples of the world: as if it were not sufficient that they oppressed us in all their lands, yet they must also oppress us in our home.

As I stood there I was driven from my place by one of the British police who carried a baton. This man was in a great rage, on account of some ailing old woman who had brought a stool with her to the Wall. The policeman jumped to it and gave a kick, throwing the woman to the ground, and confiscated the stool: for she had infringed the law enacted by the legislators of the Mandate, which forbade worshippers to bring seats to the Wall. And those who had come to pray saw this, yet held their peace: for how can right dispute against might? Then came forward that same old woman whom I knew, and looked the policeman straight in the eyes. And the policeman averted his glance, and returned the stool to its owner.

I went up to her and said: Your eyes have more effect than all the pledges of England. For England, who gave us the Balfour Declaration, sends her officers to annul it; while you only looked upon that wicked one, and frustrated his evil intent.

She replied: Do not speak of him so; for he is a good *goy*, who saw that I was grieved and gave back her stool to that poor woman. But have you said your afternoon prayer? I ask because, if you are free, I can put in your way the *mitzva* of visiting the sick. The *rabbanit* is now really and truly ill. If you wish, come with me and I shall take you by a short route.—I joined her and we went together.

From alley to alley, from courtyard to courtyard, we made our way down, and at each step she took she would pause to give a sweet to a child, or a coin to a beggar, or to ask the health of a man's wife, or if it were a woman, the health of her husband. I said, Since you are concerned with everyone's welfare, let me ask about yours.

She answered: Blessed be God, for I lack nothing at His hand. The Holy One has given to each of His creatures according to its need; and I too am one of these. But today I have special cause for thanking Him, for He has doubled my portion.

How is this? I asked.

She replied: Each day I read the psalms appointed for the day: but today I read the psalms for two days together.

Even as she spoke, her face clouded over with grief.

Your joy has passed away, I said.

She was silent for a moment. Then she said: Yes, my son, I was joyful, and now it is not so.

Yet even as she spoke, the light shone out again from her face. She raised her eyes and said: Blessed be He, Who has turned away my sorrow.

Why, I asked, were you joyful, yet afterwards sad, and now, joyful again?

She said, very gently: Since your words are not chosen with care, I must tell you, this was not the right way to ask. Rather should you have said, "How have you deserved that God should turn away your sorrow?" For in His blessed eyes, all is one, whether sorrow or joy.

Perhaps in the future, said I, my words will be chosen with care, since you teach me how one must speak. "Happy is the man who does not forget Thee." It is a text of much meaning.

She said: You are a good man, and it is a good verse you have told me; so I too shall not withhold good words. You asked why I was joyful, and why I was sad, and why I now rejoice.

Assuredly you know as I do, that all a man's deeds are appointed, from the hour of his birth to the hour of his death; and accordingly, the number of times he shall say his psalms. But the choice is free how many psalms he will say on any one day. This man may complete the whole book in a day, and that man may say one section a day, or the psalms for each day according to the day. I have made it my custom to say each day the psalms for that day; but this morning I went on and said the psalms for two days together. When I became aware of this I was sad, lest it mean that there was no more need for me in the world, and that I was disposed of and made to finish my portion in haste. For "it is a good thing to give thanks to the Lord," and when I am dead I shall not be able to say one psalm, or even one word. Then the Holy One saw my grief, and showed His marvelous kindness by allowing me to know that such is His very own will. If it pleases The Name to take my life, who am I that I should grieve? Thus He at once turned away my sorrow. Blessed be He and blessed be His name.

I glanced at her, wondering to myself by what path one might come to a like submission. I thought of the men of ancient times, and their virtuous ways; I spoke to her of past generations. Then I said, You have seen with your own eyes more than I can describe in words.

She answered: When a person's life is prolonged for many days and years, it is granted him to see many things; good things, and yet better things.

Tell me, I said to her, of these same good things.

She was silent for a little while; then she said: How shall I begin? Let me start with my childhood. When I was a little girl, I was a great chatterbox. Really, from the time I stood up in the morning till the time I lay down at night, chatter never ceased from my lips. There was an old man in our neighborhood, who said to those delighting in my chatter: "A pity it is for this little girl; if she wastes all her words in childhood, what will be left for her old age?" I became terribly frightened, thinking this meant that I might die the very next day. But in time I came to fathom the old man's meaning, which was that a person must not use up in a short while what is allotted him for a whole lifetime. I made a habit of testing each word to see if there was real need for it to be said, and practiced a strict economy of speech. As a result of this economy, I saved up a great store of words, and my life has been prolonged until they are all finished. Now that only a few words remain, you ask me to speak them. If I do so it will hasten my end.

Upon such terms, said I, I would certainly not ask you to speak. But how is it that we keep walking and walking, yet we have still not come to the house of the *rabbanit?*

She said: You still have in mind those courtyards we used to take for a short cut. But now that most of the City has been settled by the Arabs, we must go by a roundabout way.

We approached one of these courtyards. She said: Do you see this courtyard? Forty families of Israel once lived here, and here were two synagogues, and here in the daytime and night-time there was study and prayer. But they left this place, and Arabs came and occupied it.

We approached a coffee house. She said: Do you see this house? Here was a great *yeshiva* where the scholars of the Torah lived and studied. But they left this house, and Arabs came and occupied it.

We came to the asses' stalls. She said: Do you see these stalls? Here stood a soup-kitchen, and the deserving poor would enter hungry and go forth satisfied. But they abandoned this place, and Arabs came and occupied it. Houses from which prayer and charity and study of the Torah never ceased now belong to the Arabs and their asses. My son, we have reached the courtyard of the *rabbanit's* house. Go in, and I shall follow you later. This unhappy woman, because of the seeming good she has known abroad, does not see the true good at home.

What is the true good? I asked.

She laughed, saying, Ah my son, you should not need to ask. Have you not read the verse, "Happy is he Thou choosest and bringest near to dwell in Thy courts?" For the same courts are the royal courts of the Holy One, the courts of our God, in the midst of Jerusalem. When men say "Jerusalem," their way is to add the words, " – the Holy City." But when *I* say "Jerusalem," I add nothing more, since the holiness is contained in the name; yes, in the very name itself. Go up, my son, and do not trip on the stairs. Many a time have I said to the treasurer of the community funds that these stairs are in need of repair; and what answer did he give me? That this building is old and due to be demolished, therefore it is not worth while spending a penny on its upkeep. So the houses of Israel fall into disuse until they are abandoned, and the sons of Ishmael enter and take possession. Houses that were built with the tears of their fathers—and now they abandon them. But again I have become a chatterer, and hasten my end.

I entered, and found the *rabbanit* lying in bed. Her head was bandaged and a poultice had been laid upon her throat. She coughed loudly, so that even the medicine bottles placed by her bedside would shake at each cough. I said to her: *Rabbanit,* are you ill?—She sighed and her eyes filled with tears. I sought for words of comfort, but the words would not come. All I could say, with my eyes downcast, was: So you are ill and deserted.

She sighed again and replied: Yes, I am ill as ill can be. In the whole world there is no one so ill as I am. All the same, I am not deserted. Even here in Jerusalem, where nobody knows me, and nobody knows the honors done to me in my own town, even here there is one woman who waits on me, who comes to my room and fetches a drop of soup for my bedridden meal. What do you hear from my grandson? No doubt he is angry with me, because I have not written to thank him for the stove. Now I ask you, how shall I go out to buy ink and pen and paper for the writing of letters? It is hard enough even to bring a spoonful of soup to my lips. I am surprised that Tilli has not come.

If you are speaking, said I, of that gracious old woman who brought me here, she told me that she would come very soon.

Said the *rabbanit,* I cannot tell whether she is gracious: at least she is efficacious. Look you, how many holy, holy women there are about Jerusalem, who go buzzing like bees with their incantations and supplications, yet not one of them has come to me and said, "*Rabbanit,* do you need any help?"—My head, oh my head. If the pains in my heart won't take me off, the pains in my head will take me off first.

I said to her, I can see that speech is difficult for you.

She answered: *You* say that speech is difficult for me; and *I* say that my whole existence is difficult for me. Even the cat knows this, and keeps away from his home. Yet people say that cats are home-loving creatures. He finds my neighbors' mice more tasty, to be sure, than all the dainties I feed him. What was I meaning to say? I forget all I mean to say. Now Tilli is so different. There she goes, with the bundles of years heaped up on her shoulders, bundle on bundle; yet all her wits serve her, although she must be twice my age. If my father—God bless his pious memory—were alive today, he would be thought of as a child beside her.

I urged the *rabbanit* to tell me about this Tilli.

And did you not mention her yourself? Nowadays people don't know Tilli; but there was a time when everyone did, for then she was a great, rich woman with all kinds of business concerns. And when she gave up all these and came to Jerusalem, she brought along with her I can't say how many barrels of gold, or if not barrels, there is no doubt that she brought a chest full of gold. My neighbors remember their mothers telling them, how, when Tilli came to Jerusalem, all the best people here came a-courting, either for themselves or for their sons. But she sent them packing and stayed a widow. At first she was a very wealthy widow, and then quite a well-to-do widow, until at last she became just any old woman.

Judging from Tilli's appearance, said I, one would think that she had never seen hard times in her life.

The *rabbanit* replied with scorn: *You* say that she has never seen hard times in her life: and *I* say that she has never seen good times in her life. There is no enemy of mine whom I would "bless" with the afflictions that Tilli has borne. *You* suppose that, because she is not reduced to living off the public funds, she has enjoyed a happy life: and I believe that there is not a beggar knocking on the doors who would exchange his sorrows for hers.—Oh, my aches and my pains! I try to forget them, but they will not forget me.

I perceived that the *rabbanit* knew more than she cared to disclose. Since I felt that no good would come of further questioning, I showed myself ready to leave by rising from my chair.

Said the *rabbanit:* "The sweep hadn't stepped into the chimney, but his face was already black." You have scarcely sat down in your chair, and already you are up and away. Why all this haste?

I said: If you wish me to stay, I will stay. She made no answer; so I began speaking of Tilli again, and asked if I might be told her story.

And if I tell you, said the *rabbanit,* will it benefit you, or benefit her? I have no liking for tale-bearers: they spin out their cobwebs, and call it fine tapestry. I will only say this, that the Lord did a mercy to that good man when He put the evil spirit into that apostate, may her name be blotted out. Why are you gaping at me? Don't you understand the meaning of simple Yiddish?

I understand Yiddish quite well, said I, but I cannot understand what you are talking about, *rabbanit.* Who is the good man, and who is the apostate you have cursed?

Perhaps I should bless her then, perhaps, I should say, "Well done, Mistress Apostate, you who have traded a gold coin for a brass farthing." See, again you are staring at me as if I talked Turkish. You have heard that my husband of blessed memory was a rabbi, wherefore they call me *rabbanit;* and have you not heard that my father too was a rabbi? Such a rabbi, that in comparison with him, all other rabbis might rank as mere schoolboys: and I speak of *real* rabbis, look you, not of those who wear the mantle and give themselves airs.—What a world, what a world it is! A deceitful world, and all it contains is deceit and vanity.—But my father, of blessed and pious memory, was a rabbi from his childhood, and all the matchmakers in the province bustled about to find him a wife. Now there was a certain rich widow, and when I say rich, you know that I mean it. This widow had only one daughter—would she had never been born. She took a barrel full of gold coins, and said to the matchmakers: "If you match that man to my daughter, this barrel full of gold will be his; and if it is not sufficient, I shall add to it!" But her daughter was not a fit match for that holy man; for she was already tainted with the spirit of heresy, as is shown by her latter end, and she fled away from her home, and entered the house of the nuns, and deserted her faith. Yes, at the very hour when she was to be wed, she ran away. That poor stricken mother wasted half her fortune in efforts to reclaim her. Her appeal went up to the Emperor himself; and even the Emperor was powerless to help. For anyone who enters a nunnery can never leave. You know now who that apostate was? The daughter of . . . hush, here she comes.

Tilli entered the room. She was carrying a bowl of soup, and seeing me she said:

Ah, you are still here! But stay, my friend, stay. It is a great *mitzva* to visit the *sick. Rabbanit,* how much better you look! Truly salvation comes in the wink of an eye; for God is healing you every minute. I have brought a little soup to moisten your lips: now, my dear, raise your head and I shall prop up your pillow. There, my dear, that is right. My son, I am sorry that you do not live in the City, for then you would see for yourself how the *rabbanit's* health is improving day by day.

And do I not live in Jerusalem? I said. Surely Nahalat Shiva is Jerusalem?

It is indeed, answered Tilli. God forbid that it should be otherwise. Rather may the day come when Jerusalem extends as far as Damascus, and in every direction. But the eye that has seen all Jerusalem enclosed within her walls cannot get accustomed to viewing what is built beyond the walls of the City itself. It is true that all the Land of Israel is holy, and I need hardly say, the surroundings of Jerusalem: yet the holiness that is within the walls of the City surpasses all else. My son, there is nothing I have said which you do not know better than I. Why then have I said it? Only that I might speak the praise of Jerusalem.

I could read in the eyes of the *rabbanit* a certain resentment, because Tilli was speaking to me rather than to her. So I took my leave and went away.

Various preoccupations kept me for a while from going to the City; and after that came the nuisance of the tourists. How well we know these tourists, who descend upon us and upon the land, all because the Holy One has made a little space for us here! They come, now, to see what has happened; and having come, they regard us as if we were created solely to serve them. Yet one good thing may be said for the tourists: in showing them "the sights," we see them ourselves. Once or twice, having brought them to the City to show them the Western Wall, I met Tilli there. It seemed to me that a change had come over her. Although she had always walked without support, I noticed that she now leaned on a stick. On account of the visitors, I was unable to linger. For they had come to spy out the whole land, not to spend time upon an old woman not even mentioned in their itineraries.

When the tourists had left Jerusalem, I felt restless with myself. After trying without success to resume work, I bestirred myself and walked to the City, where I visited of my own accord all the places I had shown to the visitors. How can I describe what I saw? He who in His goodness daily renews the works of creation, perpetually renews His own City. New houses may not have been built, or new trees planted; yet Jerusalem herself is ever new. I cannot explain the secret of her infinite variety. We must wait, all of us, for those great sages who will one day enlighten us.

I came upon the man of learning whom you already know, and he drew me to his house, where he set before me all his recent findings. We sat together as long as we sat, while I asked questions, and he replied; or raised problems, which he resolved; or mentioned cloudy matters, which he made clear. How good it is, how satisfying, to sit at the feet of one of the scholars of Jerusalem, and to learn the Law from his lips! His home is simple, his furnishings austere, yet his wisdom ranges far, like the great hill ranges of Jerusalem which are seen from the windows. Bare are the hills of Jerusalem; no temples or palaces crown them. Since the time of our exile, nation after nation has come and laid them waste. But the hills spread their glory like banners to the sky; they are resplendent in ever-changing hues; and not least in glory is the Mount of Olives, which bears no forest of trees, but a forest of tombs of the righteous, who in life and in death gave their thoughts to the Land.

As I stood up to go, the mistress of the house entered and said to her husband, You have forgotten your promise. He was much perturbed at this, and said: Wonder of wonders; all the time I have known Tehilla she has never asked a favor. And now she wants me to say that she wishes to see you.

Are you speaking, said I, of Tilli, the old woman who showed me the way to your house? For it seems that you call her by another name.

Tehilla, he answered, is Tilli's holy, Hebrew name. From this you may learn that, even four or five generations ago, our forbears would give their daughters names that sound as though they had been recently coined. For this reason my wife's name is Tehiya, meaning Rebirth, which one might suppose to have been devised in our own age of rebirth. Yet in fact it belongs to the time of the great Rebbe Yitzhak Meir Alter, author of the *Hiddushei HaRim*, who instructed my wife's great-grandfather to call his daughter Tehiya; and my wife is named after her.

I said: You speak now of the custom four or five generations ago. Can it be that this Tehilla is so old?

He smiled, saying: Her years are not written upon her face, and she is not in the habit of telling her age. We only know it because of what she once let slip. It happened that Tehilla came to congratulate us at the wedding of our son; and the blessing she gave to our son and his bride was that it might be granted for them to live to her age. My son asked, "What is this blessing with which you have blessed us?" And she answered him: "It is ninety years since I was eleven years old." This happened three years ago; so that now her age is, as she might express it, ninety years and fourteen: that is to say, a hundred and four.

I asked him, since he was already speaking of her, to tell me what manner of woman she was. He answered:

What is there to say? She is a saint; yes, in the true meaning of the word. And if you have this opportunity of seeing her, you must take it. But I doubt if you will find her at home; for she is either visiting the sick, or bringing comforts to the poor, or doing some other unsolicited *mitzva*. Yet you may perhaps find her, for between *mitzva* and *mitzva* she goes home to knit garments or stockings for poor orphans. In the days when she was rich, she spent her wealth upon deeds of charity, and now that nothing is left her but a meager pittance to pay for her own slender needs, she does her charities in person.

The scholar accompanied me as far as Tehilla's door. As we walked together he discoursed on his theories; but realizing that I was not attending to his words, he smiled and said, From the moment I spoke of Tehilla, no other thought has entered your mind.

I would beg to know more of her, I replied.

He said: I have already spoken of her as she is today. How she was before she came to our Land I do not know, beyond what everyone knows; that is to say, that she was a very wealthy woman, the owner of vast concerns, who gave up all when her sons and her husband died, and came here to Jerusalem. My late mother used to say, "When I see Tehilla, I know that there is a worse retribution than widowhood and the loss of sons." What form of retribution this was, my mother never said; and neither I, nor anyone else alive, knows; for all that generation which knew Tehilla abroad is now dead, and Tehilla herself says but little. Even now, when she is beginning to change, and speaks more than she did, it is not of herself. We have come to her house; but it is unlikely that you will find her at home; for towards sunset she makes the round of the schoolrooms, distributing sweets to the younger children.

A few moments later I stood in the home of Tehilla. She was seated at the table, expecting me, so it seemed, with all her being. Her room was small, with the thick stone walls and arched ceiling that were universal in the Jerusalem of bygone days. Had it not been for the little bed in a corner, and a clay jar upon the table, I would have likened her room to a place of worship. Even its few ornaments—the hand-lamp of burnished bronze, and a copper pitcher, and a lamp of the same metal that hung from the ceiling—even these, together with the look of the table, on which were laid a prayer-book, a Bible, and some third book of study, gave to the room the grace and still calm of a house of prayer.

I bowed my head saying, Blessed be my hostess.

She answered: And blessed be my guest.

You live here, said I, like a princess.

Every daughter of Israel, she said, is a princess; and, praised be the living God, I too am a daughter of Israel. It is good that you have come. I asked to see you; and not only to see you, but to speak with you also. Would you consent to do me a favor?

"Even to the half of my kingdom," I replied.

She said: It is right that you should speak of your kingdom; for every man of Israel is the son of kings, and his deeds are royal deeds. When a man of Israel does good to his neighbor, this is a royal deed. Sit down, my son: it makes conversation easier. Am I not intruding upon your time? You are a busy man, I am sure, and need the whole day for gaining your livelihood. Those times have gone when we had leisure enough and were glad to spend an hour in talk. Now everyone is in constant bustle and haste. People think that if they run fast enough it will speed the coming of Messiah. You see, my son, how I have become a chatterer. I have forgotten the advice of that old man who warned me not to waste words.

I was still waiting to learn the reason for her summons. But now as if she had indeed taken to heart the old man's warning, she said nothing. After a while she glanced at me, and then looked away; then glanced at me again, as one might who is scrutinizing a messenger to decide whether he is worthy of trust. At last she began to tell me of the death of the *rabbanit*, who had passed away during the night, while her stove was burning, and her cat lay warming itself at the flame,—till the pall-bearers came, and carried her away, and someone unknown had taken the stove.

You see, my son, said Tehilla, a man performs a *mitzva,* and one *mitzva* begets another. Your deed was done for the sake of that poor woman, and now a second person is the gainer, who seeks to warm his bones against the cold. Again she looked me up and down; then she said: I am sure you are surprised that I have troubled you to come.

On the contrary, I said, I am pleased.

If you are pleased, so am I. But my pleasure is at finding a man who will do me a kindness; as for you, I do not know why you should be pleased.

For a moment she was silent. Then she said: I have heard that you are skilful at handling a pen—that you are, as they nowadays call it, a writer. So perhaps you will place your pen at my service for a short letter. For many years I have been wanting to write a letter. If you are willing, write for me this letter.

I took out my fountain-pen. She looked at it with interest, and said: You carry your pen about with you, like those who carry a spoon wherever they go, so that if they chance upon a meal—well, the spoon is ready at hand.

I replied: For my part, I carry the meal inside the spoon. And I explained to her the working of my fountain-pen.

She picked it up in her hand and objected: You say there is ink inside, but I cannot see one drop.

I explained the principle more fully, and she said: If it is so, they slander your generation in saying that its inventions are only for evil. See, they have invented a portable stove, and invented this new kind of pen: it may happen that they will yet invent more things for the good of mankind. True it is that the longer one lives, the more one sees. All the same, take this quill that I have myself made ready, and dip it in this ink. It is not that I question the usefulness of your pen; but I would have my letter written with my own. And here is a sheet of paper; it is crown-paper, which I have kept from days gone by, when they knew how good paper was made. Upwards of seventy years I have kept it by me, and still it is as good as new. One thing more I would ask of you: I want to write, not in the ordinary cursive hand, but in the square, capital letters of the prayer-book and the Torah scroll. I assume that a writer must at some time have transcribed, if not the Torah itself, at least the scroll of Esther that we read on *Purim*.

As a boy, I answered, I copied such a scroll exactly in the manner prescribed; and, believe this or not, everyone who saw that scroll praised it.

Said Tehilla, Although I have not seen it, I am sure you know how to write in a good straight script, without a single flaw. Now I shall make ready for you a glass of herb tea, while you proceed with your writing.

Please do not trouble, I said, for I have already taken something to drink.

If so, how shall I show hospitality? I know: I shall slice you a piece of sugar-loaf; then you can say a blessing, and I can add, Amen.

She gave me some of the sugar. Then, after a short silence, she said:

Take up the quill and write. I shall speak in Yiddish, but you will write in the holy tongue. I have heard that now they teach the girls both to write and to speak the holy Hebrew language: you see, my son, how the good Lord is constantly improving His world from age to age. When I was a child, this was not their way. But at least I understand my Hebrew prayer-book, and can read from the Bible, and the Psalms, and the *Ethics of the Fathers.*—Oh dear, oh dear, today I have not finished my day!

I knew that she meant the day's portion of the Psalms, and said to her: Instead of grieving you should rather be glad.

Glad?

Yes, I said, for the delay is from heaven, that one day more might be added to your sum of days.

She sighed, and said: If I knew that tomorrow our Redeemer would come, gladly would I drag out another day in this world. But as day follows day, and still our true Redeemer tarries and comes not, what is my life? And what is my joy? God forbid that I should complain of my years: if it pleases Him to keep me in life, it pleases me also. Yet I cannot help but ask how much longer these bones must carry their own burden. So many younger women have been privileged to set up their rest on the Mount of Olives, while I remain to walk on my feet, till I think I shall wear them away. And is it not better to present oneself in the World on High while one's limbs are all whole, and return the loan of the body intact? I do not speak of putting on flesh, which is only an extra burden for the pall-bearers. But at least it is good to die with whole limbs. Again I am speaking too much: but now what matters it, a word less, or a word more? I am now fully prepared to return the deposit of my body, earth back to earth.—Take up your quill, my son, and write.

I dipped the quill pen in the ink, made ready the paper, and waited for Tehilla to speak. But she was lost in her thoughts, and seemed unaware of my presence. I sat there and gazed at her, my eyes taking in every wrinkle and furrow of her face. How many experiences she had undergone! She was in the habit of saying that she had seen good things, and yet better things. From what I had been told, these things could not have been so good. The adage was true of her, that the righteous wear mourning in their hearts, and joy upon their faces.

Tehilla became aware of me and, turning her head, said, Have you begun?

You have not told me what I am to write.

She said: The beginning does not need to be told. We commence by giving praise to God. Write: *With the help of the Holy Name, blessed be He.*

I smoothed the paper, shook the quill, and wrote, *With the help of the Holy Name, blessed be He.*

She sat up, looked at what I had written, and said: Good; very good. And now what next? Write as follows: *From the Holy City, Jerusalem, may she be built and established, speedily and in our days, Amen.* In conversation I only say "Jerusalem," without additions. But in writing, it is proper that we should bring to mind the holiness of Jerusalem, and add a plea for her to be rebuilt; that the reader may take Jerusalem to his heart, and know that she is in need of mercy, and say a prayer for her. Now, my son, write the day of the week, and the Torah portion of the week, and the number of years since the creation.

When I had set down the full date, she continued:

Now write, in a bold hand, and as carefully as you can, the letter *Lamed.*—Have you done this? Show me how it looks. There is no denying that it is a good *Lamed,* though perhaps it could have been a trifle larger. Now, my son, continue with *Khaf,* and after the *Khaf* write *Bet,* and after it *Vav.*—*Vav,* I was saying, and now comes *Dalet.* Show me now the whole word, *Likhvod,* "To the honorable –." Very fine indeed. It is only right that the respectful prefix should be attractively written. Now add to that, "the esteemed Rabbi"—ah, you have already done so! You write faster than I think: while I am collecting my thoughts, you have already set them down. Truly your father—may he rest in peace—did not waste the cost of your education. My son, forgive me, for I am so tired. Let us leave the writing of the letter till another day. When is it convenient for you to come?

Shall I come tomorrow? I said.

Tomorrow? Do you wish it? What day is tomorrow?

It is the day before New Moon.

The eve of the New Moon is a good day for this thing. Then let it be tomorrow.

I saw that she was inwardly grieved, and thought to myself: The day before New Moon is a time for prayer and supplication, a time for visits to the tomb of Rachel our Mother; surely she will not be able to attend to her letter. Aloud I said to her: If you are not free tomorrow I shall come on some other day.

And why not tomorrow?

Just because it is the day before the New Moon.

She said: My son, you bring my sorrow before me, that on such a day I should be unable to go to Rachel our Mother.

I asked why she could not go.

Because my feet cannot carry me there.

There are carriages, I said, and autobuses as well.

Said Tehilla, When I first came to Jerusalem there were none of these *autobustles*, or whatever they are called. There were not even carriages; so we used to walk. And since I have gone on foot for so long, it is now hardly worth changing my ways. Did you not say you are able to come tomorrow? If it pleases God to grant my wish, my life will be prolonged for yet a day more.

I left her and went on my way; and the following day I returned.

I do not know if there was any real need to return so soon. Possibly if I had waited longer, it would have extended her life.

AS soon as I entered, I perceived a change. Tehilla's face, that always had about it a certain radiance, was doubly radiant. Her room shone out too. The stone floor was newly polished, and so were all the ornaments in the room. A white sheet was spread over the little bed in the corner, and the skirtings of the walls were freshly color-washed blue. On the table stood the jar, with its parchment cover, and a lamp and sealing-wax were placed at its side. When had she found time to paint the walls, and to clean the floor, and to polish all her utensils? Unless angels did her work, she must have toiled the night long.

She rose to welcome me, and said in a whisper:

I am glad that you have come. I was afraid you might forget, and I have a little business matter to attend to.

If you have somewhere to go, I said, I shall come back later.

I have to go and confirm my lease. But since you are here, sit down, and let us proceed with the letter. Then afterwards I shall go about my lease.

She set the paper before me and fetched the ink and the quill pen. I took up the quill pen and dipped it in the ink and waited for her to dictate her message.

Are you ready? she said. Then I am ready, too!

As she spoke the word 'ready,' her face seemed to light up and a faint smile came to her lips. Again I prepared to write, and waited for her next words.

Where did we leave off? she said. Was it not with the phrase, *To the honorable and eminent Rabbi?* Now you shall write his name.

Still I sat waiting.

She said in a whisper: His name is Shraga.—Have you written it?

I have written.

She half-closed her eyes as if dozing. After some time she raised herself from her chair to look at the letter, and whispered again: His name is Shraga, his name is Shraga.—And again she sat silent. Then she seemed to bestir herself, saying: I shall tell you in a general way what you are to write. But again she lapsed back into silence, letting her eyelids droop.

I see, she said at last, that I shall have to tell you all that happened, so that you will understand these things and know how to write them. It is an old story, of something which happened many years ago; yes, three and ninety years ago.

She reached for her walking-stick and let her head sink down upon it. Then again she looked up, with an expression of surprise, as one might who thinks he is sitting alone and discovers a stranger in the room. Her face was no longer calm, but showed grief and disquiet as she felt for her stick, then put it by, and again took it up to lean upon, passing her hand over her brow to smooth out her wrinkles.

Finally she said: If I tell you the whole story, it will make it easier for you to write.—His name is Shraga. Now I shall start from the very beginning.

She raised her eyes and peered about her; then, reassured that no one else could be listening, she began.

I was eleven years old at the time. I know this, because father, of blessed memory, used to write in his Bible the names of his children and the dates of their births, his daughters as well as his sons. You will find the names in that Bible you see before you; for when I came to Jerusalem, my late brothers renounced their right to my father's holy books and gave them to me. As I said before, it is an old story, three and ninety years old; yet I remember it well. I shall relate it to you, and little by little you will understand. Now, are you listening?

I inclined my head and said, Speak on.

So you see, I was eleven years old. One night, father came home from the synagogue, bringing with him some relatives of ours, and with them Pesahya Mordechai, the father of Shraga. When she saw them enter, my dear mother, rest her soul, called me and told me to wash my face well and put on my Sabbath dress. She put on her Sabbath clothes and bound her silk kerchief round her head, and, taking my hand, led me into the big room to meet father and his guests. Shraga's father looked at me and said: "Heaven protect you, you are not an ugly child." Father stroked my cheek and said, "Tehilla, do you know who spoke to you? The father of your bridegroom-to-be spoke to you. *Mazal tov*, my child: tonight you are betrothed." At once all the visitors blessed me with *mazal tovs*, and called me "the bride." Mother quickly bundled me back to her room to shield me from any evil eye, and kissed me, and said: "From now on you are Shraga's betrothed; and God willing, next year, when your bridegroom comes of age at thirteen for wearing the *tefillin*, we shall make your wedding."

I knew Shraga already, for we used to play with jacks and at hide-and-seek, until he grew too old and began to study Talmud. After our betrothal I saw him every Sabbath, when he would come to father's house and repeat to him all he had learned through the week. Mother would give me a dish of sweets which I would take and offer to Shraga, and father would stroke my cheek and beam upon my bride-groom.

And now they began to prepare for the wedding. Shraga's father wrote out the *tefillin*, and my father bought him a *tallit*, while I sewed a bag for the *tefillin* and another bag for the *tallit* that is worn on a Sabbath. Who made the large outer bag for both *tallit* and *tefillin* I cannot remember.

One Sabbath, four weeks before the day fixed for the wedding, Shraga failed to come to our house. During the afternoon service, Father enquired at the house of study, and was told that he had gone on a journey. Now this journey was made to one of the leaders of the *Hassidim,* and Shraga had been taken by his father in order that he might receive a blessing from his *rebbe* on the occasion of first wearing *tallit* and *tefillin*. When my father learned this, his soul nearly parted from his body; for he had not known until then that Shraga's father was of the "Sect." He had kept his beliefs a secret, for in those days the *Hassidim* were despised and persecuted, and father was at the head of the persecutors; so that he looked upon members of the Sect as if (God forbid) they had ceased to belong to our people. After the *havdala* ceremony, at the close of the Sabbath, father tore up my marriage contract and sent the pieces to the house of my intended father-in-law. On Tuesday Shraga returned with his father,

and they came to our house. My father drove them out wi[th]
whereupon Shraga himself swore an oath that he would never f[o]
us the insult. Now father knew well that he who cancels a betroth
must seek pardon from the injured party; yet he took no steps to
obtain this. And when my mother implored him to appease Shraga,
he made light of her entreaties, saying, "You have nothing to fear: he
is only of the Sect." So contemptible were the *Hassidim* in my father's
eyes that he took no heed in this thing wherein all men take heed.

Preparations for the wedding had been made. The house was
cluttered with sacks of flour and casks of honeym and the baker
women had already been engaged to prepare the white loaves and
cakes. In short, all was ready, and there lacked nothing but a bridegroom. My father summoned a matchmaker and they found me
bridegroom with whom I entered under the bridal canopy.

What became of Shraga, I do not know, for father forbade
any of our household to mention his name. Later I heard that he
and all his people had removed to another town. Indeed they were
in fear of their very lives; since, from the day when father ended my
betrothal, they were not called up to the Torah in synagogue; not
even on *Simhat Torah*, when every man is called. They could not even
come together for worship, for my father as head of the community
would not let them assemble outside the regular synagogues; and had
they not gone to another town where they might be called up to the
Torah, they would not have survived the year.

Three years after the wedding I gave birth to a son. And two
years later, another son was born to me. And two years after that, I
gave birth to a daughter.

Time passed uneventfully, and we made a good living. The
children grew and prospered, while I and my husband, may he rest
in peace, watched them grow and were glad. I forgot about Shraga,
and forgot that I had never received a note of pardon at his hand.

Mother and father departed this life. Before his death, my
father of blessed memory committed his affairs to his sons and his
sons-in-law, enjoining them all to work together as one. Our business
flourished, and we lived in high repute. We engaged good tutors for
our sons, and a Gentile governess for our daughter; for in those days

_S. Y._

nothing to do with the local teachers, who
...ing free-thinkers.

...d would bring these tutors from other towns; and
...d teachers were obliged to admit any student who
...he was not suitably qualified, tutors who had been
...n elsewhere were dependent upon those who engaged
...under no such obligation. Coming, as they did, alone, they
would dine at our table on Sabbath days. Now my husband, who
because of the pressure of his affairs could not make set times for study
of the Torah, was especially glad of one such guest who spoke to him
words of Torah. And I and the children delighted in the tuneful Sabbath hymns he would sing us. We did not know that this tutor was a
Hassid, and his discourses the doctrines of _Hassidism,_ and the tunes
that he sang us, _Hassidic_ tunes; for in all other respects he conducted
himself like any other true believer of Israel. One Sabbath eve, having
discoursed of the Torah, he closed his eyes and sang a hymn of such
heavenly bliss that our very souls melted at its sweetness. At the end,
my husband asked him: "How may a man come to this experience
of the divine?" The tutor whispered to him: "Let your honor make
a journey to my _rebbe,_ and you will know this and much more."

Some days later, my husband found himself in the city of the
tutor's _rebbe._ On his return, he brought with him new customs, the
like of which I had not seen in my father's house; and I perceived
that these were the customs of the _Hassidim._ And I thought to myself,
Who can now wipe the dust from your eyes, Father, that you may see
what you have done, you who banished Shraga for being a _Hassid,_
and now the husband you gave me in his stead does exactly as he
did? If this thing does not come as atonement for sin, I know not
why it has come.

My brothers and brothers-in-law saw what was happening,
but they said not a word. For already the times had changed, and
people were no longer ashamed to have _Hassidim_ in the family. Men
of wealth and position had come from other towns and married
amongst us, who followed the customs of _Hassidim,_ and even set up
a hassidic synagogue, and would travel openly to visit their _rebbes._
My husband did not attend their services, but in other respects he

observed *Hassidic* customs and educated his sons in these ways, and from time would make journeys to his *rebbe.*

A year before our first-born son became *bar mitzva,* there was plague in the world, and many fell sick. There was not a house without its victims, and when the plague reached us, it struck our son. In the end the Lord spared him—but not for long. When he rose from his sick-bed, he began to study the practice of the *tefillin* from the great code of the *Shulhan Arukh.* And I saw this and was glad, that for all his *Hassidic* training, his devotion to the Law was not lessened.

One morning our son rose up very early to go to the house of study. As he was about to enter, he saw there a man dressed in burial shrouds, resembling a corpse. It was not a dead man he had seen, but some demented creature who did many strange things. The child was overcome with terror and his senses left him. With difficulty was he restored to life. Restored to life he was indeed, but not to a long life. From that day on, his soul flickered and wavered like the flame of a yahretzeit candle at the closing prayer of Yom Kippur. He had not come of age for wearing *tefillin* before his soul departed and he died.

Through the seven days of mourning I sat and meditated. My son had died after the *havdala,* at the ending of Sabbath, thirty days before he came of age for *tefillin.* And at the end of the Sabbath, after the *havdala,* thirty days before I was to marry Shraga, father had torn up the marriage contract. Counting the days I found to my horror that the two evils had come about on the same day, at the same hour. Even if this were no more than chance, yet it was a matter for serious reflection.

Two years later, the boy's brother came of age—came, and did not come. He happened to go with his friends to the woods outside our town to fetch branches to decorate the synagogue on the *Shavuot* holiday. He left his comrades in the woods, intending to call on the scribe who was preparing his *tefillin;* and he never returned. We thought at first that he had been stolen by gypsies, for a band of them had been seen passing the town. After some days his body was found in the great marsh beside the woods; then we knew he must have missed his way and fallen in.

When we concluded the week of mourning, I said to my husband: "Nothing remains to us now but our one little girl. If we do not seek forgiveness from Shraga, her fate will be as the fate of her brothers."

Throughout all those years we had heard nothing of Shraga. When he and his people left our town, they were forgotten, and their where-abouts remained unknown. My husband said: "Shraga is the *Hassid* of such and such a *rebbe.* I shall make a journey to this man, and find out where he lives."

Now my husband was not a disciple of this same *rebbe:* on the contrary, he was opposed to him, because of the great dispute that had broken out between the *rebbes,* on account of a slaughterer, whom one had appointed and the other had dismissed. In the course of that quarrel a man of Israel was killed, and several families were uprooted, and several owners of property lost their possessions, and several persons ended their days in prison.

Nevertheless, my husband made the journey to the town where this *rebbe* lived. Before he had arrived there, the *rebbe* died, after dividing his followers amongst his sons, who went away each to a different town. My husband journeyed from town to town, from son to son, enquiring of each son where Shraga might be. Finally he was told: "If you are asking after Shraga, Shraga has become a renegade and rejoined our opponents." But no one knew where Shraga now lived.

When a man is a *Hassid,* you may trace him without difficulty. If he is not the disciple of one *rebbe,* he is the disciple of another. But with any ordinary unattached Jew, unless you know where he lives, how may he be found? My husband, peace be upon his soul, was accustomed to making journeys, for his business took him to many places. He made journey after journey enquiring for Shraga. On account of these travels his strength in time began to fail and his blood grew thin. At last, having travelled to a certain place, he fell sick there and died.

After I had set up his tombstone, I went back to my town and entered into business. While my husband was still alive, I had helped him in his affairs: now that he was dead, I speeded them with all my might. And the Lord doubled my powers until it was said of me, She has the strength of a man. It would have been well, perhaps, had wisdom been granted me in place of strength, but the Lord knows what He intends and does not require His own creatures to tell Him what is good. I thought in my heart: all this toil is for my daughter's sake. If I add to my wealth, I shall add to her welfare. As my responsibilities became ever greater, I found I had no leisure to spend at home, except on Sabbaths and holy days: and even these days were apportioned, half to the service in synagogue, and the other half to the reception of guests. My daughter, so it seemed, was in no need of my company: for I had engaged governesses and she was devoted to her studies. I received much praise on account of my daughter, and even the Gentiles, who make fun of our accent, would say that she spoke their language as well as the best of their own people. Furthermore, these governesses would ingratiate themselves with my daughter, and invite her to their homes. In due course, I called the matchmakers, who found her a husband distinguished for his learning, and already qualified for the rabbinate. But I was not to enjoy a parent's privilege of leading my daughter to her bridal canopy: for an evil spirit took possession of her, so that her reason became unhinged.

And now, my son, this is what I ask of you — write to Shraga for me, and say that I have forgiven him for all the sorrows that befell me at his hand. And say that I think he should forgive me, too: for I have been stricken enough.

FOR a long, long time I sat in silence, unable to speak a word. At last, wiping a tear from my eye, I said to Tehilla:

Allow me to ask a question. Since the day when your father tore up the marriage contract, ninety years and more have elapsed. Do you really believe that Shraga is still alive? And if so, has anyone informed you where he may be found?

Tehilla answered: Shraga is not alive. Shraga has now been dead for thirty years. I know the year of his death, for in that year, on the seventh day of Adar, I went to a synagogue for the afternoon service. Following the week's reading from the Prophets, they said the memorial prayer for the dead, and I heard them pray for the soul of Shraga. After the service, I spoke to the beadle of the synagogue, and asked him who this Shraga might be. He mentioned the name of a certain relative of the dead man, who had given instructions for his soul to be remembered. I went to this relative, and heard what I heard.

If Shraga is dead, then, how do you propose to send him a letter?

Tehilla answered: I suppose you are thinking that this poor old woman's wits are beginning to fail her, after so many years; and that she is relying upon the post office to deliver a letter to a dead man.

I said: Then tell me, what will you do?

She rose, and picking up the clay jar that stood on the table, raised it high above her head, intoning in a kind of ritual chant:

I shall take this letter—and set it in this jar;—I shall take this wax—and seal up this jar;—and take them with me—this letter and this jar.

I thought to myself, And even if you take the jar and the letter with you, I still do not see how your message will come to Shraga. Aloud I said to her: Where will you take your jar with its letter?

Tehilla smiled and said softly: Where will I take it? I will take it to the grave, my dear. Yes, I shall take this jar, and the letter inside it, straight to my grave. For up in the Higher World they are well acquainted with Shraga, and will know where to find him. And the postmen of the Holy One are dependable, you may be sure; they will see that the letter is delivered.

Tehilla smiled again. It was a little smile of triumph, as of a precocious child who has outwitted her elders.

After a while she let her head sink upon her walking-stick and seemed again to be half asleep. But soon she glanced up and said: Now that you understand the whole matter, you can write it yourself. —And again her head drooped over her stick.

I took up the quill and wrote the letter. When I had finished, Tehilla raised her head and enquired: It is done now?—I began to read the letter aloud, while she sat with her eyes closed, as if she had lost interest in the whole matter and no longer desired very greatly to hear. When the reading was over, she opened her eyes and said:

Good, my son, good and to the point. Perhaps it might have been phrased rather differently, but even so, the meaning is clear enough.

Now, my son, hand me the pen and I shall sign my name. Then I can put the letter in the jar; and after that I shall go about my lease.

I dipped the pen in the ink and handed it to her, and she took it and signed her name. She passed the pen over certain of the characters to make them more clear. Then she folded the letter and placed it inside the jar, and bound the piece of parchment over the top. Then she kindled the lamp, and took wax for sealing, and held it against the flame until the wax became soft; then she sealed the jar with the wax. Having done these things, she rose from her place and went towards her bed. She lifted up the coverlet and placed the jar under the pillow of the bed. Then she looked at me fairly, and said in a quiet voice:

I must make haste to confirm my lease. Bless you, my son, for the pains you have taken. From now on I shall not bother you any more.

So saying, she made smooth the coverlet of her bed, and took up her stick, and went to the door, and reached up that she might lay her lips to the *mezuza,* and waited for me to follow. She locked the door behind us and walked ahead with brisk steps; and I overtook her and went at her side.

As she walked, she looked kindly upon every place that she passed and every person that she met. Suddenly she stopped and said:

My son, how can they abandon these holy places and these faithful Jews?

At that time, I still did not comprehend all she meant by these words.

When we reached the parting of the ways, she stopped again and said: Peace be with you. But when she saw that I was resolved not to leave her, she said no more. She went up by the wide steps that lead to the courtyard of the Burial Society, and entered, and I followed.

We went into the Burial Society, which administers the affairs of the living and the dead. Two of the clerks sat there at a desk, their ledgers before them and their pens in their hands, writing and taking sips at their black coffee as they wrote. When they saw Tehilla, they set their pens down and stood up in respect. They spoke their welcome, and hastened to bring her a chair.

What brings you here? asked the elder of the two clerks.

She answered, I have come to confirm my lease.

He said: You have come to confirm your lease: and we are of opinion that the time has come to cancel it.

Tehilla was terrified.—What is all this? she cried.

He said: Surely you have already joined the immortals?

Laughing at his own joke, the clerk turned to me, saying: Tehilla, bless her, and may she live for many, many years, is in the habit of coming every year to confirm the bill of sale on the plot for her grave on the Mount of Olives. So it was last year, and the year before that, and three years ago, and ten and twenty and thirty years ago, and so will she go on till the coming of the Redeemer.

Said Tehilla: May he come, the Redeemer: may he come, the Redeemer! Would to God he would hasten and come! But as for me, I shall trouble you no more.

The clerk asked, assuming a tone of surprise: Are you going to a *kibbutz*, then, like these young girls they call "pioneers?"

Tehilla said: I am not going to a *kibbutz*, I am going to my own place.

What, said the clerk, are you returning abroad to your home country?

Tehilla said: I am not returning to my home country; I am returning to the place whence I came: as it is written, *And to the dust thou shalt return.*

Tut-tut, said the clerk, do you think that the Burial Society has nothing to do? Take my advice, and wait for twenty or thirty years more. Why all the haste?

She said quietly: I have already ordered the corpse-washers and the layers-out, and it would be ill-mannered to make sport of these good women.

The clerk's expression changed, and it was evident that he regretted his light words. He now said:

It is good for us to see you here: for so long as we see you, we have before us the example of a long life; and should you desert us, God forbid, it is as if you take away from us this precedent.

Said Tehilla: Had I any more years to live, I would give them gladly to you, and to all who desire life. Here is the lease for you to sign.

When the clerk had endorsed the bill of sale, Tehilla took it and placed it in the fold of her dress. She said:

Now and henceforth I shall trouble you no more. May God be with you, dear Jews; for I go to my place.

She rose from her chair, and walked to the door and reached up to lay her lips to the *mezuza,* and kissed the *mezuza,* and so went away.

When she saw that I still went with her, she said: Return to your own affairs, my son.

I thought, said I, that when you spoke of confirming the lease, you meant the lease of your house; but instead…

She took me up in the midst of my words. But instead, said she, I confirmed the lease of my eternal home. Yet may the Holy One grant that I have no need to dwell there for long, before I rise again, with all the dead of Israel. Peace be upon you, my son. I must make haste and return to my house, for I am sure that the corpse-washers and the layers-out already await me.

I stood there in silence and watched her go, until she passed out of sight among the courts and the alleys.

NEXT morning I went to the City to enquire how she fared. On my way, I was stopped by the man of learning to whose house Tehilla had led me. For some while he kept me in conversation, and when I wished to take my leave, he offered to accompany me.

I am not going home yet, I said. I am on my way to see Tehilla.

He said: Go; at the end of a long life.

Seeing my surprise, he added: *You* must live. But that saint has now left us.

I parted from him and went on alone. As I walked, I thought again and again: Tehilla has left us, she has gone on alone: she has left us, and gone on alone. I found that my feet had carried me to the house of Tehilla, and I opened her door and entered.

Still and calm was the room: like a house of prayer, when the prayer has been said. There, on the stone floor, flowed the last tiny rivulets of the waters in which Tehilla had been cleansed.

Translated by Walter Lever
Revised and Annotated by Jeffrey Saks

Annotations to "Tehilla"

225. *Mitzva* / A commandment, good deed.
226. *Rabbanit* / The wife of a rabbi.
227. Mount of Olives / Site of an ancient Jewish cemetery, just to the east of Jerusalem's Old City,
230. Eve of the New Moon / Special penitential prayers are recited by the faithful on the afternoon before the first of the month, a minor festival, in the Jewish lunar calendar. Many in Jerusalem customarily gathered at the Western Wall for these prayers.
230. The Place / A nickname for God, the Omnipresent who fills all places (Heb. *Ha-makom*).
230. Mandate and Mandatory Police / The British mandate over Palestine administered civil affairs from 1920-1948.
231. Balfour Declaration / 1917 British government declaration of support for the establishment of a Jewish homeland in Palestine.
231. *Goy* / Non-Jew; gentile.
231. Psalms appointed for the day / According to custom the 150 chapters of Psalms are divided into sections for daily recital over the course of the week or (likely in this case) over the course of the month.
231. Good thing to give thanks… / Psalms 92:2.
233. *Yeshiva* / Institute of traditional Jewish learning, principally of Talmud study.
234. Happy is he… / Psalms 65:5.
234. Ishmael / Biblical son of Abraham; here used as a nickname for Arabs.
237. Nahalat Shiva / One of the earliest Jerusalem neighborhoods built outside the walls of the Old City, starting in 1869.
239. Rebbe Yitzhak Meir Alter /1799-1866, founder of the Ger Hassidic dynasty.
241. Half my kingdom / Cf. Esther 5:3.
242. Writer / Tehilla is playing off the fact that in Hebrew a *sofer* is both a ritual scribe as well as a modern author.
242. Crown-paper / Special bonded stationery for use in sending official petitions or communications with the royal court of the Austro-Hungarian Empire.

245. Tomb of Rachel / Traditional burial site of the Biblical matriarch (cf. Gen. 35:9-20) on the outskirts of Bethlehem, about 5 miles south of Jerusalem's Old City.

248. *Tefillin* / Phylacteries; cube-shaped leather containers containing passages from the Bible, worn by men on the arm and head during morning prayers.

248. Sect / Pejorative description of Hassidim used by their opponents.

249. *Simhat Torah* / Festival at conclusion of the *Sukkot* holiday on which the yearly cycle of Torah reading is concluded, and each man is honored with an *aliyah*, i.e., being called up to the Torah.

250. Rebbe / Signifies a Hassidic master (as distinct from a non-Hassidic rabbi).

251. *Shulhan Arukh* / 16th century code of Jewish law by R. Yosef Karo.

251. *Havdala* / Ceremony marking the end of the Sabbath.

256. *Kibbutz* / Collective farming community.

Tehilla Timeline

We should be careful to never fall into the trap of confusing an author and his narrator. Nevertheless, Agnon often utilized a narrator who the reader is meant to believe is an autobiographical projection of the author into the story. While there's no clear time-stamp on the story "Tehilla" there are certain historical events and indicators that help us map out a timeline for the plot. If we presume that the middle-aged writer who returns to Jerusalem from a period spent abroad, settles in the Nahalat Shiva neighborhood outside the walls of the Old City, and who sometimes "found a place for myself at the Wall, standing at times amongst the worshippers, at times amongst the bewildered bystanders," is just such a case of autobiographical projection, then the story commences in the Fall of 1924, just before "the beginning of the rainy season." In fact, Agnon returned to Jerusalem (settling initially in Nahalat Shiva) from his twelve year sojourn in Germany, on October 31, 1924. Working backwards we can conjecture as to the milestones in the long life of that righteous and wise and gracious and humble woman. (To clarify, "Agnon" below refers to the actual real-life author, "Narrator" refers to the character in "Tehilla").

1820 – Shraga born (was one year older than Tehilla)

1821 – Tehilla born (104 years old in 1925)

1832 – Engagement to Shraga (one year before Shraga's bar mitzva)

1833 – Wedding to Shraga cancelled; Tehilla marries husband

1836 – First son born ("Three years after the wedding I gave birth to a son...")

1838 – Second son born ("...two years later, another son was born to me.")

1840 – Daughter born ("And two years after that, I gave birth to a daughter.")

1849 – First son dies ("My son had died after the *havdala,* at the ending of Sabbath, thirty days before he came of age for *tefillin*"; i.e., a month before *bar mitzva*)

1851 – Second son dies; husband seeks out Shraga and dies (similarly: "Two years later, the boy's brother came of age – came, and did not come.")

c. 1852-54? – Daughter engaged to Rabbanit's father and her apostasy (presumably would have been married off around this age; in all cases I place this before 1855 for the following reason: The crown-paper she wishes the narrator to write her letter on in 1925 has been in her possession "upwards of seventy years". Presumably this is the remainder of the paper stock on which she sent "her appeal [which] went up to the Emperor himself [i.e., to have her daughter returned to her]; and even the Emperor was powerless to help." Crown-paper being special bonded stationery for use in sending official petitions or communications with the royal court of the Austro-Hungarian Empire.)

1860 – First neighborhood built outside Old City; Tehilla's *aliya* before this ("The eye that has seen all Jerusalem enclosed within her walls cannot get accustomed to viewing what is built beyond the walls of the City itself.")

1895 – Shraga dies (in 1925 Tehilla tells the Narrator: "Shraga has now been dead for thirty years.")

Lag BaOmer 1908 – Agnon arrives in the Land of Israel

1912 – Agnon departs for Germany

1922 – British Mandate bans placing seats near the Western Wall ("I was driven from my place by one of the British police who carried a baton. This man was in a great rage, on account of some ailing old woman who had brought a stool with her to the Wall. The policeman jumped to it and gave a kick, throwing the woman to the ground, and confiscated the stool: for she had infringed the law enacted by the legislators of the Mandate, which forbade worshippers to bring seats to the Wall.")

October 1924 – Agnon returns from Germany; in following days or weeks, seeking out the Jerusalem Sage and the Rabbanit the Narrator meets Tehilla in the Old City

Spring 1925 – Narrator writes letter to Shraga; Tehilla dies (Earlier: "Already most of the winter had passed, and spring blossoms had begun to appear.")

1950 – Agnon publishes "Tehilla" in *Me'asef Davar*

Bibliography of Works in English

Like most of Agnon's important stories, the four novellas in this volume have been the object of analysis and interpretation by the major scholars and critics of Hebrew literature. Readers who would like to sample some of that body of scholarship and commentary, but are limited to material available in English, would find the following book chapters and essays to be worthwhile.

The most comprehensive, nearly encyclopedic, book on Agnon in English remains: Arnold Band, *Nostalgia and Nightmare: A Study in the Fiction of S.Y. Agnon* (Berkeley, CA: University of California Press, 1968). Each of the four stories in this volume are treated there, and the reader will find concise reviews of plot and theme for: "Two Scholars Who Were in Our Town" on pp. 402-405; "In the Heart of the Seas" on pp. 262-270; "In the Prime of Her Life" on pp. 115-118; and "Tehilla" on pp. 406-409.

"Two Scholars Who Were in Our Town" *

Lea Goldberg, "The Author and his Hero," *Ariel* 17 (1966-67), pp. 37-54 – Agnon's artful work as an author who speaks through a story-teller narrative to both portray an innocent

and pure ideal while at the same time creating space for two
different interpretations – as demonstrated in "Two Scholars
Who Were in Our Town" along with other stories.

Yair Mazor, "S.Y. Agnon's Art of Composition: The Befuddling Turn
of the Compositional Screw," *Hebrew Annual Review* 10 (1986),
pp. 197-208 – on Agnon's use of unexpected plot development,
as exemplified in "Two Scholars Who Were in Our Town".

Harvey Shapiro, "Multivocal Narrative and the Teacher as Narrator:
The Case of Agnon's 'Two Scholars Who Were in Our Town',"
Shofar 29:4 (2011), pp. 23-45 – explores the narrative voices
that guide the reader through the story, comparing the pious
traditional voice at the core versus the modern voice of the
framework which distances the reader from the tale.

[* *Not having been translated until now, the absence of many critical studies in English
on "Two Scholars Who Were in Our Town" is not surprising. It is hoped that this volume
will help spur the growth of such secondary literature and analysis.*]

"In the Heart of the Seas"

Sidra DeKoven Ezrahi, *Booking Passage: Exile and Homecoming in the
Modern Jewish Imagination* (Berkeley, CA: University of California Press, 2000), chapter 3, pp. 81-102 – on Agnon's use of
the contradiction between mythic and political Zionism to
"reclaim the future in the name of the past."

Roman Katsman, *The Time of Cruel Miracles: Mythopoesis in Dos-
toevsky and Agnon* (Frankfurt am Main: Peter Lang, 2002),
pp. 15-21 – the issue of myth and miracle in the novella.

Alan L. Mintz, "In the Seas of Youth," *Prooftexts* 21:1 (2001), pp. 57-70 –
proof of the value of prolonged engagement with an Agno-
nian text; demonstration of what Agnon said: "Any book not
worth reading twice probably wasn't worth reading the first
time." [Mintz revisits his earlier reading of the story in: "Agnon

on the Individual and the Community," *Response* (Summer 1967), pp. 28-31.]

Ruth R. Wisse, *No Joke: Making Jewish Humor* (Princeton: Princeton University Press, 2013), pp. 189-192 – on the amalgam of serious and comic to form an ironic statement in the novella.

"In the Prime of Her Life"

Nitza Ben-Dov, *Agnon's Art of Indirection: Uncovering Latent Content in the Fiction of S.Y. Agnon* (Leiden and New York: E.J. Brill, 1993), pp. 135-138 on the novella's web of Biblical allusions; chapter 7, pp. 107-133, on the role of the old woman ("Benign Mentor or Evil Genius?").

Nitza Ben-Dov, "Lambs in Their Mother's Pasture: Latent Content in Agnon's 'In the Prime of Her Life'," *Hebrew Studies* 29 (1988), pp. 67-80 – explores the thematic and structural function of Tirzta's dream as it operates in the novella.

Yael Halevi-Wise, "Reading Agnon's *In the Prime of Her Life* in Light of Freud's *Dora*," *Jewish Quarterly Review*, 98:1 (Winter 2008), pp. 29-40 – on Agnon's sources for the paradigm he establishes of dysfunctional generations linked by a shared love, which became such a potent template for subsequent Hebrew authors.

Astrid Popien, "Tirtza and Hirshl in Germany: S.Y. Agnon's *In the Prime of Her Life* and *A Simple Story* in the Context of the Family Novel in European Realism" in *Agnon and Germany: The Presence of the German World in the Writings of S.Y. Agnon*, edited by H. Becker and H. Weiss (Ramat Gan : Bar-Ilan University Press, 2010), pp. 115-150 – on Agnon's "realistic family novels" as adaptations and ironic transformations of the European model (as exemplified by Theodor Fontane and Thomas Mann).

Naomi B. Sokoloff, "Narrative Ventriloquism and Muted Feminine Voice: Agnon's 'In the Prime of Her Life'," *Prooftexts* 9:2 (1989), pp. 115-137 – reading the novella in light of feminist critical thought and literary interpretation.

Abraham B. Yehoshua, *The Terrible Power of a Minor Guilt: Literary Essays* (Syracuse: Syracuse University Press, 2000), chapter 7, pp. 108-130 – on the father-daughter relationship as a key to the moral map of the work.

"Tehilla"

Risa Domb, "Is Tehillah Worthy of Her Praise" in *History and Literature: New Readings of Jewish Texts in Honor of Arnold J. Band*, ed. W. Cutter and D. Jacobson (Providence, RI: Brown Judaic Studies, 2002), pp. 107-115 – an against the consensus reading which posits an ironic portrait in which Tehilla is not the exemplar of piety usually assumed.

Nitza Ben-Dov, "The Dead Do Not Praise the Lord: Alter's Psalms, Agnon's *Tehilla*, Pasternak's *Docter Zhivago*," *Hebrew Studies* 51 (2010), pp. 203-210 – the tension between belief in this world and belief in the world to come, as telegraphed through the use of (Alter's translation of) Tehillim in "Tehilla".

Theodore Friedman, "Exploring Agnon's Symbols," *Conservative Judaism* 21:3 (Spring 1967), pp. 65-71 – aims to unravel the character of Tehilla through what she might symbolize on different levels of meaning in the text.

Amos Oz, *The Silence of Heaven: Agnon's Fear of God* (Princeton, NJ: Princeton University Press, 2000), chapter 2, pp. 13-29 – a controversial book by Israel's leading contemporary novelist, which dedicates one of its three chapters to exploring religious themes in "Tehilla".

Hillel Weiss, "The Messianic Theme in the Works of A.B. Yehoshua and Amos Oz," in *Israel and the Post-Zionists*, ed. S. Sharan (Tel Aviv: Ariel Center, 2003), pp. 204-226 – response to Oz's reading of "Tehilla" in *The Silence of Heaven*.

About the Author

S.Y. Agnon (1888–1970) was the central figure of modern Hebrew literature, and the 1966 Nobel Prize laureate for his body of writing. Born in the Galician town of Buczacz (in today's western Ukraine), as Shmuel Yosef Czaczkes, he arrived in 1908 in Jaffa, Ottoman Palestine, where he adopted the penname Agnon and began a meteoric rise as a young writer. Between the years 1912 and 1924 he spent an extended sojourn in Germany, where he married and had two children, and came under the patronage of Shlomo Zalman Schocken and his publishing house, allowing Agnon to dedicate himself completely to his craft. After a house fire in 1924 destroyed his library and the manuscripts of unpublished writings, he returned to Jerusalem where he lived for the remainder of his life. His works deal with the conflict between traditional Jewish life and language and the modern world, and constitute a distillation of millennia of Jewish writing – from the Bible through the Rabbinic codes to Hassidic storytelling – recast into the mold of modern literature.

About the Translators and Editor

Paul Pinchas Bashan (co-translator, "Two Scholars Who Were in Our Town") was born to Holocaust survivors in a D.P. Camp in Vienna, and grew up in Israel. Upon completing his military service in the IDF he came to the United States where he initially worked for the Israeli Ministry of Defense in New York, working for several years in logistics and procurement, and finally becoming an executive recruiter. He went on to establish several successful executive search companies. He lives in Connecticut with his wife, Itta, and is the proud father of two daughters, Aviva and Talia, and is active in several volunteer programs.

I.M. Lask ("In the Heart of the Seas"), born in London in 1905 and arrived in the Land of Israel in 1930, was a journalist, editor and poet, but most well known as a premier translator of Hebrew and Yiddish literature to English. In addition to the works of Yehuda Halevi, Tchernichovsky, Bialik, Hazaz, Shenhar, Martin Buber and numerous poets and authors, he was one of the earliest and most prolific English translators of Agnon. Additionally, as Holocaust papers and documents started to reach Palestine starting already in 1939, he was responsible for preparing English translations for the Jewish Agency.

Israel Meir Lask, who died in 1974, was married to Luba Pevsner, and they had two daughters Ruth Rasnic and Bella Doron, both authors, and a son, Amittai, who was killed in the Israeli Air Force in 1956.

Walter Lever ("Tehilla") was born in London and came to Jerusalem in 1947 to teach English Literature at the Hebrew University and was a significant translator of Hebrew literature to English. He published a memoir of his early days in Israel under the title *Jerusalem is Called Liberty*.

Gabriel Levin ("In the Prime of Her Life") is the author of four collections of poems, most recently *To These Dark Steps*. He has also translated a selection from the poetry of Yehuda Halevi, *Poems from the Diwan*, and a book of essays, *The Dune's Twisted Edge: Journeys in the Levant*. He lives in Jerusalem.

Rhonna Weber Rogol (co-translator, "Two Scholars Who Were in Our Town"), a Montreal native, attributes her passion for Hebrew language and literature to the inspiration of her 7th grade teacher and beloved lifelong friend, the late Shlomo Jaacobi. She studied Hebrew from childhood at Shaare Zion Academy and Herzliah High School and later at Brandeis University and Hebrew University of Jerusalem. An attorney by profession, Rogol engages in volunteer work and Jewish and Holocaust education, enjoying both learning and teaching, and mostly spending time with her wonderfully supportive husband Brian, and their three children, Alissa, Joshua and Dane.

Jeffrey Saks is the Series Editor of The S.Y. Agnon Library at The Toby Press, and lectures regularly at the Agnon House in Jerusalem. He is the founding director of ATID – The Academy for Torah Initiatives and Directions in Jewish Education and its WebYeshiva.org program. He edited *Wisdom From All My Teachers: Challenges and Initiatives in Contemporary Torah Education*; *To Mourn a Child: Jewish Responses to Neonatal and Childhood Death*; and authored *Spiritualizing Halakhic Education*. Rabbi Saks is an Associate Editor of the journal *Tradition*.

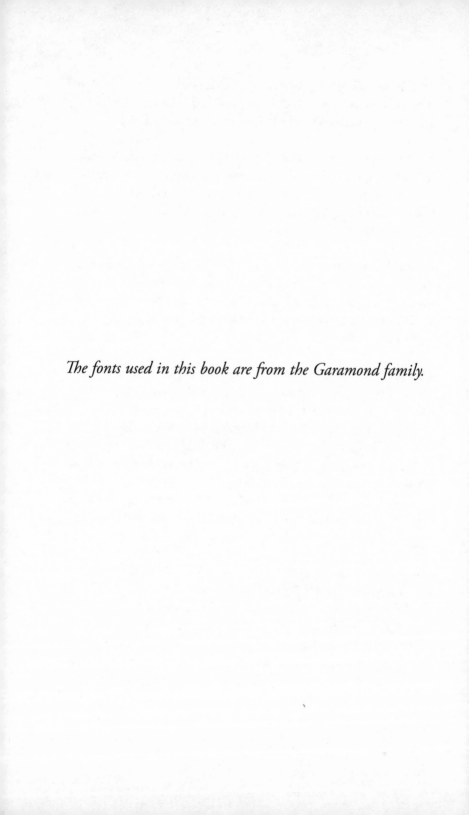

The fonts used in this book are from the Garamond family.

The Toby Press publishes fine writing,
on subjects of Israel and Jewish interest.
For more information, visit www.tobypress.com.